Praise for *An Unlikely Spy*

"Readers will travel breathlessly along with Evelyn as she navigates the treacherous waters of lifelong allegiances and new alliances, foreign dangers and secrets uncovered much closer to home. Starford has penned both a beguiling tale of espionage and a noteworthy commentary on torn loyalties and the unthinkable choices of war."

—Pam Jenoff, author of *The Orphan's Tale* and *The Lost Girls of Paris*

"A well-crafted spy novel examines the perils of espionage's foundation in personal relationships. . . . The intriguing story of a young woman's espionage career during World War II weaves in a critique of the British class system. . . . The book is rich with historical details, right down to clothing styles and furnishings. . . . The novel's depiction of Evelyn's career is exciting, but it also suggests the human cost: No matter how skilled her performances, to those above her in the social hierarchy, she's expendable."

—*Kirkus Reviews*

"Prepare to fall in awe with Evelyn Varley, the titular unexpected MI5 agent in this fast-paced thriller filled with more twists than a bag of pretzels. Set during World War II, memoirist Starford's fiction debut is a must-read for historical fiction buffs."

—E! Online

"A fast-paced tale with plenty of plot twists and enough complexity to place it somewhere between a historical genre novel and a literary thriller."

—*Guardian*

"A beguiling and compelling tale of an otherwise ordinary woman, an unlikely spy caught between the personal and the political in the machine of war."

—*The Age* (Australia)

"Class and ideologies collide in Starford's consummate debut, a clever combination of home-front drama and espionage thriller. . . . The author does an excellent job of recreating London before, during, and after the war, and in Evelyn has created a complex heroine whose sense of duty gets her in way over her head. With suspense worthy of Hitchcock and a moral reckoning straight out of le Carré or Graham Greene, this is a winner."

—*Publishers Weekly*

"A subtle yet moving story of personal and professional camouflage, of hidden selves fearing the light."

—*Booklist*

"*An Unlikely Spy* gripped me to the end: I devoured it. Rebecca Starford has created an exceptional novel about World War II, bringing 1940s England to life in formidable, compelling detail and thrusting the reader into a world of wartime spies, betrayal, and surprising revelation. What a rare treat to find a novel that offers both white-knuckled suspense and evocative, beautiful prose. I loved it."

—Hannah Kent, author of *Burial Rites*

"Rebecca Starford seems to be the inheritor of the cool narrative elegance of Graham Greene and John le Carré. Her building of the tale to reach the critical moral apogee of this book seems effortless, and she has found a fascinating and unexpected World War II corner of espionage and intelligence to exploit for a plot that runs like milk and honey."

—Thomas Keneally, author of *Schindler's List*

"A poignantly rendered narrative map of one woman's journey from misfit to spy—and a thought-provoking examination of the gently human desires that lay the groundwork for pernicious extremism. Rebecca Starford has given us a rousing reminder of the power of our choices."

—Juliet Grames, author of *The Seven or Eight Deaths of Stella Fortuna*

AN
UNLIKELY
SPY

AN
UNLIKELY
SPY

A NOVEL

REBECCA STARFORD

ecco
An Imprint of HarperCollins*Publishers*

HarperCollins books may be purchased for educational, business, or sales promotional use. For information, please email the Special Markets Department at SPsales@harpercollins.com.

Ecco® and HarperCollins® are trademarks of HarperCollins Publishers.

Originally published as *The Imitator* in Australia in 2021 by Allen & Unwin.

A hardcover edition of this book was published in 2021 by Ecco, an imprint of HarperCollins Publishers.

FIRST ECCO PAPERBACK EDITION PUBLISHED 2022

Library of Congress Cataloging-in-Publication Data

Names: Starford, Rebecca, 1984– author.
Title: An unlikely spy : a novel / Rebecca Starford.
Description: First U.S. edition. | New York, NY : Ecco, [2021] | Originally published as The Imitator in Australia in 2021 by Allen & Unwin.
Identifiers: LCCN 2021002297 (print) | LCCN 2021002298 (ebook) | ISBN 9780063037885 (hardcover) | ISBN 9780063037915 (ebook)
Subjects: LCSH: Women spies—Fiction. | Great Britain. MI5—Fiction. | World War, 1939–1945—Fiction. | GSAFD: Spy stories. | Historical fiction.
Classification: LCC PR9619.4.S725 U55 2021 (print) | LCC PR9619.4.S725 (ebook) | DDC 823/.92—dc23
LC record available at https://lccn.loc.gov/2021002297
LC ebook record available at https://lccn.loc.gov/2021002298

ISBN 978-0-06-303790-8 (pbk.)

22 23 24 25 26 LSC 10 9 8 7 6 5 4 3 2 1

For Tess Ley

And for Elinor, always

Who has not asked himself at some time or other: am I a monster or is this what it means to be a person?

CLARICE LISPECTOR, *THE HOUR OF THE STAR*

MARCH 1948

ONE

EVELYN SPOTTED STEPHEN across the busy road. He was leaning against the railing outside the Hotel Russell, a grand old building on the eastern flank of the square, reading a paperback, his collar turned high about his throat. As he pulled out his pipe and rummaged around in his pockets for a light, Evelyn felt the sluice of anticipation; it was like encountering him for the first time, though they had in fact been meeting every Friday afternoon for the past year. Walking toward him, she observed him as a stranger might, taking in his crumpled overcoat, his loosened tie, his flushed cheeks. He whipped off his trilby and gave her a lopsided smile.

"Ah, there you are, Evelyn."

He clasped the felt brim, as if uncertain about what to do with his hands now he'd shoved the book and pipe away in his coat pocket. After all these months, they still weren't quite sure how to greet one another. He finally nodded toward the hotel's *thé-au-lait* terracotta entrance.

"So, fancy that drink? I'm absolutely parched."

He held out an arm by way of invitation, and as he followed her up the stairs and through the hotel's revolving doors, Evelyn caught his familiar scent of pipe smoke, cologne, and warm, damp hair.

They were seated by the dome window overlooking the square, their usual table. Though it was nearly five o'clock, the bar was empty apart from a man beside the piano with his head buried in a newspaper. Once the waitress, a big-boned girl with a Lancashire accent, had taken their orders, Stephen began to talk about his new commission. Since the war he had worked as an Italian translator—novels, mainly, as well as the occasional cache of documents for the embassy—and he had been invited by a professor in Rome to visit the university over the summer to deliver a paper and begin a new translation of Ovid.

"They're putting me up at La Sapienza," he said, settling into his chair. "In halls, which'll be jolly. When that's done, I thought I'd mosey about. Travel down to Naples. Sorrento, maybe. Duck over to Capri."

"What about all that sunshine?" Evelyn teased. Stephen, it had become their joke, could burn in a blizzard.

"Blimey, yes." His eyes grew wide. "It will be raging, won't it, in July?"

The waitress returned, struggling under a silver serving tray laden with a tumbler of whisky on ice for Stephen and an enormous teapot, china cup, and rock cake, beige and swollen like a deformed hand, for Evelyn. It was good tea here at the Russell, none of the ersatz stuff she had to buy from her local grocer's, and fragrant with an earthy spice.

"Well, it sounds like you'll have a lovely time," she said.

"That's the thing. I'll be away for a month. At least. And, yes, it will be a fine sort of trip . . ."

Stephen paused, took a gulp of whisky, and when he set down the glass he stared at it as if it were the receptacle of an ancient wisdom. Evelyn saw something in his eyes she didn't recognize—it might have been dread. He spread his hands against the tablecloth.

"The thing is, Evelyn, I don't want to be away for a month. From you. I had rather hoped you might come with me."

The top of his ears had turned red. Evelyn sat back; he had surprised her. She picked up the blunt knife and began sawing into the rock cake. The pianist started up a playful tune in the corner.

"You don't need to answer right away," Stephen said quietly. "I've caught you unawares." He looked into his lap. "But will you think about it?"

"Yes, of course." Glancing at his thinning hair, the fine freckles across his broad nose, Evelyn felt a throb deep in her chest. "Of course I'll think about it." She reached out, grazing her fingertips over his knuckles. "I'm so pleased you asked me, Stephen, really I am."

"Mm." Color had risen in his cheeks and he wouldn't look at her.

Evelyn clasped her hands together. She had hurt him. Sometimes she forgot she could still inflict pain on others.

"Very good. Right. Well." With a rattle of his empty glass, Stephen stood up. "I think I fancy another."

Evelyn watched him as he made his way to the bar. He dragged his left foot. It had been crushed by a pontoon at Dunkirk; he had been lucky not to drown. He was shy about his disfigurement but never ashamed. It was perhaps the first thing that drew Evelyn to him: the ease with which he spoke about the past. That, and how he never asked for much in return, even when she knew he must want her to share more of herself with him.

She rubbed at her eyes. The truth was she wanted to go to Rome. But there were so many complications—her papers, for one. How could she explain it all to him?

While Stephen lingered at the bar, she turned her attention to the window and the gardens outside. It was busier now, men and women streaming from the terraces surrounding the square, batting their way through the gaggle of children mobbing the Wall's ice-cream man on the corner. Evelyn's gaze rested on a small girl and a dark-haired woman. The girl, in a smart woolen dress, was chattering away, while the woman—her mother, Evelyn presumed—flicked through a picture-card stand by one of the stalls set up along the garden fence. Evelyn watched the graceful swoop of her gloved hand until, almost as if she sensed she was being watched, the woman turned. Her eyes met Evelyn's and what followed was a moment of perfect calm, just as the air had felt before a shell dropped.

"You do like brandy, don't you? I can never remember."

Setting a drink in front of her, Stephen followed Evelyn's gaze, one hand pressed into his back. "I've never understood how children can eat ice cream in the cold."

A bus rumbled past, a few cars.

"I say, are you all right, Evelyn? You're awfully pale."

Evelyn sat up straighter as Stephen, face pinched-looking, crouched in front of her.

"Look, you needn't worry about the Rome trip, honestly. It was just a mad idea."

She scanned the square for the woman and the little girl, but they were both gone.

"I mean, I could ask Timmy Walker to come. You remember Tim? Foreign Office. He's always had a bit of a thing for the Romans . . ."

Evelyn listened to Stephen's prattle, not wanting it to stop. As long as he kept talking, she could convince herself that she had imagined it. That she hadn't seen Julia Wharton-Wells at all. But then, after a burst of laughter from the lobby and the tail end of the pianist's song, came the cry: *"Evelyn?"*

Her voice still had that breathiness, as though she had just sprinted across the street.

Turning, Evelyn saw the little girl first, and up close she recognized the straight, almost black hair and the same watchful amber eyes.

Julia stepped forward, arms outstretched, and before Evelyn knew what she was doing she was on her feet, Julia's smooth coat, cigarette smoke, and perfume caught up in their embrace.

"*Julia?* I don't believe it!"

She had aged. Of course she had; it had been nearly eight years. Still, as Julia stepped back, holding her at arm's length to look her up and down, Evelyn was shocked by the gray in her hair and the constellation of lines around her eyes and forehead.

"It's really me—*ta-da!*" Julia's grip was tight around Evelyn's wrists. She gave a sharp bark of laughter and let go, gesturing to Stephen. "And who is this?"

Evelyn introduced them, and Stephen, who had watched their greeting with bemusement, said, "You must join us for tea. I've not met any of Evelyn's pals—I'd love to pick your brains."

Evelyn glared at him. "Julia will surely have other plans."

"What do you think, Margaret, darling?" Julia peered down at her daughter as she removed her gloves. The young girl was eyeing up the rock cake. "Daddy won't mind if we're a few minutes late, will he?"

Margaret shed her green coat. "Daddy won't mind," she repeated solemnly as she took the seat opposite Evelyn. She was missing a front tooth.

The waitress appeared with more cups and saucers, and everyone watched her pour the tea. After she'd gone, Julia sat down and unwound her expensive silk scarf, eyes skating about the bar. She wore a red box coat that matched her lipstick; Evelyn had forgotten how striking she was.

"Are you staying here at the hotel, Evelyn?"

"No, we're—" She felt Julia's frank gaze. "We were just having a drink."

"I see."

"Then we're off to a film over on Tottenham Court Road. In fact, we had better be going, hadn't we, Stephen?" Evelyn glared at him again, desperate to communicate her agitation at this unexpected meeting.

But Stephen wasn't looking. His attention was on Julia, perhaps wondering if she held the answers to his many questions about Evelyn's past.

"Don't worry about that," he murmured. "There'll be a later showing."

"See?" Julia patted the chair beside her. "No rush."

Somehow, Evelyn managed to sit down and smile graciously around the table. She still couldn't believe it was Julia sitting across from her. Was this what it felt like to encounter a ghost?

"I thought my eyes were playing tricks on me when I saw you, Evelyn. After all these years—I had to come over and make sure." Julia laughed again. "But you haven't changed a bit. I suppose you're still at the same job, too?"

"Evelyn works in a bookshop," Stephen said, bringing out his pipe. "Foy's, on Store Street. You know it?"

"Store Street?" Julia glanced at Stephen, something flinty and appraising in her expression. "No, I don't think so. But I will remember to drop in sometime."

Evelyn wanted to shriek at Stephen to shut up. She imagined old Mrs. Foy, alone in the flat above the shop, Julia prowling about the shelves of Margery Allinghams, and she swigged a mouthful of brandy, feeling it burn down her throat.

"And how do you know one another?" Stephen scraped a match against the box and lit his pipe. "From Oxford, was it?"

"The war, actually," Julia said.

"Really?" He leaned forward. "Evelyn's always coy about her war years. So you were at the hospital, too?"

Julia's eyes slid toward Evelyn. She picked up her teacup, raised it to her lips.

"It wasn't quite like that. We moved in similar circles, that's all."

"Did you?"

Stephen turned to Evelyn, gave her shoulder a light nudge with his. He was enjoying himself; there was a smile playing over his mouth. Evelyn gripped her knees beneath the table, nails digging into her stockings. She had to disrupt the conversation, swerve it away from anything that might compromise her. She focused on Margaret, who was picking despondently at the rock cake. If Julia had a weak spot, surely it would be this child.

"I didn't know you had a daughter," Evelyn said. "She looks just like you."

The last bit of sun had come out from behind the low gray clouds, flooding the front bar in dazzling light. Julia set her teacup back down in the saucer.

"Margaret keeps us on our toes, don't you, dear?"

The girl looked back at her mother doubtfully.

"How old is she?"

Julia stared at Evelyn, her jaw a hard line. "Five next month." She threaded her fingers together. "We've been lucky. I never thought . . ." She trailed off, gave a shrug. "But I do like this part of town," she said, sitting up straighter. "I don't live in London anymore. We're in Kent these days and very happy there." She shook her head. "Why am I telling you? I suppose you already know. But we do like to come up to London, don't we, Margaret? The children's park over at Coram's Fields is marvelous." She paused. "You're locals, I take it? You and your . . . husband?"

"No, we're not . . ."

The pianist had stopped and Evelyn could see the waitress watching them from behind the counter, her curiosity plain as she toyed with a loose apron thread. Even the man in the corner had lowered his newspaper to peer at them. Could they sense it too? Evelyn wondered. The disquiet in the room? It was practically crackling.

"We're not married." Stephen finished the sentence for her, and Evelyn felt him edge away, a cool space flourishing between them.

Julia nodded. "I always thought I might run into you. Though I expected you to have left England years ago."

"I did think about it. But one thing led to another. Work, you see . . ."

"Ah, yes. Did you stay on long, in the end, at the War Office?" Julia brushed at some nonexistent crumbs on her dress, her eyebrows arched. "Anyway, now I know where I can find you, we must get together for a proper catch-up. I think that's long overdue, don't you? Perhaps the next time we're down. Like I said, we're on our way to meet Margaret's father." Julia was smiling, but there was no feeling in her eyes. "I don't think you ever met him. He certainly knows about you."

The hairs on the back of Evelyn's neck bristled. "Well, it's been lovely," she said as she stood up. "But we really should be going."

She looked at Stephen; this time he understood and rose to his feet with her.

"What a shame! I should have liked to talk more." All conciliation, Julia began fishing through her leather handbag. "But look, before you go, let me give you something. I picked it up at the stall across the street. It was such a coincidence to find it there. I'm sure you'll remember it."

It was a postcard, a reproduction of *Judith in the Tent of Holofernes*, and as Julia passed it across the table Evelyn felt her stomach lurch. She didn't know the gallery had the painting—the Randalls must have sold it after the war. She stuffed the postcard inside her bag as Stephen drifted off to settle the bill.

"It reminded me of a story I heard years ago . . . Anyway, I've dozens of the things in the kitchen drawer at home, but I keep buying another every time I see one. We visit the gallery when we're in town, though I'm not sure why I keep returning to that ghastly place." Julia was clutching the back of the chair, her fingers as bloodless as talons. "You always did like art, didn't you, Evelyn? And books. Clever as you were. You always thought you were so much cleverer than the rest of us. But it didn't quite turn out that way, did it?"

Evelyn took a step back. The room seemed to tilt. Around them the bar was starting to fill.

Stephen returned, and she felt his hand on her arm, though it wasn't clear if he was steering her toward Julia or away from her.

"Turned to smoke and ashes, has it?" Julia was staring at the half-eaten rock cake.

Evelyn glanced at the door. Two dozen paces, maybe less. She could make it. She took another step, conscious of the pressure building behind her eyes. The room had begun to spin and the tables roared— wild, jabbering voices. She could hear Stephen talking, his voice floating toward her as if she were trapped under water, the pale light above the surface gradually dimming, and the next thing she was aware of was his grip around her elbow as he guided her past the bar, the off-key notes of a new prelude ringing in her ears.

Stephen walked her home. After the scene at the Hotel Russell, neither of them had much desire to go to the pictures or find somewhere to eat. They made their way in silence, Evelyn one pace behind, trying to make sense of what had just happened and how she might explain it to him. But when they reached her building on Flaxman Terrace, he stood on the curb, hands shoved deep into his coat pockets. She couldn't tell whether he was angry or not; he was looking at her in the same way Margaret had as they left the bar: as if she had done something to humiliate all of them.

"Who was that woman?" he asked finally. His voice was gentle, but rounded with curiosity.

Evelyn stared at him across the pavement. "I told you. An old friend. Not even a friend, really. An acquaintance."

"But why were you so . . . ." He blew out his cheeks. "I don't know—peculiar. I've never seen you like that."

Evelyn glanced toward her flat, where the orange light of the lamp glowed at the window.

"It was a surprise, that's all. I've not seen her in such a long time. Years!"

"Years?"

"Just don't ask me how many."

She tried to smile, but Stephen took off his hat and said, "She thought you worked at the War Office."

"Did she?"

"Yes." He frowned. "You heard her, didn't you?"

"She must have been thinking of someone else. It was a long time ago."

"But you worked at the hospital."

"Yes, I did. She was confused, Stephen, that's all."

Stephen folded his arms, giving her a hard look. Evelyn began searching through her bag for her key. She couldn't stand him watching her like that, incredulity in his eyes, demanding something of her that she couldn't give.

"I'm sorry about tonight," she said. "I'm not myself, you're right. But I'm tired—that's all. So very tired."

Immediately his face softened. "Why didn't you say?"

"Because I wanted to see you, that's why."

It had taken Evelyn some time to acknowledge the depth of these feelings to herself. That come Monday morning she would already have started counting down the clock to when she would next see him.

Stephen blew out his cheeks again.

"Can I at least fix you something upstairs? You've had no supper."

"No, I . . ." Evelyn pressed her lips together, afraid she might cry. "I think I'll just turn in for the night. But will you telephone tomorrow? We can make new plans."

"All right."

Evelyn could hear the disappointment in his voice, but she was desperate to get inside; she needed to be on her own to think. From the main road came the trill of the bus, the sound of a man shouting nearer to King's Cross station, the drift of a saxophone from the jazz club down the street. London was only now waking up for the night, but giving Stephen's arm a squeeze Evelyn headed to the front door without looking back.

◦—

Later, Evelyn sat on the edge of her windowsill and smoked. From here she had a good view of the narrow street pocketed behind Euston Road. She wasn't sure what she was waiting for. She finished her cigarette and pulled down the window, trying as always to close the gap where the frame didn't quite meet the ledge. Wrapping a shawl around her shoulders, she slumped into the armchair next to the fireplace, which was a grim thing with a low mantelpiece and a blackened grate smelling of old coke. She glanced at her watch. It was late, nearly midnight, but she knew he'd still be awake.

She went to the bureau by her bed and pulled out the small leather address book from the drawer. Then she crept downstairs to the telephone in the hall and dialed. The call rang for so long she thought he wasn't home until she heard the faint click of connection and that low, scratchy voice.

"Stepney Green 1484."

"I'm telephoning for the weather report."

There was a pause and a muffled sound on the other end of the line, like a sigh.

"What have you observed?"

"I believe summer has arrived."

"And the seed?"

Evelyn screwed her eyes shut. "It's growing."

The line went silent. Evelyn gripped the receiver. She didn't know what she would do if he couldn't help. But after several excruciating moments she heard his breathing resume.

"Well, well. If it isn't Chameleon." He let out a low whistle. "Bugger me."

She slumped against the cool wall, almost faint with relief.

"Hello, Vincent. I'm sorry to call so late."

"It's no bother. I don't sleep much these days, anyway." There was more clatter and another deep, puckered inhale—he must still be smoking those awful cigars. "You're not in trouble, are you?"

"I'm not sure. Maybe." Evelyn swallowed. "Something happened tonight. I'm not sure what to make of it. I know it's been a while, but could we meet? I'm in Bloomsbury."

"I know where you are, darling." She could hear the shape of Vincent's smile. "All right. Tomorrow morning. Zafer's, Lavender Hill. Ten o'clock." And he hung up.

Back inside her flat, Evelyn returned to the window. The night outside was blotchy like spilled ink. Among the shadows she could just make out the cat belonging to the lady at number twenty scavenging through a dustbin and, farther along the street, in the direction of

Mabel's Tavern, Old Jim the street sweeper bent over his broom and shovel.

She glanced back at her bed, at the slim pillow resting against the headboard, and felt her chest ache. How long was she prepared to live like this, to be always furtive and afraid? What if Stephen didn't call her in the morning? What if her reticence that evening—a reticence they both recognized but had never brought out into the clear air—spelled the beginning of the end between them? In some ways, it would make things easier. To always wonder. To never test the strength of her feelings. Because she had told herself that if it ever came to this she would run. Pack a bag and catch the first train to meet the ferry. She still had contacts in Belgium; Christine might help her. She still knew how to become another person.

But it was too late. She couldn't leave—she didn't know how to anymore. Flight was part of the past, the old days. It sounded almost quaint how people spoke about the war now, as if they were only cracking open an old biscuit tin and not the lid of an ancient sarcophagus. Yet that was how it felt to Evelyn as she sat in the gloom, head pressed against the cool glass: as though she had been woken from a curse.

JULY 1939

TWO

FROM HER VANTAGE point beneath a marble arch, Evelyn glimpsed Sally Wesley cross from the corner of Stephenson Street toward New Street. It was a Friday afternoon and the road outside the station was banked up with taxis and buses, commuters frantic to be in London by dinnertime swelling about the grand Edwardian entrance. Clutching her small leather suitcase, Evelyn moved out of the shade and made her way along the pavement, head down, sultry air full of dust, exhaust, and the faint rot of the Birmingham canals swirling about her feet.

"*Evelyn!*" Sally gave a great looping wave. "So sorry—are we very late?"

She didn't sound all that repentant, though Sally never did. There was even, thought Evelyn as her friend rushed over to embrace her, the start of a smile in her voice. She steered Evelyn through the remaining crowds, complimenting her dress (which was a plain one) and her straw hat (forgetting that it had once belonged to her), in an attempt to appease Evelyn after the hour-long wait that had left her sweaty and dazed. For her part, Sally looked well. Her long golden hair had been done up in a loose chignon and she exhibited both the tan and languor of a relaxed summer spent in the Shropshire sun.

They dodged the young men slouching under the hotel awning smoking and kicking at loose stones; one muttered something toward Evelyn under his breath, while another, hands deep in his pockets, spat on the asphalt. Sally, who had never been one for the smaller observations of people, noticed none of this as she happily chatted away in a manner that demanded no reply, taking Evelyn's hand as they crossed the road toward the row of cars opposite the station. It seemed extraordinary to Evelyn that it had already been six weeks since they had dozed together in the shade beside the Cherwell, lulled by the gentle drone of dragonflies, after seeing off the last of the Somerville College girls at the end of term.

Sally's father, Hugh, had come around to the back of the Bentley. A pair of motoring goggles rested on top of his broad head, his white hair flared like duckling down. He also wore his old Cambridge blues, his blazer bulging at his thickening waist.

"I see you're dressed for the occasion, Hugh," Evelyn called.

"Never miss a chance to grind you Oxford girls down, eh, Evelyn? Did I ever tell you about the Eights of '09?"

"Only about a *thousand* times."

Hugh laughed and bent down to give Evelyn a kiss, his ruddy cheek smooth against hers. He smelled faintly of Caron aftershave and diesel.

"Well, isn't this fine," he bellowed, taking her suitcase as he stepped off the curb. "Just like the old days. We've missed you at the manor, Evelyn." This was the first time in many years that Evelyn had not spent July at the Wesleys' estate in Onibury. "Sallywag's been rattling round like a spare penny."

"I have," Sally confirmed, opening the passenger-side door. "Bored practically out of my skull."

Evelyn climbed sluggishly into the back seat, a faint ache pulsing behind her left eye.

"What about Jonty?" she asked, the car heaving as Hugh grunted and cajoled her suitcase into the boot.

"That's the thing, I've hardly seen him." Sally pulled her door shut. "He's been at the air base since April, though you'd think he'd been locked away in jail. He had to get special leave for tomorrow night—isn't that tight?"

"To attend his own engagement party? Yes, I should say so."

Sally reached over the seat and clasped Evelyn's hand in her sticky one, giving it a squeeze.

"I'm so glad you could make it, Ev. Seems silly, but I'm terribly nervous about it all now. Mother's invited about half of London. All these people just to make a fuss over me."

"Well, I wouldn't miss it for anything. And it certainly beats another weekend at Mrs. Banker's."

Finally, Hugh climbed back into the driver's seat. He started up the Bentley and they drove southward, down the wide road that curved around the town hall.

"And how is old Mrs. B?" Sally shouted over the engine. "She really was awful that time on the telephone. She ought to brighten up, *non*? I can't imagine how she manages to keep any lodgers."

Sally had never seen the boardinghouse on Bramham Gardens in Earl's Court—and Evelyn hoped to keep it that way. It was a tired old terrace, identical to the rest in the block, and grimy from the smog, the paintwork chipped and the front curtains always crookedly drawn.

"Mrs. Banker's not so bad," Evelyn said. "I think she's rather lonely."

"You would be too with manners like that. What did she call you again?"

"*Your most royal highness.*"

Sally laughed. It had always been difficult to make her understand the particular searching quality in Mrs. Banker that Evelyn found so unsettling.

"She's never quite got the measure of me, that's all." Evelyn stared up at the pastel sky. The afternoon had a heavy, ripe feeling like it was about to spoil, and far away fat clouds were beginning to cluster. "Imagines I'm one thing when I'm really another."

Sally folded her hands behind her head, yawning. "But who does she imagine you might be?"

On that final afternoon by the Magdalen Bridge, Evelyn had eventually said goodbye to Sally and returned to halls for her luggage, then caught the bus to London. With the help of another college friend whose father was the director of the board, she had lined up a job in the advertising department of an Old Bond Street cosmetics firm. She'd replied to the classified about the room in Earl's Court. Sally had been furious, insisting that Evelyn should stay at the Wesley family house in Mayfair, which otherwise sat empty over the summer; but with notions of independence, and perhaps a little overconfidence, Evelyn had been determined to strike out on her own, away from the cloistered safety of the university and, though she daren't say it, away from Sally.

But London was proving to be a hard city, living in it quite different from visiting. Instinctively, Evelyn scrunched her toes inside her brogues, where large blisters had swelled from the long days spent on her feet. The truth was she had no money to buy new shoes—her wage at Vivian de la Croix barely covered her room and board, her bus fare, and a sandwich for lunch. And the job, though not mentally taxing, had her trudging all day around the city's department stores to advise them on how best to exhibit their compacts and rouge in the front display windows, leaving her with only enough energy each night to return to Bramham Gardens for a supper of Mrs. Banker's potted ham and green beans. She knew it was only temporary, but still Evelyn wanted to do more, much more—she just hadn't quite landed on what that might be.

It was fortuitous, then, that she had received Sally's letter last week, a frantic scribble in smeared ink on a card embossed with the Wesley crest: *Engaged! At last! Celebration at the Manor on the 22nd—do say you'll come! x S.* Evelyn had propped the card against the ledge of her bureau and smiled at it from time to time. She wasn't quite sure how, but she had the strong sense that this weekend would offer the chance to recast her life in London. Things tended to turn out like this; knowing the right sort of people, she'd come to learn, opened many doors. Besides, her ambitions for now were modest. She wanted to use the German she had read at Oxford to find a teaching job or do a little translation, though with another war threatening that prospect was looking less likely by the day.

Still, Evelyn refused to despair. She studied Hugh's hair whipping about in the hot, dry breeze. He was bound to know someone in the Foreign Office or some other ministry and could arrange an introduction—that was the sort of man he was. Evelyn stretched out her bare legs, trying to catch some sun on her knees, and recalled her manager's advice to the new recruits on her first day at Vivian de la Croix: *Many a small thing has been made large by the right kind of advertising.* It had been a rousing speech on the office floor, followed by a round of applause as if they were in a football locker room, before the salesmen and -women of the firm streamed noisily from the building with satchels stuffed full of samples. But all Evelyn could think about as she watched them leave was something she believed Oscar Wilde once said: *Be yourself; everyone else is already taken.*

The afternoon sun pulsed across the city. The noisy traffic around the canal basin had soon banked up, and despite her hat Evelyn's face began to burn. Sally sat with her head tipped back, a pair of tortoiseshell sunglasses deflecting the worst of the glare, and Evelyn reached forward to place a hand on her friend's brown shoulder.

"So, has a date been decided for the big day?"

"Please don't get her started on the wedding." Hugh groaned, dabbing at the back of his neck with a handkerchief. Sally had spoken of little else but Jonty this past year. "Or the invitations . . ."

"Well, they shouldn't have sent the wrong paper!" Sally twisted in her seat to face Evelyn. "It's all terrifically exciting. *Mrs.* van der Hoort. Sounds awfully regal, doesn't it?"

"Sounds foreign, that's what," muttered Hugh.

"Though talk about delaying the inevitable. Really, I should have had the thing stitched up years ago and saved Daddy the tuition fees."

Evelyn smiled, though she couldn't help feeling that Sally was right. Being Jonty's wife would make her happy in a way no other occupation could—which was lucky, Evelyn supposed, because Sally wasn't much inclined to work. Still, no matter how hard she tried, Evelyn could not muster any enthusiasm for the nuptials. She had never taken to Jonty. He was blond and thick-set with two big front teeth, and spoke to Sally with drawling familiarity, as if she were an aging aunt and not his future wife.

As they idled on the Broad Street bridge, Evelyn peered down to the canal beneath them and spotted a blue and red barge. On the front deck stood an elderly man pouring water from a bucket into the river. When he was finished, he stood straighter and gazed toward the creeping shadow of the tunnel. Something about the man, perhaps his stance with his palms pressed into the small of his back, reminded Evelyn of her father.

She had been putting off a visit to her parents since she'd left Oxford; the most recent of her father's letters sat unopened on her bureau at Bramham Gardens. He had sounded disappointed when she telephoned the house last month with the news about her job at Vivian de la Croix, though he didn't say as much—neither of her parents were all that good at saying what they really thought—and after that Evelyn hadn't confided in them about her life in London. It was a habit already formed; for years her parents had shown little interest in her education, except when she announced she had decided to read German at Oxford; her father had refused to speak to her for a week, prompting her mother to remark, "Couldn't you have at least chosen French, dear?" They didn't understand: she had fallen in love with the language and the way it transported her to a different world the moment her German teacher stood in front of the class and read out passages from *Faust*. For Evelyn, another language was a means of escape. She exhaled a stream of air through gritted teeth. She knew she must visit Lewes soon, but as she watched the man on the barge potter about the bow, gathering up a heavy length of rope and dropping it down by the bucket, she swept the thought aside. She refused to be bothered by obligation this weekend.

"Anyway," said Sally, throwing out an arm along the warm leather seat back to examine her red nail polish, "*I* fancy spring for the wedding, but Jonty's keen for sooner. And the manor does look gorgeous when the leaves turn . . ." She sighed. "All depends on what old Jerry has planned, I suppose."

"Mm." Evelyn squinted against the glare. "That may throw a spanner in the works." It was shameful, really, but that was how everyone had begun to speak about the tensions in Europe: as though the world grinding toward another cataclysm was no more inconvenient than the late arrival of a train.

"I suppose if there has been a declaration, Jonty could wear his full-dress uniform, with the headgear and everything?"

"Now that's what I love about you, Sal," Evelyn said. "You'll find a positive in every situation."

Sally gave a shrug. "I'm nothing if not pragmatic."

"Jonty's a solid boy," Hugh piped up. "Maybe a bit brash at times, but he has a good heart. I'm still making up my mind about those other van der Hoorts."

Sally put her arm around her father's broad shoulders and ruffled his hair. "You've known them for twenty years, Daddy. What else is there to make up your mind about?"

Hugh kept his eyes fixed on the road. Evelyn knew little of Jonty's parents except that they owned vineyards in Stellenbosch and were, according to Sally, "filthy rich," which always conjured the image of them scrounging for grapes on their hands and knees in the chalky earth. Sally twisted in her seat again, her sparkling eyes wide as she pushed back her sunglasses and gazed at Evelyn.

"But can you believe they still won't stay over at the manor? Not even for one night. Those South Africans are peculiar, if you ask me. Too much sun."

"Too much *something*," said Hugh, and taking in his motoring goggles and blazer Evelyn tried not to smile again.

"Jonathan insists on driving back to Stokesay straight after the party. Jonty says his father hates sleeping anywhere but his own bed. Isn't that odd?"

This remark from Sally finally seemed to demand an answer from Evelyn.

"Yes," she said. "Very."

"Especially when you cop an eyeful of Hermione." Hugh met Evelyn's glance in the rearview mirror. "Can't think why he'd want to sleep in that bed . . ."

"*Daddy!*"

They all laughed, the air blowing milder as the traffic at last gained pace, each vehicle pulling away from the pack. Tipping her hat forward, Evelyn sat back and closed her eyes, the last of Birmingham's redbrick villages flitting by before the dense woodland began.

~

It was nearing dusk by the time they reached the wrought-iron gates. The far-off lights from the house glowed through a dewy gauze. Hugh took the long drive fast, the Bentley kicking up great sprays of gravel. The Wesleys owned more than a thousand acres around the manor and several surrounding farms. Most of the property was used for agriculture—cows, mainly, and some sheep as well as an orchard—but there was also a large woodland full of local native pine that began at the bottom of the lawn.

Evelyn could remember the exact moment she fell in love with the estate. It had been her first visit, during that long, wet summer of 1931 before the new school year—Evelyn's second at Raheen School. It felt odd now, but in another life Sally and Evelyn might never have met. Evelyn had been the scholarship girl in their eighteen-bed dormitory; Lewes was in the catchment area for the school's annual Harwood Prize for a local girl, and when she turned eleven Evelyn was encouraged by her headmaster to sit the exam. No one expected her to win a place, least of all Evelyn herself, but for as long as she could remember she had wanted to get far away from Lewes, from its bland high street and canal, and, if she dared to admit it, from her parents' brown stucco two-story cottage at the top of the hill. Experience, even at that young age, had always felt constrained in the sleepy, provincial town, only to be measured out in small, neat servings. She'd never been abroad, or even as far as London, but she knew another life existed, and she had read enough books to understand that going to a school like Raheen would offer her the chance to divert from the path her mother had trodden, which had left her with no real education or career, and married with a child before the age of twenty.

"What an opportunity," her mother had breathed when the letter from the school arrived, her fingertips hovering above the seal as though she was afraid it might burn her. "Haven't you done well for yourself, dear."

"I'll have to live away from you and Dad *all year*?" Amid her excitement, Evelyn had not fully contemplated what it might be like to live with so many strangers.

"Yes, but that's part of the fun, isn't it? Besides, we'll see you on visits, and when you're back at term break."

"But what about you?"

"Me?" Her mother looked up from the letter, smiling faintly. "What about me?"

Evelyn glanced at her father in his reading chair, the newspaper spread over his knees.

"What will you and Dad do while I'm gone?"

Her mother stared back at Evelyn, her smile faltering.

"Well," she said. "We'll be waiting for you, of course."

Evelyn had nodded. There was something comforting about this pledge, a picture she could hold in her mind of her parents in the house, as reliable as the sun each morning at the kitchen window.

Her father added with a chuckle, "But promise you won't go and forget us, Evelyn, once you're mixing with the finest in the realm."

He had never been much cowed by class. His father, Evelyn's grandfather, had worked as a barrel man at the local brewery and had been, as far as Evelyn could tell, an awful drunk and a bully. Still, her father had grown up clever, and liked to read, something he had encouraged in her, and though too lazy to be much of an ideologue he was still suspicious of anyone who sought to rise above their station, including his own daughter. He spent most of his spare time hunched over his newspapers, worrying about Europe. "It was the ordinary folk that kept the establishment safe during the Great War—and it'll be the ordinary folk again." He'd always look at Evelyn as he said this, narrowing his eyes, as if he expected her to come downstairs one day in fatigues with a rifle slung over her shoulder. To lighten the mood, he sometimes read out the marriage announcements over breakfast: "Listen to this, dear. *Alexandra Christabel Josephine Winifred Henrietta Gordon* of Montaigne House, to marry *Frederick Alfred William James Henry Upton-Rugg* of Ludmere Castle . . . Honestly, that's just greedy, that is. Why do these aristocrats need quite so many names?"

"Imagine the 'I do's,'" Evelyn would say. "They'll go on for hours."

"And can somebody tell me what's wrong with plain old Freddy Rugg?"

But as Evelyn had watched her mother place that letter from the school on the mantelpiece, she had seen something fleeting in her eyes, her manner almost deferential as she muttered, "We'll have to buy the girl some new clothes," before returning to the kitchen.

"What's wrong with what she's got?" her father grumbled, his own woolen jumper in desperate need of some fresh darning at the elbow. "We're not made of money, you know."

But the next week her mother had taken Evelyn to London anyway, visiting Bourne & Hollingsworth on Oxford Street, where they bought a pair of white T-strap sandals, a navy pleated skirt, and a few smart cotton blouses, and as if that wasn't enough, afterward Evelyn was treated to tea and pastries at Maison Bertaux on Greek Street before they caught the evening train home. It had been strange seeing her mother among all the noise and life of the city, wide-eyed and almost girlish in these unfamiliar, exciting surrounds. Later, after her mother had swapped her smart coat for a damp apron and pair of old plaid slippers, Evelyn wondered if the trip had given her pause to reflect on the dips in her own fate, and how her circumstances might have played out if the coin had landed differently for her, but these were questions she did not know how to ask.

Her father had accompanied Evelyn to her new school a few weeks later. Raheen stood on the Sussex Downs and the wind was blowing salty off the Channel as they crossed the front lawn. It was an enormous campus, with tennis courts, a hockey pitch, and a swimming pool, while to the west were the fenced-off paddocks of the school's farm and orchard. A dark-haired woman had been waiting on the front steps. She extended a hand to Evelyn's father.

"Frau Schneider. Pleased to meet you, Mr. Varley. I'll escort Evelyn upstairs."

Evelyn felt her father tense beside her. Taking off his hat, he blinked back at the teacher, then turned to Evelyn, almost stricken.

"I guess this is goodbye." He patted her on the shoulder and gave her a scratchy kiss, something he never did. But as he passed over the heavy suitcase, he leaned in again to whisper, "Just remember to be yourself, all right, dear? Don't mind what the others might say. Be yourself and you'll get on just fine." Then, without another word, he rammed his hat back on and stalked away, his shoulders stooped against the wind.

Evelyn watched him until he disappeared, then looked up at the clock tower. "What an opportunity," her mother had breathed again as they packed Evelyn's new clothes from London; she seemed to believe that her daughter could step from one world into another as easily as they had passed through the department store's revolving doors. But as she walked up those front steps with Frau Schneider, Evelyn knew that the abyss had cracked wide open; that while she had finally left Lewes, the town would never leave her, and she was stuck, no longer certain of who she was or where she belonged.

Evelyn had trailed after the teacher through the cold, empty corridors until they came to a high-ceilinged room at the end of a passageway, inside which about half a dozen girls were hanging up tunics and shaking down quilts. Frau Schneider directed Evelyn to the bed by the bay windows, a label inscribed *Varley* attached to the foot. As soon as she had gone, the other girls set down their things and crowded around Evelyn's bed.

"I'm Cynthia Buckland," announced one who appeared to be their leader. She had long hair in a plait and a small upturned nose. "You're local, aren't you? One of our charity cases?"

Evelyn stared back at her. "I won the Harwood Prize," she said, "if that's what you mean."

"I say, will you get an earful of *that*! We don't have a Sussex interpreter on staff, do we? *I woon de Harrwood Pryze, if that's whatcha mayne . . .*"

The other girls tittered. Cynthia peered into Evelyn's suitcase, drawing out a blouse on the tip of her finger like it was rubbish dredged from a drain. She held it aloft, turning in a circle for all to see.

"Visit the summer sales, did we, Varley?"

Cynthia gave Evelyn a hard look, but Evelyn held her gaze. With few scholarship girls at Raheen, she had expected some tiresome strutting; she knew there was bound to be a hierarchy in this place, with herself at the bottom of the pecking order. But that didn't mean she would be intimidated.

Cynthia dropped the blouse back into the case and sighed. "Dinner's at six. I'm sure you'll find your way there. Just follow the stench of boiled cabbage." Then she turned on her heel and stalked back down the aisle.

Evelyn counted her footsteps across the dormitory. *Eight, nine, ten*, her breathing returning to normal. But when she thought again of her father—*listen to this, dear*—she felt her eyes sting.

After the other girls had drifted off, Evelyn finished her unpacking, then stood at the window and stared out at the darkening sea. There was something cruel about such an outlook from the dormitory, she thought, as if to remind them there was no pathway to escape. When she heard a noise in the doorway Evelyn found a short, ungainly girl with pale hair and a babyish face shuffling along the aisle. She came up to the bed next to Evelyn's, swollen eyes briefly cast her way. The label on the foot read *Wesley*.

She sat on the edge of her bed. "You're new this term too? I think we're the only ones." The girl sniffed. "I've been told they're always harder on the new girls."

Evelyn gave her a smile before turning back to the window, her eyes fixed to the sliver of moon now hanging low on the horizon.

This was how Evelyn and Sally came into the same orbit, clinging to one another as lonely people often did. Cynthia and her friends picked on Evelyn whenever they could, about her accent, her clothes, and the perceived gaps in her education. Her crimes were not knowing anyone of importance, nor ever having traveled or eaten fine food. They laughed when she told them her father was a clerk, which finally made her weep under the lukewarm shower one night. She could bear their insults, but there was something uniquely humiliating about them finding fault with her parents.

"I know it's hard, but it's not really about you," Sally said. "They just don't like anyone different."

Sally had managed to avoid the ire of most girls at Raheen. She wasn't studious like Evelyn, failing to grasp even the most basic concepts in every subject, while some vague claim to injury always excused her from gymnastics or hockey. And she certainly couldn't hold a tune. But she was a happy person—such a rare attribute in that bluestone prison. The vagaries of school life never seemed to touch her, and Evelyn came to respect this aspect of her nature, seeing how it inured her friend from the harshest trials. And the truth was

Sally didn't care where Evelyn came from or what her father did. She valued her loyalty and her cleverness—qualities that, according to Sally, meant Evelyn was certain to go far. Sally was generous, too, sharing her clothes, her books, and the parcels of sweets her mother sent each week in the post. Of course, she could afford to be generous: her family was one of the wealthiest in England. Their money came from Sally's great-grandfather, an entrepreneur who had made his fortune in buttons, and the Wesleys, Evelyn learned on their weekend strolls along the rugged clifftop path, were acquainted with many people of importance and influence. Politicians, captains of industry, diplomats, even royalty.

"Daddy knows everyone there is to know," said Sally, pushing an aniseed-flavored gobstopper around her mouth. "Fingers in all sorts of pies. When the time comes, he'll set you right, Ev."

They had stopped at the lookout, the sea beneath them churning, the Brighton marina the size of a toy model below. This was how they spoke to one another in the depths of their isolation, picturing this great, bright future, though Evelyn had no notion of what being set right meant back then.

Still, when the Wesleys first invited Evelyn to stay she had been wary, expecting Sally's parents to be grown-up versions of the Raheen girls, full of mockery and derision. But when she had arrived at Crewe on a humid morning, Evelyn discovered the whole family waiting on the otherwise empty platform—Sally, her parents, even their English pointer puppy, Tortoise. They had all motored over from Onibury to welcome her.

"We're so pleased to meet you at last, Evelyn," Elizabeth Wesley had said before crushing her in a musky hug.

They drove back through poky villages and lush green forests, Evelyn up front, squeezed between Hugh and Elizabeth, while Sally lounged in the back, Tortoise's head out the window, his floppy brown ears whipped back in the wind. Around bends and kinks in the road, over streams and bridges—gorgeous countryside that grew more rural the deeper they traveled into south Shropshire, the road winding through the heather-clad hills of the Long Mynd. Then, after nearly two hours, they turned up the drive, Evelyn straining across Elizabeth's lap, awed by the sight of the manor sitting like a medieval castle at the top of the rise. It was made of sandstone and had more than a hundred rooms—some, Sally claimed, that even she had never been inside. The south face, which they approached at speed, was all columns and pilasters and open parapets, and as Evelyn gazed up toward them she imagined artillerymen hiding behind the stonework, cannons poised, as though the family were preparing for battle.

"Not a bad pile, is it?" Hugh said, giving her a wink, and Evelyn had felt a flutter of hopefulness that this might be a place where she could find real belonging.

Now, eight years later, Hugh brought the car around the back of the house and pulled up by the old stables near the east wing. There beneath the gaslight at the servants' entrance stood Parker.

Hugh hauled himself from the driver's seat and bent over to inspect something in the gravel, eventually raising a piece of stone the size of a cricket ball into the fading light.

"More crumbling, Parker?" he asked as the butler strode toward him.

"Yes, sir. Yesterday's wind brought down half the spire. My apologies—I thought we'd cleared the debris away."

As Hugh tossed the stone aside, Evelyn's eyes were drawn to the nearest turret, scarred with a jagged crack the shape of a lightning bolt.

She followed Sally inside and up the stairs to her bedroom. Unlike the rest of the house, Sally's room was small and plain, the cream walls bare, with only a faded pink floral barkcloth hanging at the window. Despite this austerity (or perhaps owing to it, Evelyn always thought) the room could have belonged to a child, a timelessness captured in the unmoving eyes of Sally's dolls who occupied the chaise longue in front of the pine cone–filled hearth. There were a dozen guestrooms in this part of the manor, but Evelyn always slept in Sally's room. Sally insisted on it; said it was like bunking in halls, though how that was a comfort Evelyn didn't know. Not that she ever protested—the bedroom did have a splendid view over the front lawn and the Italianate fountain of Neptune, which Evelyn studied from her position by the window seat after she had changed, her feet tucked beneath her while a warm breeze rustled the curtains.

"Is that all you've brought?"

Sitting at the dressing table and dusting her cheeks with powder, Sally pointed to Evelyn's suitcase at the end of the bed.

"I'm only staying until Sunday, remember?"

"What about tomorrow night? Your dress?"

Evelyn stood up and went to stand at her friend's side, examining the various compacts and lipsticks and blushes. None of it was Vivian de la Croix. "I thought I'd borrow one of yours."

"Did you?" Sally smiled and sprayed some perfume about her throat, watching in the mirror as Evelyn drifted across the room and began flicking through the dresses on the rack inside the oak cupboard. "Maybe the turquoise?"

"You think?"

"It goes well with your skin. I'm too chubby for it now, anyway."

"You are not." But Evelyn could see that Sally had put on a few pounds over the summer. All that rich food, no doubt. Evelyn, meanwhile, was thinner than ever. Whatever Mrs. Banker's skills might be, they were not found in the kitchen.

"Did Daddy say?" Sally murmured, applying some mascara. "Julia is home from Germany."

Evelyn's hand brushed the turquoise gown, the silk cool against her fingertips.

"Is she? Since when?"

"Arrived back in Harwich last week. We hadn't heard a peep from her in months and were starting to worry—and then *poof*! She was on her way from Rotterdam."

It was a long time since Evelyn had seen Julia Wharton-Wells, though she had heard all about her eloping to Berlin with a much older man, their wild parties in Prenzlauer Berg, and, more recently, their separation. Sally had narrated these stories breathlessly—Julia was her only cousin, almost like a sister since the death of her mother, Hugh's sister. She must be about twenty-six now; she had been in her final year when Evelyn started at Raheen.

"Is she coming tomorrow night?"

"Mm." Sally set down the mascara, blinking slowly at the glass. "I should think so. You know Julia. Never misses a party."

"What about her husband . . . Has he traveled over with her?"

"Hans? Good Lord, no. Daddy would have him shot on sight. He's a brute—like that was a surprise. Anyway, I think they have divorced. Julia has about as good taste in men as her mother did."

"She did well to get out of Germany," Evelyn said, watching Sally. "Aren't the borders closed?"

"I've no idea. All I know is that strings were pulled with Daddy's friends at the Foreign Office."

"Guide ropes, more like." Evelyn laughed.

"What do you mean?"

"Wasn't Hans quite . . . well, you know . . . friendly with German top brass?"

"Oh. I don't think so." Sally pressed her lips together, smiling at her reflection. "They're not all Hitler fanatics, you know, Ev. Anyway, Julia has nothing to do with all that. She was only a girl when she went over there. She hardly knew what she was doing."

Evelyn had only spoken to Julia a few times at school. She led a pack of tall, leggy sixth formers, barely glancing at the junior girls who scattered from their path after meals in the dining hall or before nighttime assemblies in the common room. Evelyn had watched them with a curious mix of terror and adulation; they occupied a mysterious, transitional space to her: nearly women but still girls, shrieking and giggling and pushing out their voluptuous chests beneath thick navy sweaters, something desperate and jittery about them, like fillies in the race gate before the gun was fired. But Julia wasn't like that. She never giggled or preened, and as she marched past Evelyn she was always looking straight ahead, her amber eyes narrowed in determination as though something else waited for her at the finish line.

And then, one Sunday morning in late spring, as the choral notes of Psalm 23 drifted through the air, Evelyn found Julia smoking alone under an oak tree at the back of the chapel. She looked nothing like her fair cousin; Julia was all sharp angles, her bobbed hair so dark it was almost black, something violent about the red of her lips as she sucked on that Westminster.

"You're Sallywag's friend," she observed. "Evelyn, isn't it?"

She offered Evelyn a drag on her cigarette. Evelyn took a quick inhale, a cough blooming in her throat. She had never smoked before.

"But what are you doing out here? You'll be in trouble if they find you skiving off."

Evelyn shrugged. "I'll risk it. I couldn't sit through another sermon."

Julia picked up an acorn and lobbed it across the lawn. "What is it this morning?"

"Matthew on Judas."

"Again?"

"If you ask me, it only gives us ideas."

Julia tucked some hair behind her small ear. "What do you mean?"

"Well, I think it gives us ideas about betrayal," Evelyn said. "These morality stories are supposed to be warnings, aren't they? But what if they only plant seeds in our imagination?"

There was amusement on Julia's face as she placed her hands lightly on her hips.

"You're not like the rest of them, are you," she said, smiling at Evelyn's embarrassment. "That's a good thing, trust me. I'm not like them, either."

Evelyn looked up. "You're not?"

"Don't get me wrong. I talk the same, dress the same, have the right sort of name." Julia raised a finger and tapped it against her temple. "But I'm not like them in here."

Despite the cool morning breeze, Evelyn felt her cheeks grow warm. She recalled the stories she had heard about Julia's mother. Crude stories, really, about how before she died she had gone with other men. Many men. "Hundreds," Cynthia Buckland had hissed with lurid delight. She called Julia's mother a slut. Sally wasn't aware of these stories—at least Evelyn hoped she wasn't—but as Julia stood taller, brushing down her blouse and fixing her clear gaze across the grass, Evelyn wondered if she knew her mother's reputation.

Julia smiled again, lines creasing around her eyes. "Funny, isn't it? I want to get away. You want to get in. Pity we can't help each other out."

Evelyn frowned. "Don't you want to be like everyone else?" she asked.

"Why should I want that? Wearing the same mousy dresses, grazing on the same tasteless food, spending each night in the same drafty dormitory with girls I detest . . ." Julia brushed some hair from her eyes. "This place is nothing more than a factory churning out proper little Englishwomen like tins of bully beef. Why don't we have room for something else? Something . . . *better*?" She sighed and ground the cigarette butt into the grass beneath her heel. "Still, I suppose there is some truth to that old Japanese saying: *The nail that sticks up gets hammered down.*"

"Maybe." Evelyn picked up her own acorn and moved it from palm to palm. "We haven't done Japanese proverbs yet."

Julia stared at her, then she laughed. "What an odd girl you are."

They stood in silence, the wind blowing at their legs, and after a while Julia seemed to forget that she had company. Evelyn searched for something she might say to insert herself back into Julia's consciousness. But all she could think about was how impossible the task of growing up like Julia seemed, full of so many ideas and opinions, and she felt the bright prick of fear that in the years to come she would resemble an old mangled branch on the tree looming above them, always on the brink of snapping under too much weight.

Another hymn rumbled from the chapel and a few seagulls screeched across the sky. Straightening her tie, Julia pointed to the edge of the lawn, where the earth suddenly dropped away.

"Have you found the tunnels yet?" she asked. "They lead right down to the beach. None of the other girls dare—they're scared some fellow is waiting in the dark to rape them. But I've never seen anyone else down there, so you can do whatever you like. Once I drank a half bottle of whisky and slept through supper." As Julia glanced over her shoulder, Evelyn saw something anguished pass across her face. "Some nights I gather cockles washed up along the beach. I bring them back and Cook puts them in a saucepan with some butter and garlic for me—delicious." She made a kissing gesture with her fingertips that Evelyn had never seen before but assumed she could have only learned in France. "Come too, if you like?"

"All right," said Evelyn, excited at what the other girls would make of this invitation. "I will."

But she never had the chance. Julia was excluded the following week and sent to London. Evelyn discovered there had been a long list of misdemeanors before this, but an incident with the sports master on the beach had been the final straw. Sally wept at the news, though they were angry tears. "She always has to make a scene," she cried. "Always has to stand out!" Evelyn sat beside her, rubbing her friend's back, imagining the dank, musty tunnels beneath the cliff and trying to understand what had drawn Julia to hide down there.

Of course, Julia could have never known that her experience would inspire Evelyn's quiet and careful project of assimilation at Raheen. She no longer wanted to stand out and be unhappy, so she decided to recast herself as a background player, a bit part, and go unnoticed for the remainder of her schooling. That was the way to get along, she had come to understand. That was the way to make a success of herself.

It began with her appearance, accepting more and more of Sally's old clothes from Debenhams, while saving up her own modest pocket money to spend judiciously each midterm visit to London. Then came the extra elocution and comportment lessons, which soon had her speaking with the same rounded vowels as everyone else. She no longer finished a meal, as an empty plate was uncouth ("You're not a farmhand ravenous after a day in the field, Miss Varley," Frau Schneider scolded), and tea was certainly poured before milk. And when she asked her mother and father to stop visiting each month, their bedraggled presence in the house foyer after the long walk from the bus stop drawing ignominy and hilarity, Evelyn's transformation was complete. By the time she turned thirteen, the bullying had stopped, and after Cynthia asked her to partner up for doubles at tennis and they won the House Cup, Evelyn was invited to sit with Cynthia and her friends at meals, even joining them on a few Sunday trips to Brighton.

"Looks like you've been accepted at last," said Sally one evening as they changed into their nightgowns before bed.

Evelyn threw a sock across the aisle. "Are you jealous?"

"Hardly." Sally peeled back her quilt. "I don't understand, that's all. I thought you hated them."

Looking down the length of the dormitory to where Cynthia was brushing her hair at the standing mirror, something hot and metallic rose in Evelyn. She did hate them. It was like a furnace, that loathing. It never burned out.

"Well, you know what they say: *Keep your friends close . . .*"

She smiled, but Sally only frowned and climbed beneath the covers. "If you say so," she murmured. "I'm sure you know what you're doing."

While the Raheen girls may have forgotten her inglorious past, Evelyn hadn't, and neither, it seemed, had her father. "Blimey," he declared during her visit home at Christmas. "They'll have you presenting on the BBC soon."

The next time she came down, he began commenting on her clothes, her hair, even her manners at the dinner table—"Bring out the best silver, Mum, one of the princesses has come for tea!"

It was all in jest, she told herself, but these remarks snagged like a thread caught on a branch when she realized he enjoyed making fun of her. *No*, she wanted to shout at him. *Can't you see I'm not like that? That I'm not like them?* It was one of the few things that could raise her temper, and this made her father chuckle and shake his head, as though he'd won an argument she hadn't known they'd been having. She had always expected they would laugh together about the peculiarities of the school, the spoiled girls, their small-mindedness despite all this "opportunity"—after all, this was how it had been between them before she went away. But now he didn't understand her, or seem to want to. Her mother was no better, clucking around, her conversation never venturing beyond what Evelyn might need to take back to the dorm, as if she couldn't wait to be rid of her daughter.

Sometimes, as Evelyn lay in her bed upstairs, she was racked by loneliness. She loved her parents, but now she could see them for their true selves, free from the burnish of childish idolatry or just plain youthful ignorance. She knew her father belittled her because he couldn't face the idea of her one day looking down on him, and she recognized how meager her mother's existence had become, counting out her shillings at the bakery and going without new clothes or books or an outing to a restaurant, refusing any activity that she deemed *indulgent*. Evelyn was embarrassed by this puritan denial of even the smallest forms of pleasure. She didn't want her life to be a mere transaction; she wanted to feel the workings of experience deep in her bones. She knew her parents sensed this change in her, but since she could never tell them about what really happened at school, she had to live with the knowledge that they believed she had actually become this person and was not merely wearing a disguise.

⌐

Supper that night was served in the parlor. It was cold meats with half a dozen salads, and a good deal of wine. Elizabeth Wesley sat at the top of the table still dressed in her paint-stained smock. She had spent the afternoon in her studio by the lake putting the finishing touches on a landscape that would form part of her collection due for exhibition in Edinburgh. *The Breeze Through the Trees* she was calling it, and a friend had arranged private rooms for the showing in Abercromby Place.

Evelyn loved meals with the Wesleys perhaps more than anything else about her visits to the manor. There was no formality. No matter the subject of conversation, Evelyn was always encouraged to share her ideas, and since Sally's academic career had long been perfunctory at best—never integral to her future life and happiness—Hugh and Elizabeth were always attentive to Evelyn's studies. But they talked easily about all sorts of things, and tonight the discussion flowed from the doings of mutual acquaintances to Elizabeth's recent trip to Paris and the "Farewell to the Lyceum Theatre" production of *Hamlet* in London.

"Gielgud was terribly good, wasn't he?" said Hugh. "Really the finest of the age. Shame about the theater."

"What did you think of the play, Sal?" Evelyn asked, skewering a Chantenay carrot.

"It was all right . . . Maybe when I'm your age, Daddy, I'll fall back in love with Shakespeare. How many did they make us read at school, Ev? About a hundred, *non*?"

"Some days it certainly felt like it." Evelyn smiled at Hugh. "But I should have liked to see that performance. I do think *Hamlet* is my favorite of all the tragedies and—"

"Cripes, here we go, Evelyn's off," Sally grumbled, pulling apart some lamb to feed to Tortoise, who had somehow made his way under the table. "What I want to know is why no one thinks about poor old Ophelia. Riddle me that."

"Maybe if you had focused your dissertation on that inadequacy," Elizabeth remarked, "you might have found yourself with a better grade in English." She turned to Evelyn. "Sally tells me you were also awarded a first for German. Congratulations."

"Thank you. Doesn't seem like such a wise choice of subject right now . . ."

"It will come in useful," said Hugh. "Have no fear of that."

Evelyn pushed some peas around her plate. A gust of wind rattled at the parlor windows and the candlelight flickered.

"You really think there will be another war?" she asked.

"Oh yes."

"But Chamberlain's been trying to negotiate, hasn't he? What about Munich?"

"Chamberlain won't be there much longer. Others in government don't want appeasement: they're of the mind that if Hitler wants to take a bite, why not set the dogs on him?"

Evelyn raised her eyebrows in Sally's direction. "What do you reckon, Sal—is Jonty ready to take on the Luftwaffe?"

Sally was stroking Tortoise's ears. The enormous brute had now flopped his head on the table, his flat black nose nudging at the carafe of wine, steaming up the glass.

"I rather think he's itching for it," she said. "And Jonty is the best pilot in his squadron."

Hugh laughed. "Who told him that? Wing Commander Dalgleish? He's a friend of the boy's father!" He turned to Evelyn and winked. "Still, good to have friends in high places, eh?"

"Oh, *Daddy!*" Sally groaned.

It was never like this with her parents, Evelyn thought, helping herself to more salad. Meals were to be eaten quickly, at the kitchen table, with the wireless on. At home, ideas were not contested but accepted, news remarked upon but left undebated, and Evelyn wondered with a guilty kind of sorrow what sort of person she might have been if she had grown up here at the manor with parents like Hugh and Elizabeth, and whether such an upbringing would have made her more certain of herself.

But if the Wesleys sensed any of this they didn't say, and after Hugh had told an amusing story about the Birmingham factory and his new foreman, a Welshman named Derog ("You know it means 'obstinate one?'"), Elizabeth asked after Evelyn's mother and father, as she always did, though she had only met them once at a first-year college dinner. It had been an awkward encounter, Evelyn's parents dressed in mothballed suits only ever brought out for Christmas mass, hardly knowing what to say to Elizabeth—or anyone else at the table, for that matter—having never met people quite so grand or gregarious. They'd tried their best, digging around for questions about the estate and Hugh's business (embarrassingly, her father even showed him a Wesley button on his jacket), but it had been a spiritless exchange, and to Evelyn's blessed relief her parents had declined any further invitations to the college.

Now Hugh stood up and raised a toast. "Sallywag," he cried, "it only seems like yesterday that I was dropping you off at Raheen, and now look at you—about to be *married*!"

They all clinked glasses and drank. Elizabeth headed back to the servery with the tray. She was a tall woman, taller even than Hugh, with the shoulders of a swimmer, and intricate jewelry shook from her broad wrists flecked with white paint. She had Sally's blond hair and gray, slightly bulging eyes; Evelyn always felt a tad unnerved by the way she could stare into the middle distance with an expression of contented yet still curious understanding.

"But Evelyn," she said now, "I must confess I hardly recognized you this evening. What were they feeding you at Somerville—chalk dust?"

"Well, not exactly . . ."

"Awful slop, college food," Hugh reminisced. "I always make Elizabeth take me to the Bird and Baby after those dreadful dinners. They've a decent steak-and-kidney pie at the Baby."

"It wasn't so bad at Somerville," Evelyn said. "If you were selective."

"By selective you mean vegetarian," Sally said.

Evelyn laughed. "Yes, maybe I do."

"Perhaps, Hugh, if you'd had fewer pies and more college slop,

Dr. West wouldn't have you taking those pills." Elizabeth, with some irritation, set down the carafe as she returned to the table. "Anyway, you're much too thin, Evelyn. Nobody wants a rake, dear."

"Thank you, Mummy," said Sally. "Evelyn will bear that in mind. Besides, it's not her fault. She's been working like a galley slave, didn't you know, for Charles Marsden's firm."

"The cosmetics outfit? Vivian Something-or-other?" Hugh wiped his mouth with a napkin. "What's he got you doing there?"

"I'm in the advertising department. I go about stores and suggest where they might place the Raspberry Delicate in the window." Evelyn fixed her eyes on the deep burgundy being poured into her glass. "But I'd rather like to do something different, especially if there's a war."

"Maybe Daddy could find you something?" Sally glanced toward her father.

"Hm?" Hugh's jaw was grinding at a piece of roast beef. "I'm not sure Evelyn is best suited to work at the factory, though we might be able to find something for the short term in accounts."

"What about Caro Menzies? You could always put in a good word for Evelyn with her."

"Now there's a thought." Hugh sat back, his red-rimmed eyes raised to the ceiling. "*Caroline.* She's one of Elizabeth's distant cousins. Bit of a queer duck, a real bluestocking—does some sort of work with the War Office. Dull as ditchwater, I imagine, crossing t's and dotting i's, but there might be something in it for a clever thing like you. Better prospect than paying invoices for shipments to Cork."

The War Office. A small thrill of excitement worked its way down the back of Evelyn's neck.

"Would you, Hugh? That would be splendid."

"Of course." He licked his fingertips, grinning. "*Lady, with me, with me thy fortune lies.* I'll telephone her on Monday."

"How about that then, Ev?" Sally leaned across the table, voice lowered in conspiracy. "Sounds rather spicy to me."

"Yes," Evelyn agreed. It did.

"Just mind you don't do too good a job." Sally poured herself some more wine, a mischievous look in her eye. "Daddy's been quite chuffed with the spike in consignments. All this war talk means business has gone through the roof."

"Dear, oh dear," Elizabeth said with a sigh. "War and buttons—I'll never hear the end of it."

Hugh picked at his teeth, thoughtful. "In my experience, darling, armies always need uniforms, whether we're at war or not. And this means they'll always need buttons." He flashed Evelyn a cunning smile. "But yes, I suppose we are seeing a few new orders flow our way."

"I say, Daddy, why don't you show Evelyn your old war wound?"

Elizabeth stood up again and this time rang for the footman to bring dessert. "Sally, darling, don't encourage him," she scolded. "And Evelyn, for goodness' sake, don't look!"

But they were lost in their own pantomime, Sally laughing as Hugh rolled up his trouser leg to show off where a piece of shrapnel had lodged in the back of his thigh, and even though Evelyn had seen it many times she still found herself enthralled by the scar poking through his reddish hair.

"There it is!" he bellowed.

Evelyn had once found her father's uniform wrapped in green tissue paper at the back of her parents' wardrobe. She had been nine or ten years old, and as Evelyn had no siblings to play with, the house itself had been made to act its part in an imaginary world of adventure and intrigue. On that particular morning, she had been Kimball O'Hara gleaning along the grimy laneways of Lahore. The parcel had been jammed down the back of the top shelf behind some shoeboxes and a jewelry case belonging to her mother. Placing it carefully on the bed, Evelyn unwrapped the paper to reveal a stiff brown jacket that stank of rotten eggs. Somehow she knew it belonged to her father. She ran her fingertips over the lapels and their dull brass buttons. There were some rust-colored stains around the collar and the cuffs, and a pair of trousers was also folded inside the tissue paper, along with a few creased and faded letters.

Later that night Evelyn had asked her mother about the uniform.

"Your father was a sergeant in the war," she explained. "He took a bullet in the shoulder that got infected, and then the Germans gassed his battalion." She went to the sink, where a window overlooked the small garden at the back of the house. "But it's not easy for him to remember—it's not easy for many men—so you mustn't ask about it. If he wants to tell you, he will."

As her mother stood with her back turned, Evelyn felt anger uncurl inside her. She knew her father would never say a word. Why else would the uniform have been hidden away? But that was how her family behaved toward one another, only revealing what they chose, their secrets drawn out like string beneath sand, and from that day Evelyn understood that to gauge her parents' real feelings would require a patient subterfuge.

It was in this same secretive manner that each Armistice Day her father left the house to march with all the others on the high street, then went to the Arms and drank until closing, slinking back home late to pass out on the sitting room sofa. Evelyn would tiptoe downstairs the next morning to watch him snoring, his face pale and drawn, the first bristle of dark whiskers appearing on his smooth cheeks. She knew some children would feel pity for their fathers in such a state, but she didn't. This was the one time of year when she saw that other side to him, the side that wasn't restrained or polite or controlled. It was during those cold mornings that Evelyn learned that truth was found at the edges of people, and now, as she watched Hugh throw his head back and laugh, she wondered if that scar was the only unhappy part of him.

~

Later that night, after Sally had gone off to telephone Jonty at the air base, Evelyn wandered through the grand hall, which was as cool and solemn as a tomb. She stopped to admire the paintings, some early Renaissance, some Impressionists, and a new rose-colored Venetian glasswork piece. Such a fragile thing, she thought as she tipped it from the display column, testing its weight in her hands. Next she poked her head into the oak-paneled library, inhaling the musty scent of old leather-backed folios, and leafed through a few books left out on the desk near the ladder. It was military history, Prussian War stuff—not her cup of tea at all. Then on past the billiards room and the drawing room, the smoking room and the cards room, toward Hugh's study.

Here Evelyn paused. She was always curious about Hugh's business and his friends from the club, but tonight she was reluctant to go inside. She had only been in there once before, three years ago, and turning over some papers on the desk she'd found a ledger from the Birmingham factory, full of rising figures in the expenses column. Parker had disturbed her before she'd had a chance to look around much further. To an outsider it had probably looked like snooping, Evelyn thought as she headed on toward the east wing. But there'd been no malice in it, nothing unscrupulous. She had just always been drawn to the things people didn't reveal about themselves—what they believed, she supposed, were weaknesses.

In her meandering, Evelyn had somehow arrived at Hugh's conservatory. He collected orchids from Singapore and exhibited them in an enormous glass-domed room filled with steam from the gas humidifiers stationed beneath the trestle tables. She pressed her nose against the panel and spotted him stooped beneath the staghorn fern in the center of the enclosure, pruning the leaves. He had changed into red overalls and a corn-colored shirt, and when she tapped on the glass he turned and waved, inviting her inside.

"Have you seen my new *Brassavola*?"

Evelyn's arms and forehead were immediately beaded with warm droplets as she followed him to a wooden frame attached to the back wall. There, tethered to three planks, were white heart-shaped flowers with stems thick and hard-cased like the propodus of a crustacean, something strange and beautiful about their composition, like nature had spliced together two different species.

"They're magnificent, Hugh," she said.

"Yes, I'm rather proud of them. They shouldn't really survive in Britain, but it's extraordinary what we can do to mimic their natural habitat. Their perfume is awfully sweet," he remarked when Evelyn bent her head toward the stamen. "And only released at night."

"Nocturnal flowers?"

"Splendid, isn't it? I first saw them at Kew Gardens. Remember that visit? You and Sally had a run-in with that crane at the canteen."

"Goodness, yes." Evelyn laughed.

"They're for Julia, actually. I've been cultivating them for months. I'm just so relieved she's finally home. That husband of hers . . ." He pushed away some of the white hair sticking to his forehead. "I know she hasn't always been an easy girl to handle, but my sister would have never forgiven me if something had happened to her."

Evelyn thought of Julia's sleek black hair, the sharp cut of her bob. She'd never seen a photograph of her mother around the manor, and that absence seemed conspicuous now among the dewy orchids.

"Did Julia's father help bring her back from Germany?"

"Lord Jennings?" Hugh's face grew dark. "Don't make me laugh.

Spineless fellow. Only ever out for himself." He mixed some salts into the tin watering can on the ground, then poured some liquid into a glass bottle and fixed a nozzle at the top. "He was never much of a father to her."

"Then Julia is lucky to have you."

"It's what you do for family. And for your friends." Hugh peered up at her, his bright eyes crinkling. "I've always thought you had a strong head on your shoulders, Evelyn. You found the good in my Sallywag when others couldn't." He picked up the bottle, squeezing a fine spray of water at the plants. "It's a rare quality, that. Seeing what others can't."

Evelyn watched him move on to the *Cymbidium* orchids, a pink hue through the mist on the other side of the conservatory. As she stood in the damp air, she reflected that perhaps there would come a time when she would outlive Hugh's good opinion. It was only natural, wasn't it? No admiration or respect lasted forever, and who could predict what lay in store for them all in the future? Still, she felt sadness at this prospect. There were few people whose opinion she cared for more. At her feet were the clippings from the orchid, and with a single sweep of her foot Evelyn scattered them across the floor. Through the mist, she watched Hugh spray a bright yellow stamen. At his back were a whisper of moths, rising and dipping about the flowers, their majestic flight invisible to all but herself.

THREE

A BREEZE ṢWIRLED, growing thick with the promise of rain. From the terrace at the top of the garden stairs, Evelyn rested her elbows on the wrought-iron fence to gaze out across the dewy lawn that stretched on for a couple of hundred yards before the woods began. A flock of birds—starlings by the looks of them—screeched across the line of trees, while the sky had turned violet and the air was alive with the scent of fresh grass clippings. On the other side of the peach brocade curtains behind her, the party guests danced and drank in the lavish drawing room. Bing Crosby crooned from the gramophone and every now and then Evelyn heard a whoop or a shriek of laughter.

The formal dinner had been served in the dining room, a dim, reverent space the size of a small country hall with elaborate Flemish tapestries and velvet curtains. It was a six-course banquet with ballotine of duck, filet mignon, potatoes roasted in butter and rosemary picked fresh from the garden, venison bourguignon, and soft cheeses from France, all washed down with champagne and a good French claret. Evelyn had been seated between Michael Talbert, a friend of Jonty's from Cambridge, and Jonathan van der Hoort, who was older and grayer than Evelyn remembered. Jonty sat across the table, regaling the surrounding men with a tale about Ascot and a bet on a horse that went lame, which they all laughed at because they were drunk. This was what it must feel like to be trapped in the Pitt Club after midnight, Evelyn thought. Like the others, Jonty was dressed in a dinner suit, his cropped hair oiled flat against his scalp. He didn't look much like his father; he still possessed the pompous vitality of a public school boy, but judging from the older man's occasional boorish guffaws he had inherited some family traits.

"So, Evelyn," said Talbert, swinging his head around to gaze at her blearily after the plates had been cleared. "What are you up to these days?"

"I'm working in London."

"Working?" He chuckled. "You'd be the only one at this party doing much of that."

"Speak for yourself, Talbert," Jonty protested. "Northumberland has been punishing."

"It would be with a work ethic like yours." Talbert sloshed some wine into his glass, grinning at Evelyn. "My family's a navy one. I'm finishing my cadetship in Dartmouth. I love ships and the open water, don't you?"

Evelyn peered down the long table, searching out Sally. From the corner of her eye she sensed Jonty smirking.

"Not especially," she muttered. "I get seasick."

"What about you, Jonts? Ever fancy the big, wide sea?"

"It's always been planes for me, Talbert, you know that," Jonty said. "And I've an interview for another division. Anglesea. Much larger base. Spitfires, too, in the fleet. Interview's a formality—Father is old chums with the wing commander."

"That so? Well done."

Jonty sat back, folding his bulky arms. "It's lucky us chaps are doing our bit."

Evelyn kept her expression neutral. "How do you reason that?" she asked.

Jonty shrugged. "Not sure how useful face cream will be when Jerry comes knocking. Though maybe you could translate for them, Evelyn?" To Talbert he said, "You know she read German at Oxford?"

"My sister went over there herself after school," Talbert slurred. "Spent a year or two in Berlin. And what's jolly well wrong with that, eh? They're a sophisticated people, the Germans. All that lovely architecture, music, and"—he paused to belch—"theater."

"Pity about the Wehrmacht, then, isn't it?"

"Now, now, Jonts. We're among ladies here." Talbert rested a paw on Evelyn's bare shoulder, his fingertips toying with the strap of her dress. "Let's not bring politics into the conversation. Evelyn doesn't want to listen to all that, does she?"

She shrugged him off. "Actually, I do. We all need to know what's going on over there."

"Going on?" Talbert's fist dropped to the table, rattling his glass. "It's all a lot of nonsense, that's what. Why can't we talk of something else for once? This is a party, not a Cabinet meeting."

Something warm and clammy had landed on Evelyn's leg. It was Talbert's hand, she realized, which was now creeping up her thigh.

"So, you're fluent in the old Deutsch, are you?" He leaned in, leering at her décolletage. "Perhaps you'd whisper a few words in my ear?"

Evelyn shot a glance at Jonty, but he was only grinning back at her, perfectly aware of what Talbert was doing and refusing to come to her aid. All right, she thought. If this is how it is going to be . . .

"Well, Michael, since you asked so nicely . . ." With a sweet smile, Evelyn cupped a hand over Talbert's ear and whispered, "*Du *verfluchter Widerling.*" Then she stood up, pushing back her chair, and muttered to no one in particular, "Excuse me."

The noise seemed to spike as she strode down the length of the dining table, but as she took a sidestep to slip out through the bay windows to the path below she still heard Talbert cry, "It really is such a beautiful language!"

~

The sun had sunk farther and was now just a glowing red tip behind the black outline of trees. There was movement at one of the trunks—a fox, perhaps, out for its nightly scavenge—and as she leaned against the terrace railing Evelyn recalled the visit she had made to the manor when the Wesleys opened the grounds for the annual hunt. The family had gone out on horses at dawn, leaving Evelyn, who politely objected to the sport, alone in the house. It was a rare opportunity to explore unsupervised, but she kept to Sally's room, stoking the fire and trying to read. Her mind, however, kept wandering to those woods. All morning they had been serene, a low blue mist crawling around the base of the trees, and that stillness should have been tranquil—except for what Evelyn knew was coming. And when a horn shattered the silence and the frantic baying of the hounds cut through the air, Evelyn put her book aside and went to the window. From there she had a view of the neat, empty lawn, but a moment later there came the flash of two foxes, so small and lithe they could have been cats, followed by a dozen dogs. The stage had turned eerily quiet, and Evelyn remembered wondering if this was how the final moments of life were experienced: in a cold, unnatural vacuum. She had shuddered away from the glass, but not before she saw a dog break loose from the pack, gaining on the slower of the foxes, until it launched, teeth bared, and clamped its jaws around the poor animal's flanks.

There was a noise behind her and, recalled to the present, Evelyn turned, expecting to find Sally. But it was only Jonty, a tumbler in each hand, sauntering across the terrace. Against the curtains behind him were the faint silhouettes of dancers.

"You're missing a treat, Evelyn. Hugh has brought out the cornet. He plays like a man with sausages for fingers."

He handed over a glass, then stood beside her and leaned against the fence.

"Look, sorry about Talbert. He's a great oaf, but he means nothing by it. In fact, I'm almost certain he's a homosexual, if that's any comfort. He behaves like that around women to compensate. I don't know." Jonty ran a hand over his cropped hair. "Is that one of Sally's dresses you're wearing tonight?"

Evelyn glanced at him, convinced he was teasing, but he only stared back at her, an expectant look on his face. It was suddenly very quiet out there.

"I didn't pick you as a connoisseur of women's fashion, Jonty."

"I'm not." He drank some Scotch. "It looks different on you, that's all. Fits your figure . . . better."

Evelyn kept her eyes fixed to where she knew neat brickwork ran beneath the terrace. It had always been like this between them. His condescension, coupled with a faint lasciviousness, as if she were a chambermaid and he the lord of the manor. She supposed that was exactly how he saw her—they probably all did, homosexual or not. The music from the house eddied through her head and she clutched the tumbler, tempted to hurl it into the garden.

"When will you leave for Anglesea?" she asked. "Since the job's in the bag."

"Next month."

"And what will you do there? The skies aren't exactly swarming with Luftwaffe."

Jonty took another sip from his glass. "Take pot shots at schoolgirls, I expect."

For a moment Evelyn considered walking back inside and disappearing upstairs. But something her father once said sprang to mind—perhaps she had been reminded of it as she watched Jonty, a cigarette dangling from his lips, frowning into the moonlight, that faint look of amusement never quite leaving his face. *A man's conscience never dictates his politics.* It had been a remark made apropos of nothing, which was how most of her father's wisdom was imparted. She hadn't known what it meant at the time, but now she supposed it was a question of pragmatism. Or, as her mother put it more bluntly, *It's just how the world works, dear.*

Jonty glanced toward the drawing room. The gramophone had stopped and someone started up on the piano; there wasn't a hint of Hugh's reedy cornet. Above the music came the dull throb of voices, and the din of laughter now and then drifted toward them. Jonty looked back at her, smoothing down his hair again.

"We've never really had the chance to chat, have we, Evelyn? After all these years. Funny, isn't it? But I am sorry for that."

"Are you?"

"Yes. I mean, you are Sally's closest friend. She's told me so much about you, but I still don't feel like I know you well at all."

Evelyn looked away, unsure what sincerity sounded like in his voice.

"I wouldn't believe everything Sally tells you."

Jonty smiled, wolfish all of a sudden. "I don't."

He took out his cigarette case and offered her one. She was careful not to touch his hand as she lit up from his match. They smoked in silence, but it wasn't uncomfortable between them, and Evelyn began to think that it was indeed funny how little they knew of one another. She supposed he wasn't all that bad—no different from most young men at Oxford. She studied the hard line of his jaw.

She imagined he'd be a rough lover, and she allowed her mind to wander toward the possibility of him putting his arms around her, and before she knew it she was imagining the feel of his lips against hers. Where all this came from she didn't know—it had to be the wine and whisky. But he must have had some hint of her thoughts, because with a quick look over his shoulder he flicked his cigarette away and moved forward to kiss her, his lips knocking against hers. For a brief moment, Evelyn felt something leap inside her, but she quickly pushed him away.

"What?" he growled, his grip still firm on her shoulders. "*What?*"

"You can't."

"Why not?"

"Because . . . Well . . ." She couldn't think. "I don't want it, that's *why*."

Jonty released her and edged backward, refusing to look at her as he swiped at a lock of blond hair.

Evelyn's eyes grew dry, itchy; she was too tired for anger. She considered saying something, but why must she placate him? Instead, she stubbed out her cigarette and resumed her view over the lawn even though the atmosphere had been spoiled.

"You don't like me much, do you, Evelyn?"

Jonty was watching her, his left eye bunched up as he kneaded his forehead. There was something menacing in that look—Jonty had always seemed to Evelyn like a man with thin skin, as if his flesh and organs and ebullience were so near to the surface you only had to prod to see the life of him. It frightened her, and she recalled the rugby match at Cambridge last year when he'd had his nose broken. He had been guided off the field by the wingers, blood gushing, bruises gathering like dark clouds across his cheeks, but he had raised a fist in triumph. Pain was an accolade to him, something to be earned, and something to be inflicted.

"You're . . ." He hesitated, grasping. "I just can't work you *out!*"

"Then don't try to," Evelyn said in a clear, glassy voice. "I can't imagine it will trouble you for long."

But he still took another step toward her, and she hoped he wasn't about to kiss her again.

"What is going on out here?"

A dark-haired woman stood on the edge of the terrace. Jonty glanced at Evelyn, and she knew he was wondering how long she had been there.

"We were just taking some air. Awfully stuffy in that drawing room." Straightening his bow tie, he flashed his teeth. "But I'm ready for a dance now. Maybe I'll see you both back in there?"

Evelyn followed his swagger down the path beneath the windows, a dull throb starting up behind her eye. When she looked back, she found the woman watching her.

"It's Evelyn, isn't it?"

She was tall, like Evelyn, though with a fuller figure, and her complexion was clearer, heartier. She had thick, almost unruly eyebrows, and her red lips were wet-looking in the dark. She wore a black felt dress with short sleeves and a narrow belt pinching in at her waist, her loose hair longer than it had been all those years ago.

"Julia? I'm sorry, I didn't recognize you . . ."

Julia blew out a long stream of smoke, laughing, as she made her slow way toward the fence.

"It's quite all right, I must have changed. You've certainly grown up since I last saw you."

"Have I?" Evelyn hid her hands behind her back, embarrassed to realize that, after the confrontation with Jonty, they were trembling. "I'm not sure I feel it."

She watched Julia remove the stub of her cigarette from the holder and flick it into the air, tracking the orange spark as it sailed into the rose garden below the terrace. She may not have been as sharp-featured as Evelyn remembered, something now softer around her mouth, but she still had that determined look in her eyes, as if she were looking past Evelyn in search of something behind her.

"You must be pleased to have made it home for the celebrations," Evelyn ventured.

"Worked out well in the end, didn't it?" Julia nodded at the drawing room window. "And old Sallywag will do all right with Jonty. I don't think he's much chop, but she's always liked him. They'll have very blond, very dim children. Hundreds of them."

"Yes." Evelyn smiled. "You're probably right."

"How are you enjoying the party?"

"I'm having a marvelous time." She held up her Scotch. "Though I fear I've drunk too many of these."

"Others certainly have." Julia cupped a hand around her lighter as she lit up another cigarette. "I was watching you at dinner. Jonty really should have left Michael Talbert tied up in the stables."

"Oh." Evelyn took this in. Usually she was the one doing the observing. "He's not so bad."

Julia made a face. "Englishmen really are horrendous when they drink. All their worst impulses come rushing to the surface."

Evelyn wondered how much Julia could really know about Englishmen after so many years in Germany, but perhaps she had more intuition than most—anyone who could line her eyes so expertly with kohl was bound to have that kind of knowledge hidden away somewhere.

"You know," Julia pointed toward the dark hint of woodlands at the end of the lawn, "there's a pretty little creek through those trees. When we were girls, Sally and I would play down there for whole days at a time. Like a couple of wildlings, we were, forever coming back to the house covered in dirt and scrapes. I liked playing Robinson Crusoe best. Sally was always Friday."

Evelyn followed the line her long finger made and they stood like that, staring in the direction of the creek, until a burst of noise erupted from the drawing room and the curtains flapped and rustled.

"So how did you get on at school in the end? You were . . . unhappy."

"You remember that?" Evelyn smiled, her curiosity stirring. "It was fine. I studied hard. Went on to Oxford."

"You found a way to fit in?"

Evelyn blinked. She wasn't quite sure how to answer that.

"Yes," she said eventually. "I suppose I did."

Julia nodded, though there was something distracted about it. Far off, Evelyn made out the sound of birds in the woods, owls perhaps. In the muddy light, she thought she saw Julia grip the railing before suddenly tilting back her head to inhale the humid air.

"I have missed this." She sighed. "*A body of England's, breathing English air.* I rarely got into the countryside when I was in Berlin."

"It is glorious, isn't it," Evelyn agreed. "I think if I lived here I'd never want to leave."

Julia glanced at her, then back to the dark lawn. "Hugh tells me you've been a fixture at the manor." The corner of her mouth twitched. "He likes you. Thinks you're awfully clever. But Hugh thinks everyone's clever, so my real bellwether is Elizabeth. She's a harder nut to crack."

The Scotch had taken hold, burning around Evelyn's blood. Sally's stories of her cousin had painted a picture of a cold, restless woman, all mink coats and coral pink nail varnish, but as Evelyn watched Julia smoke she wondered if Sally had got her wrong; if there wasn't in fact something more candescent inside her. She supposed Julia must have given up on whatever had kept her in Germany for so long—or it had given up on her—and she felt that curiosity quickening, sharpening, like an ax sparking against the grinder.

"And what does Elizabeth say about me?" she asked.

But Julia didn't have the chance to reply. There was a rapping at the drawing room window and there at the glass stood Sally, waving, while in the background the Wesleys' guests moved around the floor, now more like the swell of a rough sea, all taffeta, lace, and silk in the dance.

"Looks like we've been rumbled," Julia murmured.

⌒

It was bright and muggy the next morning as Evelyn strolled with Sally and Julia across the east lawn, an old knapsack of sandwiches and a thermos of coffee banging at her knee. At the bottom of the lawn they followed the creek toward the lush canopy where Wesley Farm began. There were workers in the fields tilling, while in the next allotment a few young hands were tending to the apples in the orchard that would soon make cider. The last of the party guests had left an hour ago, and Hugh and Elizabeth had motored over to the Birmingham factory, which meant the young women had the estate to themselves.

On their walk they dissected the party, and the dancing, which had gone on until dawn. Aside from Michael Talbert throwing up in the foyer, they agreed, the event had gone off without a hitch. Eventually Sally found a plush spot beside the stream and the three of them sat on the bank with their feet dangling. They ate the sandwiches and drank the peaty, bitter coffee, and after sharing an apple Evelyn threw the browning core into the current, watching it fly over the rocks and eddy around the scummy shallows by the ferns. As the day's heat peaked, the three of them stretched out under the shade of the enormous beech trees and slept until the afternoon sun crept along the moss, scorching their bare legs.

Evelyn was the first to wake, her shoulder tender from a protruding root, and she sat watching the light strike in shards off the water. A few paces away, Julia had her back to a sycamore tree, eyes closed, smoking. The stream gurgled, spat, and a breeze fluttered at the base of the trees. Evelyn closed her eyes again, breathing in the warm, enlivened air. There had been few moments that she wanted to capture and contain as much as this one; it felt as though her life had been placed on a languorous, delicious pause.

"Do you know Jonty left this morning without saying goodbye?" Sally suddenly croaked. "I thought that awfully mean of him. We won't see each other for weeks."

"He probably felt filthy, Sal," Evelyn said. None of them had woken up sprightly after only a few hours' sleep.

"Maybe." Sally sighed, raising a hand against the glare. "Did things change, Jules, between you and Hans? When you got engaged, I mean?"

"Well, we didn't have an engagement party at the manor, did we?" Julia said.

"No. But then you did cause a bit of scandal." Sally tipped her head toward Evelyn. "I've told you, haven't I, how she eloped to Germany? It caused such a scene—I thought Daddy was going to have a stroke. I was only fifteen, which meant you were, what, twenty-one?"

"Twenty." Julia ground out her cigarette. "It was romantic for a time. Everything is when it's forbidden."

Evelyn studied the honeycomb shadow dancing by Julia's legs and asked, "How did you meet your husband?"

"I was visiting an old school friend in Berlin," said Julia, crossing one foot over another to admire her toes. "Her father was the consul general and they lived in an apartment overlooking the Wörther

Platz. They had lots of parties, full of artists and politicians and all the diplomats from the Foreign Office. One night they invited a cabaret singer named Honey and she sang Lilian Harvey songs—that's when I met him. Hans. He was accompanying her on the piano . . ." She paused, her eyes fixed on the surface of the stream. "He played so well, and with such variety. Mahler, Brahms, von Sauer. I've always thought music can transform a person, though later I learned he wasn't such a gentle man by nature. Still, it was all rather magnetic . . ." She smiled, her mind snared in the memory. "From the moment I met him I wanted to be always near him." The smile wilted. "I thought he could offer me a different life."

"What does he do in Berlin?"

"He was a sergeant in the army when I met him. Now he's a lieutenant in their security police."

Sally laughed. "Which I always thought terrifically amusing as Julia has never been much good with rules." She craned her neck to look again for Julia in the shade. "You were excluded from how many schools? Three, wasn't it?"

"Four." Julia frowned, her attention drawn back to the stream. "I wanted to get away from all that. Boarding school. England. It's all so conventional, so predictable. But after a while I realized Hans wasn't the man I thought he was, and Germany wasn't the place I thought it was either. It changed while I was there. Became . . ." She sighed. "I don't know. It was like horses get before a thunderstorm. Everyone had a wild look in their eyes."

"And that's why you came back?"

Julia's gaze drifted toward Evelyn. She shrugged. "This is my home. Sometimes you need to go away to remember where you belong."

Watching her chew on her bottom lip, Evelyn wondered just quite how Julia had done it—turned her back on her old life for a man she barely knew. Was that what love did to a person? Made them so . . . reckless? But Sally wasn't like that; if anything, her love was grounding, solidifying. Evelyn scratched at the damp hair behind her ear. Perhaps Julia would have gone anyway, and she supposed it was easier to take those risks in the knowledge that family and friends would always welcome you home. What would her parents and the townspeople of Lewes make of such an expedition, Evelyn wondered. It was hardly worth thinking about.

They sat for a while longer, the air silent except for the drone of the insects hanging above the stream.

"Do you think you'll ever marry, Ev?" Sally asked.

Evelyn was doing up the straps on her sandals, wincing at the burn on the bridge of her feet.

"I don't know. Why?"

"You never seem interested, that's all. I always thought maybe you and Philip . . ."

"Yes, well." Evelyn sat up, rubbing at her face. She didn't want to talk about it. "The less said about him the better."

"Who is Philip?" Julia asked.

"He was Evelyn's boyfriend at university," Sally said. "Very serious chap—I'm sorry, Ev, but he was. And there was a touch of the red about him."

"He was a communist?"

Evelyn snatched up a tuft of grass, the strands sticking to her sweaty hands. "No, he wasn't a communist—he'd read Marx, that's all, and joined the Labour Party for a time. He wasn't my boyfriend, though."

"But he wanted to be?"

"I suppose. Only I didn't feel that way about him."

"Poor Philip." And for a moment Julia looked genuinely sad.

They had taken a couple of English literature tutorials together at Oxford. Philip wrote poetry, some of it published in the university magazine. He was softly spoken with gray eyes, and with his northern accent and his unionism he wasn't like the other students. Evelyn had been attracted to him, but while there had been many shy looks, many stilted exchanges, she had never been quite sure of the depth of her feelings for him; it certainly wasn't love, but there had been tenderness. Later, that's how thinking about Philip always made her feel: tender, like someone had pounded at the flesh around her heart.

He had invited her to a ball at Christ Church, and once or twice they had a pint in town. One night, at the end of term, they went to the birthday party of a boy in their class where there had been dancing and a lot of red wine, and afterward Philip offered to walk Evelyn back to Somerville. She remembered leaning her head on his shoulder, the rub of corduroy at her cheek, and how it had smelled of wood smoke. At the gate, he had kissed her, gently at first, but then with more eagerness, his hands gripped around her hips, drawing her toward him. He was making noises she'd never heard before: moaning, almost as if he were in pain. The kiss went on for a minute or so until Evelyn felt the press of his erection right there against her leg. She couldn't help it—she pulled away. It wasn't that she didn't want to stir these feelings in him, but she felt nothing back, no rush of warmth, no thrill of wanting, and suddenly that evening, and every other evening they had ever spent together, felt spoiled and tawdry, leaving them both embarrassed at his desire.

"What's the matter?" Philip had asked, but when she stayed silent he shook his head, something mean passing across his face. They didn't see each other again before the term break. Evelyn wrote to him once or twice from Lewes but received no reply, and when she passed him in the Radcliffe Quad the first day back he simply nodded and looked away. This brush-off had hurt her more than she expected;

she'd cried about it back in her rooms, but they were resentful tears that soon dried, and she didn't think much about Philip again.

"We used to have a name for Evelyn in halls," Sally said, rolling onto her back and folding her arms behind her head. "Do you know what it was?"

"Oh, don't say it," Evelyn groaned. "Please, Sal."

"Cold Fish. Because she'd never let a chap get near her!"

Now Evelyn felt herself blush to the roots of her hair and waited for Julia to join in with Sally's laughter, but she only stood up and brushed down the back of her legs.

"I've never understood why we idealize one form of love over others. Romantic love has never brought me much happiness."

"Isn't it obvious?" Sally said. "Romantic love keeps the world turning. You know—sex, babies, all that."

"And is that how Jonty makes you feel? Giddy, like you've been on a waltzer? Because he makes me feel a bit sick, too."

Sally had also climbed to her feet, face flushed, her pale hair curling at her temples. There was a dark patch of sweat on her dress and she gave the hem a grumpy tug.

"Perhaps, Julia, you should think more about who you give your love to. Then you might find real happiness."

"Maybe." Julia watched her mildly, then turned to Evelyn and held out her hand. "It was Shelley, wasn't it, who asked, *What is all this sweet work worth, if thou kiss me not?*"

Peering up at her, Evelyn was aware of the bruise at her lip where Jonty had tried to kiss her, and she grew afraid once again that Julia had seen them. But when the sun dipped between the trees, flaring at her back and concealing her face, she somehow knew that Julia was smiling.

They began to stroll back. The sun was about to disappear behind the manor, but the air was still weighed down with the afternoon heat. At the tall reeds Julia stopped, admiring the few ducks bobbing about in the middle of the lake.

"Why don't we swim?"

"But we've no costumes," Sally said. "I could grab something from the house . . ."

"No need for that."

Julia stripped down to her underwear and ventured into the shallows. Her neck looked very brown above her white shoulders.

"Julia! What if someone sees?"

"No one will *see*. Come on! Evelyn?"

Evelyn gazed at the lake. It was the color of long-steeped tea. She watched Julia wade out, a few threads of hair coiled about her throat. She eased off her sandals, then pulled off her dress. Her skin felt raw in the last stripes of sun.

Sally stared at her, arms folded. "Well, I'm not going in," she muttered. "You're both mad."

"Suit yourself."

Evelyn took a few steps into the chilly water, the silt squelching between her toes. She could hear Sally, petulance in her voice, as the water rose to her waist. Evelyn wasn't a strong swimmer, but she still felt safe. Julia floated nearby on her back, her feet in the shape of a vee. Evelyn dived deep beneath the shiny surface of the lake. It was glorious, like slicing through the dark, and she swam out farther, doing a few lazy strokes toward the impervious ducks. Behind them the manor watched on, its rectangular shadow stretching wide across the lawn.

⌒

Parker drove Evelyn and Sally into Birmingham. By now the weather had cooled down, and heavy rain fell all the way to the station.

Evelyn had said her goodbye to Julia in the drawing room, her hair still damp from the lake. In the next few weeks Julia would be traveling up to London, where Hugh had arranged some work for her at the Benevolent Society, and she asked Evelyn to telephone her at Curzon Street. They'd go out for dinner, she promised, or to a show. Sally had stood in the doorway during this exchange, chewing at the end of her plait, sullen as though she had been scolded.

It was a quiet journey to London. The first-class carriage was almost empty, as was the dining car, which they visited after Rugby. Sally ordered the fillet of trout followed by blue cheese, and Evelyn had rib-eye steak then apple-and-rhubarb strudel. The waiter brought a carafe of cabernet franc to the table.

"This trout isn't too bad," said Sally, piercing a head of asparagus with her fork. "You can have bad luck on these trains. I remember once on the way to Edinburgh I had the worst soup of my life—Windsor, I think it was."

Evelyn sipped at her wine as the train lurched from side to side.

"I suppose you'll be very busy in London," Sally said. "Too busy to play with me."

"Awful, this employment business, isn't it? Next I'll be joining a union." But when Sally only stared glumly out the window, Evelyn said, "There's plenty you could do too, you know. Volunteer, perhaps? Take a class. You could even join Julia at the Benevolent Society. Serving tea and biscuits to the downtrodden could be the making of you."

But Sally wouldn't yield. "Oh, it's all so dreary!" She sighed. "And we know she's only doing that as a kind of penance. Julia only ever does something if there's a reward in it."

"Why do you say that?"

"Because it's true! I adore her, you know I do, but you must take her as she is. And she's a wolf! There's never enough for her to gobble up." Sally set down her fork, eyes fixed on her plate. "When we were little girls she would come over to the manor and steal all my things. Toys, books, even food at the table, if you can imagine it . . . It became a great joke to my parents. But I hated it. And the thing was, she didn't want any of it for herself. She only wanted it because it belonged to someone else."

Countryside streaked by in a dark blur, the occasional spark of a streetlamp or fireplace through the window of a cottage.

"She seems an intriguing person to me," Evelyn said. "Someone who has turned her life around."

Sally snorted. "You're worse than Daddy."

"What do you mean?"

"Around her finger." Sally made a twirling motion. "She's smarter than she looks, Evelyn. Was a prefect, for a time, at Wycombe Abbey. Bet she didn't tell you that."

"Well, no . . ."

Folding her arms, Sally made a face, as if an obscure point had been proved, and Evelyn sat back, trying to reconcile this picture of Julia with the woman she'd just encountered. She knew she should believe Sally, but somehow she couldn't.

After coffee, they returned to the compartment. An elderly woman had joined them, though she was asleep beside the sliding door. Evelyn edged past her to the maroon-colored plush seat beneath the luggage rack and read her book while Sally dozed in her spot opposite. But as the train neared Euston, Sally woke with a start and straightened, pressing her nose to the window.

"What is it?"

But Sally wouldn't look at her, and after a few moments Evelyn thought she wasn't going to answer.

"You won't forget me, will you?" she said finally, her face pale and closed off as she sat back and toyed with her mantilla comb.

Evelyn set aside her book. "Why are you asking me that?"

"Remember that time at school, when we went to Brighton for the day and visited the Palace Pier? Lucy Kingston-Smith was there, and Cynthia Buckland—oh, how I *loathed* her."

Evelyn blinked. "Yes."

"Well, you probably don't recall, but when I went to buy tickets for the organ show at the Dome, you all ran away, leaving me on my own in the street . . ."

Sally's face was caught in such anguish that Evelyn felt something pitch inside her. She did remember, mostly how being included in this excursion had felt like the momentous arrival at some longed-for destination, and then it all being spoiled by Sally's tears afterward on the long walk back to the school. Sally had never understood why it had been so important for Evelyn to get along with those girls, or what it meant to feel like an outsider. Evelyn leaned forward, taking her friend's hand.

"Why are you bringing all this up now?"

Sally smiled, a brief gleam against the glass. "I don't hold any grudges, Evelyn. How could I? I don't care about what happened. It was fine in the end, wasn't it? I found you on the pier, eating ice cream. Cynthia was talking to that man with the dog . . . But whenever I think of it, it's not with any kind of anger or even pain; it's always with the same surprise I felt all those years ago."

She sat back, pinch-faced, as Evelyn shook her head. She wondered if all the excitement of the weekend had sent Sally over the edge.

"Surprise at what?"

"At how easily you were persuaded to go along with it all." She sniffed, her eyes never leaving the window and the rush of houses, high streets, and depots as the train surged deeper into London.

Evelyn leaned into her seat, gently rocked by the movement of the train, uncertain how to reply.

"I say this only because I care about you—" But Sally was drowned out by a blast of the horn. The train was arriving.

They sat like that, heads tipped back against their seats, watching one another, almost wary, Sally fixing up a stray clump of blond hair, while her arms, Evelyn saw, had broken out in gooseflesh.

⁓

The platform was crammed from the disembarkation of another commuter train. With no porters about to help with the luggage, they had to force a path through the steam and press of bodies, the shrill whistle ricocheting around the station. Evelyn was nimbler than Sally as they made their way toward the Great Hall, and they became separated on the stairs.

On the street, the night air was cold, almost raw, and a light drizzle had begun to fall, making the bitumen glitter. Evelyn took huge, gulping breaths, her lungs expanding, her chest rising; she was tall among the crowds. As she hailed a taxi, she turned at the sound of her name, having forgotten all about Sally, and it took her a moment to recognize her friend through the rain.

LATE SEPTEMBER 1939

FOUR

THE BUS PARKED outside the Victoria and Albert Museum looked like any other Regent double-decker only it had no route name or number on the front panel, nor any advertisements fixed to the bright red flank. Evelyn crossed the road quickly, weaving between the soldiers at the Cromwell Road checkpoint sandbagging the museum, and climbed on board. There were a few other young men and women already seated inside, but they didn't acknowledge her as she made her way down the aisle and sat on a fold-down seat near the driver's cabin. Nobody spoke as the bus made its way along Queen's Gate, snaking around Kensington Gardens before continuing in a north-westerly direction.

Evelyn kept her hands in her coat pockets, every now and then running a fingertip over the sharp edges of the telegram. It had been waiting for her on the hall table when she'd come home last night to Bramham Gardens. With no postmark or return address, the telegram had instructed her to be at the whistle stop across the road from the museum at nine o'clock the next morning, where she was to board the unmarked bus. There was no sign-off or further instruction, other than: *Tell no one.* Evelyn had read over the message twice before stuffing it inside her blouse. Then she had gone to the front door and poked her head outside, as if a clue might be found in the dark. But only a few cars had trundled by, then the paperboy on an old bicycle doing his evening round; this was a quiet enclave in Earl's Court, away from the commotion of the train station and the nearby thoroughfare.

Later that night, as she sat at Mrs. Banker's dining room table, pushing the slab of potted ham and string beans around her plate, half listening to the Newcastle twins' excited chatter about joining up at the exchange, Evelyn wondered if it had been a prank. It was all too wild, too mysterious, to happen to her; not even the declaration, it seemed, had shaken up her life in any material way. In fact, apart from the soldiers on the street and the new Anderson shelter in the boardinghouse's back garden, you'd hardly know there was a war on at all. Yet here she was on an unmarked bus hurtling through Shepherd's Bush.

After another twenty minutes, the driver pulled up at an ornamental iron gate. Evelyn peered through the grimy window toward the cameo emblem on the gatehouse entrance, then at the uniformed guards standing beneath it. It seemed they had stopped outside a fort. A few crows perched in a nearby tree had their eyes trained on the bus as steam from the exhaust gathered below the glass like mist.

"Where are we?"

A tinny voice, male, from near the front.

The driver came out from his booth as he tilted his cap. "Didn't they tell you?" His smile was toothless. "This is Wormwood Scrubs. The prison."

That got everyone talking in urgent whispers. Alone at the front of the bus, Evelyn shot another look toward the menacing facade and shivered. Why had she been brought here? There'd been no mention of prisons in the telegram. So it was a prank—but before she could dwell on this she was on her feet with the others, marching down the aisle and out into the bright morning. It was there, on the thin strip of grass beside the road, legs trembling as an officer in green fatigues barked out some instruction, that Evelyn recognized Caroline Menzies, dressed in a smart naval uniform with brass buttons, standing among the soldiers by the gate.

True to his word, Hugh had telephoned Caroline after the engagement party, and the following week Evelyn had received an invitation to the War Office, the enormous neo-Baroque building on Horse Guards Avenue in Whitehall. Caroline was in her early thirties, tall with a scoliosis stoop, wavy auburn hair, and spectacles. "I manage the female staff at the Ministry of Supply," she explained as they sat in her makeshift office on the second floor and shared a pot of weak tea. Caroline had been fidgety—telephones kept shrieking unanswered outside the door and the noisy clatter of typists' heels charging up and down the shiny marble floor perforated the balsawood partition wall like gunfire—so Evelyn made her case efficiently, describing her typing expertise (one hundred and fifty words per minute, she boasted) and exaggerating her aptitude for shorthand. She had experience in neither activity, but planned to enroll in a course. But it was her German studies that Caroline seemed most interested in; she even made a note of it in her small leather book. She had promised to keep in touch, but Evelyn hadn't heard another word—not even after she joined Mrs. Banker's other lodgers around the wireless that first Sunday morning of the month as Chamberlain made his emergency broadcast.

Now, siphoned off into a separate group, the young men were marched away through the iron gates, leaving the handful of remaining women on the grass verge. They all watched the big doors of the main building creak and slam shut, the air soon growing still once more.

Caroline came over with a clipboard pressed against her chest and gave them a stern smile. "Ladies, do come with me," she said.

But rather than head through the gatehouse entrance after the men, Caroline guided them down a cobbled lane adjacent to the brick fortress, stopping at a large blue door guarded by another soldier, who waved them inside. It was like entering a frigate, thought Evelyn, shuddering from the slap of metallic cold that greeted them. They pushed on, trailing beneath the open stairways, and passing row after row of dullish cells. On the first floor, the landings rattled with the barrage of men and women leaping up and down those metal stairs, while the scraping of chairs, shouts from officers on other blocks, and the inmates' muffled replies were all audible amid the horrendous din. They could have been crossing Paddington station at a quarter past five, the shrill, cavernous echoes like the shouts of paperboys, the bang and buckle of cell doors as noisy as an approaching train, and the farther they walked, the more the girls around Evelyn flinched and muttered unhappily.

Finally they reached another set of gates, opening onto a hall, and Caroline asked them to wait while she fetched a supervisor. Evelyn stood with the others in a small circle, exchanging shy smiles. The air smelled rank, like old urine mixed with feces, and a few yards away she saw a low-fitted sink with flies gathering around the plughole. There didn't seem to be any natural light or fresh air.

"It's awfully sinister, isn't it?" remarked a pretty redhead, and they all tittered, though their laughter was cut short by a noise directly above them. An inmate had come careening down the walkway, screaming at the top of his lungs, *"You fuckin' cock!"*

Three guards came after him and he was tackled to the floor, where he writhed about for a moment or two, still swearing, until one of the guards drew back a fist and punched him in the stomach, a solid clock of knuckle against flesh. A few girls whimpered, burying their faces in their hands, but Evelyn found herself edging forward, neck craned, fascinated—she rarely saw violence of any kind, and here it was, so close she could almost smell the man's blood. The scuffle was over in seconds, though most girls still had their eyes clenched shut by the time Caroline returned.

She pointed to Evelyn. "Miss Varley, this way."

As the girls looked her up and down, Evelyn imagined they were wondering what she had done to be singled out like this, and once they had set off she waited for Caroline to explain. Caroline, however, was silent on their way through a low doorway opening into another corridor; she didn't mention their meeting at Whitehall, and Evelyn began to wonder if the woman even remembered her.

It was quieter down here, squirreled away from the commotion of the ground floor and its elevated walkways, and they went on for a few more minutes until Caroline stopped outside a cell door.

"Listen, Evelyn," she said, her voice low and strained as she turned to face her. "I'm sorry for all this cloak-and-dagger stuff—it must all seem a bit . . . I don't know . . . barmy to you. When we met, I didn't mean to deceive you. It just makes everything easier if we recruit under the guise of the War Office." Tugging at the cuffs of her jacket, she offered Evelyn a hopeful smile. "All right?"

Evelyn didn't reply. They were interrupted by a raised voice inside the cell, the noise coming from a man standing beside a desk, a telephone jammed between his shoulder and ear. When his bloodshot eyes settled on Evelyn he muttered, "I'll call you back, David," and slammed down the receiver.

"I've brought Miss Varley," Caroline said, peering around the jamb. Then, to Evelyn, she added, "This is Mr. Chadwick."

Chadwick stood with his hands on his hips, breathing hard, a pulse beating wildly at the base of his throat. He didn't look much like a bureaucrat; dressed in a crumpled brown suit and surrounded by acrid ashtrays and half-drunk coffee cups, he could have passed more convincingly as a Soho bookie. His eyes were enormous behind a pair of bifocal glasses.

"Thank you, Caroline."

He yanked out a desk drawer and rummaged around, finally producing a packet of cigarettes. He lit one and stood there smoking furiously for several moments, then nodded at the chair.

"Take a seat."

But Evelyn didn't move, and her mouth was dry when she tried to swallow. This was fear, she realized. Cold, bright fear. Not because she was afraid of what might happen to her in this cell, but because she was alert to the understanding that she had stumbled upon something extraordinary. That, quite possibly, her life was about to change.

"What's the matter, girl? You look dazed."

Evelyn nodded. She supposed she must—but then who wouldn't after what she'd seen this morning? She looked around; Caroline Menzies had gone, her footsteps receding down the corridor, and when she turned back Chadwick had ground out his half-smoked cigarette and immediately lit up another.

"I beg your pardon," she said slowly. "But I wonder if you might tell me what I'm doing here? The bus driver said this was a prison, but how can that be true? When I first met Miss Menzies, we spoke about positions at the War Office . . ." Evelyn made a sweep of her arm around the cell. "But unless I'm dreaming, I'm not back in Whitehall."

From somewhere in the building came the loud clack of a typewriter and the rattle of keys in a lock. Chadwick watched her carefully, his eyes so dark the pupils had disappeared, then dropped into the chair behind his desk.

"No, you're not in Whitehall, Miss Varley. This is Section 5. Intelligence. I'm head of the Transport division."

"*This* is MI5?"

Chadwick blinked at her. "We had to move quickly," he said. "That's why we bused you all in today like farmyard fodder. If I'd had my way, recruitment would have been stitched up months ago, but the ministry wanted to wait until a declaration before staffing provisions were made for this office." He paused, something guarded about him now. "I'm sure you can understand the need for discretion."

With her back pressed hard against the chair, Evelyn realized she had also sat down. She wished she could smoke, but he hadn't offered her a cigarette, and in the flurry of the morning she'd forgotten to buy more of her own. Chadwick continued to watch her and she wondered if he was enjoying her discomfort. It was difficult to tell; his face betrayed little emotion.

"And what do you do here?" she asked when it became apparent he wasn't going to volunteer any further information.

"We look after the transportation of classified material. Shipping consignments, dispatch riders bearing top-secret communications, petrol coupons, arranging travel for those in government office. That sort of thing. It's not especially glamorous work, but we liaise closely with the other divisions in Section 5, and they use our intelligence in their own investigations."

Evelyn glanced around the cell again. It really was a wretched little room, with poor light and only a single tiny window made up of three panes of glass near the top cornice. Against the desk leaned a set of foam-backed blackout curtains. Evelyn shuddered; she couldn't help it—there was such a chill. Still, behind all that, she felt a tingle of excitement. She had been invited to MI5, and for a moment she imagined Sally's feathery voice in her ear: *Sounds rather spicy to me!*

"Well, it's certainly a unique working environment," she said.

Chadwick smiled grimly. "This location is only temporary. And really, it's not so bad. Be thankful you're here today and not last week, when we still had prisoners' chamber pots lying about the place." He reached across to search through his drawer. "Most of the brutes have been moved elsewhere, but there are still a few on A Block—for God's sake, don't ever talk to them if you can avoid it. They've gone quite fruity since clapping eyes on women again."

He brought out a manila folder and slapped it down on the desk. "Your file."

He seemed to be waiting for a reaction, but Evelyn kept her face still. It made sense that they had a file on her, and she was curious about what they knew. What they deemed important enough to record.

"Makes for some impressive reading," he said.

"Does it?"

"Yes." Chadwick cleared his throat. "Born 1917. Only child. Mother a housewife; father fought in Belgium, now a solicitor." He scratched his chin. "Only he's not a solicitor, is he?"

Evelyn clasped her hands together, squeezed. She could feel the blood rising to her cheeks.

"I beg your pardon?"

"I imagine that's what you told the registrar at Somerville College and your Oxford chums. I understand. We live in a world where appearance is everything. But Dad's not a solicitor, is he? He's just a humble clerk." He peeked at her from behind the file, his face implacable.

"I meant no harm by it," Evelyn said.

"But you lied."

"I exaggerated. I think you'd agree there's a difference. What I said hurt no one but allowed me a little more . . . dignity." She offered a conciliatory grimace. "Is there much wrong with that?"

They stared at one another until Chadwick returned a small smile.

"We trade in secrets here, Evelyn. There's no shame in having a few of your own. Our only concern is for who might discover them."

He read some more. "Home in . . . Lewes. That's Sussex, isn't it?"

"Yes. Near Brighton."

"And how did you like growing up there?"

Evelyn hesitated. It was not a question she had ever been asked.

"It was nice enough. Maybe a tad quiet for my liking."

"And then on to Oxford," Chadwick continued. "Did well there—very well. Firsts in German and Literature. Other interests are . . . *Art*, it says. What kind?"

"Painting, mainly."

"Favorite painter?"

"Well, I'm not sure I have just one . . ."

Chadwick raised his eyes. "Indulge me."

"Liss, maybe," she said.

"Flemish?"

"German, actually."

Chadwick had a chuckle. "I'm a philistine, Evelyn, don't mind me. More at home at the London Palladium than the Tate."

Evelyn studied him across the desk. Yes, she believed that. Despite her first impression, she could see he wasn't a threatening sort of man; there was something crumpled about him, in fact, as if some event had bent him out of shape. She tried to guess his age, but it was impossible—he could have been anywhere between thirty and fifty, with gray hair standing on end, while the lines etched deep into his face seemed to contain their own complex stories.

"Good references from the principal and the debating master."

They had done their homework. Evelyn wondered what old Roly-Poly Wilson had told them, with his bad breath and wandering hands. Not much of consequence, surely. That she was persuasive, probably. Sharp. Adaptable. That she could see both sides of an argument no matter how repugnant.

"And a glowing character reference from Hugh Wesley. Is that Wesley of Wesley Buttons?"

"Yes, sir. I'm a good friend of his daughter."

"Says here you're working at the present." He squinted over the top of his glasses. "Cosmetics, is it?"

"Vivian de la Croix. Advertising department."

"Hm." It was an unimpressed sound. "You wouldn't be sad to leave?"

Chadwick looked at her frankly. He had grown calmer, his voice now carrying a pleasant, gravelly timbre, and she had an image of him at home, fireside, with a book and a good single malt, and perhaps a dog—no, a cat—as his reading companion.

"The thing is, Evelyn, I need an assistant," he said, once he'd closed the file. "It's secretarial, mainly. Answering the telephone, making tea, typing up reports. But it's all going to get pretty hairy soon, don't mind what other people tell you, so I need a girl who is reliable." They both looked to the lamp, which crackled for a moment. "There will be many opportunities in the Service for a clever thing like you."

Outside, an elm tree scratched at the glass of the small window set high into the wall. Evelyn wondered how anyone could discern her reliability after such a brief meeting. Did Chadwick plan for her to sit a test? She'd already been caught out in a lie about her father, but he didn't seem to mind. Perhaps it didn't always follow that to be of good character meant being wholly honest too. Besides, maybe something else in her file pertained to her general trustworthiness, an epitaph from the revered Somerville principal—*As loyal as a dachshund*—and this endorsement was sufficient, like the royal imprimatur. Or perhaps it was none of these things. Perhaps it was as simple as Chadwick having a sense of how they might work together—he must have long ago developed an instinct for whom he could trust.

"I think it's fair to describe myself as reliable," she said.

Evelyn watched him lean back and light up another cigarette, the gray smoke drifting toward the ceiling. It would be untrue to say she wasn't intrigued by it all, or flattered that she had been singled out, and she thought of the gaggle of girls arriving on the bus, flinching away from the prisoner on the landing. Chadwick had seen something in Evelyn that set her apart; she could feel that in her bones. Something steely, she supposed, even ruthless.

"It's a rigorous day here—no time for a chinwag with other staff." He pointed to the empty doorway where Evelyn imagined few people ever lingered for a chat. "But the wage is three pounds a week. What do you think?"

Chadwick grinned then, deep creases etched in his cheeks. *Three pounds.* That was almost twice her wage at Vivian de la Croix.

"I think it sounds like just the ticket. Thank you, sir."

With a nod, Chadwick reached for the drawer again. This time he pulled out a piece of paper and pushed it across the desk, along with a fountain pen.

"All that's left is your autograph. It's fairly straightforward: once you sign you are bound by law never to speak about your work here at the Scrubs or with any other division of the Service."

Evelyn read the bold header: *Official Secrets Act.* If there had been more time, she might have hesitated before picking up the pen and thought about what her signature might bind her to. If there had been more time, she might even have reflected on what had brought her to the Scrubs in the first place. But there wasn't. All she had was the certainty she could do well here, that she could make a real contribution to the war and to her own fledgling career, and with a scribble and a flick she handed the signed paper back to Chadwick.

"So what can I tell other people, sir, about where I work?" she asked as he folded up the document and returned it to the drawer.

Chadwick glanced across the desk. "I find it prudent to have a cover that's uncomplicated. Something formal, respectable, but one that others won't care to probe into much." His smile was almost a sly one. "So I'd tell them you work at the War Office," he said.

There was a team of eight in Transport, many of whom came in and out of the prison wing at various times that first morning—drivers, runners, and a couple of cipher experts. Chadwick set Evelyn to work on new petrol orders that were delivered in batches each hour to the head of division's secretary on the other side of the prison. Her job was to assess each order, make sure the figures matched, record the sums in the ledger, type up the consignment, and give the stamp of authorization. But the truth was that figures had never been her strong suit and she had to check her calculations at least twice, while her typing wasn't nearly as good as she'd told Caroline Menzies it was. This slowed her down, and by midmorning she was only partway through the overflowing tray.

At one o'clock Chadwick invited Evelyn to join him for lunch in the staff cafeteria. They headed over to the east wing together and sat at a table next to the window with a view of the empty exercise yard, a concrete strip stretching the length of three tennis courts. The prisoners were only allowed outside for half an hour early each morning.

"It's a miserable system, prisons," Chadwick said. "I was in the colonial force in India for nearly fifteen years, and for half that time I was on duty at the watch house. You learn a man's true nature when you have him in isolation." He nibbled at his fish-paste sandwich, then gave up. "I've never got used to British food again. In Bombay, we ate like kings—even at the police station. *Idlis, batata vada, ragda pattice* . . . Delicious it was. Some weeks I went without a bite of meat."

Evelyn glanced down at her indeterminate stew with a film of yellow fat congealing on the surface. "You enjoyed India, then?"

"Oh yes," Chadwick said, "very much. But I met my wife on leave here in London." He folded his arms, the cuffs riding up to reveal surprisingly hairy wrists. "Daisy didn't like India."

"She must be pleased to be back."

Chadwick nudged his plate away, his gaze returning to the window. Evelyn could feel the dull energy coming off him now, like the mildest swell of sea.

"She would have been," he said quietly. "She died over there. Typhoid."

"Oh." Evelyn set down her fork. "I'm very sorry, sir."

Chadwick nodded, his eyes fixed to the lazy flight of a gull outside. So there it was, Evelyn thought sadly. What had bent him out of shape. They sat for a moment, staring at that desolate exercise yard, until someone approached the table with the alert of a telephone call for Chadwick, and he excused himself to return to the block.

The cafeteria was emptying out and Evelyn felt a little lonely sitting there by the fogged-up window. Chadwick had been right: so far there hadn't been a moment to chat with her other colleagues, but she had glimpsed a few harassed-looking assistants during her busy morning, and the smiles exchanged had been accompanied by a sense of camaraderie. She hadn't seen any of the young women from the morning bus.

"So you're Chaddy's new girl, then?"

A dark-haired man with chafed lips and a pale blue cravat stood by her table. He stuck out his hand and introduced himself as Vincent Meyer, Chadwick's decryption analyst. It turned out he worked from the cell next to Evelyn's.

"And how are you finding your first day?" he asked.

"I must have broken a record somewhere for typing." Evelyn

massaged her aching hands. "Who knew we needed so many couriers? I counted around eighty of your reports alone."

"Wait until we start on the enemy alien stuff." Vincent sat down and pulled out a flask from his jacket pocket, pouring a splash of tart-smelling liquid into his enamel mug. He offered some to Evelyn, but she shook her head.

"Enemy aliens?"

"Abwehr agents. German spies. The ministry has a bee in its bonnet about infiltration. They're interning any Jerry they can get their hands on."

"Are there really German spies in London?"

"Bennett White seems certain of it." He leaned forward. "Have you met the Master?"

"I don't think so."

"He's head of counterintelligence. Very dapper. That's where this war will be fought and won—in the drawing rooms of the English noblesse." Vincent sat back, smiling to himself. "Chaddy says you speak German. It'll be good to have another in the team. You spent much time over there?"

Evelyn shook her head. "More of an armchair expert, really. I read it at university."

"Oxbridge? Quite a few of you around here."

Vincent had his arms crossed, but it wasn't belligerent; in fact, he was appraising her quite unashamedly, his gaze moving over her hair, face, apricot blouse, all in a dispassionate sort of way, as though she was a coat in a shop he was thinking about buying.

"What about you, Vincent?" Evelyn asked when his eyes finally flicked back to hers. "You must pass as a native to do all that decryption."

"That's because I am, darling. A native."

"You're German?"

"Was." He took a mouthful of booze, wincing. "I'm a naturalized British citizen now. My parents got me and my brother out years ago. Sent us to live with my mother's relatives in Cambridge."

Evelyn stared at her tea. The wind howled at the window, a branch scrabbling at the glass. She looked at Vincent's fingers wrapped around his mug. They were long and delicate; more suited to playing a piano, she thought, than using a typewriter.

"Is that usual here, at MI5?"

"What?" Vincent's top lip curled. "To have a Hun on the team?"

"I didn't mean . . ." Evelyn found herself floundering; his skittish manner made her feel like she was rounding up a stray cat. "What I meant was you must bring very useful insight."

"I'm not sure about that. I don't understand what's going on over there any more than the rest of the Section. Sometimes the best perspective comes from an outsider." He stood up, his chair scraping against the tiled floor, and as he brought out an orange tin of small cigars he rested a light hand on her shoulder briefly. "But I am looking forward to us working together, darling."

That afternoon, Evelyn typed up a stack of decoded reports due for dispatch with the evening couriers. She didn't see Vincent again, but she thought she heard his voice from time to time echoing along the corridor. Chadwick popped his head in occasionally, but most of the afternoon he locked himself away in the phone booth near the gate on a private line to Whitehall. Once she'd finished the reports, Evelyn moved on to her own telephone calls to the depots and other fuel-supply companies.

At six o'clock a bell rang through the wing signaling the end of the working day. Evelyn looked up to the small, high-set window. It had grown cloudy outside without her realizing it, though she had been working by lamplight since teatime. Still detecting the faint sound of Chadwick in the phone booth, she hurried upstairs to the small kitchen in B Wing to make him some coffee. By now most of the floor had gone home and the prison was uncannily quiet, the only noise coming from the inmates on the other side of the building. But Chadwick wasn't at his desk when she returned, so she left the steaming mug by the pile of papers and gathered up her coat and handbag. This time, as she made her way down the long corridor, it was with arms raised, fingers twitching, as a blind person might, the only light coming from the distant cell door, the dull bulb in the lamp burning like the last star of the night.

⌒

It was nearing dusk by the time Evelyn walked back toward Bramham Gardens from the bus stop near Old Brompton Road. She took off her hat and coat in the vestibule and hung them on the stand by the front door, collecting a letter addressed to her from the hall table. The house was dim and quiet, like a place of bereavement, though Evelyn could make out some sounds of frail life as she walked upstairs to her bedroom on the second floor: a dry cough, the tired springs of a mattress, jetting gas. The waft of boiled cabbage from the kitchen followed her to the landing. The floorboards creaked.

Her bedroom smelled of damp. Evelyn went to the small stove and put on the kettle, then opened her window a fraction to allow in some fresh air. The small park behind the line of terraces was empty except for the solid outline of a man and woman pressed together beneath a plane tree, his head buried in her neck. Evelyn eased off her tight leather brogues and pushed them beneath the bed. Her feet felt clammy inside her stockings.

When the kettle had boiled, she made herself a cup of tea and wandered over to the bureau by the window. The room had been advertised as furnished, which Evelyn discovered had meant only a small single bed, a rickety cupboard, and a two-shelf bookcase, but she found herself in luck when the departing lodger gifted her the antique desk. She unlatched the writing stand, breathing in the aroma of resin, and sat down. She picked up her father's letter, slipped the paper knife under the seal, and sawed it open. Evelyn read the short note, which mentioned the local girls in Lewes enlisting in the WVS and wondered whether she might do the same in London, and began a reply.

Dear Mother and Father,
Some good news from me today. I am leaving my post at Vivian de la Croix to join the War Office. I am now the assistant to a fellow named John Chadwick in the Ministry of Supply. My wage is £3 . . .

Evelyn tipped back her chair and stared at the chipped cornices and mold stains on the ceiling. There wasn't much more she could write, and though her parents wouldn't detect any censorship, the thought of how much she would now have to conceal from Sally filled Evelyn with unease. She scribbled a few more lines, then went to the sink beside the window. After she had run the tap and splashed icy water on her face, she stood bent over the basin for another moment, feeling the blood rush to her cheeks, until a knock sounded at the door.

It was Mrs. Banker come to collect the rent. She bustled her way inside, her beady eyes roaming about as they always did, snagging on the rack by the bookcase where Evelyn kept her best blouses, blazer, and woolen coat. Tonight the landlady wore a flannelette dressing-gown, her misshapen ankles bulging over the sheepskin trimming of her mauve slippers. When Evelyn handed over the notes, Mrs. Banker counted them right there in front of her, making a clucking sound, before stuffing the money inside her pocket.

"Dinner will be ready at eight. Remember, Miss Varley, I don't tolerate lateness."

Evelyn watched her scuttle off toward the door.

"Cabbage again, is it?"

Mrs. Banker looked over her shoulder. She had the kind of weathered face that spoke of a hard life, though Evelyn had little sympathy for the old woman. She knew Mrs. Banker had always been suspicious of her. Evelyn wasn't like her other lodgers—the landlady had said as much the day she moved in—and Evelyn had since learned that Mrs. Banker didn't like peculiarity of any kind.

"Picked from my very garden, your most royal highness."

As she said this, the moan of the air-raid siren started up, rattling the glass in the windowpane. Evelyn gripped the back of her chair. This was the second time the siren had gone off that week. She waited for it to quieten down, signaling another false alarm, but the low wail continued. Without another word, Evelyn strode toward the door, urging Mrs. Banker ahead of her along the narrow passageway and down the heaving set of stairs. They headed for the parlor, where Mr. Buckley from the top floor was already handing out gas masks to the other lodgers from a pile on the settee. He had been appointed the local air-raid warden and made nightly rounds of the block of terraces dressed in a pair of heavy cotton overalls and a steel helmet.

"We've got two minutes before a bomb lands on our bleeding heads!" he shouted.

When the masks had been distributed, he marched them downstairs to the basement kitchen and out the back door and onto the concrete patio, calling them to a halt at the brick wall. He pointed to the rockery at the far edge of the yard where the Anderson shelter stood.

"Surely that flimsy tin shed is next to useless," someone called.

"It's built into the ground," Mr. Buckley pronounced indignantly, as if he had designed the contraption himself, "and will keep us safe during any raid."

In the stark moonlight, the shelter looked a lot like a dog kennel disguised beneath a pile of rocks, and as Evelyn studied it more closely she saw it was made from little more than corrugated iron. She glanced at Mrs. Banker. The poor woman was shaking.

"We'll be safe in there," Evelyn said, putting an arm around her. "Mr. Buckley is right."

"And how can you be so sure, missy?" But there was no malice in her voice and she shrank into Evelyn, grabbing at her hand.

They filed into the shelter one by one. The roof was so low they had to sit slumped over with their heads almost in their laps—it was lucky the Newcastle twins, great hulking lads, had never returned from the exchange. The siren wailed relentlessly and the air inside soon grew thick and stale. Evelyn could hear sobbing—Mrs. Banker, maybe—and someone broke wind. She closed her eyes, aware of the tremor in her lips, and in her hands, which she clasped together in a kind of prayer. She had never imagined any danger would touch her here, in the middle of London, and she was rocked by her own naivety. Imagine, she could die in Earl's Court tonight, and it felt savage to be confronted by her own mortality while pressed against these wriggling strangers. There was so much of her life she still had to live; she hadn't realized how desperate she was for it until that very moment, and trapped inside that pitch-dark shelter she experienced an awful mix of despair and gratitude for the revelation.

She wasn't sure how much time had passed before the first siren stopped and the all-clear commenced a stirring cry—half an hour, perhaps, though it felt longer. After spilling back out into the fresh night air, they all stood in a circle in the middle of the patio, grinning at one another and staring up at the sky. There was no hugging or crying, as one might expect; no false sentiment, though Mr. Buckley did raise a fist and holler, "It'll take more than that, you friggin' Boche bastards!" before he took off to inspect the other houses on the street.

Within a few minutes, order had been restored, with Mrs. Banker complaining that her dinner would be ruined. But while the rest of the lodgers filed inside, Evelyn stayed out in the garden, pretending it was for a smoke. Instead, she prowled about the paved courtyard, kicking at the tall grass, swiping at the low-hanging ivy. She felt queer, something almost inflamed coursing through her, as if she could walk into the street and flip over a taxi or snap a lamppost in half, and she fought the urge to howl at the twinkling night with the joy of it all, and the terror.

It was only later, after she had climbed into bed, that she remembered the letter to her father propped against the bureau ledge. She got up and placed it in her handbag for the morning. Then she went to the window, wondering about the couple beneath the tree. For some daft reason she expected them to still be out there, tangled in their embrace, amid the threat of bombs falling from the sky. But she couldn't see them; the gardens were as murky as a pond, the only movement the faint whisper of a squirrel in a low branch, the glimmer of a fox.

MARCH 1948

FIVE

IT WAS SPITTING fine rain as Evelyn headed toward Euston Road. Last night felt distant, like a long-forgotten dream, and in the pale light she could see how conspicuous a woman like Julia would be in this part of town. Still, Evelyn checked over her shoulder on each corner, relieved to find the streets empty. The butcher's and the grocer's, on the other hand, were crowded—the locals came early for the best fresh meat and vegetables—and as she browsed Evelyn was pushed around as though she'd strayed into the middle of a rugby scrum. In the end, she bought a loaf of bread, a small square of butter, milk powder, a cut of lamb, something off the bone for a stew or a broth, and some beets, carrots, and a turnip. It wasn't much for the week, but she never had much of an appetite. She had hoped for some coffee, too—the proper kind, richer than the horrible silty stuff served everywhere now—but Mrs. Grundy had run out, and so she asked for a small box of tea and cigarettes instead, tucking it all away in her basket.

Evelyn trailed back toward the flat, her head bent against the bitter wind. Most Saturdays Stephen wandered over from his small bedsit on Tavistock Place to accompany her to the shops. Though it had usually only been a matter of hours since he'd last seen her, he was always in a talkative mood, describing the latest book he had been reading or relating some story from the morning newspaper. Evelyn enjoyed these conversations, admiring the way his mind worked; there was something unpredictable about it, and having set aside that part of herself for so long she found her own mind gently exercised once again. She wondered if he spoke to his friends in the same eager manner. She'd met a few of them—one time at a dinner party, another at a pub in Highgate—and they had displayed such polite, wide-eyed curiosity that Evelyn wanted to know just quite what Stephen had told them about her.

Evelyn paused beneath a shopfront awning to adjust the bulk of her wicker basket. If the sky was clear, Stephen sometimes managed to coax Evelyn over to Clerkenwell Road where a few Italian grocers still ran their weekend stalls—many had been interned during the war, but they were slowly returning to London. After packing her basket full of onions, garlic, and tomatoes, Stephen would steer her toward the vendors wearing tweed *coppolas* who sold cured meats, olives in jars of oil, and blocks of pungent-smelling cheeses. When he spoke Italian to them, Stephen's manner changed—he became loud, cheeky even, making them laugh. Everyone seemed to know him; the old men called him *Stefano*, and Evelyn *bella ragazza*, stuffing her already overflowing basket with sprigs of dried basil and oregano, smiling and patting her hand. And through all this garrulousness, Evelyn would catch Stephen watching her with a warm intensity that made her stomach flip. Later he'd cook for her back at the flat, simple but delicious meals like gnocchi in a rich tomato sauce with a fresh green salad, while Evelyn read by the fireplace and drank wine.

"Don't you men all hate cooking?" she once remarked as he stirred the pan on the stovetop.

Tea towel flung over his angular shoulder, Stephen had smiled her way and said, "I love cooking for you."

It was in those moments that a visit to Rome seemed like the most uncomplicated thing in the world, thought Evelyn as she stopped on the corner of Euston Road, waiting for the traffic to pass. That the past was well and truly behind her.

After dropping off her groceries at the flat, Evelyn took a bus toward Pimlico. The weather had turned foul, rain sleeting in violent bursts across the street, but as she hurried across Vauxhall Bridge, she still paused at the railing to gaze at the brown river churning beneath her. It was not a thing of beauty, the Thames, but there was something mesmerizing about the way the current moved in different directions. Evelyn couldn't understand how the water did that, following its haphazard course beneath the granite arch. It was a long way down. She had heard that hitting the river from such a height had the same effect as landing on concrete—a person could split their stomach open with a belly flop—and she clenched her eyes shut against the thought of it.

Evelyn waited in the empty bus shelter on Wandsworth Road. The rain began to ease, though the wind had picked up, sending old sheets of newspaper scraping along the street. Ordinarily, if she wasn't working Saturday afternoons at the bookshop, Stephen would collect his car after their visit to the shops. He liked to take day trips, and if the weather was fine they'd often motor over to Guildford for lunch by the canal. Evelyn looked forward to these outings all week, though now she wondered if Stephen knew this. She wasn't exactly effusive, never being quite sure how to express her feelings, but she wished that she had said something, anything, to make him understand what that time away from London meant to her, how it took her out of her own head. She had hoped Stephen might have stopped by the flat this morning, or telephoned, but somehow she knew he wouldn't. She tried not to think about what it would mean if he never got in touch.

When the bus arrived, Evelyn sat upstairs, studying the view of the Chelsea riverbanks as they lurched along Nine Elms Lane. The Battersea power station came into view, smoke belching from its enormous white stacks. The bus stopped at the dogs and cats' home opposite the park as the sun hid farther behind the dark clouds. She got off at the next stop and walked through the underpass at Clapham Junction, an inbound train rattling and groaning on the tracks overhead. The morning had grown colder, and Evelyn drew her coat tight as she strode on toward Lavender Hill. The area was a poor, rough one, the houses desolate—row after row of dingy, low-set terraces built right up to the edge of the pavement. The air looked thick and dirty, and Evelyn glanced around for any garden, trees, or even a bit of grass, finding none. There were a few scruffy children playing hopscotch at the top of one street on the edge of an estate. It was still odd to see children outside; Evelyn always assumed there weren't any left, as if, like so many of those young men, they had never come back to London after the war.

Vincent was waiting inside the greasy spoon on the corner. Evelyn spotted him through the front window as she crossed the quiet street. He hadn't changed: still tall and stooped, still dapper in his Oxford shoes and Italian coat, still pale and dark, though with some steel-wool gray in his hair. There was something comforting about the familiarity of him, even after all these years. Evelyn swallowed at the painful lump in her throat, a bit of weak sun finally reemerging as she pulled open the cafe door.

Presided over by an elderly Cypriot, Zafer's was a clean, unassuming establishment with formica tables spaced evenly around the narrow interior. A few down-and-out-looking men sat hunched over their plates of eggs and beans, half-drunk mugs of tea beside their trays.

The air was humid with the pong of old socks and unwashed bodies. It was not somewhere she imagined Vincent spent much of his spare time, but there was also no chance of running into anyone either of them knew, which was probably why he had suggested it.

Now, sitting across the sticky table from one another, Evelyn finally got a better look at him under the fluorescent lights and saw that the years had not been kind to him. His skin was not so much pale as jaundiced, and his forehead, which he dabbed at now and then with a silk handkerchief, had a damp sheen to it. After adding a few sugars he drank his tea with elbows planted on the table, a gesture not of nonchalance, Evelyn realized, but in an effort to keep himself upright.

"How have you been keeping yourself, Evelyn?" he asked after coughing into the handkerchief. "Still at the bookshop?"

She had a sip of tea. Of course he knew. They had probably sorted it for her, the job, like a belated going-away present.

"I'm glad Mrs. Foy kept you on. She's a good old stick."

"And you?" Evelyn set down the tin mug. "Still with Section 5?"

"Good grief, no. I moved over to Special Branch years ago."

"No more decryption?"

"I still dabble. But I hunt reds now—or haven't you heard?"

She had heard—it was hardly a secret. It didn't matter to people like Vincent who the enemy was, as long as there was one.

"And do you still see much of Bennett?" she asked lightly.

Vincent shook his head.

"He's no longer in the Service?"

"No. At the BBC, actually. Does some program on the wireless all about birds." He peered at her with his red-threaded eyes. "He's rather good, I'm afraid. Just recherché enough to be charming."

"And did you two ever . . ."

"*No.*" Vincent pressed his lips together. "No, that finished some time ago. Never really started, in fact—so not all that much to end."

He spread his hands across the checkered tablecloth; they were even thinner and bonier than she remembered, a blue vein pulsing at his knuckle. "So, you had a little run-in. Who was it?"

"Julia Wharton-Wells."

Vincent raised an eyebrow. "I see. Did she recognize you?"

Evelyn nodded. "We spoke for a few minutes. About nothing of consequence." She picked up her mug then set it down again, suddenly incredulous. "She has a daughter."

"Yes." His mouth twitched. "You sound surprised."

Evelyn stared at the oily surface of her tea. "I suppose I always thought her life would have stopped." She didn't add, *like mine did.*

"Do you think she's still in play?" Vincent asked. "Only we haven't heard any chatter."

Evelyn thought of Margaret and the way Julia had looked at her, like her own heart was beating inside the little girl's chest.

"I doubt it."

"And did she threaten you?"

"Not directly. But she gave me this." From her handbag, Evelyn drew out the postcard of *Judith in the Tent with Holofernes* and handed it across the table. Vincent scowled, giving it an impartial shake.

"It was . . . it was in the Onslow Square house when I visited Randall. The original . . ." Evelyn paused. "It's Judith betraying Holofernes—don't you know it? It's an allegory, for goodness' sake." She was growing agitated, exasperated even, as she sensed Vincent's interest waning. "Julia knows it means something to me."

"All right, all right. I'll file a report, though I'm not sure Section 5 will do much for you, all things considered. I could be in strife just for meeting you. Too many cobwebs . . ." Running a hand through his hair, he tried to smile. "Meanwhile, I'd lie low for a while if I were you, maybe take a trip somewhere. Have you friends who could put you up outside London?"

"*Friends?*" She laughed, and Vincent had the good grace to look embarrassed.

They finished their toast and ordered another mug of tea. As Vincent dabbed at the crumbs on his empty plate, Evelyn thought about when she'd last seen him, at Chemley Court. How long ago that seemed—and she was glad for that distance, although there had been a period in her life when she would have given anything to fold the passage of time into minute portable squares. Vincent knew all this, of course, had made this calculation when he offered to meet her, and she could feel his familiar appraisal of her dry lips, her brown coat. It was a curious bond they'd once had, that flimsy intimacy, like old lovers knowing each other's deepest secrets and their silent vow to always keep them.

"Did anyone else see you with her?" he asked.

Evelyn nodded. "Stephen Glover."

"Who is that?"

"A friend." Evelyn hesitated. "A close friend."

"Does he know—"

She shook her head.

Vincent frowned. "Does he know you're here now?"

"No. I haven't heard from him since last night." Evelyn fidgeted with the canister of sugar. "I was . . . *scared.*"

There, she had said it, though she felt no better for it.

Vincent casually brought out the orange tin where he kept his cigars. "What were you scared of, darling?"

"I thought Julia might say something . . ."

"Would that be so terrible?"

Evelyn stared back at him. So this was how Vincent approached the past: incisive, diagnostic. He was lucky enough to be in the position where he could view it with such detachment, but it made her want to shriek.

"Terrible? After what happened? It would be *ghastly*."

They sat watching one another, the air between them unmoving, until Vincent sat back, smiling faintly. "I've often wondered what became of you, Evelyn. What it all did to you. It was all so very unfair . . . I'm sorry I didn't keep in touch." He puffed away on the cigar, thoughtful. "Do you care for this chap, Stephen?"

"Yes."

"You love him?"

Beneath her coat, Evelyn could feel the exact pressure of Stephen's arms around her when they went dancing, the certainty of him but also the bulk of him as they glided around the hall, as if he were bracing for impact. Perhaps that was what he'd been doing: waiting for the blow that would tear them apart.

"I don't know," she said. "I don't know what that feels like."

"Rot. We all know what it feels like." Vincent let this hang, perhaps considering what it had meant for him in the intervening years. "And now he thinks you're keeping something from him? Some part of yourself?"

Evelyn nodded.

"Well then, it's simple. You need to tell him. Everything. Start at the beginning. How can anyone really love you if they don't know you?"

"But it's not that simple."

"Why not?"

"Well, I'm not supposed to talk about—"

Vincent leaned forward, snatching up Evelyn's hands, his own blue and hard like they had just come out of Zafer's chiller. But his eyes were the same color as the Thames, and Evelyn's mind wandered back to the river and all the silt that lay beneath it.

"You don't have to be loyal to them anymore, Evelyn, for Christ's sake! Not them, not anyone! Do you understand?" His bottom lip trembled as he slumped back, rubbing at the faint map of broken capillaries across his cheeks. "What's the use of scurrying around in the shadows like you're still a damned spook? Some things you have to bring up from the ground or they will kill you. You of all people should know this."

And it was absurd, after all this time, to still be afraid of the war and its long shadow hanging over her—Evelyn knew that. But it wasn't fear like the men would have felt in the boats or on the beaches. Not the same fear as when the German bombs rained down across London, picking out targets like indiscriminate skittles—she could remember that particular visceral terror, with its airlessness and the static whistle at the back of her head. This fear was made of quicker, steelier matter; it was sleek and icy, working its way inside Evelyn's blood. It was the same fear she felt when she first met Nina: of being *seen*.

Afterward, they stood out the front of the cafe. Vincent offered a hand to Evelyn and they stood looking at one another, squinting in the gray light.

"You will think about what I said, won't you, Evelyn? About getting away?"

"Of course."

"Your parents . . ." Vincent was winding a scarf around his neck. It had started to rain. "They lived outside the city, didn't they? Could you stay with them?"

Evelyn bit her lip. She looked past him to a group of children gathered in a circle in the lane. She hadn't spoken to her mother and father in years.

"They're dead." The lie, like all those from the past, came easily.

Vincent made a face. "Oh, darling, I'm sorry. I had no idea." But then he was struck by another coughing fit, so violent he was bent over by it, and when he straightened she saw a glob of bright blood in his handkerchief.

They didn't hug or kiss on parting. There was no promise of another telephone call. It was still easier to say nothing, Evelyn thought, watching Vincent walk away. He looked frail as he made his way back up Lavender Hill, head bowed, as if a sudden gust of wind might sweep through and take him away. But later, as Evelyn headed back across Vauxhall Bridge, the grit and rain howling around her, she gripped the rail for a moment, rocked back on her heels with the force of it, and realized she was the one in danger of flying away.

NOVEMBER 1939

SIX

EVELYN WALKED UP the hill to High Street and turned off toward the Ouse and the cobbled walkway through the market stalls. She passed the brewery and St. Thomas's church on the corner. It wasn't a long walk from the station, but she soon stopped by some sparse shrubs at the side of the road to catch her breath. Through the spindly branches she could make out the slate-colored triangular roofs of South Street, and tucked away behind the trees the old pub, the Dorset. The town didn't extend far; beyond it a patchwork of green and brown and gray farmland moved in a gentle incline toward the horizon. Behind that land was Falmer. This view was Evelyn's favorite thing about Lewes: it reminded her of life beyond the town. When she was a girl she used to fancy she could see all the way to Brighton.

Veering into the next laneway, Evelyn glimpsed her parents' house. Not a large dwelling by any means, it was a two-story cottage clad with brown stucco, and she could make out the ivy creeping up the wall outside the kitchen and the thread of smoke from the chimney. Still, it was imposing from this distance. Perhaps that had something to do with its proud stance, tall along the hemmed-in lane, elevated on the mound of lush grass, and the large Regency-style windows overlooking the valley. The lawn looked to have been recently clipped and the pheasant grass and foxtail barley planted by the verge were thriving. As Evelyn strolled up the stone path she caught the strong, earthy scent of Michaelmas daisies growing in pots on the patio.

The front door was unlocked and Evelyn let herself in. She called out, but there was no reply. She set down her suitcase and went through to the sitting room where she found her father on the sofa, the morning newspaper spread across his lap.

"Hello, Evelyn."

"Did you not hear me at the door, Dad?"

The room was cluttered with his books, stacks of old magazines, and her mother's knitting unspooling from a box on the chaise longue. The grandfather clock in the corner ticked above the fizz and crackle from the fire in the hearth, and a few knitted lace doilies had been cast over the arms of the sofa. On the wall above the fire hung the portrait of Evelyn's grandfather and beneath it two photographs in silver frames stood on the mantelpiece: one of her parents on their wedding day, the other of Evelyn when she was about four years old, dressed in a white slip dress, clasping her toy rabbit, Bunny. She gazed at the soft curl of her hair, the solemn pout, her cold eyes. It wasn't a flattering portrait; there must have been others in her parents' collection, and she wondered why they had chosen to display this one. Nothing much else in the room belonged to Evelyn—no sketches or papers or books of her own. She recalled all the times her mother had complained about her leaving her socks, shoes, hairpins, brushes around. Now it was as if she had never lived in the house at all.

"Hello, dear. I thought it was you. I'll fetch an extra cup."

Her mother had appeared in the doorway with tea and biscuits and brought the tray to the small table in front of the sofa. Once her father had set aside his reading she began pouring out the tea.

"Now, how is the new flat? Are you settled in?"

Peering over his glasses, her father looked smaller than Evelyn remembered, his cardigan hanging limp from his shoulders.

"Oh, yes," she said. "It's much nicer than Earl's Court."

Evelyn had moved from Mrs. Banker's earlier that month. The new flat was on the corner of Berwick and Broadwick streets, on the third floor above a small public house. On a clear day, the terrace was almost attractive, and with its olive-painted dormer windows and slate mansard roof Evelyn often felt that she could have been living not in Soho but in the twelfth arrondissement of Paris. Ivy grew up the left side of the facade, hedge boxes hung from the first-floor ledge, and a lantern swung at the pub's entrance. The flat was a Service one, which meant the landlord had been vetted. Chadwick even had someone already there for Evelyn to share with, a switch operator from the Scrubs. "You'll be much happier lodging with another MI5 girl," he reasoned. "And Fay's a good sort—trust me."

But the building had known better days. The stairs leading up to the flat were rotten, each step felt precarious, and on the landing outside the front door, where the wallpaper was stained and curling away from the skirting boards, the peaty stench of mildew often lingered. Nonetheless, Fay Harding, a friendly, freckly girl from Bolton, had made the place homely with old rugs, Indian lampshades, and joss sticks burning in the hall. A good sort, as Chadwick had promised, she was also a social creature, out most nights with the other switchies from the Scrubs. Evelyn was always invited to join them, and she had gone along a few times to the revue at the Windmill Theatre, to please Fay as much as anything else. They were nice enough girls, but Evelyn was never quite comfortable with them, unable to shake the feeling they preferred it when she wasn't around.

"And Sally?" her mother asked. "I hear she's getting married."

"Yes, that's right." Evelyn blew on her tea and set it down on the table. "The wedding's in early March."

"March?" Her mother made a face. "She's taking a gamble on the weather." Then, frowning, "She's not, well, you know . . . ?"

"No, nothing like that." Evelyn could feel irritation surging in her veins. How could her mother do this to her after only a few minutes in her company? "Jonty, her fiancé, he's in the RAF. It's all about his deployment and whatnot."

Her father snapped a malt biscuit between his teeth and munched on it contentedly. "Now, tell us about this government job of yours, dear," he said. "I'm not sure Mum and I are quite certain of what you actually *do*!"

"I'm Mr. Chadwick's assistant in the War Office."

"That's in Whitehall, isn't it?"

"That's right. He's head of Supply."

"And I suppose you're working on some intriguing stuff?"

Evelyn shifted against the sofa. She realized if she couldn't speak about work, she couldn't really speak about London, and that didn't leave much to talk about. Her father didn't seem to notice, already drawn back to his newspaper, his obligatory queries discharged, but her mother had been watching her from the armchair as one might watch a bird whose aviary door had been left open.

"I'm not sure how intriguing it is," Evelyn said. "We keep an eye on all the army consignments and deliveries around the country. Fuel logs, dispatch riders, that sort of thing. But there's a fair amount of administration too. Posting letters and answering the telephone."

Her mother frowned. "They should be putting you to better use than that."

"I'm doing good work, Mum. Important work."

"What about your plans for teaching? Or have you given up on them?"

"No." Evelyn clenched her jaw. "They're just on hold for now. Like many people's plans."

But this wasn't enough. Her mother stirred her tea and set down the spoon. "All men, then, is it? The War Office?"

Evelyn couldn't tell if her tone was approving or reproachful.

"No, it's not."

Her parents stared back at her.

"Well, I'm sure you know what's best," her father said finally, reaching for another biscuit.

Evelyn looked out the window, her eyes drifting over the neat garden hedge. A bird had nested in the brambles near the back gate. It began to whistle, the shrill noise penetrating the glass, and Evelyn and her parents went quiet, listening.

"I say, it's a waxwing," said her father, rising from his chair and moving to the window. "We thought all the garden birds were gone for the season, didn't we, Mum? But this chap looks fairly plump and well feathered."

He tapped on the glass and the bird turned its black and white eyestripe in their direction. Evelyn admired it for a moment. When she was a girl she used to walk with her father up the Malling Down reserve, an old pair of Brevete field binoculars bumping against her chest, to watch the first arrival of the serins, her favorite finch with a bright yellow plumage.

"The garden is looking healthy. Is that your work, Mum?"

"Mum has been spending a lot of time out there," her father murmured, returning to his chair as her mother stacked the cups and saucers on the tray. "It's something of a passion of hers." The wisps of his eyebrows shone gold as he glanced back at Evelyn. "So, how long do we have you?"

"I'll take the last afternoon train back on Tuesday."

"Till Tuesday," he mused. "Not too bad, is it, Mum?"

Her mother had paused in the doorway but didn't reply. Evelyn watched her leave the room, taking in the straight line of her back, the fragile gray of her bun.

"We thought we might head out tomorrow to Eastbourne," her father said. "Make a day of it, like we used to when you were a scrap. We could even have fish and chips on the promenade? Remember that time—"

"—with the seagull? He wanted your cod."

"He got it, all right, and half my chips." Her father laughed. "Didn't get your pickled egg, though, did he? You kept that safe like the Praetorian Guard."

"Mum said it served us right for eating out there by the beach."

"Well, sometimes your mother doesn't see the value in a bit of fun. But we won't hold that against her too much, will we?"

He winked, reaching for his newspaper again, and Evelyn felt the dull throb of her heart. She leaned back on the sofa, but she couldn't settle, distracted by the sound of clattering crockery, knowing her mother was at the sink furiously scrubbing. She wouldn't come out of the kitchen until every last plate, spoon, and teacup was spotless—it had always been like that; she had always preferred to spend time at the sink rather than with her own daughter—and as she stood and went to the window, Evelyn became aware of another feeling behind that throb, hot and swift and sharp, like a swoop of the waxwing perched in the brambles.

~

The next day they traveled to the seaside. The sun was out and crowds had flocked to the promenade; some children were even running through the shallows beneath the pier. After a stroll and a baked potato from the van near the new bandstand, her father found a quiet tavern tucked away from Grand Parade, and they sat on a terrace overlooking the gardens of St. Mary the Virgin and drank dark ale. Her parents talked about the town and the renovation of the clubrooms at the golf course. They didn't ask about Evelyn's work again, or much about her life in London. Perhaps they're afraid of what I might tell them, she thought, tracing the rim of her glass.

Evelyn sat in the back seat on the return drive to Lewes. She could see that her father was happy; his family, if only for the duration of the journey, had been reunited. But her mother remained tense and watchful, gripping the handle above the car door all the way home.

⌒

The next morning, after her father had walked into town, Evelyn joined her mother in the garden as she pruned the roses. The sun was out again but the wind had bite. Evelyn watched her mother move from one bed to the next, her gait springy, her face fixed in stern concentration. Normally Evelyn would have joined in without hesitation, but something held her back. Perhaps it was the wariness her mother had adopted since she had arrived home, tiptoeing about Evelyn as if she were a stranger. Once the roses had been attended to, however, her mother called, "There's another pair of secateurs somewhere in the shed if you'd like to help me?" and Evelyn followed her to the kumquats and the strawberry patch, where insects had nibbled through most of the leaves, and they spent another hour laying a compost of loam, peat, and sand over the plants.

At midday, her mother brought out some lemonade and cheese-and-chutney sandwiches, and they sat shivering on the patio, a white cast-iron table between them. When they were finished, her mother fetched a pot of coffee, which they drank from the small glazed cups Evelyn had made in a school pottery class, her spidery initials, *E.V.*, carved into the base.

"He misses you," her mother remarked. "Your father. He likes having you home."

Evelyn blew on her hands, gazing out over the lawn. She felt her lips curve in a smile, a reluctant one.

"I really think he never got over you going away to school." Her mother sighed. "It was almost like he knew."

Evelyn turned to look at her mother, pushing the hair out of her eyes. "Knew what?"

Her mother took a sip of coffee. "That you were more interested in other people. That our family was never quite intriguing enough for you."

Evelyn sat up straighter in the cold seat, waiting for her to say more, but instead her mother went to the lime tree in a terracotta pot and began pruning. When she'd finished, she rose to her full height and began tossing the dead branches into a pile by the boot-room door.

"I just hope you know what you're doing," she said, her back to Evelyn. "War can make everyone . . ." She didn't seem to know how to finish this. "It can make people reckless. And you're only a young girl. Some would take advantage of you. Especially in London."

Evelyn laughed. "I'm twenty-two years old! I think I know my own mind by now."

"You may know many things, dear, but I'm not sure you've ever known that."

Something malicious had slipped into her mother's voice when she turned around again but also something raw, and as she stood like that, almost challenging her to retaliate, it occurred to Evelyn that she was trying to reveal something, however oblique, about her own experiences.

"Is that what happened to you?" she asked. "When you met Dad?"

Her mother shook her head.

"Then what?"

Evelyn stared at her mother. How alike we are, she thought. She had never considered herself to be an image of her mother, but there it was, plain to see: the long, fine shape of their faces, the dark hair, that proud bottom lip.

"Sometimes I wish you'd never gone away either," her mother muttered, tugging off her gloves. "I had always hoped for something bigger for you, grander, but perhaps it was a mistake."

"Mother, don't be so obtuse."

She shrugged, finality in the gesture. "Never mind."

"Never mind?"

Evelyn threw up her hands. How long were they going to continue like this, talking around one another whenever the conversation strayed somewhere dangerous, like steering clear of a raving stranger on the footpath? When would her mother stop believing that Evelyn would cast her aside—or, worse, forget her?

"I don't understand you, Mum, I really don't. Why won't you say what you're thinking?"

Her mother hesitated. "All right. Since you asked. I don't understand the appeal of this War Office work. It sounds so menial to me."

"I work for the government. I'm trying to play a part, however small, in this war. How is that menial?"

"And why on earth do you want to be doing that? You are an Oxford graduate. You could be doing anything. You could be *married*."

"For goodness' sake."

"And always trying to run away. Was it so awful here? Were your father and I so terrible?"

"Mum . . ."

"Well." Her mother shrugged again. "You wanted to be a teacher the last I knew. That, at least, is a respectable profession, even if your father and I had hoped for something more for you. Isn't that why you studied German? And I needn't remind you what trouble that caused. But now you come home and we discover you're a glorified errand girl. What was it all for, your education, if you only planned to do something like that?"

Evelyn leapt to her feet. Rage had flooded her entire body, though she had no idea what to do with it, except perhaps to break something. Instead, she strode to the edge of the patio, picked up her secateurs, and threw them across the lawn. It felt good to see them fly from her hands; to release, even for a moment, all that pent-up fury. Her mother watched them sail through the air and land near the roses. Then she turned back to Evelyn.

"Now why did you do *that*?"

Her eyes were shining and her mouth twitched. But when Evelyn took a step toward her, she flinched, strands of dark hair whipping against her forehead in the breeze, and the awful understanding that it was possible to frighten her struck Evelyn like a slap. She took a sharp breath, tears smarting at her eyes, but she marched inside the house before her mother could see them.

They didn't speak about what had happened. When her father returned from town, Evelyn was locked away in her room with the comfort of the *Children's Hour* on the wireless while her mother sat crocheting in the sitting room. Evelyn listened to the sounds of him moving around downstairs, his rumbling one-way conversation. He wouldn't notice anything different, she thought bitterly; he had never been aware of the nuances of the house. And her mother, Evelyn realized, was good at keeping secrets.

The evening she was due to return to London, Evelyn found her mother stooped over the sink scrubbing at a pan. At first she wouldn't be drawn away to say goodbye, but when she finally put down the scourer and eyed Evelyn's dark green pullover and brown monk strap shoes, she seemed to struggle with a new emotion, and she crossed the kitchen with arms outstretched.

"You travel safely, dear," she mumbled, damp hands on Evelyn's sleeves. It took Evelyn another moment to realize she was crying.

"Mum?"

Her mother pulled away, covering her face. "Don't mind me. It's only . . . You're so far away."

"But London isn't far. You could visit."

Her mother shook her head. "What would I do with myself in London?"

She dabbed at her eyes with the corner of her apron. It would be unbearable, Evelyn thought guiltily, to share living quarters again, to see in the stark light all that her mother had missed out on after half a lifetime in quiet and inconsequential Lewes. And what if she ran into someone she knew? Someone like Julia . . . Evelyn had worked so hard to build this version of herself that she couldn't have it threatened like that. Still, as she stood there, Evelyn wished she could shake some courage into her mother and into herself to push past these limits of imagination. Each had created a part in the other's life they had no idea how to play. There was so much Evelyn wanted to say, so much she wanted to ask, but a rigid, unyielding wall had sprung up between them, and this felt like grief to Evelyn as her mother turned back to the sink, as if she had lost something that could never be replaced.

⌒

It was a clear night as Evelyn and her father walked to the station. A crescent moon hung low to the west. Evelyn's nose stung from the cold.

"Life is quiet without you in the house," her father said as they made their way down the sharp incline toward the main road. "I keep myself busy, but I think Mum feels it keenly."

Evelyn didn't reply, recalling the pressure of her mother's embrace in the kitchen.

"Maybe you could send just a few more letters? Or telephone, perhaps? Is there a telephone at the flat?"

Evelyn felt herself grow heavy. She longed to be on the train, away from this blithe needling. But she managed to say brightly, "Yes, Dad. And I will call, I promise," and this seemed to mollify him as they turned the corner into Malling Street.

There were only three other passengers waiting on the platform for the London-bound express. Evelyn boarded, and a few minutes later the train began to pull away. She waved to her father as he jogged alongside the carriage, then sank back into the seat, closing her eyes.

SEVEN

AFTER GETTING OFF the train at Piccadilly, Evelyn walked up Shaftesbury Avenue, turning left at the Globe Theatre to head north along Rupert Street. It was darker in Soho, seedier, with derelict houses, empty plots, and stray cats—the difference stark from the wide, well-lit streets that merged at the Circus. But Evelyn preferred this part of town; she liked its illicit mood, its danger. As she strode on in the direction of Berwick Street, the buildings started to improve, with bars and cafes dotted along the footpath, the smell of olive oil, onion, and garlic sizzling in the pan wafting from every second window. Evelyn, however, could also feel the eyes of men loitering in open doorways; she sensed a hunger in them, and she kept her own eyes firmly ahead as she approached the pub on the corner.

Once she had arrived back at the flat and hung her coat on the hallstand, she slipped quietly into her room. It was the smaller of the two bedrooms overlooking the street. It might have belonged to a maid once; there was only enough space for her creaky bed and a wardrobe made of pine. On the mantelpiece, Evelyn had put some red cyclamens in a Chinese vase to jolly up the place. But no matter what she did, the room reminded her of her childhood doll's house, everything in miniature. It's hardly the room of a grown woman, she thought as she kicked off her shoes.

She walked down the narrow hall. The rest of the Broadwick Street flat was just as poky. There was a kitchen and a sitting room with a couple of sofas and an old leather armchair, and a tatty rug in front of the fireplace. In here, the walls were covered in framed pictures of forts and castles and some Yorkshire landscapes, a few pastoral prints, and one or two portraits from last century. They were in the flat when Fay first moved in and she didn't want to get rid of them ("I'm superstitious like that," she explained), but these remnants of past lives made Evelyn uneasy, as if the previous occupants still lived behind the glass.

"Hullo?" she called.

Fay glided out from her bedroom into the sitting room. She was dressed in a silk kimono and her hair was set in rollers. Music from the gramophone drifted about the room; something American, by the sounds of it.

"All right, Evie? You look done in."

Evelyn slumped into the armchair and watched Fay pour some brandy and a splash of water into a glass.

"Where are you off to tonight?" she asked.

"Tony's taking me to the pictures. *The Spy in Black* is showing at the Troc. I'm rather keen on it."

"Oh yes?"

"Mm. You see, I plan for a cuddle in the back row, maybe a smooch. And then . . . Well, we'll see, won't we?" Fay giggled, sashaying back to her room to get dressed.

Tony was a tall, droopy fellow who never quite looked Evelyn in the eye. He worked as a car salesman in Clapham. He thought of himself as rather fashionable with his pencil mustache and black hair smoothed back with Murray's. Evelyn had only met him twice, but each time he'd shaken her hand with curious deference, as though she were Fay's father and he sought her approval.

"And what about you?" Fay called a few minutes later as Evelyn made her way back toward her room. "How are you spending the evening?"

Normally Evelyn enjoyed a night on her own, but she felt despondent as she reached her door. In some ways, living with Fay reminded her of the life she was missing out on, and with Fay following her down the hallway they soon found themselves standing together at the cramped entrance to the flat. Fay peered into the mirror hanging beside the hallstand, adjusting her headscarf. She eyed Evelyn in the glass.

"Pretty girl like you shouldn't spend her nights cooped up," she murmured. "You should have a chap." She checked her purse, coy all of a sudden. "Tony has loads of pals. I could . . . Well, we could see you right with one of them."

Evelyn tried not to flinch at the suggestion. "I don't know . . ." Her voice was airless. Why couldn't Fay just leave her be?

Fay opened the front door and tottered on her heels toward the top of the stairs before turning to raise her hand like the Queen at a parade.

"You think on it, Evelyn," she instructed. "It might be fun."

⌒

After a bowl of onion soup and a few crusts of yesterday's bread, Evelyn went downstairs for a bath. She sat naked on the cold edge of the tub, listening to the sounds of footsteps clomping along the street and the shouts from the restaurateur at Ley On's, before easing herself into the water.

As she lathered up her arms with a leftover sliver of Lux, Evelyn thought about what Fay had said about having a chap. She supposed it was something she ought to consider. She looked down at her long legs growing dark hairs again, her concave stomach, her small, high-set breasts, and added some more hot to the milky bath. The pipes groaned, shuddering in protest, as water eventually spluttered from the tap. She lay back, resting her head against the cool enamel, and as she did her fingers strayed over the top of her legs, down the groove of her hip bone, and across her soft pubic hair. She let her hand rest there. She wondered what had become of Philip. He had been interested in teaching too, hadn't he? She could see him in that profession, at an austere grammar school, with horn-rimmed glasses and a pipe, always believing himself cleverer than his colleagues. For a moment, she pictured meeting him on the street, his surprise at finding her dressed so smartly and striding along the pavement with such purpose. Imagine if he knew what she did now!

Evelyn edged her fingers down to the soft, warm part of her. She hesitated, her pulse quickening, and continued stroking herself. At first nothing happened, and she thought about stopping, but she didn't, and soon she felt something rise in her. She closed her eyes, aware of her breath shortening and the small, steady waves moving around the bath. Soon she felt like she was on top of a wave herself. Philip popped into her mind again and the press of him against her leg. What would it have felt like inside her? Her arm slowed, faltering.

"*God.*"

She slapped her hand against the hard surface of the bath. What was the matter with her? The light hanging above her flickered, a moth hovering at the bulb. By now the water was tepid and, shivering, Evelyn reached for her towel.

⌒

She had already turned out her bedroom lamp when a loud banging sounded through the flat. Supposing it was only Fay (she was always forgetting her key), Evelyn dragged herself out of bed and slipped on the velvet dressing-gown hanging from the back of her chair. But when she pulled open the front door she found Sally and Julia crowding the mat.

"What on earth are you two doing here?" she cried as they swept in, bringing the cold air with them.

"We're taking you out. The Four Hundred Club. It's all arranged, no excuses!" Julia held up a finger to silence Evelyn. "I don't care if you've got Herr Hitler himself in the War Office basement. Tonight, you're coming with us."

"And we've brought wine," Sally said, thrusting out a bottle. It was already half empty.

They wandered through to the sitting room. Evelyn wished she had known they were coming. She would have done the dishes, or at least made sure Fay's bedroom door was closed to conceal those rumpled sheets and stains on the duvet. She would have dressed! But they didn't seem to notice, the sitting room already clogged with Sally's cigarette smoke as she threw herself across a sofa, while Julia paced up and down on the rug in front of the fireplace. At first Evelyn thought she was trying to warm up—it was a bitter night, after all, with snow predicted—but then she recognized the restlessness in that gait, like a cat in a cage.

She went to the kitchen to pour them each a glass of wine. It was awful, and her stomach prickled at the vinegary aftertaste, but, rallying, she had another mouthful, then another, and her palate started to relent.

"Nice place," said Julia, smiling faintly. "Very cozy."

"Yes, very cozy, Ev," Sally agreed. "They found you these digs, didn't they? The War Office?"

Since the wine would soon be gone, Evelyn brought out Fay's bottle of brandy and took it over to one of the sofas.

"I like it here," she said. "It's cheap as chips and Fay's a terrific girl. It works out well for me." She sat on the edge of the cushion, pulling her dressing-gown tighter around her shoulders. "Besides, I'm really only here to sleep."

"Mm." Julia peered at the lithograph hanging above the mantelpiece. Somewhere in the dregs of Evelyn's memory she recalled the title: *The Wreck of the Atlantic.* "They're working you hard, then, at Whitehall?" She turned around, her eyes bleary in the dim light from the lamp, and Evelyn wondered where the pair had been before arriving at the flat.

"Quite hard, yes," she said.

"How strange to think of you in that drab building," Sally said, flicking through a tattered copy of a French *Marie Claire* that Fay had bought from the pawnshop on Berwick Street. "But I have missed you. Soho is just too far away!"

"It's hardly far." Evelyn had a sip of the brandy and made a face—it was sweet, nasty stuff—but she was already feeling quite tipsy. "Half an hour at a brisk pace."

"Well, it's far when you have a pal in the next room." Sally patted Julia's dark head as her cousin sat down on the rug. "Julia is staying on at Curzon Street for a while. Did I tell you?"

"It's only temporary, Sallywag, remember."

"Yes, I suppose it is—until you elope again!"

Julia blew out some smoke and smiled across the rug at Evelyn.

"She's found herself another man," Sally elaborated. "But at least this one's English."

"Oh yes?" An image of Jonty's lean face flashed in Evelyn's mind. "Now that does sound promising."

"Go on," Sally said, nudging her cousin with the tip of her high heel. "Spill the beans to Evelyn."

"There's nothing to spill." Julia put out her cigarette in an empty glass. "He's a friend, that's all."

"Will he be at this club tonight?" Evelyn asked.

"No, he's out of town for a few weeks. Up north."

"He's some army man," Sally said quietly. "Tall, apparently, and very handsome."

"If you say so." Julia rested back on her elbows, stretching out her long legs. "And it's navy, not army, but let's not quibble."

⌒

Somehow they made it to Leicester Square and found Rupert Street. There was a long line at the top of the staircase at number twenty-eight, but Julia walked them straight to the front. She knew one of the men on the door, and when they made their way into the basement they discovered their table was right by the band, with Jonty and Michael Talbert sitting on either side, each dressed in neat blue suits and drinking Taittinger from shallow coupes.

"Is this your doing, Sal?" Evelyn hissed.

"What?"

"Talbert!"

"Oh, don't mind him." Julia took Evelyn's hand, steering her toward the table. "Jonty needed a chum. I'll keep an eye out for you." She gave her a wink. "Besides, Michael's paying. Might as well make a night of it."

"You remember Talbert, don't you, Evelyn?" Jonty said. "He arranged this handy spot for us by the music."

"Evelyn," Talbert slurred. "Jolly good to see you again. You're the German, aren't you?"

"I'm sorry?"

"That Boche girl, from the party at Wesley Manor. Lovely arse."

"Michael, do behave." Julia guided Evelyn to a seat farthest from Talbert. "And do keep your voice down. Evelyn is not German. Do you want to have us all arrested?"

"Beg pardon, beg pardon," Talbert muttered, his head swaying out of rhythm to the music. "See, we're celebrating tonight, Evelyn. I'm being shipped out next week to HMS *Ramillies*. It's escort duties in the North Atlantic for me."

They finished the champagne and Talbert went to order another bottle, but as he returned from the bar a group of smartly dressed men and women approached their table, old friends of Julia it seemed, and she was soon drawn away, though promising it wouldn't be for long. There was dancing next, followed by more drinking. Talbert was a surprisingly handy dance partner, but after the third bottle Evelyn began to fade. With Talbert's arm firmly around her lower back, she must have put her head on his shoulder and closed her eyes, because when she opened them again she wasn't on the dance floor with Sally and Jonty or even back at their table, but pressed against a wall in the dingy corridor near the cloakroom, the music thrumming through a set of velvet curtains, Talbert's hand inside her underwear. He was fumbling about, his fingers working in a furious stabbing motion, while his other hand grasped Evelyn by the throat, his big thumb tracing her bottom lip.

"Michael, what on *earth*?" She tried to push him away, but he was too heavy.

"Don't you like it? Doesn't it feel right?" He mashed his face against hers, all stubble and sour breath. "Come on. I might be fish food in a few weeks. Don't know when I'll get another chance to—"

Evelyn pushed him away again. "Will you stop it!"

"What's the matter?" He stepped back now, blinking at her, his mouth hanging open. "*Evelyn?*"

She stumbled back to the dance floor, elbowing through the

remaining couples, desperately searching for their table and her handbag. Scrabbling around behind the stools, she found it tucked beneath one of the curtains, and as she went to stand up she heard a laugh and saw Julia dancing just a few meters away. Evelyn crouched down farther, raising her handbag to her face like a mask. She watched Julia moving to a quick foxtrot. Her partner was a short, dark-haired man in a tuxedo, a small, waxy mustache imprinted in a line above his lip. He looked Mediterranean, Spanish perhaps, and when he released Julia's hand in a flourish, making her pirouette, she cried, "*Andreas!*"

Evelyn got to her feet and rushed past, her legs moving of their own accord, then she was upstairs and bursting into the fresh night air—only it wasn't night but the washed-out gray of dawn. She had a moment to register her relief at being outside before she scuttled toward Shaftesbury Avenue and vomited in the gutter.

She crouched like that for several minutes, retching and spitting, until she felt steady enough to stand. Her head was throbbing. If Julia came out now, Evelyn believed she actually might die of shame. But she didn't, though Evelyn spotted Michael Talbert across the street, gripping a lamppost and straining forward like a dog on a leash.

"I take it you don't fancy another jive?" he called.

Then came the sound of heels on the pavement; Julia had appeared at the top of the stairs in an enormous mink coat.

She gave Talbert a filthy look. "Do bugger off now, Michael," she snapped. "There's a good boy."

She strode over to Evelyn and pulled her into a fierce hug. She smelled of stale smoke and perfume, and something else sweet, like grapes.

"I'm sorry," Julia whispered.

She took off her coat and wrapped it around Evelyn's trembling bare shoulders. Then she reached for her hand and they began walking. Evelyn thought Talbert might come after them, but when she glanced behind her she could see he'd already disappeared back inside the club.

"Are you all right?"

Julia was watching her, concern in her amber eyes. There was a faint smear of kohl on her cheek.

"I'm fine." Evelyn swallowed. Her head was still pounding. "You're not cold without your coat?"

"No. I love it. Makes me feel alive."

"What about Sally?"

"She's gone home with Jonty."

"And your other friends? Won't they miss you?"

But Julia only gave Evelyn's hand a squeeze.

"Listen, I know a place where we can get a decent cup of tea," she said. "It's just down here. They should be open now. Shall we?"

"All right." Evelyn felt her voice shake. "Thank you."

Julia gave a brisk nod and on they went.

At the corner, waiting for a taxi to pass, Evelyn raised her face to the sky. As she did, she closed her eyes, and felt the tender scratch of snow on her lips, her cheeks, her eyelids. The snow would fall thick over London that morning.

EIGHT

THE WORK AT the Scrubs continued through the last scraps of autumn. There were more reports and more memos, though Chadwick soon began Evelyn on new tasks. Once a week, she prepared documents for his meetings with the interior minister and the undersecretary, who later made inspections of the wing, and after they'd gone Chadwick would appear in the doorway, a relieved smile tugging at the corner of his mouth as if he were a schoolboy and had just escaped a caning.

"Looks to be a nice day out there," he might say, standing on tiptoe for a glimpse of life through their smudged cell window. Evelyn never knew quite how to reply. When it wasn't raining, she would spend her lunch breaks rugged up on the bench beneath the birch tree. Sometimes Vincent would join her and they would share one of his little cigars, and afterward he would bring out the newspaper and they would take turns reading the headlines in absurd German accents.

Vincent was her only real friend at the Scrubs, and she found herself thinking about him while she made a cup of tea upstairs or touched up her lipstick in the loo by the common room. He wasn't like Jonty or Michael Talbert, or even much like Philip. He was handsome in a Byronic sort of way, but she found she liked looking at him and talking to him for the sake of it, not because she felt any attraction to him. She couldn't imagine ever kissing him. She got the sense he didn't want to kiss her either.

Some evenings they met for a boozy supper at Quo Vadis around the corner from her flat. Vincent knew the owner of the restaurant, Mr. Leoni, who after tiramisu often brought them over a bottle of grappa that they usually finished there at the table, the ashtray overflowing with Evelyn's cigarettes. She liked getting drunk with Vincent; it meant they could talk uninterrupted for hours. And he was always interested in the reports she made, the files she read, and what she thought about the work they did at the Scrubs. Apart from Sally, she'd never had a friend who cared quite so much about what she had to say.

"You know, Chaddy thinks you're the best decrypter in the Service," she told him late one of these nights as the old waiter began sweeping the tiled floor. They had been the only patrons for the past hour, but no one seemed in a rush for them to leave. Evelyn dreaded the arrival of the bill, but Vincent paid every time—somehow he was never without a wad of pound notes clipped together in his pocket. "So go on, tell me: how did you get so good at those codes?"

"Well, it's all a game, isn't it?" Vincent said as he struck a match, his face suddenly ghoulish in the tawny light. "They're just cryptic crosswords, really, and I've always been good at them."

"You should join the Eccentric Club." Evelyn grinned. The table didn't feel quite steady beneath her elbow; she really shouldn't have drunk all that Poli. "It's only a few blocks from here."

"Hm," said Vincent, tapping at some ash. "Not sure how amenable they are to my sort, no matter how much decryption I'm doing for King and country."

"Why shouldn't they be? You're an Englishman."

Vincent set his cigar down on the lip of the ashtray. "Because I'm Jewish, darling. Or didn't you know?"

Evelyn felt her smile waver. "Actually, I don't think I did."

Vincent held her eye, then shrugged. "Only I thought you must have heard." He filled their glasses with the last of the grappa. "The occasional jibe, the odd snipe?"

"No . . ." Evelyn remembered those looks across the caf from time to time, usually from one of their older, sterner colleagues. She had assumed they disapproved of Vincent's youthful extroversion or his flamboyant lavender cravat, but could it have been something darker, meaner? Surely not. She had heard worse at school, anyway, she recalled dimly, and at university—such as from that awful gray-haired librarian when Evelyn borrowed a folio of *The Merchant of Venice* ("Have you read this?" the woman had asked, nudging a copy of *The Kingdom of Shylock* across the desk. "Very illuminating about the Yids . . ."). Evelyn pushed away her glass. With no Jewish friends of her own, she'd never had reason to pause and consider what these attitudes might mean, and she was now ashamed to realize that it had been language so ubiquitous it had hardly made an impression on her.

"Are you very observant?" she asked.

"Not especially. Though my aunt and uncle are quite devout, and when they come up from Cambridge it can be awkward. They're always going on about the Sabbath and nagging me to attend the synagogue off Bevis Marks." Vincent tipped some grappa into his mouth and stared at the empty glass. His eyes were very red. "I just can't make them understand how believing seems so pointless. What kind of God allows all this horror in the world?"

Evelyn felt a low drone start up at the back of her head. Despite all the drinking, she was now astonishingly alert. She sat forward, moving around in her mouth the words that she dreaded having to ask.

"And your parents—what do they think?"

Vincent was gazing at the tablecloth, stained from the excesses of their meal, and turning over the teaspoon that had accompanied their coffee hours ago—grateful, it seemed, for something else to fix his attention on.

"They don't think anything," he said quietly. "Last year they were killed in Berlin. It happened during the pogrom of Kristallnacht. The Sturmabteilung came into their apartment and bludgeoned them to death." He let out a shaky breath, almost like a laugh. "They used sledgehammers, I'm told. Mama and Papa were in bed. They probably didn't know what was happening, which I suppose I should be thankful for. Nearly a hundred Jews were murdered that night, and barely a month after the Munich Agreement." Vincent peered at Evelyn from beneath his dark fringe, smiling grimly. "And still people think Hitler can be trusted on appeasement."

Evelyn stared back at him, her heart pummeling at her breast. Until that moment the war had felt abstract, mere spy craft of no real consequence played out at the Scrubs between well-mannered men and women. But now she finally absorbed the blunt reality that this was no game. That people were dying. Perhaps this had been Chadwick's test for her—to see if she could adapt to this understanding without fear or equivocation. To see if she could live up to her responsibility.

"Vincent, I'm so sorry," she said. "I had no idea about your parents. This is just awful."

Vincent sniffed and sat back, and when he pressed his lips together Evelyn saw something defiant in his expression. She felt a throb of tenderness for him. What courage it must take to sit down each day and work on that decryption, to unpick those messages typed up in the language of his childhood, all the while knowing what those people—his people—had done to his own parents. She felt sick at her own ignorance.

"That's why our work is so important," Vincent said. "We can't let this happen to another family." He reached into his jacket pocket for a moment before bringing out a small black-and-white photograph. "It's the only picture I have of her. My mother. She was only forty-three. They ransacked the apartment and all my family's albums were destroyed. But somehow this survived."

Evelyn stared at the dark, haunted eyes gazing out from a porcelain face framed by a black bob. But there was something steadfast about his mother's expression that compelled Evelyn to consider just what she could see beyond the photograph.

"What was her name?" she asked.

"Anna."

Evelyn swallowed. Her throat was dry. "She looks like a very good sort, Vincent."

"Yes, she was." He gazed at the portrait, then tucked it away again, keeping his hand pressed against the pocket as if to protect it. "She understood me. How many people can you say that about?"

Evelyn watched Vincent run a hand through his hair. Then he twisted in his seat and called for the bill, his somber mood vanished. As he chatted with the waiter, she admired the neat line of his suit, the gentle slope of his proud shoulders. She wanted to say, "I understand you," but she knew it would be a lie.

⌒

The next morning, Evelyn arrived at the Scrubs to find a neat pile of pale blue papers on her desk with the words MOST SECRET stamped in red at the top. It was the transcript of an interview between an officer and a woman referred to as 'Dunlin'. The woman, a postmistress, had been passing on communiqués to a German national in Manchester.

Evelyn read the interview. It was short, about five pages. Dunlin began with clumsy bravado ("I've got rights" and "It's still a free country"), but by the end she had been reduced to tears, begging for forgiveness. Evelyn flicked back through the transcript and gleaned a few key details: the woman lived alone, had never married or had children, and had met the man through a lonely hearts agency.

"Did you interview her, sir?" Evelyn asked when Chadwick appeared in the doorway later that day. "This Dunlin?"

"Yes, at Latchmere House."

"The estate on Ham Common?"

"That's right. We've set up an interrogation center there."

"What happened to the lover?"

Chadwick rubbed at the pouches beneath his eyes. "He went to ground, funnily enough, as soon as he got a sniff of trouble."

Evelyn stared at the transcript. "Are they all like this, these assets? Women exploited?"

"Generally."

"And what will happen to her? Is she looking at prison?"

Chadwick shrugged. "That's not for us to decide, but I imagine the judge will sentence her to two years, at least."

Evelyn shook her head. "She's hardly a threat to the nation . . . She's just a lonely old woman."

"Hm." Chadwick was rummaging around for his cigarettes in the drawer. "If that were the case, perhaps she should have joined her local Women's Institute instead."

Evelyn returned to her desk and began another report, but her mind kept straying back to Dunlin from Aberdeen. It was all such low-grade stuff. The case hadn't hinged on much—a few letters from Berlin, some questionable information about a freighter at the docks. Surely it would have been better to cultivate this woman and her connections to lure her lover out again? It seemed like a wasted opportunity, and glancing toward Chadwick, Evelyn realized with perfect clarity that she wanted to get inside that interrogation room.

A couple of days later she approached Chadwick with another transcription, this time involving a German national arrested in her bakery in Hackney. Coded messages rolled up inside a film canister had been found baked into blueberry muffins. The detained woman had wanted to speak in German to her interrogator, but they had denied her an interpreter at Latchmere House, meaning the transcription was a mess of broken English and a few phrases of muddled German.

"There are quite a few mistakes in this document," Evelyn said, handing Chadwick the typed-up pages. "*Versandbehälter* is actually a shipping container, not a parcel, which I suppose has a bearing on the intelligence?"

"Hm." Chadwick, with a grunt, snatched the paper away.

"And would it not, I don't know . . ." Evelyn searched for a delicate way to phrase it. "Would it not be beneficial to interview some of these foreign nationals in their own language? This woman's English is very poor. More information could have been sought in German."

Chadwick blew his red-looking nose. "Yes, I suppose it could have. Chap that did it only had a smattering, I believe."

Evelyn stood a little straighter. "Sir, I think I could be useful in cases like this. I've still not put my German to use, and I've more than a smattering of it." She swallowed. "And it might be helpful to have a woman speaking to these suspects—whether they're men or women. Offering, perhaps, a gentler touch?"

Chadwick folded his arms. "Aren't we keeping you busy enough?"

"I'd like to do more."

"All right." He gave her a slight smile. "I'll bear that in mind."

When she got home that night, Evelyn telephoned Sally at Curzon Street. She longed to speak to her friend, to learn news of the world outside the echo chamber of Wormwood Scrubs. But Sally was out; she had been out all week, in fact, going to dress fittings and speaking to caterers. There was a letter from Julia, however, waiting on the hall table, inviting her to tea next week at the Dorchester—*I'll keep an eye out for you in your War Office regalia, I'm sure you look strapping in fatigues*—and Evelyn took it up to her room and propped it on the mantelpiece.

The following week, Evelyn traveled with Chadwick to Latchmere House to interview a young man named Jacob Vermeer. Four Dutch parachutists had been picked up off the east coast of Ireland and brought to London—well, three now, as the fourth had swallowed cyanide on the flight back across the Irish Sea. Two of the Dutchmen had already given up intel about their mission, but Vermeer had so far held out. Believing this was because he had information about the next man-drop, Chadwick suggested Evelyn take part in the interrogation. "He won't speak to us in English or even Dutch," he'd explained on the drive from White City. "So let's see what he'll tell you in German."

The director of the interrogation center met them on the gravel driveway in front of the house, a brown folder held tight to his chest. A short, wiry fellow in service dress, Captain Toby led them around to the east wing, where they traveled along a chilly corridor that smelled of antiseptic and then climbed a flight of metal stairs. At the top stood an armed guard who gave a salute and stepped away from a heavy door.

"He's in here," Toby said.

Evelyn came forward and put an eye to the cell peephole. The room was gloomy, with only a glint of light from the high-set windows, but it was enough for her to make out the shape of a couple of chairs and a table, and the man—young, by the look of it—hunched over the end of it. He was dressed in brown overalls and his face, which he raised suddenly as if sensing Evelyn on the other side of the door, was swollen and bruised.

"He looks the worse for wear," she remarked.

"I'd say so." Toby handed Evelyn the folder and jammed his hands in his pockets. "You'll see in there how he had the gumption to tell us he'd soon be in charge of everyone in London."

Evelyn turned back to the peephole. The boy inside had stood up and begun pacing about the cell.

"Why did they send him over?"

"Same reason the Germans always do," Chadwick said. "They want intelligence about land movement. Distribution of troops, armaments, planes, ships in the ports, civilian morale—as if they'd find all that out, for goodness' sake."

"These boys could have landed in a bucket of nipples and still come up sucking their thumbs," Toby barked. "The Fallschirmjäger drop them out of their planes with absolutely no training. Most of them have been picked up around Berlin or Amsterdam by the Nazi talent spotters and then blackmailed, which of course makes it easier for us to turn them."

"And is that our plan?" Evelyn asked, glancing to Chadwick for confirmation. "To make him one of ours?"

He smiled back at her dourly. "Ordinarily, yes. His friends have already been spectacularly forthcoming."

"Forthcoming?" Toby laughed. "We only had to dangle a noose at them and they squealed quicker than I could say *pannenkoeken*. We know who sent them, their mission, their cover stories, their MOs. There's never much originality to it—this lot were told to pass as Norwegian sailors shipwrecked near Bangor. They've got false papers, Norwegian kroner, but they can't speak a word of the lingo. They'd have been found out in hours. All except for this one." He tapped against the latch. "This one isn't for turning."

Toby put a key hanging around his neck in the lock and pushed open the cell door, motioning for Evelyn and Chadwick to follow him inside. He pointed to the wooden chairs at the table where he wanted them to sit.

The Dutch boy was frozen in the corner, half-crouched like a cornered animal, shivering violently. His auburn hair was matted with black blood, and his right arm, Evelyn now saw, hung limp, the shoulder bulging at an odd angle.

"Good morning, Jacob," Toby said loudly. "Are we in the mood to talk today?"

Vermeer shuddered and stared at the floor. His lips were blue.

Toby sauntered over to the table and sat down on the edge of it, his legs dangling wide, facing the prisoner. "Now, Jacob, let me remind you of a few facts. Your friends have already told us a great deal about your mission. We know which German colonel put you on that plane, and we know you were ordered to spy on the Belfast ports. We even know how much they promised to pay you—about a thousand Reichsmark, wasn't it?" He sat back, folding his arms, and made a *tut-tut* sound. "That's not much money for a life, now, is it?"

The boy looked up with bloodshot eyes and spat on the floor.

"Fuck you," he said in English. "You and your whore."

Toby twisted around, his jagged eyebrows raised.

"Did you hear that, Miss Varley?" He tipped his head back and shouted, "Did you hear that, sparrows?" He chuckled, bringing his face down level with Vermeer's. "We're recording everything you say, Jacob. They'll read it all back to you at the Old Bailey." He stood up and clapped his hands together. "Rightio, I'll leave you to it. I'm just outside if you need anything. But remember"—he peered down at Evelyn, and she could see each of his nose hairs, as coarse as twine— "this cretin was planted for the invasion. Don't forget that when he bats his lashes at you." With a laugh, he slapped Chadwick on the back. "I say this as much for Chaddy as you, Miss Varley. Everyone knows John's soft. Come along, then?"

Chadwick looked at Evelyn, and after she had given him a brisk nod he stood up and followed Toby out of the cell door, which they slammed shut. Evelyn turned back to Vermeer, who was now staring at her with curiosity. His shivering had stopped. The air in the cell went still.

"Right," Evelyn said. "Right."

Her pulse fluttered. She could feel her color rising. Suddenly the idea of interrogating a suspect seemed mad. She wanted to laugh. What on earth was she going to say to this boy? How could she ever make him talk?

"Ah . . . *sprichst du Deutsch?*" she stammered.

The boy sniffed, hoicked. A gob of brown phlegm landed on the floor.

"*Was ist, wenn ich es tue?*" he said.

"I thought you might prefer to speak in German." Evelyn nodded to the wall where she imagined the tiny microphone had been implanted between the bricks. "They won't understand, anyway."

Vermeer ran a hand across his swollen nose. "*Dummköpfe,*" he sneered.

"Yes." Evelyn felt herself smile. "They are fools."

She brought out her cigarettes and the boy's gaze flickered across the silver case. She offered him one and he snatched it up greedily and waited for a light. Then he sat back, watching her as he smoked. The dossier said he was twenty-five, but he looked younger than that—barely out of his teens. On his chin were a few wisps of a soft beard, and where they weren't cut and split and bruised his cheeks bore a rash of pimples. His eyes were pale, washed out, and his lashes were as long as a girl's. But his hand was steady as he brought the cigarette to his plump lips. Perhaps Toby was right. Perhaps he wasn't for turning.

"You are alone here, Jacob," Evelyn said quietly. "Your friends have turned on you."

Vermeer shrugged, sucking on his cigarette.

"And we have enough intelligence to secure a conviction in our courts. The judge won't show leniency." She paused. "Do you want to be hanged?"

Vermeer flashed his teeth. "*Was macht es aus?*"

"It matters a great deal. Your life has value, meaning."

The boy swallowed, his Adam's apple juddering. "What do you know about my life?"

"Why don't you tell me?"

"Isn't that enough?" He nodded at the dossier. "What else is important? Do you want to know when I first pissed the bed? The first girl I fucked? Hm?"

"No," said Evelyn. "I'd like to know why you traveled to Ireland."

Vermeer scoffed. "So you can trick me?"

"So I can understand you."

Evelyn edged forward, her hands planted on the table. He glanced at her fingers, at her red nail polish, and she saw his eyes widen a fraction. She knew she had to walk a careful line to make him trust her, to affect him as she knew she could. She had heard that men on the gallows often cried not for their wives or lovers but for their mothers. Soft femininity was required. Powder, not rouge.

"I know what it feels like to be angry, Jacob," she said quietly. "What it feels like to want to belong."

He raised his eyes to hers, looked away.

"You're English," he said. "You always belong."

"I don't know if that's true. I've often felt lost."

"I'm not lost." Firmer now, his shoulder turned toward the wall.

Evelyn sat back, picked up her cigarettes, lit one, and as she sat there smoking they both watched the purple trails of smoke drift toward the ceiling.

"But you're away from your family, your friends, Jacob. You're a prisoner in another country far from home." She smiled, hoping her eyes were kind, because she did feel a rush of pity for him. "Doesn't that make you just a bit lost?"

Vermeer stared at the floor. Beneath the baggy overalls, she could tell he was slight, fine-boned, and there was something oddly graceful about the way he leaned back and crossed one leg over the other. Not one of nature's typical fighters then, Evelyn reflected. Not for the boxing ring. A brass-knuckle fight, perhaps, in the back lanes of the East End, the price of an underworld wager gone wrong.

"I never wanted to come here," he muttered. "I never wanted to get involved in any of this shit. But I had to, didn't I? I had to do what he asked me."

Evelyn threaded her fingers together. She waited, listening to the sounds of Vermeer's sodden breath through his mangled nose.

"My father . . . he owed money. He made some bad debts with some bad people. But the Gestapo, they promised to help. *He* promised to help our family . . ." Vermeer looked up, rage and despair flashing in his eyes.

"If you helped him in return?"

"Yes."

She watched him suck on the cigarette like he was drawing air from it, and thought about her parents. Would she jump out of a plane for them? Captain Toby had sneered about these recruits, but Evelyn couldn't help admiring their courage. To be faced with such a choice.

"This man," she said carefully. "He was your handler?"

Vermeer nodded.

"And now he has betrayed you?"

Another flicker passed across his face. The boy swallowed, his lips a tight line. He looked for a moment as if he might cry.

"What is his name, Jacob?"

He shook his head.

"He's not here to help, Jacob. He's abandoned you, just like your compatriots. You owe him no loyalty."

As Vermeer ground out the cigarette, Evelyn saw the slump in his shoulders.

"Where did he recruit you?" she asked quickly.

"I can't tell you."

He was retreating from her now, a carat of ice loose from the drift. She sat forward again.

"You know, Jacob, it is possible for us to change our way of thinking. To admit to our mistakes. We can find forgiveness if we're open to understanding this about ourselves, if we're willing . . ."

He snorted. "What are you, my priest?"

"No, but I am trying to help you. To make you see there is another way."

He narrowed his eyes at her and she could see the fresh calculation going on behind them—an animal instinct.

"Where's the next drop, Jacob?"

"And if I tell you, what then? You might catch those men and bring them here, but there will be more after that. Hundreds of us, thousands."

The boy raised his good arm and looped it around the back of his battered head. He was gloating. Evelyn smiled tightly, but she could feel the first flutter of panic in her breast.

"You can still save yourself, Jacob. The people who put you here don't care if you live or die."

"And you do?"

Evelyn blinked back at him. The truth was she had no answer for that—not one she could speak, anyway.

"Give me a cigarette," he said.

She passed over the case. He took one and put it behind his ear, then took another and waited for Evelyn to hold up the lighter. He inhaled deeply then sat back, his face concealed behind the smoke.

"I will be safe," he said, "if I tell you?"

"You have my word."

He scoffed. "Your word." He pointed to his shoulder. "You English have always believed you have more honor than the rest of us. More decency. A gentleman's handshake and all that bullshit. But your gentleman wouldn't piss on most of his fellow Englishmen if they were on fire. You're as depraved as the rest of us."

He stared at her for another moment, his eyes flickering toward the door. He ran his tongue over his teeth and tapped some ash into the tray.

"The drop is tonight," he muttered. "Firth of Forth. More Dutchmen, I don't know how many. They are watching the docks."

Evelyn breathed out, counting her heartbeats. *Three, four, five.* She had done it. Somehow she had made him talk, and now she had information that would make a real difference to Captain Toby's operation. She watched Vermeer smoke for another minute, then she went and banged on the door, and after she had stood in the doorway and told Toby and Chadwick what she had discovered, Toby pushed his way back inside the cell.

"Scotland, eh?" He glared at Vermeer, hands planted on his slight hips. "Now that wasn't so hard, was it?"

Vermeer only shrugged, silent once more.

"Right." Toby clapped his hands. "I had better get back to the main house and telephone through to the Admiralty. And while I'm doing that, the sergeant outside will help you get scrubbed up for the Old Bailey, Jacob. Can't have you looking like this when you come before the judge." He glanced over to Evelyn, gave her a wink. "What do you think, Miss Varley, fancy a wager?"

"I'm sorry, Captain?"

"A wager. On the black cap for this one? Odds on, wouldn't you say?"

Vermeer looked at Evelyn. He must have comprehended something in Toby's tone because for the first time he looked afraid.

"Well, I don't know . . ."

Evelyn tried to smile, clinging to the thread of hope that this was a joke, until she saw Chadwick's eyes fall to the floor.

"He gave us the intelligence," she stammered. "He told us about the next drop. I'm sure the judge—"

"I'd still put money on the noose," said Toby cheerfully.

"What did he say?" Vermeer was now looking wildly from Toby to Evelyn. "What did that bastard say?"

When he tried to stand up, Toby pressed down hard on his injured shoulder, making the boy cry out.

"You stay there until I say you can move," he snarled. "The rope's too good for garbage like you."

"Jasper," said Chadwick, taking a step toward him. "Perhaps we should—"

But he didn't finish. From the doorway, Evelyn saw a hard glint enter Vermeer's eyes and she shrank back, struck by a pulse of hatred so swift and powerful it was almost visible across the width of the cell.

Suddenly Vermeer bucked in the seat, the brute force of it knocking Toby aside, and he sprang to his feet, raising his good arm in a salute.

"Zum Glück sprichst du Deutsch, Schlampe!"

In a flash Chadwick had crossed the cell and pinned Vermeer against the wall. The boy thrashed against him, shouting and swearing, his teeth stained pink. Toby hollered to the guard outside, and when the young man rushed in, his pistol was out of the halter and he began beating Vermeer with it.

"I told you," Toby cried, as though Evelyn were to blame for this. "There's no point in softly-softly with this sort. No *point!*"

The sergeant was still belting Vermeer, who had by now slumped against the wall, one arm raised to protect his face, his body shuddering with each clock of the pistol butt. Evelyn was aware of Chadwick at her side, his hand on her shoulder, giving her a shake. There were tears in her eyes.

"Evelyn?" he was shouting. "What did he say?"

"What?"

"The boy—just now. What did he say?"

She could feel the fruitcake she'd eaten earlier that morning rising up the back of her throat. Glacé cherries, walnuts, brandy. Evelyn stared at Chadwick, at those deep lines etched into his face. She had believed she had come here to make a difference to the way these interrogations ran; to do a better, fairer job of them. But now she understood that any small victory would always be at the expense of others. That her success today had been paid for with this boy's misery—and his blood. This was the terrible, inescapable equation of the work she did, and looking away from Chadwick, Evelyn squeezed her eyes shut.

"He said, 'Lucky you speak German, bitch.'"

NINE

AS SHE STOOD at the pristine basin in the Dorchester restrooms and stared at her waxy reflection, Evelyn hoped Julia wouldn't sense death hanging about her like a bad smell. She had thought about canceling their afternoon tea, but she knew that was a dangerous route: it would only encourage her to bury herself deeper and deeper in her work. Conscious of her red eyes, Evelyn splashed her face with cold water and ran a coat of fresh lipstick over her lips, patting some powder on her cheeks to finish. Afterward, her eyes were a little brighter, and she thought about what Chadwick had said on the drive back from Latchmere House: that you could put an awful memory in a box and throw away the key. She wasn't sure she believed him about that, but she would give it a try.

Julia was already sitting on a high-backed divan at the far end of the oval bar when Evelyn walked in from the lobby. She watched Evelyn peel off her gloves and sit down, then pushed a glass toward her. "You look quite done in," she said. "Have you had an awful day?"

The patterned wallpaper behind Julia's head seemed to shift as Evelyn swallowed some Scotch, afraid that she might cry.

"Yes, I have rather," she said. "But let's not talk about work or the war or anything else dreary. I want to hear about you."

Afternoon tea arrived on a tiered stand. There were finger sandwiches with cucumber and cream cheese, chicken and mustard, smoked salmon and dill. Sweets were warm raisin and plain scones, with homemade jams and Cornish clotted cream, as well as pastries. Evelyn ordered Darjeeling tea, Julia had champagne. The food cheered Evelyn up, and they spoke a little about Sally and her parents. Hugh had been busy at the factory, while Elizabeth was presently ensconced at the manor, entertaining another party of friends. Julia didn't eat or drink much but smoked a great deal, a pile of cigarette butts already overflowing from the ashtray. She had started at the Benevolent Society under the guidance of "a rather pious old duck from Glasgow" and had been put to work planning their annual gala, which seemed to cost more to host than it raised for the charity— "Which is why the rich should never be in command of other people's money," Julia concluded.

Evelyn enjoyed her company. Julia was also a reader and liked talking about books and plays, though she wasn't pretentious about it as some of the students at Oxford had been. There was a meandering quality to her mind, like a kite cut free from its string; it was hard to keep up with her. She was learning about trade unions, orchids ("for Hugh"), and she had attended a few lectures at the Royal Institute of Philosophy in Gordon Square—curious about how other people lived, she said.

"So you feel more settled now you're back in London?" Evelyn asked when the empty serving stand had been collected.

"Yes, I suppose I do. More settled than before, in any case." Julia smiled. "Problem is, I've never been much good at being told what to do. That's why school wasn't for me. I don't like rules. Unbridled and lawless, that's what my parents always said. Practically a barbarian.

Must have Viking blood somewhere in there. Have I ever told you my father's pet name for me? *Foxling.* He gave it to me when I was a girl." She tapped her canine tooth, which protruded fang-like from her mouth. "He says as soon as he clapped eyes on these gnashers he was convinced I'd been swapped by my mother and the vixen of the den. Probably explains why he's never much liked me."

She stared moodily at her empty glass, while a man at the piano started playing Debussy. Then she looked up.

"What about you? What do your family call you?"

"Me?" Evelyn felt herself smile. "I don't really have a pet name, which I rather regret now. It softens you, I think. Gives a sense of intimacy."

"Or the veneer of one." Julia tilted her dark head. "Anyway, I think Evelyn suits you. It's grown-up. I've always thought some people keep the shape of their face from childhood, and then one can chart a pathway through their life . . . But you're not like that. In fact, I'm not sure I can imagine you as a very small child, all impressionable and malleable. It's like you arrived fully formed."

She turned to watch the pianist, something almost wistful in her expression, while Evelyn brought out her cigarette case, her hand not quite steady as she struck the match against the box. Julia couldn't have known how she had touched upon the truth of her: that at times Evelyn felt hollowed out, as if there was nothing beneath her shiny exterior at all.

~

Afterward, Julia offered to walk with her to Grosvenor Square, where Evelyn was to deliver a file to the American embassy. It was already getting dark as they headed up South Audley Street, a few stray stars appearing low in the sky.

"You're not much alike, you and Sally," Julia said after a while, pulling her coat tighter around her waist. They cut through the Mount Street Gardens behind the chapel. "I wonder why you ever became so close."

"What do you mean?"

"Well, Sally's . . . How shall I put this?" Julia glanced at Evelyn, appearing to weigh up something in her mind. "Let's just say she's not much engaged in the currents of the time. I wonder what it is you find to talk about."

"I think you're being unfair to Sal," Evelyn said. "She's just not that political. And she's always been kind to me, and generous—the whole family, in fact, has treated me like I was practically one of them. I have a lot to be grateful for."

"Yes, and you've been a good friend to her," Julia said. "That means a lot to Hugh. He stakes everything on friendships—it's one of his best qualities."

They walked on, quiet for a few minutes, until they came to the edge of the square. Evelyn gazed up at the embassy, seven stories tall, resplendent in the dusk, the last glimmers of light at the bay windows outlining the Corinthian columns.

"Have you been inside?" Julia asked.

"Only to the foyer," Evelyn said.

"It's awfully ostentatious, isn't it? Mind you, that's the Americans for you." Julia chuckled. "You don't have much to do with them, then, at the War Office?"

"No. They're keeping well out of things for now. But further up the ranks I believe it's all very much jump-how-high sort of stuff from us."

"Mm. I hear old Joe Kennedy has built a replica Oval Office in there—to inspire his brats to achieve the highest office. Who said the

Yanks were egalitarian, eh? They crave empire as much as we do . . ." Julia brought out another cigarette and was about to light up in a pool of violet lamplight when she paused, her head tipped again with a new thought. "You know, you ought to come to the family home in Ludlow after the wedding. Stay with me in the old barn. Wesley Manor is just down the road and I could introduce you to my new friend, the navy man." She smiled, but there was some uncertainty in it this time. "He'll like you." She raised a hand to flag an approaching taxi, the downcast headlights flaring at her stockinged legs. "And let's go out again. Next week, maybe? I'll telephone."

TEN

THE FLAT WAS on the third floor of an imposing redbrick apartment building called Chemley Court set back from the Thames. It had two bedrooms, an open dining room with an alcove, a sitting room, and a galley kitchen at the back. Bennett White greeted Evelyn at the front door in a pair of old corduroys and tatty felt slippers, a few toast crumbs clinging to his burgundy sweater—a far cry from the dapper suit he'd worn when they first met. His study, which he ran out of the second bedroom, was just as disheveled, she discovered as he steered her down a hall overrun with piles of old papers, and had stained wineglasses and mugs dotting the floor. Several plates of half-eaten sandwiches had been squeezed into the oak shelves like bookends. Near the door sat White's assistant, Ted Young, a slight, harried-looking man of about thirty with a shock of crinkly hair, bashing away at a typewriter. The room reeked of sweat and mold, but beneath all this was another, even more peculiar smell. White pointed to the metal cage under the window seat.

"It's my northern short-tailed shrew." He frowned. "You're not squeamish about these sorts of things, are you, Evelyn?"

"Not at all." Evelyn swallowed. "I'm just more familiar with domesticated animals. Cats and dogs. I manage horses, at a pinch."

"I've always been more interested in wild animals," White remarked. "What can you do with a dog? Teach it to sit, command it to stay. There's no art in that. But a creature that you must tame . . . *that* is fascinating."

Of course, she had seen White around the prison before he had invited her to lunch at the Ritz last week—in the corridors, outside Chadwick's cell, once or twice across the noisy caf—but he had appeared taller and more solid than she remembered as he sat smoking at a table beneath a bronze chandelier. Evelyn had judged him to be in his early fifties, wearing tweeds and odd-colored socks (one blue, one red), but all very stylish; certainly not like most of the drab ex-army men drifting around the Scrubs.

They had eaten in the Marie Antoinette suite, a room as big and grand as a ballroom. It wasn't exactly to Evelyn's taste, but White assured her they would get a decent feed there, which they did, enjoying salad niçoise and beef stroganoff, and a very good bottle of chardonnay from Touraine. On the overmantel next to their table was a basket of white roses—floral motifs, in fact, were positioned all around the suite—and fixed to the walls were lamp holders propped up by miniature Apollonic lyres. Everything else was decorated in ostentatious gilt, and beside their table was a floor-to-ceiling mirror, which meant Evelyn had the peculiar feeling of watching herself throughout the meal.

While they ate, White had spoken warmly about his division, which ran three case officers from a flat in Pimlico; he described their idiosyncrasies as he might those of his own family, and Evelyn began to see that there was something disarming about him. He drank heartily, tearing off great chunks of bread to mop up the creamy sauce, and though he asked her many questions about university, her childhood in Lewes, and her parents, he was never probing. He seemed genuinely interested.

"Now look here, Evelyn," he said finally, when the plates had been cleared and their coffee arrived. "You've been patient, but I'll cut to the chase. I was impressed with your recent work at Latchmere House, very impressed. You got good intelligence from the Dutch boy—it seems you have a knack for it. So I'd like you to come and work for me."

His face had turned red from the wine, which made his eyes smaller and darker, and Evelyn thought how much he resembled one of those birds he was said to know so much about. A magpie, perhaps, on the lookout for its next scrap.

"What about Mr. Chadwick?" she asked.

White took a neat drag on his cigarette, then another, before grinding it into the ashtray.

"John and I agree that you would be better placed in counter-intelligence. Besides, I need another girl on my team."

Evelyn felt herself nodding. *Another girl.* She wanted to do something with her hands, which she'd placed on the tabletop, to stop them fidgeting.

"And I would be your assistant? Answering the telephone, typing, that sort of thing?" Her voice sounded flat.

White's eyes widened. "Good Lord, no. I will run you as an agent."

"An agent?" Evelyn had the urge to laugh at the sheer surprise and delight of it, but when she saw his face, the intensity of his expression, she felt instead a bolt of fear. "But I've no experience."

White sat back. "I've read your file, Evelyn. It's not unique. There's the usual good report from the Somerville principal, strong grades, another language, and other distinctions. Captain of the college tennis team, wasn't it? These records never tell me all that much about a person. We have, after all, different identities around different people.

I imagine a scholarship girl from Lewes has many . . ." He smiled blandly. "But I suspect you've always been good at making people like you. That's why I wanted to meet you. And now I can see you are indeed calm and self-assured. Attractive. Not enough to draw attention to yourself, but certainly enough to charm. And, like all good spies, you never give away too much of yourself."

He had offered her a cigarette and they sat there smoking. White finished his coffee and wiped his mouth with the napkin.

"I have a mantra for agents handling their subjects," he said. "*Formed of their own image.* Imitation is, after all, the highest form of flattery. I tell all my agents this. How we must adopt the precise attitudes of our interlocutor."

"And is that what you would have me do in your team?" Evelyn asked. "More interrogations?"

"Perhaps in time. But first we will place you somewhere to gather information. Reporting on what you see, what you hear. Counterintelligence is about distraction, deception, but at its core is truth. You must make your subjects believe in you and your convictions."

Before they parted, White bent down to retrieve a file from his satchel, slapping it down on the table. TOP SECRET was stamped on the cover. "Read this," he said. "And then come and see me next week."

Watching him leave, Evelyn caught a glimpse of her own reflection. It was unsettling—she didn't look herself at all, dressed as she was in a blue tambourine beret, her brown felt suit, her lips painted very red. Her face was still pink, but she didn't mind that; it gave her vibrancy, as though you could almost see the blood being pushed through her veins. She stood up and stepped away from the table and as she did her reflection moved toward the partition where the pieces of mirror met, splitting her in two. She stared at the glass, transfixed, while the suite slowed almost to a standstill; even the waiters by the door had fallen silent and motionless, as if they too were waiting for her next move.

～

By midafternoon, the study was already growing dark. White reached over to flick on the lamp, but it was a weak bulb, casting the room in deeper shadow. Evelyn watched him pull a tobacco pouch from the desk drawer and begin the careful ritual of filling his pipe.

"What do you think of our little spy den?" he asked.

Evelyn peered about the room, aware of Ted muttering under his breath as he replaced the ink ribbon in the Royal.

"It's . . . unconventional."

This elicited a smile. "You probably think we're all mad. But the thing is, Jack Littleproud is away on a case right now, leaving me a man down, so we're scrambling to keep on top of things." White pointed across the room. "I recruited Ted from Oxford, actually, though it was a few years before your time. He was monitoring some undergraduate students. Awful rabble, campaigning for pacifism, weren't they, Ted?"

"That they were," said Ted with a sigh, giving Evelyn a pained look.

"So"—White squinted across the desk as he struck a match—"you read that case file?"

"Yes, sir." Evelyn brought out the folder and handed it to him across the desk. "It was most instructive. Clearly you don't nab the founding member of a Soviet spy ring overnight."

The case related to an investigation of communist espionage conducted by an agent code-named "Posey." The infiltration had started back in 1930, when Posey made contact with an Englishman named Frederick Gibson, a member of the Friends of the Soviet Union. He took a liking to her, the report said, as she reminded him of his sister, and they soon formed a friendship. But years had passed before

Gibson asked Posey to rent an apartment in Kensington, where he would meet with other communists and share documents he'd stolen from the Woolwich Arsenal, and the substance of the case had been gathered from there.

As she had read the file over the weekend, it became clear to Evelyn that White wanted her to absorb the tactics of Posey—cautious friendship, ingratiation and, ultimately, betrayal—but she found herself most intrigued by the black-and-white photograph pinned to the front page. It was a portrait of a young woman in a dark cardigan and blouse, her hair drawn into a plait. A scribble on the back read *S.G. 1934.* Evelyn couldn't believe that this was the agent who'd been embedded for years in a communist cell. She couldn't have been more than twenty years old. According to the file Susanna Grey had worked at Chemley Court until earlier that year.

White stood up and went to the window where he smoked solemnly, his eyes fixed on the street below.

"Eight years," he muttered. "That investigation took its toll on all of us, but Susanna in particular. Some days I wondered if we would ever come out the other side of it. That's the thing about this job: there's no room for even a shred of doubt, no room for conflicted loyalty." White scowled. "You need that certainty to guide you like a beacon, otherwise . . ." But when he turned back toward Evelyn his face had cleared. "In any case, you'll have seen that Susanna used no magic or disguise to infiltrate that group. Authenticity is always the best method in espionage. Truth with just the lightest shade of dark. I want you to do the same with your investigation into the Lion Society."

"The Lion Society?"

"It's a group made up of fascist sympathizers, mostly renegades from the Establishment. Nasty pieces of work. The MP Andrew Randall is the founder. Apparently he keeps the names of his members in a red leather-bound ledger. We have knowledge of some of these people but not all, and it's already quite a list. The Duke of Wellington, Lord Lymington, B. L. Chesterfield . . . There are two branches of the club: one for women, one for men. The women meet each week at a Kensington restaurant owned by a Russian émigré family called Ivanov."

Evelyn knew the place on Queen's Gate. "And what does the club do?" she asked, lighting a cigarette.

"At first we thought Randall only wanted to expose the activity of what he calls the organized Jewry. They all loathe Jews—it's the raison d'être of the club—but it had been fairly innocuous stuff until now. Distasteful posters around London, anti-Semitic graffiti, that sort of thing. Lately, however, we've heard whispers of more troubling ambitions. Randall is now actively collaborating with Nina Ivanov, the leader of the women's group, to create a groundswell of support for Germany from within the political establishment. It's our belief that they already have direct links with the Nazi leadership in Berlin and that they have begun to leak crucial intelligence out of Britain to undermine our campaign. We've had our eye on a particular broadcaster for some time. He fled to Germany last summer and has since worked for the Rundfunkhaus radio station run by the Ministry of Propaganda. We think the Lion Society is feeding him top-secret information about the British war effort and taking instruction from him."

Evelyn glanced at the unsmoked cigarette that had burned down almost to her fingers. She stubbed it out.

"What do they hope to achieve by doing that?"

White offered her a grim smile. "It's simple, really. They plan to form an alliance when Hitler invades Britain."

"Invasion?" Evelyn repeated it softly, thinking of Jacob Vermeer. *Lucky you speak German, bitch.*

White tapped a finger against the desk. "That's why we need you inside this organization. We need that membership list and we need to know who is leaking intelligence. Find the name and address of every wretch who has ever paid a penny to the Lion Society so we can build a case for the Home Secretary to issue the internment orders. As many of these men and women as possible should be locked up—and if I had my way, we'd throw away the key."

Evelyn was aware of a curious vibration in the balls of her feet, like she was standing on an air vent above the underground, until she realized it was her heart thudding away like that, making her whole body hum.

"But how would I join this club?" she asked. "I can't very well walk in off the street . . ."

"I already have an agent planted on the inside," White said. "Mrs. Armstrong, a top-notch old duck—she's been embedded in there for years. She reports that the women's leadership group are looking to recruit from the War Office; they want moles in the bureaucracy to help their cause. Mrs. Armstrong has already supplied a paper on *The Merchant of Venice* and Zionism that Nina Ivanov was told you wrote. It was rather good, actually, and she thought so too." White flashed a brief smile. "We plan for Mrs. Armstrong to introduce you to Ivanov at the restaurant, for her to take a liking to you in person, and everything else to follow from there."

"All right."

It didn't sound all that different from how Evelyn had behaved at Raheen—hiding who she really was and what she really thought, and adopting the manners and attitudes of those around her. It was a performance, nothing more complicated than that, and she had an instinct for this kind of disguise.

"The thing to remember about Nina Ivanov is that during the reign of Nicholas II, her family was one of the most influential in

Russia," White continued. "And I mean *influential*. The mother was a lady-in-waiting to the Empress, and Nina's father, the admiral, was once the naval attaché at the Russian embassy in London. After the revolution, they had no choice but to remain here in exile. So while they might appear content with their little restaurant, they're extremely bitter about everything they've lost."

Evelyn nodded. "And once I'm friendly with Nina, I'm to then make her believe I have something useful to the Lion Society, like access?"

"Yes," said White. "You must encourage her to believe that you can use your position at the War Office to assist her activities. She might ask for anything. Files, telephone numbers, names. Whatever she wants, we will give it to her." He began digging around in the top drawer, finally pulling out a small piece of card. He scribbled something on the back of it before pushing it across the desk to Evelyn. She turned it over to see another portrait photograph, this time of a rather glamorous-looking young woman with fair hair and pert lips.

"That's Christine Bakker, an attaché with the Romanian Legation. She's worked with me for years. I've given you her telephone number. She may come in handy in this investigation. If the chance ever arises, you can tell the group you have a diplomatic contact. Christine could be useful for a range of things, including liaising with other embassies and even smuggling material out of Britain. The Lion Society will know we're watching the Allied embassies, so Christine has good cover with the Romanians, who are still neutral. Please memorize that number and destroy the photograph."

"Thanks." Evelyn tucked the photograph inside her purse. "I will."

White pressed his fingertips together. "And now to your transformation."

Ted Young came over and dumped a pile of documents on the desk.

Evelyn peered at the old newspaper on the top, *Völkischer Beobachter*, the daily for the National Socialist German Workers' Party.

"Today you read," White said. "Because before you can gain this group's trust, you must start thinking like them and sounding like them. You must, essentially, become like them."

Evelyn raised her eyebrows and White smiled. "You know, I once believed in fascism myself," he murmured. "It's no secret, but there you have it, the folly of youth. However, the more I look back on it, the more I realize it wasn't a folly, not really. I was driven by an entirely rational desire to destroy communism—I would have done anything. I think that's why I've always found the love of one's country has its limits; we need to see our love reflected in something, or someone. In my experience, the most zealous patriot has had no one else to love. An absent father, a dead wife . . ." He smiled again, his bright eyes alert. "That's why in war, and in death, that love can be immortalized. It's a powerful urge."

"It reminds me of a Wallace Stevens poem I read as a child," Evelyn said. "*Death's nobility again; Beautified the simplest men; Fallen Winkle felt the pride—*"

"*—Of Agamemnon; When he died . . .*" White nodded. "Yes, I like that. War is one of the few opportunities for men to become equal."

But not for you, thought Evelyn, as he sucked away on his cigarette. You're not immortal. You're all flesh. Thick, blood-red lips, hooded eyes, flabby jowls. It was almost impossible to imagine that any foreign agent could trust him—surely one so fond of indulgence could never be dependable? Still, unlike Chadwick, there was something magnetic about White. His manner was mercurial, and she could see how deftly he steered, convinced, manipulated; how easy it was to talk with him. But pressing behind this feeling was another, sharper sensation, like a sudden fleck of boiling water on her skin. If he was this kaleidoscope of different people, how could she ever be certain of his loyalty to her?

⌒

Evelyn's new desk in the alcove overlooked St. George's Square and she glimpsed a hint of river off to the right. Fat black clouds hung over Embankment. She didn't mind the quiet, but she missed the companionable noises of the Scrubs, and she missed Vincent poking his head around her door to invite her outside for a smoke; she couldn't hear anything from White's study on the other side of the flat. She imagined Chadwick alone in his cell. He'd barely raised an eyebrow when she packed up her desk. He'd known all along why White had wanted to have lunch with her, of course. "You'll do very well with Bennett as a mentor," was all he said, though Evelyn had sensed admonishment in his tone, as if she could have chosen to stay, which was unfair, because when she looked back on that strange meal at the Ritz there had never really been a question about her joining counterintelligence, no real decision to be made at all. Bennett White, Evelyn had since learned, was not a man to whom many people said no.

After Evelyn had read some of the German newspapers, she listened to the recordings of the propaganda broadcasts from Berlin, which began with the preening greeting '*Jar-many calling*' and did little else but urge the British people to surrender to Hitler. When she'd had enough of that, she pored over notes made by an agent called "Dove" planted at one of Oswald Mosley's London rallies. This had turned violent, with a few men hospitalized and a woman raped in a West End lane. Evelyn glanced at the remaining reading piled up on her desk—White planned to test her on the Molotov-Ribbentrop Pact, the Nuremberg Laws, and *Volksdeutsche* in the morning.

She leaned back and rubbed at her sore eyes. It was ghastly stuff, and being immersed in it was like being lowered into a pit of molten tar and ordered to swim. It didn't seem possible that ordinary men and women thought this way. White had suggested she draw on things she may have heard at Oxford to give authenticity to her new persona, yet it wasn't anyone from college she thought about as she sat at the desk but her own mother. All this preparation must have dredged up a forgotten memory, because she recalled an afternoon the previous year when, flicking through the local newspaper, her mother had raised a hand to her mouth and made a small noise of astonishment. Evelyn had gone to her, afraid to hear of a death or some new disaster abroad. But her mother had only folded over the newspaper and with a great sigh put it to one side.

"Do you remember Harriet Graham from number twelve?" she said. "The publican's daughter?"

Evelyn nodded. She and Harriet had been in the same class at primary school.

"She's engaged . . . to a *Jew*."

Evelyn hadn't known what to say. She had never heard her mother speak like this. She looked to her father, expecting some rebuke, but he only cleared his throat and continued reading by the fireplace.

"But what does it matter if he's Jewish?" Evelyn asked, following her mother into the kitchen. "Isn't their happiness what's important?"

"Yes, dear," said her mother patiently. "Only, it's a pity she's chosen that path. It will make her life so much more difficult."

"But why?" Evelyn still didn't understand. It had always been her belief that men and women should love whomever they pleased. Wasn't that freedom what made them all human?

"Well, dear, you know *why*. It's just not the done thing, is it? This intermarrying."

Afterward, Evelyn had gone upstairs to her bedroom with a greasy feeling sliding around in her stomach. She knew her mother didn't mean to be unkind—perhaps it was only ignorance, though this didn't sit well either. Despite her lack of education, her mother was an intuitive woman, and liked to be on the right side of public opinion on moral matters. But that couldn't be right either, could it? The more Evelyn pondered it now as she sat there at the desk, the more confused she became, and nagging at her behind this feeling was the concern that her father hadn't said anything. Did his silence mean that he agreed? And what of her own complicity? As the sky turned grayer at the window, Evelyn remembered how she had never challenged her mother or tried to find out what had made her think like that and, perhaps worst of all, had forgotten the incident by the next day.

~

By midday the flat had grown cold and damp. Evelyn wandered through to the kitchen to make herself a cup of tea. There was no milk, and she opened the tin for a biscuit, though all that remained were a few stale crumbs. She went to the sitting room and drank her tea overlooking the satiny river.

Another hour passed, and Evelyn was immersed in yet more reading when she heard a key in the front door. Assuming it was White, she didn't immediately turn at the creak in the hallway or the flop of a hat when it landed on the stand.

"So, you're Bennett's new girl, then?"

Evelyn twisted in her seat, the grin already stretched across her face. "Vincent!"

"*Guten Tag,* darling." After depositing his briefcase on the dining table, he strolled over to the desk and bent down to kiss Evelyn's cheek. The tips of his hair were flecked with rain. "Can't get enough of me, can you?"

"You're working with White too?"

"Poached as the best egg. All this drama at the Home Office with enemy aliens has meant there's decryption coming out of Bennett's ears. I've been coming over from White City every other day this week, but now it's permanent. Chaddy's none too pleased."

"Poor Chaddy."

"Yes." Vincent walked to the old leather armchair by the empty fireplace in the sitting room. "Still, it's much jollier here than at the Scrubs, don't you think?"

"Working out the front of Parliament would be jollier than the Scrubs. And it's quiet. You can actually hear yourself think!"

"Don't get too cozy," Vincent warned her. "You do know Mosley lives in the building? Somewhere on the ground floor, goosestepping about. Not that he's much in residence."

Evelyn fetched the corned beef sandwich she had packed for lunch and rejoined Vincent in the sitting room, pulling out the chair paired with the Louis XVI desk. She handed him half the sandwich. "And the other agent, what's he like?" she asked.

"Jack? That's Jack Littleproud—I can't really say. He's on a case, I believe, and has not been in much. Nor Bennett, come to think of it." He looked her way, winking, as his lean jaw worked away at the day-old bread. "You must have made an impression."

⌒

At the end of the following week, after three tests, much berating, and some play-acting in front of Vincent and Ted, Evelyn was called into White's study and told she was ready to be introduced to Nina Ivanov. The meeting had been arranged for Thursday morning at the Arbat Tea House; Mrs. Armstrong would collect her from the front of South Kensington station at ten o'clock.

White had been standing by the window as he explained all this, hands linked behind his back, his gaze shifting southward. Perhaps he had seen something on the Thames, and after a fortnight confined indoors, Evelyn suddenly longed to be out there in the cold, breathing in great lungfuls of fresh air far away from Chemley Court. But then he did something strange. Setting his pipe on the window ledge, he bent down to his shrew's cage, opened the latch, and reached inside. Evelyn watched as the tiny thing, no bigger than a powder compact, scurried into his palm. White brought a fingertip to the creature's back for a gentle stroke, all the while making gravelly soothing sounds. Evelyn took a quick breath. The truth was that she didn't much like any animal, let alone those with a long pointed snout, and fancying she could hear the swish of his scaly tail made her queasy. White walked back to his desk, the shrew cupped in his hand.

"This morning I read about the farmers in Norfolk," he said. "They've started shooting birds on the migration to Europe. Thousands have been slaughtered."

Evelyn glanced at the newspaper spread across the desk, making out the headline: SKYLARKS THAT SING TO NAZIS WILL GET NO MERCY HERE. She looked at the shrew. He sat placid and unassuming in White's hand, but Evelyn could see how those small eyes were wide and shining. There was a readiness in the span of his minute pink feet, as if at any moment he would launch himself across the desk.

"Surely they don't believe the birds have somehow betrayed them?"

"That's exactly what they think," said White. "You and me, we're students of history, and students of history always make good spies. We're interested in the small eruptions of change, always with an eye to avoiding the next catastrophe. But these farmers, they only understand the land, the sky, what's right there in front of them. It's not so eccentric—I've known men who went to war because they wanted to defend the mallards and teal nesting in the reeds along the Devon coast."

The shrew snuffled, his eyes trained on Evelyn. How strange it was to see White like this, so caring and so delicate; she wondered if Posey had had the same induction.

"Huxley said something on the wireless the other day that has stuck with me," White continued. "That the yellowhammer song is the best possible expression of a hot English country road in July. Isn't that marvelous?"

"Yes," said Evelyn. "I've never quite thought of it that way."

"But it is not a question of thinking, my dear. It is a question of *feeling*. Don't you see? You must understand the emotions of others if you're to seek their trust. After all, any old landscape can be made to look like an English one. But it is the birds, first and foremost, that will make you believe this is home."

As he stood there, blinking at her, willing a sign of apprehension, Evelyn began to wonder what he saw in her. Was she a small, insubstantial thing like his shrew? Was she something to be tamed?

"To train a wild animal, you must first build up its confidence," he said quietly, as though he had divined her thoughts. "Without it there can be no trust, and the animal will never be gentle or tractable; he will never feed as you want him to, or stop biting or trying to escape. But when he becomes compliant, you know he has accepted you as his own."

He extended his hand toward her, and Evelyn raised her own palm to his fingertips. Still the shrew stared at her, unmoving, and she felt a tremble work its way along the length of her arm. White watched her with a crooked smile and resumed his seat.

"Deep breath," he said.

And so she inhaled and exhaled slowly, and her hand grew steady. They sat like that, on opposite sides of the large oak desk, their fingers almost touching, a tiny mammal the subject of their urgent fascination. At last the shrew took a sniff of the air and edged toward

Evelyn. He stood on the tips of White's long fingers, his whiskers twitching. Then he scurried into Evelyn's palm, where he remained still but for the steady thrill of his tiny heartbeat pulsing against her skin, the almost imperceptible quiver along his flanks with each surreptitious breath.

"What a dear little thing!" Evelyn's throat felt tight.

White leaned back, admiring his work, and as he folded his arms across his broad chest Evelyn wondered if she had misjudged him too.

"See?" he said. "See how easily you can do it?"

ELEVEN

WITH HER TWEED suit, white ringlets, and horn-rimmed spectacles hanging loose around her neck, Mrs. Armstrong looked more like a school dinner lady than one of White's agents. But while they sat at a window table overlooking Harrington Road sharing a brass samovar of tea, which Mrs. Armstrong had been drinking through a cube of sugar set between her front teeth—it was the Russian way, she explained with some enthusiasm—Evelyn recognized the flintiness in the old woman's eyes as they surveilled the dining room, the doddering spinster disguising an incisive operative.

The restaurant was empty apart from another couple in front of the fire who spoke now and then to a distinguished-looking man with a thick white beard wearing a dark jacket and a naval cap. This must be Admiral Ivanov, Evelyn thought. When his brooding gaze strayed their way he called out something in Russian and a tiny old woman in black stockings and an apron materialized with a bottle on a tray. Mrs. Armstrong had been talking amiably about her dog, an Irish wolfhound named Jessie. It was only the illusion of chatter, of course, but there in the snug dining room, the gramophone playing a Vertinsky arietta, the smell of goulash cooking in the kitchen, a cup of sweet tea thawing her chilblained fingers, Evelyn found herself so drawn into the story that she almost didn't notice Nina Ivanov emerge from the kitchen to join her father by the fireplace.

"Look," Mrs. Armstrong whispered.

Amid the preparation in advance of the meeting, Evelyn had not given much thought to what Nina might actually look like. She had supposed her to be a tall, athletic sort of woman, someone who wouldn't look out of place throwing a javelin, for instance, but when Nina came out from behind the bar Evelyn was surprised to discover she was no more than five feet tall, dressed in a black crepe dress and polished heels, her severe face softening as she recognized Mrs. Armstrong from across the room.

"I've been promising my friend Evelyn for some time that I would bring her to your delightful restaurant," Mrs. Armstrong explained after the introductions had been made. "And now here we are!"

"Have you had Russian food before, Evelyn?" Nina's voice was cool, clipped, with only a faint trace of an accent.

"I'm ashamed to say I haven't," Evelyn said with a smile. "I'll have to come back and hold Mrs. Armstrong to her word. She says you make the best *rassolnik* in London."

Nina tapped the tabletop with a black-painted fingernail. She wore no other makeup, nor any jewelry. A faint scar ran from her hairline to her left eyebrow.

"And are you a student?" She frowned over Evelyn's plaid dress and satchel.

"No—well, not anymore." Evelyn laughed. "I work at the War Office, actually."

"Ah, yes." Nina glanced at Mrs. Armstrong. "Gertrude has mentioned you. That must keep you busy."

"Not especially. I'm in the filing department—it gets rather dull, to tell you the truth."

There was a glimmer of interest in Nina's dark eyes. "And how long have you been there?"

"Only a few months. In fact—"

The bell sounded at the door. The lunchtime rush was about to begin, and with a quick shrug of apology Nina went to greet new guests on the other side of the dining room.

"Come along, then." Turning back to Mrs. Armstrong, Evelyn saw the old woman finish her tea and stand up.

"Is that it?" She wasn't ready to leave. She'd had a taste of this infiltration and it was like an adrenaline hit. She watched Nina guide the group of men in smart suits toward a table near the fireplace.

"Yes, pet," said Mrs. Armstrong. "There is nothing more for us to do today. But visit again soon. Nina will remember you, I'm sure of it."

⁓

Evelyn returned the following week. She came alone and sat by the front window again with an outlook to the busy street. But after an hour of flicking through the newspaper and drinking so much tea she thought she would burst it became clear that she wouldn't encounter Nina.

"On own today?" the admiral called from his seat by the fire. "Not with mother?" His accent, unlike Nina's, was still thick.

"Yes," said Evelyn as she approached the counter to pay. "Though Mrs. Armstrong isn't my mother. She's just a friend. An old friend of *my* mother's, actually. But I do enjoy dropping by. You have a very fine restaurant."

The admiral nodded. "We do our best. We have been in England now more than twenty years. I am proud of my family business."

"I met your daughter the last time I was here." Evelyn peered along the bar. "Is she not working today?"

The admiral pointed the clip of his pipe at the ceiling. "She up there. Dressmaker. Very good. Very talent." He grinned behind his enormous beard. "One client is Duchess of Windsor!"

Evelyn raised her eyes. A small chandelier hung from the elegant latticework and she could see, very faintly, the crystals vibrating with movement upstairs. She imagined Nina moving about the room, that stern, serious expression fixed to her white face, a needle caught between her teeth, a measuring tape threaded around her wrists. It was an incongruous image, one that troubled Evelyn for the rest of the day—that someone with such virtuosity could also have so much hatred stored away behind her calm facade.

⁓

On her third visit, Evelyn brought along Sally Wesley. It was a Friday night, but the snow-laden streets were quiet, the blackout in this part of London keeping most people indoors. It was busy in the restaurant, however, and lively with music from the quartet playing Russian folk tunes by the bar. Evelyn and Sally ate savory dumplings called *pelmeni* filled with mince and topped with sour cream, and for mains they ordered dressed herring. Sally enjoyed the food and the wine, and spent most of the meal talking about Jonty's deployment to engage German surface ships in the Heligoland Bight in the same happy tone as she might have used to describe a friendly rugger tour to the Continent.

Only toward the end of dinner did Nina appear at the kitchen door with a white apron tied around her waist. She began making her way through the crowded dining room, pouring each of her guests a glass of amber-colored liquid from a jug. As she came nearer to their table, Evelyn felt the familiar kick of her pulse and her blood rise, as if she was poised for a sprint, the starter's gun raised to fire.

"Evelyn, how lovely to see you again." Nina filled their glasses. The drink smelled earthy, like beetroot pulled fresh from the soil. "*Kvas*," she explained. "A traditional Russian refreshment. Fermented from black rye bread. It's not for everyone, but I do like our guests to try it."

Evelyn glanced at Sally, and they both drank. It was sour and slightly salty, though there was a hint of mint in the aftertaste.

"Lovely," she said.

"Really?"

"Well, no . . ." Evelyn laughed. She was a little tipsy—they both were—and it made her feel bold. "But the rest of the meal was splendid. If I'd known how well you cooked, I would have come weeks ago!"

"Well . . ." Nina shrugged and nodded toward the kitchen. "I do have some help."

"You're too modest," said Sally, rising to her feet. "Excuse me, but may I use your telephone? I think I'll call our driver before the snow really comes down again."

Evelyn and Nina watched her walk off to the booth near the front door.

"She's nice," Nina said. "How do you know each other?"

"Sally's an old school friend, actually." Evelyn paused, dropping the crumb lightly. "Her family are the Wesleys, the button manufacturers."

"Are they indeed?" Nina raised her eyebrows. "I must have used a thousand of them on my dresses."

Evelyn watched her squint across the room in Sally's direction again. The snow through the window outside fluttered about the low-lit streetlamp.

"I'm lucky to have Sally here in London," Evelyn continued. "It's not always easy to meet new people in big cities. Especially those with similar interests."

Nina stared down at her, her dark eyes seeming to weigh Evelyn up in that long, drawn-out moment. She was almost pretty with some color in her cheeks. Then, with a glance over her shoulder, she set down the jug.

"Since you enjoy our Russian food, perhaps you'd like to drop by again on Sunday evening? I'm having a small gathering of friends in my flat—Mrs. Armstrong will be there. I'll make my special omelettes."

The noise of the restaurant seemed to roar and mute in quick succession, the strangers eating and drinking around them slowing almost to a halt. From the corner of her eye, Evelyn saw Sally hang up the telephone.

"It will be very relaxed," Nina was saying. "Very welcoming."

Sally stood in the restaurant doorway, a tall young man now at her side. She said something, and with a laugh he began to accompany her back toward the table. There wasn't much time.

Evelyn looked up at Nina and smiled. "I'd be delighted. Thank you."

"Eight o'clock?"

"Eight o'clock."

Nina nodded, her eyes bright once more. She reached for the *kvas* and moved on, passing Sally and the young man. He paused midway between the tables and gestured politely to Evelyn.

"Don't forget: try the admiral's *kizlyarka*." His voice was loud, American. "It's a grape vodka—you'll love it, trust me," and Sally gave him a wave of thanks as she sat down again.

"Flirting, were you?" Evelyn asked. "You're shameless."

"Hardly. I'm practically a married woman." Sally studied Evelyn. "You could do with some of it, you know."

"What?"

"Flirting." She gestured toward the young man. "Those Americans, they're a good-looking bunch. You never know who you might meet."

"Hm." Evelyn had never shared Sally's ideas about what constituted good-looking. "I'll have to take your word for it."

"But some excitement, some danger." Sally picked up her bag and held it to her chest. "It might brighten things up. Better than spending all your time with Julia."

Evelyn's attention snapped back, and she frowned at Sally. "What do you mean?"

"Only that if you spent less time with her, and more time out and about, you might snag yourself a man too." Sally folded her arms, something smug flickering across her face. "I know you've been seeing one another, Ev, you needn't be so clandestine. I don't mind, of course; I've been so busy and she does need another friend."

"Well, as long as I have your permission . . ."

Evelyn watched Nina pause at the next table to talk to more guests. She wondered if they were Russians, friends of the family. They didn't look Russian, but then Evelyn wasn't really sure how to tell if they were. Or maybe they were only men and women who thought the same way Nina did. Evelyn felt sick at this possibility, like the herring had worked its way up from her stomach. She had always imagined it would take a rupture, a calamity, for someone's perceptions to be so wildly altered; to be so *corrupted*. But now she saw it could be as simple as a home-cooked meal. She studied Nina's movement about the tables, her face reset to a severe, appraising expression, all that gaiety gone. She had been painted with such clear lines, Evelyn thought, but tonight as she stood there in the firelight her outline seemed to blur and shift, like the first shimmer of a mirage.

⟋

The preparation continued at Chemley Court. The files from the Home Office had finally arrived with dossiers on about a dozen women who White believed might be at the supper on Sunday, though it soon became clear that Evelyn should concentrate her efforts on Nina and Isadore Randall, the wife of the Lion Society founder, Captain Andrew Randall. It was her money, the files recorded, that largely funded the club and its operations, and she'd earned some notoriety earlier in the year after telling the Arbroath Business Club that an international group of Jews was behind every recent revolution across the world. Evelyn studied the photograph attached to the file, taken outside the couple's home, Mrs. Randall about to climb into the back of a motor car, her hair a wiry pompadour. She had a cruel face, it had to be said, with a small, sneering mouth and the round, owlish eyes of a dowager.

"Ooh, are these your new chums?" Vincent peered over Evelyn's shoulder. "Don't they look like fun. I do hope I'll get an invite to supper!"

"Mm." She closed the file. "I feel grubby just thinking about them."

Vincent strolled back to the dining room, a hand in his pocket.

"The funny thing is, they probably have quite a few Jewish friends," he called. "Extraordinary, isn't it, but they're never hateful about the people they know, these anti-Semites. It's always the other, nasty, hook-nosed lot scurrying about in the East End, not their solicitor or their colleague or that nice banker next door . . ."

He slumped into the chair at the head of the table. While Evelyn had been preparing for her infiltration, Vincent had been forced to set aside his usual decryption work to assess new reports flowing in from the public on suspected enemy activity, a ten-inch stack waiting for processing in his tray, another outside White's study door. Every curtain-twitcher in London had spotted *something*, he told her that morning over tea and a few biscuits she'd managed to scrounge from the back of the kitchen cabinet. The latest memo related to a retired schoolmistress in Clapham who had reported unidentified marks on a telegraph pole outside the local bakery.

There were concerns these marks might be a code designed to guide the German invasion.

"Most files we chuck out straight away, but White thinks this one is worth chasing." Vincent took a bite from the biscuit and made a face. "Just be thankful you're not on the pigeon case."

"The *what*?"

"We've called it the Somerset Pigeon Case, after all the reports from the local plod about their good constituents capturing pigeons suspected of secret dealings with the Boche."

"I've always found pigeons to be a most untrustworthy bird," Evelyn muttered. "It's the eyes. Too beady for me by half."

Vincent grinned. "And they give nothing away in the interview room, the blighters."

At the end of the week they took a late lunch at the pub on Lupus Street, a rowdy drinking stop, full of workingmen congregating at the front bar. Pushing his way through the boiler suits and flat caps, Vincent found them a booth by the back near the loos, where the wallpaper was peeling and the worn mauve carpet was a little less sticky underfoot. They ordered steak and chips, and pints of Guinness. Evelyn supposed the other patrons might think they were lovers, the way they bent their heads together, the knowing looks they exchanged, and when they spent time like this she did sense a thread between them grow taut, a little like what she supposed love might feel like.

"My brother's one of them," Vincent said, nodding toward the lads playing darts by the bar. "A proper member of the proletariat. Or thinks he is. Worships Marx like he was the real messiah. Works for a tenants' union."

"You don't talk about your brother much. Is he in London?" Evelyn asked.

"No, New York. He emigrated to America a few years ago. We were never all that close, but we still write to one another now and then."

"So you're on your own at Stepney Green." Evelyn chewed on a cold chip. "Does it get lonely?"

"Yes, it can." Vincent paused. "Though sometimes I stay at the flat."

"What, Chemley Court? But where?" Evelyn started to smile. "There's only one bedroom."

"Well, I stay with Bennett . . . In his room."

Evelyn blinked. "Oh. I see."

Vincent was staring at her, color spreading up his throat. "It's only been a couple of times," he mumbled.

"But is he . . . ?" Evelyn hesitated, uncertain how to ask. "His wife, does she . . . ? He's not, well . . ."

Vincent looked miserable now. "Do you mind, Evelyn?"

Evelyn felt her own face flush hot, and she was filled with pity for Vincent—not for what he had told her but for the fear she had detected in his voice.

"Don't be so silly. Why should I ever mind about a thing like that?" She sat back, hands around her pint glass. "I was going to say I'm surprised, but I don't believe I am." She laughed then, covering her mouth, and Vincent laughed too—in relief, perhaps. "Sorry, is that awful?"

"Not really." He rubbed his nose. "You wouldn't be much of a spy if you hadn't spotted it."

Evelyn finished the watery dregs of her Guinness. "Have you always liked men?"

"Yes, I think so." Vincent smiled grimly. "I'm not sure I could live any other way, even if it would make my life easier."

"Yes." Evelyn understood that. But it was unpleasant to think of

White knowing Vincent's vulnerabilities, though she supposed they were his vulnerabilities too now. "I hope he's nice to you," she said. "Treats you, well, like a princess."

Vincent gave a shrug. Then he reached across the table and took Evelyn's hands in his. "But you mustn't say anything, Evelyn. Please. Bennett's not . . . Well, this knowledge of himself doesn't sit quite comfortably."

"Of course. You can trust me."

We all have our secrets, Evelyn mused as they strolled back along Lupus Street, the wind whipping about their faces.

MARCH 1948

TWELVE

MRS. FOY WAS STILL upstairs when Evelyn arrived at the bookshop on Monday morning. She stood for a moment by the rosewood cabinet displaying the first editions, her eyes drawn to the front window where, just below the gilded sign that read *Foy's Books & Collectables*, the sun had been flinting at the glass. There were boxes of books from the weekend deliveries blocking the doorway—one from Faber, another from Penguin, the rest from Mrs. Foy's secondhand supplier in Hammersmith. Evelyn dragged them to a corner to clear a path toward the desk. Alix, Mrs. Foy's Russian blue, slunk downstairs, eyeing Evelyn imperiously as she removed her coat and hung it on the stand.

Foy's on Store Street was one of the few buildings in the block undamaged after the war. The shop was on the ground floor of the terrace, positioned between tearooms and a boarded-up gallery, and on the two floors above lived Mrs. Foy, who had run the business since her husband died. Evelyn had worked for Mrs. Foy for nearly two years. Though the shop was close to the British Museum, they weren't bothered by many customers, and this meant Evelyn's days passed with little cause for nuisance or surprise. And she liked the quiet, which she supposed wasn't good for business, but Mrs. Foy never seemed concerned by it.

"Is that you, Evelyn?" Mrs. Foy called from upstairs. "I'm just finishing breakfast."

"Hullo," she called back, blowing on her hands. Winter had returned overnight, covering Bloomsbury in an icy mist. Evelyn's breath came out in a fog—the shop was as cold as the street, and smelled musty. She bent over the paraffin heater and lit up last week's oil, while from the first floor came the sound of Mrs. Foy's hip knocking against the dining table, rattling the china. The pine floorboards above Evelyn's head groaned.

"Shall I bring down some tea?"

This was their ritual. Every morning Mrs. Foy called down, arranged the tea, and they sat together at the small desk with the cash register, drank weak Tetley, and waited for the first customers to arrive. This could take hours. Sometimes Mrs. Foy had baked the night before and they might share a piece of fruitcake or a scone, and then she would bring out her knitting while Evelyn read. Mrs. Foy was always knitting—socks, scarves, pairs of booties. Evelyn didn't know what she did with all these woolen creations, for she had no family to give them to. Her latest project, a red balaclava, hung lifelessly from the hook above the stairs.

Usually this was a pleasant way to start their morning, but today, when Mrs. Foy paused her chatter to refill their cups, Evelyn moved away from the desk and began stacking the shelves near the front with the new stock.

"Is everything all right, dear?"

Evelyn kept her eyes on the books. "Oh, yes," she said, making her voice bright.

"Only you look a bit peaky." Mrs. Foy set down her cup. "Busy weekend, was it?"

"No, nothing like that."

Evelyn rubbed some dust off her nose with the flat of her palm. The stock from Hammersmith stank; it must have got wet in the truck and would have to be returned. Evelyn balled her hands into tight fists. She hated telephoning the account manager—he could talk for England.

"And your young man?"

"Stephen? He's fine."

"You must invite him to come by the shop." Mrs. Foy gathered up the tea things and returned them carefully to the tray. "I'd like to meet him."

Evelyn didn't say anything. She stared at the dark spines, the edges of her vision blurring. She wished Mrs. Foy would shut up.

"I said I'd like to meet him, dear."

"Yes, I heard you." Evelyn inhaled, held the breath, and forced a smile. "Maybe one day soon. We'll see."

She wandered back toward the desk, but Mrs. Foy was already halfway up the stairs, straining under the weight of the tray.

"*We'll see, we'll see,*" she was muttering. "That's all you young people say, isn't it, when you can't make up your minds."

"I'd like to," said Evelyn, holding up her palms to Mrs. Foy's back, almost beseeching. "But it's not so simple . . ."

"Sometimes I don't understand you at all, Evelyn. You were given a second chance. Most weren't so lucky . . ."

Mrs. Foy stopped on the landing. Her cheeks were pink, her calves inside a pair of charcoal-colored tights bulging like prize hams. She had once been a school matron and Evelyn thought her voice, especially at moments like this, still carried some of that prim reproach.

"You shouldn't leave it too long. I was lucky to meet Mr. Foy when I did, but he was a lot older than me." She stared past Evelyn to the

Indian rug at the foot of the stairs. "That's where he fell dead. Heart attack. One morning he got up, walked down these stairs, and never came back up them."

Evelyn had lost count of the times she had heard the story of Mr. Foy's demise. She stared at his portrait hanging above Mrs. Foy's head. There were many around the shop, but this was the best. It must have been taken before the first war, because he still possessed the slim languor of youth, a full head of fair hair, and a strong profile, turned away from the lens as had been the fashion, his left thumb hooked inside his waistcoat pocket. It was curious to imagine this man as Mrs. Foy's husband: it was almost impossible to believe she had ever been young.

As the old woman trundled on up the stairs, Evelyn went to the desk and began filing away the receipts. The ceiling groaned again with Mrs. Foy's pottering; she spoke to Alix and the crockery clattered in the sink. Evelyn stopped what she was doing and ran a fingertip over the cash register's metallic keys, an ache of regret in her chest. Mrs. Foy had only ever been kind to her, even when she knew her most shameful secret.

The morning remained quiet. A gentleman came in at eleven looking for some books on antiquity and eventually bought three of the rarer hardbacks for eight pounds. Afterward, two small boys came in asking for comics, but they left empty-handed, and Evelyn took an early lunch break in the square. She sat alone on the bench, nibbling at her stale sandwich. A chilly wind whipped along the path, skirting around her ankles; it wasn't at all pleasant outside. The rest of Bloomsbury must have felt the same way: apart from a disheveled-looking woman pushing a wailing child in a pram up and down the path, the gardens were empty.

She wondered if Stephen was nearby. They had met in this very square on a day when the sun had been out for the first time in weeks. Evelyn had been sitting on a different bench, near a rash of tulips, finishing her lunch. A few yards away two gardeners in rolled-up sleeves and waistcoats had been cutting the lawn with scythes, and as she listened to the whoosh of the blades slicing through the grass she had heard a tread on the gravel and found a man standing over her, his hat casting his face in shadow. He'd held up a brown paper bag and a thermos.

"Mind if I share your bench?"

It was only when he sat down that Evelyn saw his smooth face. He was younger than her and had a wispy blond mustache. She studied his careful movement with the sandwich—his long fingers, his delicate wrists—and when she looked up she was surprised to find him watching her, those hazel eyes amused, fine lines at their corners as he smiled.

Now, Evelyn wrapped up her lunch. She would finish it later. The woman with the pram had stopped at one end of the gardens as she tried to shove a bottle into her screaming child's mouth. Evelyn leaned back on the bench, observing the sparrows foraging about in the crumbs at her feet. They were awfully tame, though she supposed they knew danger when it presented itself. She watched them peck about between the pebbles, then raise their heads to her inquisitively, but when no further food arrived they flew away.

Evelyn peered up at the washed-out sky. It was her birthday next week, she realized. Last year Stephen had taken her on a day trip to Bath. They caught the early service from Paddington. The morning was fine, the air mild and full of the scent of fresh spring flowers. Stephen, who knew Bath, having spent every childhood summer at his grandmother's house on Wells Road, took her on a tour of the Abbey and the Roman baths, the Assembly Rooms in Bennett Street, and finally Royal Crescent, a sweeping arc of Georgian townhouses built from honey-colored stone, which they admired from an enormous grassy lawn across the street.

They had lunch at Sally Lunn's, sharing a main course of a chicken and ham hock trencher, with Evelyn trying one of the famous buns with cinnamon butter for dessert. While they ate, Stephen told her stories about his grandmother, who, among other things, had been a governess in Milan and had in later life shared her house on the hill with half a dozen cats. The rest of her family found the old woman difficult, but she had been fond of Stephen, and his visits were an opportunity for her to indulge in their shared passion: literature.

"She'd have great boxes of books waiting for me in my bedroom," he told Evelyn. "Milton, Dostoevsky, the Brontës, Conrad, Kipling, Austen of course. Once I'd read them we would have long discussions as we walked around town. About the characters and their experiences, but also their different ways of living. Gran was something of an eccentric herself: she had a cane and liked to wear a monocle, which I know some found a bit odd. But she was a rather frustrated person, I think. Very creative, and more free-spirited than she was allowed to be. Not well suited to her times. But never one to judge others, either."

"I suppose that outlook is handy when you live with six cats," said Evelyn.

"Yes." Stephen had laughed, but his eyes were tender. "I do miss the old dear. I should have liked her to meet you."

After lunch they perused the shops on a stroll over Pulteney Bridge ("It was inspired by the Ponte Vecchio in Florence," remarked Stephen, "but I think it's the more beautiful of the two"), then came back down Manvers Street toward the station. Stephen had stopped out the front of the George Bayntun bookshop and bindery.

"I thought we might quickly duck in." He looked up at the grand arched entrance. "Or is it too much of a busman's holiday for you . . . ?"

"Of course not," Evelyn said.

They went inside. While Stephen disappeared to find the bookseller, Evelyn browsed the rare editions in the glass display cabinets—there were a few prayer books, a Dante, and an elegant edition of *The House of Life* by Rossetti in straight-grained green goatskin. When Stephen returned he had a brown-paper package wrapped in string under his arm, but without further explanation he guided Evelyn from the shop, and they continued on toward the station. When they arrived on the platform, however, he pulled off his hat and ran a hand through his sandy-colored hair. He seemed nervous all of a sudden, tugging at his tie and shuffling his shoes. Eventually he handed Evelyn the package.

"I wondered if the bookshop would have it," he said, watching as she slowly loosened the string. "You see, it was the last thing Gran and I read together before . . . well . . ." He cleared his throat, his eyes shining. "I thought you might like it."

It was a copy of John Dryden's *All for Love*. It was a fairly recent edition from Stourton Press, no more than twenty years old, with gilt lettering on the spine and deckle edges.

"Gosh," Evelyn said, careful to keep her tone light as she turned the book over in her hands. "This is very thoughtful, Stephen. Thank you."

"It's only a small gift. But since it's your birthday . . ."

The London train had pulled into the platform and Stephen helped Evelyn climb aboard. Later, as he dozed in the seat next to her, the flattened land empty apart from the occasional stone cottage and field of barley flashing at the window, Evelyn thought again of the book in her handbag. She was touched by Stephen's gift and the sentiment attached to it, but it was hard not to feel some disquiet. After all, it contained the story of the final hours of Antony and Cleopatra, an ill-fated couple so tested by war, betrayal, and lies.

⌒

"Ah, Evelyn, you've just missed her."

Mrs. Foy stood behind the desk, flipping through the sales ledger, her eyes rheumy behind a pair of reading glasses.

"Who did I miss?" Evelyn asked, unwinding her scarf and hanging it next to her coat.

It was finally warm in the shop, almost snug. Evelyn smiled at Mrs. Foy, still feeling contrite after her brusqueness earlier; she resolved to make more of an effort with the old woman, starting with an invitation to the pictures. They could go on Friday, even have a late supper. After all, Mrs. Foy had been kinder to her than almost anyone else in London—and for once Evelyn wanted to show her some gratitude.

"She didn't leave her name. Well-bred lady. Dark hair. Nicely dressed."

Evelyn's vision crowded in an instant, and she put a hand against the door, her legs weak. So Julia had come for her.

"What did she want?"

"Hm?" Mrs. Foy was flicking through the ledger again.

"The woman." Evelyn tugged at her collar, the air in the shop thin. "What did she want?"

"Oh . . . It was about the Baudelaires, I think. Yes, that's it. She said she spoke to you last week." Mrs. Foy looked up, her eyes widening. "She's French, isn't she?"

Evelyn almost screamed. "You mean Mrs. du Cru?"

"Is that her name?"

"But why didn't you say?"

"Well, I didn't . . ." Mrs. Foy whipped off her glasses. "Are you quite all right, dear? You're as white as a ghost."

Evelyn had forgotten that the schoolmistress had arranged to collect the volumes of poetry for her pupils. She sagged against the door, almost faint with relief, as Mrs. Foy hurried over, grasping her by the shoulders and steering her around behind the desk. She went to fetch a glass of water and they sat together, Mrs. Foy rubbing Evelyn's back. After a few minutes like this, Evelyn said she was feeling better, and Mrs. Foy frowned and said, "I don't know about that!" But when Evelyn insisted, she finally relented, and went upstairs for her afternoon nap.

Evelyn waited a little while longer before she began to clean shelves toward the back of the shop, keeping an eye on the door. No one came in. She could hear the lilt of a violin—Brahms always sent Mrs. Foy to sleep. Alix basked in the small patch of light in the front window, licking one of her dainty silver paws. Eventually Evelyn went to the front door and flicked the sign to *Closed*. Mrs. Foy wouldn't mind; the morning sale was more than Evelyn had made all last week. She returned to the desk and picked up the telephone, dialing through to Stephen's office in Russell Square.

He picked up after a few rings, his mouth full; he must have been eating a late lunch at his desk. Something about this made Evelyn feel teary again.

"Stephen, it's me." She swallowed thickly. "It's Evelyn."

"Oh. Hello."

There was a pause as the line crackled.

"How are you?"

"Yes, fine, fine."

Evelyn heard rustling, the sound of a door closing, and she pressed the phone hard against her ear. She realized she had no idea what his office looked like, or what he might look like in it, and this ignorance panicked her, the past twelve months they had spent together slipping through her fingers like grains of sand.

"I thought . . ."

But what did she think? What on earth did she expect she might say? That she had wanted him to come over to the flat on Saturday? That she needed him? Evelyn had never asked anything of him before; what would he make of this request now? Her hand began to shake.

"I thought you might have telephoned. On the weekend. But you didn't, so . . ."

Stephen cleared his throat. He sounded very far away. Evelyn thought again of those hazel eyes, how they crinkled with his smile. He smiled so easily—and laughed. He was always laughing, though she never understood what he found so funny. Now she couldn't believe she had never asked.

"Listen here, Evelyn. I'm quite busy today with this Ovid stuff. If there was nothing else?"

"No," she said. "Well, I mean, there is . . . But it can wait."

"What is it?"

Had his voice softened? She couldn't tell. The telephone receiver grew warm in her grip.

"I wondered if you'd like to come by the flat tonight." She had lowered her voice to a whisper, worried that Mrs. Foy might hear; she wouldn't approve of these assignations, no matter her opinion of Evelyn. "I'd like to see you."

She listened to Stephen's even breath at the other end of the line. It was unbearable. Why wasn't he saying anything?

"I have to work late," he muttered finally. "But I might be able to pop around afterward."

Evelyn thanked him and rang off. Then she sat there, her head resting against the desk, shivering with raw cold. But amid that feeling was some sense of renewal as she raised her head and looked at the portrait of Mr. Foy, then at the place on the rug where he had died. Perhaps that was what upset Mrs. Foy so much: that her love had been snatched away, while Evelyn kept her heart closed to the man who wanted to share himself with her. She looked into her bag lying beneath the desk. There inside was the copy of the Dryden that Stephen had gifted to her in Bath. He couldn't know it, but she had carried it around with her ever since, bringing it out to read a passage or two, though always resisting the urge to plow on to the final act. Something about the book, emblematic as it was, meant that Evelyn needed to keep those last pages unread.

But that had all changed, she thought grimly as she turned toward the window where speckled light now filtered through the glass. The time had come for Evelyn to find a new kind of courage. Vincent had been right, after all. Some things did have to be brought up from the ground.

⌒

Evelyn left the shop at five o'clock and caught the train to Green Park. The early spring air had grown almost warm by the afternoon, though the wind still had bite, and a few flecks of rain struck her face as she emerged from the underground and wandered up Clarges Street.

This was the first time she'd been back to Mayfair since the start of the war. She stood out the front of number twenty-nine, eyes fixed on a second-floor window. Curzon Street was quiet and full of long shadows as the sun dropped and the sky lit up in an indigo haze. A taxi rolled by and Evelyn stepped back around the corner, where she waited until the lamp on the front porch came on and Sally Wesley appeared in the doorway. Though it had been nearly eight years since she had last seen her old friend, Evelyn would have recognized her silvery-blond hair anywhere, and the way she tilted her head as though she were always on the verge of asking a question. Sally spoke to someone inside, then closed the front door with a bang. Evelyn shrank back further as Sally marched down the pavement, her fur coat dwarfing her slight frame. She wore a black hat and her hair had been cut short, resting just above her shoulders; it suited her.

When it was safe to do so, Evelyn followed her. On Sally walked for perhaps a quarter of a mile, past South Street, until she stopped at the Grosvenor Chapel, a plain rectangular building with a portico on the west side and a short turquoise-colored spire containing the clock and bell that now struck for the six o'clock Eucharist.

Puzzled, Evelyn watched Sally stride into the chapel. She lingered on the other side of the street, reluctant to venture further—she had always hated the cloisters, the stonework bearing down on her, the hard pews—but she was curious about what she might find in there. After a quick survey of the footpath she strode across the road and in through the great oak doors. The pews were half full, not a bad congregation for a weeknight, and Sally was seated toward the front. Evelyn found a spot at the back and the service began. After some singing and a sermon, the congregation filed up the aisle for their fill of the blood and body of Christ.

Evelyn watched the parishioners. Faith could have found a place in her life once, and she saw the appeal of the sublimation, the submission, the trust in a higher power, especially after everything the world had slowly come to understand about the war. The absolving of responsibility, the abstract explanation for the most unspeakable wrongs . . . that could have suited her very nicely. But it wasn't an honest way to live—not for her, anyway. Besides, she'd never trusted anyone enough to believe in something she couldn't see.

When it was Sally's turn to approach the altar, she kept her eyes on the floor with an air of piety that struck Evelyn as false. She looked thin, almost gaunt, and like Julia she had aged; her face had somehow grown longer, pouchier. Evelyn watched the vicar perform the rest of the sacrament. As she returned to her seat, Sally raised her eyes toward a low-lit chandelier before they settled on Evelyn, and in that brief moment Evelyn felt a blister of pain run along the aisle before she glanced away to her hymnbook. When she looked again Sally had sat down, her attention once more directed toward the vicar. Was that it? After all this time, was there to be no shouting, no clamor, no scuffle? Evelyn waited for a few moments, but Sally just stared resolutely at the altar.

As "When I Survey the Wondrous Cross" resounded through the chapel, Evelyn edged out of the pew and slipped outside. She began pacing the block, stamping her feet against the cold. She wondered now if it had been a mistake to come, but still she strode around the perimeter of the Mount Street Gardens at the back of the chapel.

About twenty minutes passed before Evelyn heard voices near the doors and the congregation spilled out onto the pavement. There was some mingling beneath a lamp, and amid the crowd Evelyn saw Sally speak to a couple before breaking away and walking down the road in the direction of Curzon Street.

Evelyn followed, lagging a hundred or so yards behind for the rest of South Audley. On the corner, however, Sally stopped. She didn't turn, but her head was cocked, listening. Evelyn slowed and stopped too.

"I thought you might do a better job of tailing me than that." Sally's voice came out almost as a sigh. She spun around, her hands planted on her hips. "Or have you suddenly found an interest in religion?"

Evelyn's arms hung limp at her sides. Sally was staring at her, waiting.

"I know it's been a long time, but I thought we might finally have more to say to one another." Evelyn hesitated, fumbling over her words, as Sally began to shake her head. Had she really thought she could just turn up here and tie up threads of the past like ribbon around a box? "But I can see that won't be possible."

"And why is that?"

"I suppose because we both see what happened differently."

She might have aged in the years since they last saw one another, but Evelyn still recognized the spark of curiosity in Sally's round blue eyes.

"You go alone, then, to church?" she asked.

Sally shrugged. "Jonty doesn't care for it."

Evelyn nodded. The breeze whistled around them, receded. "How is Jonty?"

"He won't believe I've run into you . . ." Sally narrowed her eyes. "He's left the air force and joined his father's company. We have a son now. He's three."

"A son."

"Yes. Hugh."

Evelyn felt faint. There was so much she wanted to ask, but Sally would never let her. They stared at one another across the shadowy pavement. It was getting late. Evelyn was cold and hungry. She thought of the house on Curzon Street—the soft light, the plush furnishings, all that warmth—and indulged in the daydream of Sally asking her inside, pointing to the room on the second floor where a bed had been made up, reminding her that this would always be her home.

"You shouldn't be here." The spite had left Sally's voice. She sounded as tired as Evelyn felt, and as sad. And it *was* sad, what had been lost between them—Evelyn had let go of enough anger over the years to appreciate that. She took a step forward.

"I wanted to hear you say it, that's all," she said. "I thought if we ever saw each other again, you might have it in your heart to say it."

"Say what?"

"That you understand why I did it." Evelyn swallowed. "That you forgive me."

They were standing in a pool of milky moonlight. The surrounding houses were dark and quiet, but lights shone in a few windows at number twenty-nine. The front door opened and Jonty stepped out onto the porch. Evelyn recognized his broad shoulders, his flat face, though she doubted he could make her out from that distance. When she looked back to Sally and saw tears in her eyes, Evelyn felt herself transported with a lurch back to that train ride from Wesley Manor after the engagement party when Sally had warned her about her willingness to overlook the faults of those awful girls at Raheen. Sally had been right, in the end, though not in the way she had imagined. No one could have predicted that future, Evelyn thought bitterly.

"I stopped being angry with you years ago, Evelyn. What's done is done." Sally took a few quick steps away but paused, and when she spoke again her voice was barely a whisper. "I don't care about why you did it, or about what you told yourself that made it right in your own head. You betrayed me and my family, and though I loved you I can never forgive you for it."

They stood gazing miserably at one another. It was true: the past was behind them. They could never go back. Life marches you forward no matter how hard you dig in your heels. It had taken Evelyn a long time to understand that too—but this was the first time she had acknowledged the truth of it to herself. If she had done so earlier, she would never have come to Mayfair and sought Sally out. She would have saved herself from the wretched feeling squeezing the breath out of her. Because she had come looking for absolution tonight, no matter what she told herself, and Sally couldn't give it to her—no one could.

She watched Sally turn and sprint across the road, pushing past Jonty, and a few seconds later Evelyn heard the slam of the heavy front door. Then she glanced along the cold street, where shadows like spider's legs made a pattern through the old birch, and set off toward the underground.

JANUARY 1940

THIRTEEN

NINA IVANOV'S LARGE dining room was painted white and decorated with a single armorial plate mounted on the wall, while a portrait of the Tsar had been propped against the mantelpiece. A fire in the hearth warmed the room, and sounds and smells of cooking were coming from the kitchen, the air full of the aroma of butter, onion, and something else fragrant, like cinnamon.

Evelyn smiled around the table. Nina had made the introductions when she first arrived, Evelyn's heart hammering in her chest, legs so flimsy she feared they might collapse beneath her. But she had managed to remember a few names—Mrs. Guthrie and Miss de Crespigny, for instance—while those belonging to the other women glancing at her now and then with a mix of curiosity and wariness she would need to get later from Mrs. Armstrong, who sat at the other end of the table. Everyone was a lot older than Evelyn, with gray hair and crepey skin at their throats, and as they spoke about their recent Christmas celebrations ("So dreary this year!" they bemoaned), their wayward children, and problems with the tutor or the cook, she began to relax. It was familiar, this quiet snobbery, like an old language she hadn't spoken in a while. She could have been back at university for one of those dreadful parent dinners, or at a gathering of the local Women's Institute; Evelyn half expected someone to bring out baskets of oranges and invite them to make marmalade. It hardly felt like a gathering of German sympathizers, but she knew that she must remain on her guard. Even a moment of complacency could blow her cover.

Evelyn had been seated next to Isadore Randall at the head of the table. Mrs. Randall picked at her food uninterestedly, not talking much to the other women, but whenever a remark was lobbed her way she'd give a nod or a grunt of regal assent, and the conversation would continue.

"How nice for you all to get together like this," Evelyn said once Nina had finally sat down to her own supper. "It must be lovely to have such a large group of friends."

Nina brushed away a few strands of hair coiling at her temple. "We enjoy it," she said demurely.

"And how do you know one another?"

"Well"—she turned to Mrs. Randall—"it has mainly been through other clubs, hasn't it?"

"And my church. Crown Court, in Covent Garden."

"That's right." Evelyn nodded toward the other end of the table. "That's how you know Mrs. Armstrong."

"Andrew and I have been friendly with Gertrude for years," said Mrs. Randall. "Nearly ten, it must be. She's been so helpful on the committee; our longest-serving secretary, in fact."

"And is that what brings you all together?" asked Evelyn, sipping on her wine. "Faith?"

"In a way." Nina cut her omelette into small pieces and placed one delicately in her mouth. "But mainly we talk about culture and ideas, like in a salon. Our model is the Literaturnoye Kafe in Saint

Petersburg. Sometimes one of us will read from a novel, or recite a bit of poetry."

"But it isn't all books. You do know Nina is also famous in the world of fashion?" said Mrs. Randall, setting down her knife and fork and turning her stern gaze on Evelyn. "You'll have heard of Nina de Ivanov Haute Couture Modes in the West End?"

"Of course—that's you, Nina?" Evelyn wiped her mouth with the napkin. "How very impressive. First-class cook *and* dressmaker."

"Oh no, she's a genuine *couturier.*"

"I don't know about that," Nina said, pouring herself a glass of water. "I sold a bit of everything there, remember—frocks, hats, evening gowns, and jewelry—though it was to some of the wealthiest people in Europe. But the business suffered when the Litvak tailors moved in, and then I lost my financier, Major McPhee. Still, one must make the best of a bad situation, and working from home means I now have a more select clientele."

"You're too modest," Mrs. Randall cried.

"I don't like to boast."

"My dear"—Mrs. Randall rested her claw-like hand over Evelyn's, the jewels on her fingers shimmering cruelly under the light—"Nina has more friends of influence than the rest of us combined. Your mother still takes tea with Queen Mary, does she not?"

"It's true." Nina's eyes had grown brighter; evidently she did like to boast. "And of course another good friend is a well-known attaché to the Italian embassy."

"And doesn't he throw the best parties!"

"Yes," Nina said, almost tittering. "Very gay."

"Very wicked, more like." Mrs. Randall raised her eyebrows at Evelyn, and she made sure to look appropriately scandalized. Some transgressions, it seemed, were acceptable to the Lion Society.

They made an odd pair, Evelyn thought. The nervous, suspicious Russian and the aloof, meandering patrician. Where Nina's manners were sober (she hadn't touched any wine nor smoked), her gestures abrupt and skittish, Mrs. Randall had that rambling way of talking common to the upper class, as if she were conducting the conversation with herself, only to suddenly sharpen her focus on a particular word or phrase and almost flay Evelyn with her fierce attention.

"You must tell us some more about yourself, dear," she instructed as a *korolevsky* cake was brought out for dessert.

Evelyn shifted in her seat. They had already talked around the edges, with Evelyn explaining what she did at Whitehall with the inventory logs, the telephone calls, sprinkling some details about the rumored internments. Nina and Mrs. Randall had appeared cautious—they never showed too much interest, but Evelyn sensed that Nina, in particular, had been storing away everything she said to be picked over later.

"You're not from London, originally?" Mrs. Randall prompted her.

"No, I grew up in a town called Lewes," Evelyn said. "Then I went on to Oxford after Raheen. I enjoyed my time there; in fact, I rather miss it. There was so much more I wanted to learn."

"You're not learning at the War Office?" Nina watched her slyly. In the bright dining room her pinned-back hair shone auburn.

Evelyn smiled. "I'm certainly learning about the limits of our government," she said casually. "There's no real leadership, for starters—if I'm honest, it's chaos."

"How so?"

"Well, for one thing, no one was prepared for Chamberlain's declaration. There weren't enough staff, not even enough desks, if you can believe it. That set us back months." Evelyn drank the last mouthful of wine in her glass; what was that—her third? Her head was beginning to feel like it had been stuffed with candy floss.

"I'm not the only one who thinks like this. Morale is low, which gets all sorts of rumors going. I've seen some vicious rows, too. The undersecretary—"

"Johnny Lyttelton?" Mrs. Randall raised an eyebrow. "Why, he's a good friend of ours!"

"Oh yes?" Evelyn wasn't sure where to go with all this, but she had no choice but to push on. "The thing is, we're all a bit fed up on our floor, me and the other girls. The typists. It's like no one is listening . . ."

Glancing at Mrs. Randall, Nina frowned, some color leaving her cheeks. "What do you mean?"

Evelyn felt herself falter. To hide it, she reached for her glass of water and took a gulp, but all that wine had made her sluggish. She could feel heat creeping across her face. She had come on strong; revealed too much too soon—she must have, or else why would Nina be staring at her like that, expectant, a hand raised to that faint scar on her temple?

"Well, I suppose what they really want is a better Britain," she finally said. "It's what we all want, isn't it? They just don't quite know where to look for it." She paused, smiling grimly. "I tell them it would be best if Chamberlain had held firm on appeasement. I hear things they don't, of course, so I suppose they are inclined to believe me."

"That can't be a popular opinion in the rest of Whitehall," said Nina as someone brought out coffee with a jug of cream, and a box of Rowntree's Black Magic was passed reverently around the table.

"Yes, you could find yourself in a lot of trouble if you expressed those views outside this flat," Mrs. Randall agreed.

With a shrug, Evelyn accepted the chocolate box, choosing a marzipan. She handed it on to Mrs. Randall.

"Maybe. But it's what I think, and I don't care who knows it."

Again Nina glanced at Mrs. Randall, frowning, until the older woman laughed, her crowded teeth glistening.

"Well said, dear. The fish stinks first at the head, as the Turks say. Little wonder we're losing this war." She bit into her chocolate and made a face. "Oh, it's ghastly cherry. I had hoped for caramel!"

⌒

By eleven o'clock, most of Nina's guests had gone, abandoning the round of backgammon that had commenced at the dining table after brandy, the few remaining now smoking by the fire with Mrs. Randall.

Evelyn said her goodbyes, but as Nina accompanied her to the front door she stopped midway down the shadowy hall. "May I show you something?"

She opened a door that led into a room with a long, rectangular table in the middle covered with measuring tapes, scissors, canisters of pins and tacks. A sewing machine sat at one end. Lining the back wall were shelves of wools, trims of leather, silk, rayon crepe, and Moygashel linen, every color and texture imaginable, and on the left wall were two racks sagging under the weight of dresses and shawls on hangers. In the far right-hand corner, where Nina now stood, was another white wooden door, with a latch and bolt, which must at one time have led to the kitchen.

Evelyn went to the black velvet dress studded with elegant gold buttons hanging from the rack nearest to her, running the hem through her fingers.

"How is it fair you have more than one talent?"

Nina leaned against the back shelf, toying with a piece of violet-colored silk. "Are you not talented, Evelyn?" she asked.

"Oh, I don't know. I do a few things quite well, but nothing exceptionally."

"Not your work?"

"I'm diligent, if that's what you mean. But this—it's creative. It's enterprising."

"Do you want to be a dressmaker?"

"Well, no, but . . ."

Nina folded her arms, smiling faintly. "Then isn't it pointless to be envious of what you don't want?"

It was a strange sort of logic, thought Evelyn, her eyes drawn to the bulb hanging from the ceiling. A few moths hovered nearby, nudging against the glass.

"I suppose I don't know what I want," she said.

She watched Nina go to the worktable, where she reached for the silver scissors. Then she picked up a piece of wool that had frayed at the tip, examining it beneath the light.

"I shut myself away in here after my shop closed," she said quietly. "Day, night, no sleep, barely a bite to eat. My parents tried to coax me out, but I wouldn't budge. I just couldn't accept that I had failed. But somehow I managed to convince myself that if I worked hard enough for long enough things would go back to how they were—that my shop would reopen and thrive; that I would be someone again. It was all I cared about, because I didn't know what to be without the shop. Then, one day, it must have been months later, I woke up and understood my mistake. I had believed the failure was my own doing. That I had done something wrong."

Nina raised the scissors and with a firm snap severed the frayed wool.

"When something is stolen from you, it's only natural to seek reparation," she murmured, turning her dark eyes to Evelyn. "You understand this, I think."

After Nina turned off the workshop light, she guided Evelyn along the hallway toward the front door. Slipping on her coat, Evelyn hoped another invitation would be issued, but Nina was silent, only reaching for the latch. Then she paused and looked over her shoulder.

"You mentioned your colleagues at the War Office," she began. "The typists . . . "

"Yes?"

"Well, as you know, I'm always on the lookout for new friends." Nina blew out her cheeks, giving a shrug, as though it was of little consequence to her. "Perhaps I might get their names and addresses from you? I had in mind to write them a note, perhaps invite them to tea." She laughed, a scratchy sound that Evelyn hadn't heard before. "If nothing else, it will bring down the average age of our group by a decade or two. But it's no trouble if . . ." She trailed off.

Evelyn felt herself smile inwardly. Here it was. The first bargaining chip. The first proof of loyalty, and the first betrayal. She almost felt pity for Nina, except for the trace of reticence in her face as she pulled open the door, peering around the jamb. Evelyn hadn't won her over yet.

"I'm sure I can arrange it," she said.

Nina gave her a curt nod. "Good. And listen, Evelyn. Next Sunday afternoon B. L. Chesterfield is giving a lecture at Caxton Hall. Would you like to come? I think you'd enjoy it."

"All right," said Evelyn. "I'll put it in my diary."

"Good." Nina nodded again. "*Dobroy nochi.*"

It was as much a dismissal as a farewell, with a brisk kiss on each cheek, and Evelyn found herself moving fast down those stairs, the air outside hitting her like a slap, the shudder of snow on the passing terrace roofs the only other movement as she hastened along the footpath toward the underground, desperate to be home.

When Evelyn arrived at work on Monday, she found the flat empty. There was a note, however, on her desk from White, instructing her to meet him at the Press Club at eight o'clock that evening. After typing up her daily report for Ted, Evelyn locked up and left, catching the bus at Lupus Street to Whitehall Place. The club was hidden away at the end of a narrow lane and accessed via a set of stairs. She was greeted by the maître d'hôtel and guided away from the dining tables in the main reception area to a darkish room at the back of the building. There, by the large window, sat White, a small candle in the middle of the table, a half-empty bottle of champagne chilling in a bucket of ice nearby.

"Good evening, Evelyn. I hope you don't mind that I've already eaten." He tapped his wristwatch. "I need to be at the Savoy by ten to brief the Home Secretary on your investigation."

After the waiter had brought over two coffees, Evelyn described her first encounter with the women of the Lion Society. "To be honest, it was all rather anodyne, sir," she said. "Most of the night I felt like I had stumbled on a WI meeting, not the latest collective of the Valkyrie. Still, Nina put in a request, as you predicted: a list of typists from the War Office. She's obviously eager to recruit."

"Good," White said. "I think half a dozen names should do it. Won't be too tricky for the Ministry of Supply to rustle that up. And the next meet?"

"Sunday. Nina invited me along to Caxton Hall for the Chesterfield rally."

White nodded. "You're making progress, Evelyn."

"I had also hoped to arrange an introduction to your old agent, Posey? I'm keen to pick her brains about the Woolwich Arsenal case."

White stirred some sugar into his coffee then licked the spoon.

Wind groaned at the glass. "Susanna? I'm afraid that won't be possible."

"Has she moved departments?"

White leaned back in his chair. He studied Evelyn as she drank from her small cup, something bleak moving across his features.

"She's no longer in the Service," he said. "In fact, she doesn't live in London anymore. She emigrated to Australia after the trial." There was a long pause and White's eyes grew wide. "Didn't I say?"

Evelyn stared at the grainy silt left in the bottom of her cup and shook her head. White spread his hands, a shrug his only apology. Outside, the wind had died away and the snow began to collect on the sill. As White sat there quietly, fiddling with the pewter candlestick holder, Evelyn wasn't quite sure what to say. Finally he pushed out his chair and stood up.

"You don't need to talk to Posey," he said. "Everything you need to know about her, all her methods, was in that file. Even, if you needed reminding of it, the toll such an investigation can take on a person. Focus on that membership list, Evelyn—and on exposing the leaks."

"All right." Evelyn watched him turn toward the door. "By the way, do I have one, sir?"

White turned back. "One what?"

"A code name. In the reports that Ted is compiling from my investigation?"

"Oh, yes . . ." White tugged at his collar. "It's Chameleon. Rather apt, wouldn't you say?"

After he'd gone, Evelyn sat alone at the table, the coffee churning in her stomach. She had always thought it strange for Posey's portrait to be in the file, but she wondered now if it had been an oblique message. Or perhaps even a warning.

FOURTEEN

AFTER A VISIT to the fruit and vegetable stalls at the Berwick Street market, Evelyn got changed back at the flat and made her way to Panton Street. She had arranged to meet Julia at the theater. They had tickets to the Saturday matinee of *They Walk Alone* by Max Catto, a play set to music about a servant girl who begins murdering young men from her village.

"It's a comedy, then?" Evelyn asked as they found their seats in the loge.

"Do keep an open mind. I've heard terrific things, especially about the lead, Emmy." Julia rubbed her hands together as the curtains rolled back. "I really did miss the West End when I was in Berlin," she whispered. "Of course, they have plenty of theater and music too, but they go for all that feverish Mahler and Wagner, which I don't like at all. And you know I can't bring Sally to anything. She's like a child, forever asking when she can be taken out for her ice cream."

Evelyn smiled. "How is old Sal? She's gone awfully quiet."

Julia rolled her eyes as the lights dimmed. "She's hardly been quiet at Curzon Street, I can assure you. Let's just say if I hear the word *wedding* again I may go on a killing spree myself."

Evelyn enjoyed the play. It was melodramatic, which was unsurprising, and the austere orchestral music was rather jarring alongside the high-pitched dialogue, but it was fun sitting up there in the box with Julia laughing at her side, aware of the admiring looks from the other theater-goers; Julia, dressed as she was in a gray pantsuit, a heavy necklace of jade against her slim throat, looked a little like an actress herself, Evelyn thought.

Afterward they walked over to Regent Street. Julia may not have wanted to hear about Sally's wedding, but it was only six weeks away and Evelyn needed to find herself an outfit. They visited a few department stores, and then found a small modiste, Laurent & Co., down Regent Lane on Warwick Street, near the Catholic church. Evelyn had a look through the dresses, growing more and more dispirited, until she found what she wanted hanging on the end of the rack. It was made of pale blue silk, with silver buttons down the front and an apricot sash tied in a loose bow at the back. She checked the label—House of Worth—and asked the proprietress the price. It was twenty-five pounds, more than she could ever hope to afford.

"We'll take it," Julia said, sweeping past Evelyn toward the counter.

"What? No, Julia, we won't."

Julia brought out her checkbook. "What else should I spend my allowance on?"

"I don't know. Certainly not on me."

Julia looked at her and frowned. "But you're my friend," she said, as though she were explaining something very simple. "And it will give me pleasure."

Evelyn felt her cheeks burn. She didn't want to be Julia's charity case. But the dress really was exquisite, the silk slipping through her fingers as cool and sleek as a stream. She'd never owned anything so fine, and with a pang she wondered what her mother would do in this situation.

Such an opportunity . . .

"I really can't," she said. "Please."

But Julia put her hand on Evelyn's arm. "Don't think on it too much. Sometimes life gifts us beautiful things—and all we must do in return is enjoy them. Do be careful, though . . ." She bent over the counter to scribble her signature on the check. "You might just upstage the bride."

"Goodness, don't say that!" Evelyn covered her mouth. Sally could be capricious when she least expected it.

"Come on." Julia handed over the large box tied with a lilac ribbon. "You can buy the wine at dinner to say thanks."

They strolled the half-mile over to Covent Garden. The streets were quiet: it was that lull of the late afternoon, the sky a swatch of color as the sun sank, right before the evening roared to life. They headed up Southampton Street and stopped at Boulestin, a restaurant decorated with circus-themed murals, and took a table inside by the windows.

"It's just like being in Paris." Julia sighed happily. "You know André Groult did the decorations?" She snapped the menu shut. "Why am I looking at that? I know exactly what I'm having!"

They ordered a bottle of wine, a white from the Loire Valley, and Julia ordered the Basque piperade for herself, the escalope de veau Choisy for Evelyn, and the tarte Tatin to share for dessert. It was strange seeing Julia with an appetite; Evelyn wasn't sure she had ever seen her eat.

"Hans and I used to go to Paris in the autumn," she said, tearing into a fresh bread roll. "We'd stay in this little hotel in the fourth arrondissement around the corner from his favorite jazz club on Rue de Rivoli. It's built into a twelfth-century vaulted cellar." She paused, chewing. "We did have some good times together."

"The fourth arrondissement," Evelyn said. "That's in the Marais, isn't it?"

"Yes, the Jewish quarter." Julia reached for her wine, watching Evelyn curiously. "Have you been to Paris?"

Evelyn shook her head. "Actually, I've never been out of England."

Julia set down her glass. "Not even with your parents?" She stared, incredulous. "But you are so worldly, so clever."

Evelyn laughed. "Is that something only achieved through travel?"

"I think so. If I had stayed in England, I probably would have ended up in a gutter somewhere, penniless and disgraced."

"I find that hard to believe."

"Well, disgraced, certainly." Julia rested her chin on her hand. "I don't think I knew myself until I went to Berlin, and in an odd way I came to better understand others too. What we want as people, what we desire. What happens if we can't get it."

"Don't we all desire the same sort of thing?" Evelyn said, drinking some wine. "Good health, an education and vocation, opportunity for our family."

"Yes, I think so," said Julia. "But what frustrates me is that we don't need wealth for all that."

"We do in England," Evelyn murmured. "There is a great divide between the rich and the poor."

"I agree. And that is the fault of government, isn't it? We need strong leadership to bring about more opportunity, and stronger controls around our economy. It's unbelievable what I've seen during my time at the Benevolent Society. The squalor of the Peabody Estate in Shadwell, for instance, where English children are literally starving to death. What kind of country can live with that on its conscience?"

Some people, Evelyn's father included, would think Julia frivolous, spoiled even. Yet though it was true that Julia had led a privileged life, she seemed to Evelyn like someone willing to test the structures that shaped the world they all lived in rather than simply accepting them. Evelyn knew enough to understand how rare that was, and raising her eyes to the silk balloon lights hanging from the ceiling, she felt a warm spread of happiness.

"We must go," Julia was saying as the waiter brought over their meals. "To Paris. When this ridiculous war is over. We'll stay in the Marais and we'll go to that jazz club." She clapped her hands, excited. "Wouldn't that be splendid?"

"What about your navy man?" Evelyn asked. "Wouldn't he like to travel with you?"

"Yes, I imagine he would."

"Is he coming to Sally's wedding?"

"I don't know." Julia turned her face toward the window, squinting a little. "I haven't decided."

"And your father?"

"Oh, yes. He'll be there." Julia's mouth twitched. "Along with his child bride."

Evelyn glanced down at the table. Here was a sore point. She had heard from Sally that Julia's stepmother was young—younger, even, than Julia.

"How long have they been married?"

"Two years. Being in Germany meant I missed the wedding. Everyone was relieved about that, especially my father."

"You don't get along, then—you and your stepmother?"

Julia picked up her knife and spread some butter on the roll. "She's not my mother," she said. "Why should I pretend to have any affection for her? Or for my father. I only ever loved him because my mother did."

Evelyn stared at the glint of Julia's knife. "How old were you when she died?"

"Ten."

"And you were close?"

Julia blinked. "I don't know," she said. "I'm not sure I ever really knew her. I had a nanny, then a governess, and then I went away to school. I never spent more than an hour at a time in her company. She never visited me at school, barely wrote, but she did summon me home before she died. She knew, I think, how sick she was, even if my father didn't. I was there in the room with her at the end . . ." Julia smiled faintly, but her eyes had grown glassy. "We're told from childhood to love our parents. That it is unconditional, that it must never waver. A bit like love of one's country, isn't it? Oh, but what am I like!" she suddenly cried, dabbing at her eye with the corner of the napkin. "Did you put a truth serum in the wine, Evelyn? I never talk about my mother, not to anyone!"

"It's quite all right," Evelyn said, pleased that Julia had confided in her, and she signaled for the waiter to refill their glasses.

When he was gone, Julia began spooning the piperade into her mouth, and after a minute she sat back, her hands folded in her lap, a look of contentment returning to her face. Evelyn thought about her own mother standing at the kitchen sink, the slope of her shoulders, that fragile bun. She could see the course of their estrangement like footprints trailing down the hallway and out the front door, but for once it didn't feel as though she had done something wrong.

FIFTEEN

ON SUNDAY, EVELYN walked through St. James's Park and took the path alongside Horse Guards Road into Westminster. It had been a cold morning, the low, gray sky threatening rain, but some blue had now crept in among the clouds. Crowds of well-dressed men and women in dark suits and coats were swirling beneath the marquee signage of Caxton Hall as though arriving for a gala or theater show.

Evelyn met Nina by the front steps and they went inside, pausing to inspect the pamphlets being sold from a trestle table on the edge of the foyer before heading up the wooden staircase beneath the long stained-glass window. Their seats were in the western parterre box where Mrs. Randall already sat, her opera glasses out, smiling and waving as she recognized faces in the crowd. Mrs. Guthrie and Miss de Crespigny from the Lion Society sat in the row behind.

Evelyn gazed over the expanse of the hall, craning her neck to take in the stalls. The venue was full, there must have been three thousand people there, and the room vibrated with the cacophony of shrill voices. All of a sudden, the main lights went out, a spotlight pierced the stage, and a man shuffled out to the microphone by the stalls on the right. After thanking the Anglo-German Fellowship for sponsoring the lecture, he introduced B. L. Chesterfield, an unremarkable-looking man in a brown suit. The audience clapped excitedly as he brought out his notes.

"Some of you are probably wondering if this war will ever start in earnest," he began, squinting into the black sea before him. "And you have a right to wonder. We have been kept in this purgatory for months now and are still no closer to breaking free. Of course, we all know how the tension began. Herr Hitler invaded Czechoslovakia; there is no denying that. But invasion and colonization are the story of empire. Of *our* empire. They are what make nations like ours great powers of this world. And so what should have been considered as an inevitable, even favorable, expansion by our friends in Berlin was taken up as an emblem of fear by the hysterical left-wing press." He paused, dropping the papers to stare into the audience, and when he spoke again it was without his notes. "I am not alone in this belief. Not only is this war a needless one, it is an immoral one. And whom should we blame when our sons are killed in battle? The Jew, my friends, who has stoked tensions here and on the Continent, hindering our efforts to secure peace with Germany."

The crowd cheered and stamped their feet. In the dark, Evelyn could make out Mrs. Randall's furious nodding, while Nina was leaning forward, her hands gripping her knees as she stared down at the stage. A smile fluttered on Chesterfield's thin lips as he held up a hand for quiet.

"Let me give you an example of their lies," he cried. "Some of you may have heard of Kristallnacht, when the Nazi stormtroopers entered Jewish quarters across Germany, Austria, and Sudetenland. It was a bloody affair, to be sure, with Germans and Jews both killed in equal numbers. The newspapers, your *Mirror*s and your *Daily Herald*s, blamed the Sturmabteilung, which was to be expected, since our press is almost entirely run by Jews and their supporters. But what these newspapers didn't tell us was the truth: that the Germans only acted in retaliation; that the pogroms began after the German official Ernst vom Rath was murdered in Paris—not by a deranged Pole, but at the behest of a secret Jewish cabal based right here in London. The conspiracy starts on our very doorstep, my friends, and we must stand together to rid our country and our people of this pernicious, filthy stain, and seek peace with Germany to end this war."

The crowd roared again, louder and more febrile.

It's mad, Evelyn thought, peering into the stalls. The worst kind of propaganda, trawling the sewers of a depraved mind. But his audience didn't care, she realized, her blood running cold. Truth didn't matter. These people had come because they knew they would have their insane beliefs confirmed.

Evelyn could sense Nina's gleaming eyes searching out hers in the dark, her small hands finally coming together in vigorous applause. Tears pricked Evelyn's eyes as she joined in, louder and more raucous than the rest of them, her thoughts fixed on Vincent and his mother, and that haunted look in the photograph, as if Anna had had some terrible knowledge not only of her own fate but of the place to which she had sent her sons.

Chesterfield continued, lambasting Fleet Street, the War Office, and Westminster itself for harboring the enemy, people he called "greasy little Jew-boy pornographers." It went on like this, growing wilder and more vulgar, until the crowd were on their feet, screaming, "The King, the King," and giving Nazi salutes. The hall seemed to swell like a dreadful tide, and then everyone started singing along to a recording that blasted through the speakers mounted beneath the empty house seats, and it took a moment for Evelyn to recognize the trumpets of "Das Lied der Deutschen," the German national anthem.

As row after row of men and women stood with hands over their hearts, Evelyn could not look away, as if she herself were in a weird trance, and for some reason she recalled a bonfire night when her father took her to watch the procession from the Waterloo site in Lewes. It had been bitterly cold—Evelyn recalled the whip of wind at her cheeks and the end of her nose, and how her father had wrapped her in his great woolen coat as they stood with a few hundred other townsfolk in the lush field next to the Ouse. When the procession approached, Evelyn had seen how the leaders of the carnival club, each dressed in the red coats of the British regiments with rifles slung across their shoulders, bore an enormous flaming cross. Behind them came a drum platoon, sounding a throbbing beat that Evelyn felt in her back teeth, stirring up something deep and unfathomable. Soon enough the pack of spectators began to swell and push, and she was torn loose from the shelter of her father's coat.

He had hoisted her onto his shoulders after that. He wasn't a big man; she could feel his sharp bones beneath his coat, and his legs buckled for a moment before he steadied the weight of her. From that height Evelyn could see everything: the leering guy doll, as big as a giant from *Gulliver's Travels*, the smaller, wrinkled pontiff, and the dozens of burning crucifixes like something from a nightmare as they blazed through the dark.

Perhaps her father had sensed her trembling, because he strained his neck to ask, "Are you all right?" But she hadn't been afraid. Something else had awakened in her, a quickening of the blood. She had stared at the guy, at the deep wells of his eyes, and felt a thrill work its way from the bottom of her spine to the top of her head.

"*Evelyn?*"

It was Nina, hands gripping her shoulders, shaking her just as her father had that night.

She looked around. Chesterfield had left the stage and their box had begun to fill up with people from the adjacent alcove.

"Come along." Nina took her arm. "Let's catch up with the others."

But outside men and women were spilling from the entrance, making it impossible to break away and locate their companions in the crowd.

"Never mind," said Nina as they were borne across the street by the movement of the throng. "We're all meeting at the flat later anyway."

They continued on through St. James's Park. The assembly comprised several hundred people, those up the front holding placards and banners, Chesterfield himself leading the procession. Nina and Evelyn stayed toward the back, happy to walk at a more sedate pace through the gardens, which were still busy despite the approaching dusk.

"Are you all right?" Nina stopped to examine Evelyn's face, her own unusually animated. "You look quite dazed."

"Yes, I'm fine." From the corner of her eye, Evelyn glimpsed children throwing bread to the ducks on the lake. What did they make of this ghastly parade? "But it was incredible, wasn't it? I've never seen anything—heard anything—like that in my entire life!"

"Nor me," said Nina. "It certainly lifts the spirits."

"You think it's true, then, what Chesterfield said about the pogroms and the press?"

"Oh, yes." Nina stared resolutely ahead. "We had the same problem in Russia. It was the Jew creditors, in fact, exerting all that pressure on the peasants that led to the overthrow of the Tsar. They control everything, you know. The press, the banks, even the monarchy." She sniffed. "Because of them my family was forced from our home and from our position in society. The Jews ruined our lives."

They rounded the corner, Buckingham Palace looming on the left. In a few minutes, they would cross into Green Park and make their way toward the underground. Evelyn paused to gaze up at the gilded bronze of *Winged Victory* standing there on her globe, a victor's palm in her hand, but a moment later she regretted it—if she hadn't hesitated, she would have missed the clear, bell-like cry of *"Evelyn!"*

She stopped dead. It was Julia on the other side of the roundabout by the grass, her bulky coat dragging almost to the ground, a lead looped over her wrist, Tortoise attached to the end of it and sniffing at a lamppost.

"I thought it was you! What a coincidence finding you here." Julia came toward them, smiling wide in delight.

"Isn't it!" Evelyn's voice sounded off kilter, like the pin had been set wrong on the gramophone. She stood there like another statue, paralyzed by indecision. Tortoise gave her thumb a half-hearted lick.

"And who is your friend?" Julia asked pleasantly.

"I'm sorry." Evelyn shook herself back to life. "This is Miss Nina Ivanov."

"Pleased to meet you." Julia raised a finger as though testing the wind. "*Ivanov* . . . That's Russian, isn't it? And where have you both come from?"

"Caxton Hall." Nina stood a little taller. "Mr. Chesterfield was giving a lecture. Rousing, wasn't it?"

She glanced at Evelyn, who let out a small, strangled laugh. "You could say that."

"Chesterfield?" Julia shook her head. "Not heard of him. What was he speaking on?"

"Oh, well . . ." Evelyn's blood was squealing through her veins now and she was aware of sweat gathering at the back of her neck. "This and that."

"I suppose that's where this crowd has come from." Julia waved a hand behind her. "Great rabble, chanting and carrying on with placards."

She watched Evelyn uncertainly, not bothered by Tortoise tugging on the lead, probably eager for his dinner. The sun had fallen behind the trees; they would soon be standing in shadow. Evelyn was peering down The Mall, wishing some distraction might be summonsed from the gleam of cars cruising east, when she saw the outline of a man by the fence of Lancaster House: dark-haired, woolen suit, loping across the lawn. The scene had a surreal element to it, like encountering a leopard in Trafalgar Square, and when he hit the walking track the man accelerated, his long legs hardly touching the ground. He was gesturing madly, hollering something Evelyn could not catch, and then she saw that behind him were a gang of half a dozen men, all dressed in black trousers, belts with big brass buckles, and black turtleneck sweaters. They were gaining on the man, who flew past Evelyn only to trip on the hedge a few dozen yards ahead and career into the rose garden.

"Oh my . . ." Julia, dropping Tortoise's lead, rushed over to him. "Are you all right, sir?"

He got himself up, swiping away the brambles tangled around his arms. His nose was bloody, eyes wild. He was only a boy, seventeen, eighteen at most.

"Please, miss," he cried. "You must help me."

Julia glanced at Evelyn, her own eyes wide in alarm. "But of course we'll help. Just let me—"

She didn't get to finish. The big-shouldered men had pulled up, and Evelyn caught a glimpse of the insignia on their red armbands, a black disc shot through with a bolt of gold lightning. Fascist thugs, Mosley's lot, out for blood after the rally. One of them said something to Nina and pushed his way toward the boy, sending Evelyn stumbling off the curb.

"I beg your pardon." Julia turned on them, giving the leader a poke in the chest. "Just what are you doing?"

"*Julia.*" Evelyn's voice was a plea. A warning. But Julia wasn't listening.

"Now, look here. I don't know what this young man has done, but you're to leave him alone."

"I'd move out the way if I were you, miss." The tallest of the group, a great hulking man with red hair, took a menacing step forward.

"Don't be so ridiculous." Julia sized him up and gave a disgusted shake of her head. "You can't go around attacking whomever you like."

"Julia, I think we ought to leave this," Evelyn said, firmer this time.

"For God's sake." Julia was on her tiptoes, searching about the road. "Where are the police when you need them?"

As she said this, the redhead reached out and gripped Julia by the arm, wrenching her aside.

"We've got no problem with you, lady, but he's ours. So I suggest you move along and leave us to it."

"This is extraordinary." Julia looked to Evelyn in the twilight. "Are we going to stand for it?"

Evelyn could feel Nina's glare on her as though it was scorching fire into the center of her brain. She hadn't imagined that her moment of reckoning would play out to this particular script, but here she was, worlds colliding—and now she had to choose. She thought of the texture of that silk dress, the watery slip of it through her fingers, gone. Maybe in time she would tell Julia the truth. Maybe in time Julia would forgive her.

"No!" Evelyn hadn't meant to shout it, and Julia reared back as if she had been bitten. "Leave him, Julia. Just leave the boy to them."

"What on earth are you talking about?" Julia, a strange glint in her eyes, looked beyond Evelyn to Nina, as if she might know the answer. "He needs our help. Those brutes will tear him in half."

"He does not need our help," Evelyn shot back. "He's nothing but a filthy little Jew."

Julia blinked at her, astonished. "A *what*?"

"You heard." It was Nina, her low voice cutting across the lawn. "We've no business here and nor do you." She stepped forward and placed a soft hand on Evelyn's back. "Come along," she said. "We should be going."

"Evelyn." Julia was staring at her. "I don't understand. This isn't like you."

Evelyn linked her arm through Nina's and began walking away. With the defense weakened, the men were on top of the boy in seconds, laying into him with their fists and steel-capped boots. "Dirty Yid," she heard them hiss as the blows rained down. "You filthy fucking scum."

⌒

An hour later, Evelyn's legs still felt hollow as she sat with the others at Nina's kitchen table drinking lemon tea. She tried to eat one of the *pryaniki* biscuits from the plate in front of her but couldn't; her stomach was churning with fright. Someone was recounting their favorite lines from the rally, which elicited murmurs of agreement, and Evelyn was glad that Nina hadn't mentioned the boy, nor how they had met Julia in the park—it was already taking all Evelyn's willpower to refrain from putting her head down on the table and clenching her eyes shut. Nina hadn't said much at all, in fact, and once the cups had been cleared she went through to the living room, loaded a Bruckner symphony on the gramophone, and turned the volume right up.

"In case they're listening," she whispered on her return, pointing to the far wall.

"*Listening?*" Evelyn followed the line of her finger. "The neighbors?"

"No, MI5, of course."

Evelyn's eyes snapped back to Nina's. They held one another's gaze for a beat, Evelyn's face aching from the tight, determined set of her smile.

"Why should MI5 want to listen to you?" she asked.

"Can't you guess?"

Evelyn swallowed. The lemon tea had left an unpleasant aftertaste. Clasping her hands together beneath the table, she noticed for the first time what looked like posters and tins of greasepaint stacked against the skirting board. One poster had been propped up on top of the pile, showing an enormously fat man in a suit and bowler hat leering from behind a Union Jack, his big lips downturned, his nose hooked. From his lapel swung a gold chain with the Star of David. Beneath this image ran the large print: THIS WAR IS A JEW WAR.

Evelyn turned back to Nina, then to Mrs. Randall and the others, a shiver working its way down her spine. They were all watching her, waiting. She was close now—she could feel it.

At her feet was her handbag containing the list of typists from the War Office, folded away inside a sealed brown envelope. She reached for it. "Before I forget, Nina, I have that list you asked for . . ." She slid the envelope across the table.

Nina snatched it up, and Evelyn watched the women crowd around for the opening, smiles spreading over their faces.

"Excellent work," Mrs. Randall remarked as Nina stood up and went to hide the envelope in the sitting room. When she came back to the kitchen she stopped at the pantry and brought out a carton of eggs and a glass bowl, placing them on the table. After cracking the eggs into the bowl, she reached for the whisk beside the sink.

"When you were last here, Evelyn, you talked plainly about the war," she said quietly. "I admired that honesty—we all did. Here was a young woman who shared our beliefs. Here was an ally in our fight."

Nina started beating the mixture in a fast, smooth rhythm, the whisk never once touching the bottom of the bowl.

"Chesterfield spoke to you this afternoon," she continued. "He got inside your head. I could feel that, sitting there beside you, and I could see it as we marched through the park. Which is why I invited you back here again tonight. And it's why we have decided to share something very special with you."

Evelyn glanced around the table, the blood roaring in her head. "Oh yes? What's that?"

A smile flickered across Nina's face. "The truth is, Evelyn, that we're part of a secret organization. The Lion Society, we call it, and if MI5 ever got wind of what we do they'd come after us in a flash. We meet here each week, though I flatter myself that my cooking is an additional incentive."

The others chuckled as Nina stepped over to a different cupboard, bringing out a plump clove of garlic and a small onion, which she started peeling. When she was done, she swept the skin from the board and pointed to the posters by the wall.

"For months we've been spreading our message that the war is a Jew war. But it's not enough—the government isn't listening. They refuse to see that prosperity can be found in appeasement and adopting more of Hitler's attitudes to nationhood. So we need to take a different approach; something more cunning, more subversive. To effect real change we need people on the inside of institutions that are working against the British people. Inside places like Parliament, the judiciary, even the War Office . . ."

Evelyn raised a hand to her clammy brow. "The War Office?"

Nina looked up. A pale blue vein pulsed at her forehead. "Will you work with us, Evelyn? Will you join in this fight? We can have a tremendous impact. We could even alter history . . . How many people will be able to look back on their lives and say that?"

They all stared at her, waiting. Evelyn watched as Nina picked up the knife and began slicing the onion, the *thwack* of the metal striking the board oddly grounding, the smell of butter in the warming pan almost a comfort. Her heartbeat grew steady.

"You know what inspired me most about Chesterfield?" she began. "His convictions. He wasn't *afraid*. I've always been afraid of what other people think. But not anymore. Not after today. Now I understand the difference one person can make. That through my actions I can shape a better world. I suppose that's what makes a real revolutionary." Evelyn made herself look up, her face flushed, her hands trembling in her lap. "It's what makes me grateful to have met you."

"And that's what Britain needs, isn't it?" Nina said, her eyes bright. "Our very own revolution."

"Yes!" someone cried, and the table burst into shrill applause.

Nina went to fetch something from a kitchen drawer. When she returned to the table she pushed a small felt case over to Evelyn.

"Go on, dear," Mrs. Randall said. "Open it."

Inside was a silver badge about the size of a penny engraved with an image of a glorious eagle swooping down to attack a spitting viper. Nina unclipped it from the casing and pinned it to Evelyn's cotton blouse.

"Do you like it?" Mrs. Randall asked. "Everyone gets a PJ when they join."

Evelyn glanced down at the repulsive thing, her skin crawling. It was like having a tarantula in her breast pocket.

"PJ?"

"*Perish Judah*. Clever, isn't it?"

"There you are." Nina sat back, pleased. "Doesn't she look the part, everyone?"

The women all nodded.

"And I think it's time you met my husband." Mrs. Randall leaned across the table, her breath sour as she whispered to Evelyn. "Andrew's heard a lot about you. Perhaps you'd like to come by the house on Friday evening? We're in Onslow Square. There's much you could share with him."

"I'd be honored," Evelyn said.

She had done it. She had arranged the meeting with Randall. But how much had it cost her? She glanced over to Nina now pouring the omelette mixture into the pan on the stove, and through the fragrant mist the other woman returned a small, tight smile.

⌒

Later, once everyone else had gone home, Evelyn walked with Nina along Brompton Road, each of them carrying a tube of rolled-up posters under one arm, while Nina had the tin of greasepaint in her other. There was hardly any traffic about, the night very cold and clear. Nina wasn't saying much but it wasn't awkward, and Evelyn was grateful for the quiet. Her own head was a horrible jumble, every new thought looping back to Julia and wondering how on earth she would ever explain herself, or what she would do if the Wesleys found out about what had happened in the park.

"I suspect we're rather alike, Evelyn," Nina said as they waited for a taxi to pass near the square. "We've both made a home for ourselves in places we wouldn't normally belong. Who would have thought a Russian could inspire such patriotism in the English? We live in a topsy-turvy world."

They crossed the road, passing a young man walking a pair of scrappy terriers in tartan jackets.

"You still don't think of yourself as English?" Evelyn asked.

"I consider myself both Russian and English, but you English will never accept me as one of your own. Not really. You've always feared foreigners. Always sought to conquer rather than live alongside them."

"And what's wrong with that?"

"Nothing at all. But I've always thought you need to understand your own nature if you're to have dominion over another."

They had stopped at the corner opposite Harrods. Evelyn took the glue tucked under Nina's arm and strode across the road. When she reached the facade she laid a hand against the stonework.

"Here," she called with a quick glance over her shoulder. "This is as good a spot as any." She popped open the tube, slid out a poster, and unfurled it. "Keep a lookout, won't you?"

Evelyn pulled the cap off the glue with her teeth and squeezed out a cross onto the back of the sheet. Then, in one swift motion, she pivoted, pressed the poster against the wall, and smoothed it down from top to bottom with her forearm.

"This glue is good stuff—where did you find it?"

"A friend used to do costumes at the Alhambra," said Nina. "The RAF use it too, apparently!"

To a passerby, it might have looked like a schoolgirl prank. No less innocent than covering dorms in confetti, wrapping toilet paper around the dining hall, or locking Matron in the broom cupboard. But after what she had seen in Caxton Hall, what she had felt blistering around the audience and spilling into the streets, Evelyn understood the danger of it. Where did all this hatred go once it had been unleashed? She wondered what had happened to that poor boy in St. James's Park, and her mind turned yet again to Julia—what must she think of her? Evelyn pushed that worry away, and once she had finished a second poster she found herself urging Nina on with the rest, until there was a dreadful line of them along the stone. Then Evelyn heard a noise: the sound of a car and a man's cough.

"Do hurry, Nina!"

"What's that?" Nina stood back to admire her handiwork, her head tilted in appreciation. "Now hasn't that brightened the place up?"

More sounds followed. Footsteps. Nearer, louder.

"There's someone coming!" Evelyn breathed.

"Who?"

"I don't know who!"

A strange, terrified giggle erupted from Nina. Evelyn grabbed her arm; her flesh was wiry and taut beneath her coat.

"Come on!"

"*Hey!*"

There it was. A voice; she wasn't imagining it. Nina's eyes grew wide, the whites shining in the dark, fear in her pupils for the first time. They took off, running for a few hundred yards, ducking down Lancelot Place, before they had to stop, doubled over and wheezing, at the start of Trevor Square.

Evelyn checked the street. No one had followed.

"Come along," Nina said. "It's just over here."

Somehow they ended up outside a terrace. The identical houses on either size of it were cast in blue shadow, though a faint light glowed in a window at number thirteen. Nina walked up to the front door, gesturing for Evelyn to join her.

"Isn't it a little late for house calls?"

Evelyn watched Nina use the knocker to strike against the door before pressing an ear to the wood, listening for life as she might for the sea in a shell. Then, with a nod, she began fishing around in her coat pocket. She brought out a penny, which she used to crack open the lid on the greasepaint tin before passing it to Evelyn.

"The rot begins in Parliament, you know," muttered Nina. "The festering filth of it all. If I had my way, I would destroy Westminster and rebuild it from the ground up, with a strong leader with strong English values. It's bizarre, isn't it, how we forget that humans are a tribal species—happiest with our own kind. When it all boils down to it, we can't really accept difference. We won't. The sooner everyone else accepts that, the sooner we can bring this sniveling war to an end."

Evelyn looked away down the street, something heavy pressing against her spine. "Whose house is this?" Her voice sounded weak, barely a whisper.

But Nina didn't answer, and when she heard a tread inside, first down the stairs and then along the hall, a pink light shining through the leaded glass, Evelyn felt her face harden, her shoulders curve.

The door opened. An elderly man stood there in checkered pajamas and a navy dressing-gown with a crest on the breast pocket. It was Leslie Baden-Marr, the member for North Islington; Evelyn recognized him from a photograph she'd seen in *The Times*. A Jewish MP. Behind him stood a short, chubby woman in a hairnet—his wife, presumably—who gripped his sleeve.

"Ladies, do you have any idea what time it is?" Baden-Marr peered into the gloom, though there was nothing reproachful in his tone, and Evelyn noticed that his feet, which were slim and very pale, were bare.

"I beg your pardon, sir," Nina said, all deference, "but we have a package for your wife, Rachel."

Perhaps it was Nina's smooth voice; perhaps it was the fact that the women on his doorstep were young and well dressed, but after a moment of deliberation Baden-Marr stepped aside for his wife, who, though clearly tired and a bit wary, nevertheless looked intrigued as she edged forward. "For me?"

Nina's dark gaze flickered down to the tin. Somewhere, a clock struck the hour and a dog barked, and Evelyn imagined she could even hear Mrs. Baden-Marr's congested breathing. She raised her eyes to the empty sky. Evelyn had always valued obedience, order, discipline, but now she found herself in a place where she would not be punished for her actions. It was dreadful how remorseless she felt, how free. She launched the paint, the black liquid tracing an arc in the air, like the billow of Nina's cape caught in the wind.

~

When she arrived home at Broadwick Street, Evelyn let herself inside quietly and stood in the hallway, her forehead pressed against the cool panel of her bedroom door. Though it was late, Fay was still up; she must have caught the evening train back from Bletchley, where she had spent the past week. Jazz played softly on the wireless and the smell of simmering broth and fresh bread floated from the kitchen, reminding Evelyn so much of her mother's cooking that she was afraid she'd break down right there in the dark.

"Hello, darling," called Fay, as Evelyn finally made her way over to the sofa. "You're not usually such a night owl."

"It's been a long day." Yawning, Evelyn kicked off her shoes. "How was your secondment?"

Fay took a swig from a bottle of beer and made a face. "They're a funny old bunch down there. Square, you know? No sense of humor. Mind you, I wouldn't have one either if I had to stare at numbers all day."

Evelyn studied Fay. She was dressed in her silk kimono, her hair wrapped in a turban, and Evelyn wondered how she was able to find such easy happiness in herself and in others. She found herself wishing she'd made more of a confidant of her; Fay could have been the real friend she needed through all this. Chadwick had been right, she thought spitefully. She should have been happier sharing with a fellow MI5 girl, and she considered telling Fay about the investigation. But what to say? That she felt guilty? That she felt scared? That she wished she had never agreed to the assignment because she was starting to forget what was real between people and what was false? It was all so hopeless—it made her want to weep again—so she stood up and moved toward the stove, drawn by the aroma of the soup. She couldn't remember the last time she'd had a home-cooked meal.

"You don't look so hot, Evie," Fay said. "Have you been looking after yourself?"

"Oh yes." Evelyn poured herself a glass of milk. "Pining for you, that's all."

"More like working too hard," Fay muttered, but she was also wan beneath her rouge. "Have you managed to have any fun while I've been away?"

"You know me. Allergic to a good time."

"There's nothing else?" Fay leaned against the bench. "You can talk to me, you know."

"It's just . . ." Evelyn hardly knew where to start. "It does wear you down, rather, this pretending." She rubbed at her eyes, seeing stars. "Maybe I'm just tired. I'm sure I'll be myself again when the case is done."

"Your problem is you've given over too much of yourself," said Fay, folding her freckled arms across her chest. "You've got to keep that real part of you hidden away. This is only a job for me, it's not a life. I'm heading back to Bolton after the war and leaving the Service for good. I've got plans, you see. I'm going to open my florist shop and I want to get married and have kids—three little ones. But that person who'll leave London, she never comes out at the Scrubs. No one sees her; she's precious. I have to protect her, like I would those kids."

Evelyn smiled sadly. "You can see what your life will look like, then, when this is over?"

"It's all that keeps me going." Fay frowned. "Some people cling to the past, but I've always been looking forward, ever since I was young. I mean, take Dillwyn Knox's girls down at Bletchley. Do you know what they call themselves? Dilly's Fillies. And they're clever, Evie, we'll have them to thank when they crack the codes. But you can bet they won't ever see much glory for it, and they'll resent that for the rest of their days."

Evelyn stared at the kitchen window. The curtains shuddered like a sneeze with each draft of cold air.

"Yes," she murmured. "I can't imagine the chaps letting them take the credit."

Fay sighed. "Still, it wasn't all bad down there. In the evening they put on dances in the mess hall and got in a local brass band. I met an intelligence officer from Dundee. We danced together every night. Bruce, his name was, and I could just about listen to him say it all week. *Brrr-uuuss*." She giggled.

"What about Tony?"

Fay planted her hands on her hips. "Oh, well, he's joined up, actually."

"He has?"

"I had a letter from him before I went to Buckinghamshire. He's probably on his way to the Belgian border right now."

Evelyn considered this, recalling Tony's thin mustache, his impatient eyes.

"He probably did it on a whim—that's Tony all over," Fay said. "Thought he'd look smashing in the uniform or something equally ridiculous." She laughed, but it was brittle, and when she brought her hands to her mouth Evelyn saw that her red nails had been bitten down to the quick. "I mean, how bloody *stupid*. What use is he going to be over there? He'll get himself killed, that's what."

"Oh, Fay." Evelyn started toward her but stopped, not quite knowing what to do next. "I'm sure he'll be fine."

But they both knew she couldn't be sure of that, and after swiping at her eyes with the back of her wrist Fay returned to the soup, stirring it with renewed vigor until a loud knock on the door startled them both.

Evelyn checked her watch. "Who could that be at this hour?"

But it was only the landlord, dressed in his pajamas, his shock of white hair untidy from his pillow. There was a call for Evelyn. "A gentleman," the old man grumbled, though he was by now accustomed to these late-night disturbances.

Evelyn headed downstairs to the telephone in the hallway, aware of the landlord's soft tread behind her, the rise and fall of his raspy breath. She picked up the receiver.

"Hello?"

"How did you get on tonight?"

It was White. The line was poor, crackly with background noise; he must have been in a restaurant booth somewhere. But his voice sounded strained, unlike himself. She wondered if he'd been drinking.

"It went very well, sir. You're speaking to an official member of the Lion Society. I have the badge to prove it."

"Bravo!"

"And I've been invited to the Randalls' house on Friday. I'm to be introduced to Captain Randall himself."

"Have you indeed? Well, this is quite the development."

There came another muffled sound down the end of the line, as though White had covered the mouthpiece, and Evelyn heard laughter, then, *You never told me that!*

"His wife thinks I might have some useful insights," she said. "I wouldn't be surprised if they wanted me to act as some sort of conduit at the War Office. They were pleased with the list I gave them of the names of the typists and—"

"Yes, that is likely," White interrupted. "But remember, censorship has been enforced, which now blocks any correspondence through the usual channels. So it may soon be time to offer up my Belgian agent, Christine Bakker."

"Yes." Evelyn recalled the waxy part in Nina's hair as she fixed the badge to Evelyn's blouse, the weight of it tugging at the lace. "I thought so too."

"We're very close to that membership list, Evelyn," White said through another crackle. "We'll talk more tomorrow at the flat."

"All right—but, sir—"

He had already rung off. Evelyn hung up the telephone and leaned against the wall, trailing a finger down the gap between the sheets of wallpaper, tugging at a small tear. Her eyes stung. She wanted him to call back, but how could she describe the dull weight of grief dragging at her heels?

Evelyn sighed. There was no room for compromise in what she was doing. She had done a good job—she had convinced Nina she believed in her cause, and the women of the Lion Society had welcomed her with open arms. That was all that mattered. So why did she feel quite so miserable?

⌒

Later, in her bedroom, Evelyn wrote a letter to her father. It was the first in weeks; despite her promise, she hadn't been in touch with her parents since her visit to Lewes back in November. Her father had written to her three times; each letter had been put unopened in her bedside drawer. She had avoided the blunt intrusion of her parents, but tonight she knew she must confront these feelings if she were ever to understand what had drawn her to this job with White, what had compelled her to live like this. She pictured her mother and father in their sitting room, evening creeping over the sofa and the chaise longue, their backs turned from the last color at the window; though even that image was growing blurry at the edges, fading, almost as if they were disappearing from her too.

But when she read back over the letter, a chatty note about work, the flat, and how she'd been spending her time in London, Evelyn couldn't detect the lies. It really was truth with just the lightest shade of dark, and Evelyn reflected bitterly that White would be proud to know just how far his protégé had come.

She put the letter in an envelope, sealed it, and placed it in her handbag to post in the morning. Then she went to the kitchen sink to wash her hands with the steel-wool scourer, but no matter how hard she scrubbed, the black greasepaint stains under her fingernails wouldn't shift.

As she climbed into bed, Evelyn heard Fay humming from the sitting room. She was probably crocheting the blankets and booties she sent to her sister-in-law back in Bolton. But there was something mournful about the tune, and Evelyn found herself wrapping her flimsy pillow around her head. She thought about Tony, marching along some gray beach. He'd be telling a yarn, making the other soldiers laugh—that was how Evelyn always imagined the men: laughing in their toil, as if they were at a holiday camp. All these mind games had obliterated her capacity to picture the actual war, with all its blood and bones and tanks and guns. Michael Talbert appeared too, and Evelyn remembered him at the nightclub, his dry, forceful hands. She could almost feel the pressure of his mouth, almost smell his cologne and the hint of sweat about his collar, but she could not recall his face. She ran a finger over her lips, banishing the memory. For once sleep did come easily, thick and deep like the falling of a stage curtain.

SIXTEEN

EVELYN ARRIVED AT the Randalls' house just as the bell of St. Augustine's struck nine. Without a word, the maid led Evelyn upstairs, past the Impressionist paintings and the Chinese vases, to the drawing room at the end of a long, gloomy hallway.

Captain Randall himself greeted her at the door. He was dressed in a pinstripe double-breasted suit and brown soft-leather brogues. Evelyn had imagined someone taller, brawnier, but as he made a small bow she saw that he was slight and almost waifish, his bald head shining under the purple shade of the hall lamp.

"Welcome, Evelyn," he said. "Come in, please."

The drawing room was dark, like the rest of the house; the only light, in fact, came from the fire in the hearth. In the far corner Evelyn could make out Nina, who acknowledged her with a nod. She couldn't see Mrs. Randall.

"Scotch is your poison, isn't it?" Randall asked, returning from the drinks cabinet with a tumbler. There was another man sitting on the sofa in front of the fire. "I don't suppose you've met Tom Weston? He's our chap in the American embassy."

Weston turned toward Evelyn and flashed a pearly smile. He wasn't much older than her, and there was something familiar about him, too. Evelyn realized with a shock that he was the young man who had flirted with Sally at the Arbat Tea House. But there had never been mention of an American, or any dossiers revealing links between the Lion Society and the embassy. How had they missed this?

"What do you do at Grosvenor Square, Mr. Weston?" she asked as she joined him on the sofa.

"Cipher clerking. I'm an assistant to Ambassador Kennedy. I work closely on the details from Washington." His eyes had a glazed, unfocused look to them, and she saw he was drunk.

"And how do you like London?"

Weston gave a shrug. "It's all right. I'm used to making new cities home. New York, Berlin. I was in Moscow for three years before my transfer here."

Nina spoke up from the corner of the room: "You like Moscow best, don't you, Tom?"

"Yeah, I guess so." Weston chuckled. "But I've been lucky. I found my place at the restaurant with Nina and her family. Wonderful people, aren't they?"

Evelyn smiled politely and nodded. She watched Randall standing by the fire, one elbow propped against the mantelpiece, twisting the signet ring on his slim finger. Like the mood in the room, he was difficult to read. His file had described him as one of the most dangerous subversives in the United Kingdom, but seeing him here, in his home, calm and well mannered, she knew many would struggle to see any violence in him—he was all respectability. But she recognized the darkness lurking beneath the surface, and her eyes were soon drawn to a gold-framed painting hanging above the fireplace.

"Is that a Liss?" she asked.

Randall arched his neck. "Mm. My wife bought it." He smiled tightly. "Do you know it?"

"Yes. It's *Judith in the Tent of Holofernes*. One of his most celebrated works."

The painting was shadowy, Judith's pale, sculpted shoulders iridescent in the dim light. Beneath her extended arm lay a headless corpse, blood gushing from the stump of its neck like a fountain.

"It's gruesome," said Weston. "I'll give it that."

Evelyn continued to peer at the frame, afraid now to look elsewhere. "I'm rather surprised you own it, sir," she said.

"Oh? And why is that?"

Randall was staring at her with such a blank, unfeeling expression that, despite the heat from the roaring fire, Evelyn felt a cold prickle at the back of her neck. She glanced at Weston, but he was gazing into his empty glass, while Nina still had her eyes fixed on the painting, her forehead creased; if they knew what the work represented, they weren't saying. But Randall—did he know?

"It's an Old Testament story," she murmured. "Judith is a heroine of the Jews. One night she penetrates the camp of the Assyrian general Holofernes. The Assyrians have been plundering her homeland for months and she offers to help his army in the siege of Bethulia. But after waiting for Holofernes to drink himself unconscious, she takes his sword and cuts off his head." Evelyn paused. "She'd been planning her attack for some time. She caught Holofernes completely unawares."

"Not the first fellow to fall into that trap!" Weston snorted.

Evelyn looked at the fire, sensing Randall's eyes on her as he reached for the poker hanging from the stand, and realized she had no idea what he was capable of. Could he have set her up? The door was only a dozen paces away. If she moved fast, she could be on the other side of it before they had the chance to react.

"But why on earth did Isadore buy this for you, Andrew?" Nina's sneering voice cut through the room. "She mustn't have known it was Jew art, surely?"

Randall gave a wan smile. "Oh, she knew. My wife is nothing if not meticulous."

Evelyn saw his mouth twitch beneath his mustache as he raised the poker, gazing at the sharp tip.

"I hang it here to remind me. About complacency. That our enemies are everywhere—even in our own ranks. That given half a chance they will destroy us in our own homes."

There was plain menace in his face now, real animal hatred, and Evelyn felt a bright stab of fear in her gut. He knows, a voice bellowed inside her head. *He knows.*

"My wife tells me you are a champion of our cause, Evelyn," Randall said, facing the fire again to prod at a log.

Evelyn somehow nodded. She daren't speak—she couldn't.

"And your work in the War Office provides an opportunity to advance our plans at the Society?"

Randall reached across the hearth and hung the poker on the stand. Then, with his back still to her, he rested both hands on the mantelpiece while one foot was planted forward, as though he were about to spring into the flames. But when he finally looked back at Evelyn, she saw that he was smiling.

"That is my belief, yes," she said, exhaling slowly in relief.

"The government continues to ignore my warnings about the Jew problem," Randall muttered. "No amount of negotiation, wrangling, or even begging will persuade Chamberlain to shift an inch. They're so eager to misunderstand—to think the worst of us, as if *we* were the enemy. But all we want is stable government, safety, and security for our nation. Safety in our beds." He pointed to the painting. "But to do this we have to rid ourselves of these corrupting forces and recognize how much can be gained by peace with Hitler."

The fire hissed with the abrupt explosion of a log. Randall crossed the carpet to close the drawing room door.

"To make matters worse, I have MI5 watching me like a hawk. It's been like this for weeks. They're surveilling anyone with connections to the British fascists. Tom must take precautions, too—the Americans have eyes everywhere." Randall returned to the edge of the rug. "We've known for some time the danger our cause faces if the bulldog gets his way and becomes PM. It's no secret that Churchill's argued in the Cabinet for stronger measures against the Germans—he wants full-scale war. But this outcome would be a disaster. British troops are already depleted; the German army is more organized and more powerful. It will be a bloodbath. And now we have proof of something we've suspected for many months: that Churchill has been secretly agitating for American involvement in this war."

Evelyn sat forward. "What kind of proof?"

"Highly classified cables between Churchill and Roosevelt. They reveal that while the Americans have been making false overtures about peace and appeasement, Churchill has been doing everything he can to entice them into the war."

Evelyn blinked. Such an alliance required the cooperation of many agencies of British government, including MI5, yet she had heard nothing about it. Could it be true?

"Quite a shock, isn't it?" Nina said with a grim smile. "To have been lied to so comprehensively by the government?"

"And the cables?" Evelyn asked. "Where have they come from?"

Randall pointed at Weston. "Direct from the American embassy. Nina arranged to make copies. I have the originals."

"I used a fellow named Sidorov, a Russian photographer," Nina confirmed. "Very good, very discreet."

"But the Americans," said Evelyn, shaking her head, "they won't be drawn in, will they? They've nothing to gain, nor any appetite for another world war."

"They're as mendacious as Churchill," Randall said, now pacing the rug. "But I've read the advice from Roosevelt and his intelligence agencies, as well as correspondence direct from the Admiralty. The Americans are already involved. They're sourcing radio detectors and sharing signaling with MI5. Their preparations for war have begun. And they must be stopped. *Churchill* must be stopped. If he topples Chamberlain, we will never forge peace with the Germans, and Britain will be razed to the ground."

He marched toward the desk, unlocked the slatted tambour top, and rolled it back to reveal two small drawers, several letter racks, and a few pigeonholes. The top drawer contained a sheaf of papers, which he tucked under his arm, and a red leather-bound ledger. *The membership list.* Evelyn caught only a glimpse of it before he slammed the top of the desk shut.

"There." Randall thrust the documents into her lap. "These prove the extraordinary deception of both governments."

Evelyn leafed through the papers, each bearing the American embassy seal and the stamp TOP SECRET. She read quickly, taking in as much as she could. It was just as Randall had described. When she was done, she sat back, deflated. If these were leaked, they would further destabilize the government, dealing an enormous blow to public morale in the process. But White, she thought angrily—he must have known about this all along and kept it from her. Why? She studied Tom Weston. He hadn't said much, an arrogant smirk fixed to his handsome face. Just how had he stolen the cables right from under the Americans' noses?

When she asked as much, he replied, "It wasn't difficult. I have high-level clearance at Grosvenor Square; I just took them home one evening a few weeks ago—I bet no one'll ever notice they're gone. I like to think Kennedy would approve of our activities in his own way. Old Joe wants appeasement almost as much as we do."

"The man's been trying to meet with Hitler for months!" Nina added.

"Yeah, well, from where I sit, it's all a question of trust," drawled Weston, standing up to pour himself another drink. "On the one hand, Roosevelt tells the American people that this war is Europe's problem, that the United States will not enter the conflict under any circumstances, while on the other he's cozying up to Churchill and laying the groundwork for deployment. They leave us with no option but to alert the public. We all deserve to know the truth."

Evelyn found herself nodding, though she didn't know what she was agreeing with anymore. Everything had become scrambled in her head.

"And there is still time, still opportunity, to negotiate an honorable peace with Germany," Nina put in. "Hitler is a reasonable man. He has made these overtures. We can form an alliance, work toward a greater, purer Britain. We all know this is preferable to another war."

"Which is why this duplicity must be exposed," Randall finished smoothly, "and why I will take the original cables to Parliament. I will expose the hypocrisy of the lot of them and show just what Churchill plans to do if he gains power."

Evelyn felt her eyes grow wide. She had not counted on this development.

"And the copies," she asked, her voice hollow in the high-ceilinged room, "what do you plan to do with them?"

"Several have already been smuggled to Berlin," Nina said. "I had a contact, a most trusted ally in the Italian embassy . . . But his position was compromised and now we're in something of a fix."

"Where was he taking them?"

Nina glanced at Randall, nodded.

"To the Rundfunkhaus radio station," he said. "The head of our operation is a British fellow based in Berlin."

"He's a broadcaster?"

"Yes. We communicate through a system of code words. They travel in a note alongside the cables. It's clever, really: to let us know the package has safely arrived, the broadcaster delivers the code word during his program. And the next time the code word is broadcast I'll know he's ready for me to take the cables to Parliament the following day for the afternoon session."

Evelyn swallowed. So White had been right: the cables were going to this German propaganda broadcaster, and Nina, Captain Randall, and Tom Weston were responsible for the leak. She stared at the fireplace, a low rumble of terror working its way up from the balls of her feet. She had the proof, here in this room, not just of the theft of the classified documents but of the existence of the membership list itself. Evelyn felt like she was standing on the top of a rugged mountain peak, staring at the swaths of desolate landscape below. One ill-timed step now . . .

"I'm so sorry," she said. "You may not have heard, but the Censorship department has moved into the War Office. I'd really like to help, but I couldn't get this material out for you myself—they're just too scrupulous." She sat forward and frowned, her chin in her hand, as if considering. "But I do have another contact who might be useful."

"Yes?"

Evelyn couldn't bring herself to look at Nina; it was like watching someone tiptoeing into the path of an oncoming train. Evelyn glanced at the door, knowing what she needed to do but wishing in that moment she could walk away and never look back. She gritted her teeth and took a long, slow breath.

"She's a Belgian girl," she heard herself say. "Christine Bakker. Very reliable. We were friends at the War Office, but she works for the Romanian Legation now and still has diplomatic immunity, which means no army personnel are authorized to search her at the border. She travels regularly to the Continent—I believe she's due to leave London again next week. I know she would be amenable to our plans."

"And we can trust her?" Randall asked.

Evelyn nodded. "Absolutely. We can put any material in her correspondence satchel and it is guaranteed to be delivered. No one will suspect her."

She stared at the ice dissolving in her glass, her rapid heartbeat thudding in her ears. Could the others hear it too? If they did, they would surely know the truth, and when finally she looked up she saw Nina inching toward her.

"When?" she said. "When can I meet Christine?"

Evelyn's stomach clenched. "Monday?"

"No," said Randall. "It must be sooner."

"Tomorrow?"

"And she will get the cables to Berlin?"

Nina's hands were extended, beseeching, as if she would at Evelyn's command prostrate herself there on the rug. Even Randall looked queer, chewing on the corner of his thumb, his eyes fixed on the fire. Only Tom Weston was undisturbed, swigging the rest of his drink and loudly smacking his lips. Foolish boy, Evelyn thought. He has no idea what he has done.

She turned to Nina and nodded, hoping the Russian woman

didn't see the twitch beneath her eye, the first tremor before the earthquake struck, while Randall raised his glass and drank. From above the mantelpiece Judith loomed large, her gaze no longer one of triumph but of resignation.

"They will get to Berlin," Evelyn said. "I can promise you that."

⌒

The trip to Chemley Court was a blur. Somehow she managed to climb into a taxi, mumble the directions to Pimlico, and before she knew it she was hammering away out the front of the flat, half out of her mind. White wrenched open the door.

"*Evelyn?* What on earth is the matter?"

But her teeth were chattering so hard she could hardly get the words out.

White brought her inside and led her over to the sofa. He fetched a glass of brandy from the cabinet and made her drink it.

"Are you quite all right?" He was wearing pajamas and his reading glasses hung at the top button, dragging the plaid down to reveal a triangle of pink flesh. "Did something happen at Randall's? Are you hurt?"

"No, I'm fine." Evelyn rested her head against a soft cushion, feeling some calm return. How she wished she could close her eyes and make everything disappear. It was too much. She couldn't do it, could she? Their plan was certain to fall apart. White regarded her sternly, and behind him Evelyn glimpsed a light glowing beneath his study door and the quick movement of a shadow.

"I'm sorry, I didn't know you had guests," she said.

"Never mind about that. What happened at Onslow Square?"

"*Is* there someone here?" Evelyn sat up. "Is it Vincent?"

White blinked and looked away, but not before she caught a flash of rage in his eyes. She hadn't meant to say it, but she needed some truth to cling on to now, especially as she knew how closely White guarded his secrets.

"What is going on, Evelyn?" he demanded, turning to face her once more. "Why have you arrived here in such a panic?"

She stared back at him. "We got it wrong," she said finally. "Not about the membership list—that's locked away in Randall's bureau. It's a red-leather ledger, like you said. Top left-hand shelf. He keeps the key on him." Evelyn took a deep breath. "But we missed the Americans' involvement. There's an embassy cipher clerk named Tom Weston working for the Lion Society. I actually encountered him a few weeks ago at the restaurant but didn't know at the time that he was part of all this. Turns out for the past few months he's been stealing cables between the Admiralty and the American government. Nina Ivanov and Captain Randall have been making copies and sending them on to Berlin. You were right: it's all part of their propaganda effort with the Rundfunkhaus radio station to disrupt the Allied war effort and organize support for Germany in the event of invasion. The Lion Society had a man in the Italian embassy delivering these cables to the Continent, but somehow his cover was blown. Which is lucky for us: I said that Christine Bakker can help transport the latest batch . . . I've told Nina we can meet her at the Arbat Tea House tomorrow morning."

White went to his small writing desk, where he rummaged in the drawer for a moment before producing a notepad and pen. She thought he might make some notes, but he only sat there at the desk, his unlit pipe gripped between his teeth, and Evelyn registered that this was the longest she had ever spoken without him interrupting.

"But, sir, I'm afraid that's not all—Randall is threatening to bring these cables into Parliament once he has the go-ahead from Germany. He wants to expose Churchill and his secret dealings with Washington."

"Fuck," White whispered. "*Fuck it!*"

"Did you know? About Churchill and the Americans, I mean?"

A lock of White's silver hair had fallen in a curl over his eyes as he furiously massaged his temples. He let out an odd noise—laughter, Evelyn supposed, though it sounded more like a bark.

"Of course I bloody knew," he snapped. "I wouldn't be doing my job if I didn't. The Americans have been equivocating for months, we need to pull them over the line." He stood up, his face now bright red. "But I didn't know that a mole in the American embassy had been smuggling out our top-secret communiqués . . . *Christ!* The Home Secretary will be apoplectic that we missed this. It could put these negotiations at risk."

He marched toward his study and returned with a manila folder that he slapped down on the desk.

"Those damned Yanks at Grosvenor Square," he growled. "There when you don't want them and always sloppy. You see?" He opened the folder and stabbed at the sheet of paper inside. "Ted already had a file on this Weston; I knew I'd heard his name before. Seems he's been on Special Branch's radar since he arrived in London." He scanned the document and exhaled. "Look. He'd only been here a few weeks before inviting a suspected German agent to his flat."

"That doesn't surprise me."

"Flashy fellow, is he?"

Evelyn nodded. "Certainly more highballs than neat whisky. But why wasn't he brought in?"

"The Americans—here." White read, gave another sigh. "They pulled rank, citing diplomatic immunity. We were told to back off. Bloody fools!" He rubbed at his temples again. "All right, all right. We can contain this. Not the cables going to Berlin, but we have our opportunity to catch out Randall and the others. You said Ivanov wants to meet you and Christine Bakker tomorrow at the restaurant?"

Evelyn nodded. "I thought that the best place. I know it means we can't get any surveillance in, but it's safe territory for Nina. She'll be less twitchy somewhere familiar."

"Good, good," said White. "Then it is all arranged."

Evelyn sank farther into the sofa. She felt achy, like something metallic had been slipped into her bloodstream.

White took her empty glass. "You did very well tonight, Evelyn. At last we have the Lion Society right where we want them. Now go home and get some rest. You must be as sharp as a tack tomorrow." He frowned at the telephone on the stand. "I'll make calls to the Home Office and the Director General, but first I must speak to Christine."

~

The lights were out when Evelyn returned to Broadwick Street. She stumbled along the dark hallway until she found her door, so tired she was dizzy, and kicked off her shoes. She managed to scrabble about and find the lamp switch on the table by her bed, but when she flicked on the light she screamed.

"*Evelyn?*"

When Fay rushed in, Evelyn was still shaking, tears streaming down her face, eyes squeezed shut as she thrust her hand toward the bed.

"Who is it?" she moaned. "Who *is* it?"

"What?" Fay wrapped her arms around Evelyn, reaching up to stroke her hair. "Who, darling?"

"That . . . *body*!"

"The *what*?"

Evelyn opened her eyes. The pale blue dress Julia had bought for her looked rather like a body, laid out across the quilt. She had tried it on earlier that morning and forgotten to hang it back up in her wardrobe. Evelyn stood over it, fighting the urge to rip it to shreds. Instead, she threw it over the back of the chair and let out a weird, strangled laugh.

"Are you all right?" Fay asked, a warm hand on her arm. When Evelyn didn't answer she pulled back the covers and guided her into bed. "You're exhausted. Here." She tucked Evelyn's feet in, smoothing down the quilt, and then she sat on the edge of the bed, humming something tuneless under her breath. A few minutes passed like this until Fay stood up and turned out the lamp, gently closing the door behind her.

Lying there beneath the covers, Evelyn stared at the moonlight peeking in through the slim gap in the curtains. Am I really going to do this? she wondered. Throw Nina to the wolves? It didn't feel right to even question herself, and she shuddered to imagine what White would say if he were privy to these thoughts. The problem was she had nothing to weigh this dilemma against, no way to test her own judgment. Evelyn shut her eyes, listening to the faint breeze rattling at the glass. She may have had the backing of MI5, but tonight she felt entirely on her own.

SEVENTEEN

CHRISTINE BAKKER WAS waiting out the front of the Arbat Tea House when Evelyn arrived in South Kensington the next morning. "So, you're White's new girl," she said, looking her up and down. "You're pretty. He like them pretty. Like row of little china dolls." Then she laughed.

Christine was herself very beautiful, with straw-colored hair and creamy Flemish skin, though in the harsh early light there were dark bruises beneath her glittering blue eyes. She was dressed in a mink coat and black stockings, and in a pair of high heels still only came up to Evelyn's shoulder.

Evelyn peered toward the shopfront where the *Closed* sign hung in the window, then down the length of the empty street. "Has White briefed you?" she whispered.

"*Ja.*" Checking herself over in her compact mirror, Christine wiped a smudge of kohl from her cheek. "The mark gives me documents, I take to White, he does his magic decoding, and I travel on to Antwerp for delivery. It's a piece of cake. I done it many times, sweetie." She yawned. "But I am just famished, you know? I had no breakfast before I come. Do you think this Russian will feed us?"

Finally there was some movement behind the glass, and Evelyn saw the admiral flip over the sign and the restaurant's green door opened.

Nina was waiting for them at her father's table in front of the fireplace, where a tray of tea things and a plate of *hvorost* had been set out, but like a queen at court she neither stood as they approached nor introduced herself to Christine. This didn't seem to bother Christine, who sat down and immediately lit up a small black cigar, stuffing one of the biscuits into her mouth.

"Oh, these are *good*."

Nina began pouring the tea, but didn't touch hers when she was done. She just sat there, as unmoving as a statue, except for the flutter of a pulse at her throat.

"Christine has agreed to post your mail from Belgium, Nina," Evelyn said. "She's traveling across the Channel tomorrow night."

Christine pushed a curl out of her eye and gave a quick nod. "Yes, I do this for you. It is not difficult to send on to Berlin from Antwerp. I have people there to help me."

Nina ran a fingertip over the scar at her eyebrow. "And what do you want for this—money?"

Christine ate another biscuit, her small face puckered in ecstasy. "I really must get recipe . . ."

"*Christine*," said Evelyn.

The Belgian dismissed the admonishment with a flick of her wrist and reached for the cigar smoldering on the edge of her saucer. "No payment."

"But why?" Nina shook her head. "You're risking so much . . . You don't even know me."

Christine looked up and frowned. "What I need to know? Evelyn is my friend, I trust her, and when she need favor, I help." She sat back, picking at her teeth. "I don't care for politics, but I know rats when I see them. I know what filth they spread." She tapped her nose, gave a laugh. "Best rid of rats, *ja*, Miss Ivanov?"

Christine smoked some more of her cigar, the spicy smoke rising in a plume above the table. As the silence stretched out between them, Evelyn had the curious sensation of drifting, like being on a barge suddenly untethered from its mooring. Then there was a small quiver of movement at Nina's lips, a flash of white teeth, and her eyes shifted back to Evelyn.

"Yes," she agreed quietly. "Best to be rid of the lot."

She took a pale blue envelope from her lap and pushed it across the table.

"This is all?" Christine asked.

"Yes."

"And it's what, exactly?" Christine made an impatient gesture as she looked inside. "I need to know, sweetie, in case anything go wrong."

Nina glanced at Evelyn again, who returned a slight nod of reassurance.

"It's cables between the embassies for the Rundfunkhaus radio station to broadcast. Top secret. Copies of letters from Churchill to Roosevelt and Hoover. And there's a note for our friend in Berlin. He makes his broadcasts every Thursday night at ten o'clock—we'll be listening carefully to make sure the package has reached him."

"*Ziezo.*"

Christine ground her cigar into the saucer and tucked the envelope inside her coat. Then she stood up and walked out of the restaurant, the transaction complete with a brief handshake and a nod of farewell. Evelyn watched as Christine stalked down Queen's Gate and disappeared around the corner, then let out a slow breath. But when she turned back she saw something feverish in Nina's pallor, and all of a sudden the Russian reached across the table to clasp Evelyn's hands. "She won't let us down, will she?"

Evelyn swallowed at the rusty taste in her mouth. She tried to prize her hands free, but Nina's grip was strong.

"Of course not," she managed to say. "We've nothing to worry about."

At last Nina sat back, smiling, and drank some of her tea. How much she's changed since our first meeting, Evelyn thought, when I sized her up from the far corner of the dining room. Gone was the calculation, the wariness; gone was the suspicion. She supposed this was as close as Nina would ever come to trusting another person, and there was a part of Evelyn that wished she hadn't. She'd imagined she'd feel vindication in betraying Nina, but all Evelyn felt as she walked away that morning was wretched.

⌒

Vincent had begun the decryption of the note by the time she arrived at Chemley Court. The Society had used a Cyrillic alphabet and numerals, and spread across the table were dozens of his scrunched-up attempts at the decoding. Ted Young had already taken photographs of the cables for their files. White stood beside Vincent while he worked, and Christine sat hunched on the windowsill overlooking the square. Evelyn made coffee and passed it around, but no one really drank any of it; the atmosphere was tense. Another half hour ticked by, and when it became too much White took some files from his desk and went to sit in the dining room, while Evelyn joined Christine by the window.

"So," said Christine, her eyes on the lackluster gardens below, "you like it here in London, with these men?" She had removed her mink coat to reveal a faded floral-print dress.

"It's better than being stuck behind a desk," Evelyn murmured.

Christine gave her a frank look. "You know he takes all credit. White. I see it every time. His agent always stays in the dark." She shrugged, examining the cheap ring on her index finger. "No one would do what we do if they had choice, *ja*? The Master handles us too, remember."

"Have you known him long?"

"Three years. He found me in Amsterdam. In club. Dancing." Christine gave a husky laugh. "Don't look surprise, sweetie. I had many important client in De Wallen—people no one else accesses. Politician, royalty." She wrapped a piece of dry hair around her ear, thoughtful. "Men will tell woman many things when they want to go to bed with her."

"And did you know Posey? The agent before me?"

"Susanna?" Christine's bright eyes narrowed. "Yes, I knew." She sucked on her cigar, her expression a mean one. "Chewed up, spat out."

"What do you mean?"

Christine looked at her, then shook her head. She rolled up the sleeve of her cotton dress to the elbow and when she turned over her arm Evelyn saw a rash of what looked like needle marks in the groove of her yellowy skin.

"I tell myself this is last assignment for White. It's too long living like this. Susanna learn the hard way, *ja*? Years and years of her life to that case—for what? White isn't too much a bad man, but he is loyal to his England above all else." She sniffed, shifting off the window ledge and stretching out her legs. "I won't come back to London again. I go to Bruges and live in apartment near the market square. You should do same."

"Leave?"

Evelyn had never thought about what it might mean to leave all this behind, but before she could explore the idea further, Vincent shouted, "I've got it! I've bloody got it!"

Evelyn leaped up from the windowsill as White rushed in from the dining room, all of them converging on Vincent's desk.

"It's *Carlyle*," Vincent cried. "It spells Carlyle. That's our code word."

White slapped him on the back. "Well done, my boy. We've got the bastards now." He looked up. "Right, these cables can go on to Antwerp. I've already briefed the Home Office and here is the plan: the arrest warrants will be issued the moment the code word is broadcast on Thursday night. On Friday, Special Branch teams will bring in Randall and Tom Weston, and raid the Onslow Square house for the membership list. Meanwhile another team will make its way to the Russian restaurant on Queen's Gate. I'll telephone you that morning with your instructions, Evelyn. The intention is to round up as many of the Lion Society ladies as possible, including yourself and Mrs. Armstrong, to protect your cover. It's best if the agents can arrest you there at the restaurant so Nina Ivanov doesn't suspect anything."

While he went to telephone Whitehall again, Christine carefully placed Nina's letter and the cables inside a leather satchel, and then gave Evelyn a long hug. She smelled of smoke, stale wine, and another, flowery smell—a scent by Jean Patou, perhaps—and when at last she pulled back to hold Evelyn at arm's length she bestowed on her an enchanting smile. "You take care, sweetie," she said. "And think about what I said." Then she was gone.

EIGHTEEN

THE DINING ROOM in the Arbat Tea House was empty on Friday afternoon. That's one blessing, Evelyn thought, as she took a seat at the window and ordered a coffee from the waitress. Her coat and dress were damp from a sudden rain shower that had burst from the sky as she hurried along Harrington Gardens. But it was warm inside the restaurant and for a time, hands cupped around her mug, her gaze fixed on the slick street outside, Evelyn could almost forget what was about to unfold.

After Vincent's decryption, she had been moved from her flat to an MI5 safe house in Bethnal Green as a precaution until the circulation of the arrest warrants. It had been a grim few days: she hadn't been allowed to leave the dilapidated terrace or even talk to anyone else in the building. She spent most of the time lying on the lumpy bed, staring at the mold on the ceiling and trying not to remember how Nina had looked at her after Christine had departed with the envelope, the entreaty in those dark eyes.

She had tried not to think about Julia, either, or what it meant that she hadn't heard from her. These thoughts unraveled fast, sending Evelyn into an anxious spiral. She grew convinced that Julia had said something to Hugh and Elizabeth, precipitating the inevitable and inglorious end to her tenure as Sally's friend . . . Then, that morning, she had received the telephone call from White. The broadcast in Berlin had contained the code word "Carlyle," and the arrest warrants had been issued. Special Branch had organized the raid for three o'clock today: Captain Randall would be confronted on his way into Westminster while agents raided his house for the cables and the membership list, and Tom Weston, his diplomatic immunity finally waivered, would be arrested at the American embassy.

And shortly, thought Evelyn, taking a shaky sip of coffee, Nina Ivanov and I will be picked up here at the restaurant.

The admiral sat by the fire, reading his newspaper. A half-empty bottle of vodka was at his side. After a while he called to Evelyn, "I get my daughter?"

"Is she working?" Evelyn pointed to the ceiling. "I'm happy to wait . . ."

"No, she with friend." The admiral smiled and stood up. "But I get her. She want talk to you, I'm sure."

He limped across to the door near the gramophone, which opened onto the stairwell leading up to Nina's flat. Evelyn checked the time: two minutes to three. She heard the floorboards above her groan, voices too faint to distinguish, then a moment later Nina appeared in the doorway, smiling. Her hair was tied back in a high bun, a few loose strands brushing against her cheeks. A pair of glasses hung around her neck on a silver chain and there was a line of blue ink on her chin.

"Evelyn, you're here! Are you hungry? Can I fix you something to eat?"

"No, no." Evelyn stood up, overwhelmed by Nina's warm greeting. "I'm fine, really."

Nina joined her at the table, pouring more coffee from the jug and encouraging Evelyn to drink it.

"Captain Randall is very happy, dear, very happy indeed," she said quietly. "We're expecting more cables next week, so if you can arrange it we would like to use Christine again . . ."

There was movement outside, and through the window Evelyn caught a glimpse of a figure hurrying across the street away from the restaurant. It was a woman, her head down and covered with a dark hat and lace veil, a voluptuous fox fur draped over her shoulders. Something about her posture, the confidence of it perhaps, made Evelyn set down her mug and stare. The woman stopped on the curb to adjust her veil, and in that brief moment before the lace dropped back she saw that it was Julia.

Evelyn was aware of the steady rise and fall of her chest. She took another sip of coffee and checked her wristwatch again. Special Branch were due to arrive at any moment. If Julia were to see her being arrested, how would she ever explain *that* away? Everything would come out, the whole nasty mess, and she would have failed. She clenched her jaw. She couldn't fail, she *wouldn't*—not when she was so close. She watched Julia pause at the intersection to push back her veil and light a cigarette, the match taking an interminable time to flare, but when it did she turned the corner and was gone.

Evelyn sat back, drawing in a ragged breath. She sensed Nina across the table following the line of her gaze, her face caught in a frown, until two black cars pulled up on Queen's Gate and three men in dark suits and hats climbed out. They hurried along the footpath beside the window and thrust open the restaurant's front door, coming toward them.

"Nina Ivanov?"

It was the tall one in the middle, holding his warrant card aloft. The admiral slapped down his newspaper and cut him off by the bar.

"*Chto eto?*" he barked.

"Papa." Nina moved forward, her hands outstretched. "I am Nina Ivanov. How can I help you, gentlemen?"

Evelyn eased back in her chair. She was staring at Nina's shoes, the way the tip of her high heels rose as she pressed on the balls of her feet, like a sparrow ready to take flight. Perhaps the men saw this too, as suddenly they lurched at her.

"*Ho!*" the admiral cried. "What you doing?"

Nina struggled, hair spilling from her bun as they began dragging her toward the door. The admiral was shouting now, and Mrs. Ivanov appeared by the gramophone in the corner. She too began to wail.

"Evelyn," Nina shrieked. "*Evelyn!*"

She was lashing out at tables, at chairs, knocking over her father's bottle of vodka, which smashed against the hearth.

"Get your hands off me! You filth! You sons of whores!"

The admiral flung himself at the men, but he was pushed aside and lost his footing, tumbling heavily to the floor.

Spotting Evelyn across the dining room at last, the tall agent with the warrant card strode toward her, his knowing wink almost lost in the pandemonium.

"Evelyn Varley?" He yanked her arms around her back and she felt the cool snap of handcuffs on her wrists. "You're under arrest for violating the Official Secrets Act."

⁓

The sun shone bright against the glittering wet pavement. The agent hauled Evelyn along the street, Nina just ahead, still crying and raging against her captors. The road was empty except for a scruffy-looking boy near the corner, his bicycle tipped over, staring open-mouthed at the spectacle unfolding before him. The agents opened the back door of the first car, shoving Nina inside. She immediately threw herself at the window.

"Please, Evelyn, don't tell them anything!" She pummeled at the glass, her face filled with such dreadful fear and confusion that Evelyn couldn't bear to look.

In the background, the Ivanovs continued shouting from the green doorway, pleading with the agents.

Evelyn found herself being shoved into the second black car. She huddled on the back seat, knees drawn up to her chin as the engine rumbled to life, the tires screeching as they made an abrupt U-turn then sped down Onslow Gardens. They drove through Chelsea, turning onto King's Road. In the front passenger seat, the Special Branch agent removed his hat and wiped his brow. He peered into the rearview mirror, searching out Evelyn's reflection and laughing when he found it.

"What are you sniveling about? Show's over, love. You needn't pretend anymore."

White had made a pot of strong black coffee. He poured a cup and steered it across the desk. Evelyn glanced blearily around his study. It had been tidied, and the shrew and his cage in the corner were gone. When her eyes strayed toward the window she could just make out the pebbles and brown mud of the riverbank, and for a moment she pictured herself standing above gray silky water, inhaling a breeze thick with brine.

"So," White said, lighting up a cigarette. "You did it."

Evelyn's face felt bruised, like she had aged years in a single afternoon. She reached for her cup. "Yes, I did."

"And are you all right?"

She bit down on her lip, not saying anything.

White continued to stare at her, though something in his expression had softened. "These cases test us, Evelyn. They test our resolve and our loyalty. And you've come to know these women. You gained their trust. But you did the right thing. *We* did the right thing—we always do. They're not good people, you must remember that. They are traitors."

Evelyn remained quiet as White peered at her, tapping ash into a saucer. "And nothing else happened during the arrests?" he probed.

Evelyn felt her gaze glide again, seeking out the patch of white light in the cloudy sky. She knew she should mention that she thought she'd seen Julia across the street, but what was the point? Why drag her into all of this, and the Wesleys too?

"Nothing else to report," she replied. "It all went like clockwork."

"Good." White leaned back in his chair. "The Ivanov woman has gone straight to Holloway. They'll bring forward the trial, next month I'm told, and hold it in camera; these espionage cases are always tried in secret. The others—Randall and Tom Weston—they've also been charged with violating the Official Secrets Act, so prison is certain. Five years, I'd say. And you will need to provide testimony."

"But that means . . ."

"Yes." He watched the smoke drift toward the window and dissipate. "Your cover will be blown, I'm afraid. With these fascist groups, in any case—but we've a little more time up our sleeve before that. Most of the others arrested were released without charge, so no one should be suspicious if they find you out and about in the coming days."

"I see. And after the trial?"

"You'll go back to the Scrubs. John Chadwick is run off his feet in Transport and needs another girl." White smiled sympathetically; it was not a natural expression for him. "This is just the way it is with counterintelligence, Evelyn. It's not personal. You have done excellent work."

"Just not good enough to keep me here." Evelyn's throat grew thick, tears welling in her eyes. How could she not take it personally? She didn't want to return to Wormwood Scrubs and that dreary little cell she had shared with Chadwick.

"We may have you back again, in time, and as I said you'll stay on until the trial . . ." Trailing off, White stood up and went to the window, staring out thoughtfully, one hand pushed deep into his pocket.

"I've just come back from briefings at Whitehall. Chamberlain is worried these arrests will bring on a spill. I don't imagine the old boy can hold on much longer." His breath made a fog against the glass. "Still, we roll on. You'll be happy to know I've got a new investigation for you in the meantime."

He pointed to a creased leaflet on top of a pile of papers on his desk. Evelyn picked it up and read the headline: *End Manchester Capitalism!* She had a quick read. There wasn't much to it; the leaflet promoted collectivism and the German welfare state under Hitler, arguing that by declaring war on Germany the British government sought to keep its own poorest citizens in poverty. There was a small swastika in the top left corner.

"We had a tip-off last week about someone distributing this propaganda at the Raven Inn over in Battersea," said White. "Seems the publican is warehousing the leaflets in the keg room before letterboxing them around the neighborhood. As you can see it's fairly low-grade, but it needs to be shut down. I'd like to know who is responsible for getting the stuff printed."

"All right," said Evelyn. "How would you like me to run this?"

"Bring Vincent along to the pub to start with. Pretend he's your brother. Work on the surveillance together. Watch the regulars and the publican. No one needs to know much about either of you except you've recently lost your jobs and feel hard done by—it will endear you to the mark. You're not political but you don't mind old Adolf. You'll assume a new name for this investigation, too. Evelyn Varley doesn't patronize the Raven, but Bea Henry does."

Evelyn nodded. "And how do I get these men to talk?"

White's expression was harder now. "I'll leave that for you to decide. I don't think there's much you couldn't do if you put your mind to it. So wear something nice, won't you, in the field? And some lipstick, some rouge. That hat you wore when we first met."

Evelyn gripped the corner of the desk, feeling color surge to her cheeks. Deep down she had been expecting this day; perhaps there had even been a hint of licentiousness during that first lunch at the Ritz. And now, after everything she had done, everything she had achieved, White expected her to put herself forward like a piece of meat. It was humiliating. All the same, she made herself smile. If she did a good job, perhaps he would reconsider her transfer back to the Scrubs.

"Fine," she said. "If I must."

White turned to the window again. "You'll thank me for this, Evelyn, you really will. It's best to keep yourself busy after an investigation like the Lion Society. You don't want to go dwelling on the particulars—that way madness lies."

After he'd gone, Evelyn sat in the grim silence, the flat groaning with the push and pull of wind. She gazed toward the window, wondering what White had been looking at outside. A solitary light twinkled somewhere far off, but the rest of the city was black.

⌒

Later that night Evelyn stared at the watery shadows shifting against her bedroom wall, all the while alert to an instinct that the flat was being watched. She got out of bed a few times to press her nose to the window, but there was nothing to see on the street below, and she closed the blinds. Eventually she tiptoed downstairs to run herself a bath.

When she returned to her bedroom, she changed into her flannel pajamas and wandered through to the sitting room. Fay was out again, but her door was ajar, giving Evelyn a glimpse of her cluttered dressing table and the corner of an unmade bed. She sat on the sofa and flicked through a few magazines, but her mind wouldn't settle. The silence was like the slow drip of a tap. She switched on the wireless, turning up the volume as far as it would go, making the sound ricochet off the walls and shudder in her ears. For a while it drowned out her thoughts, but eventually she flicked it off and made her way back down the hallway to her bedroom.

As she climbed into bed, her mind strayed to her parents, and she considered telephoning them in Lewes. If she told them the truth, there was a chance, however slim, that they might offer some words of understanding, of comfort even. They might even tell her to come home, that they would look after her, and how could she refuse an imperative like that? From downstairs, the telephone continued to beckon like a weak sonar signal. For that was how Evelyn had started to feel: cast out somewhere on a dark ocean, desperate for someone to find her.

This time the tears came—great racking sobs, so loud she had to put a pillow over her face to smother them. Finally, having exhausted herself, she yanked the covers to her chin and closed her eyes. Her last thought was of that sliver of the Thames she could see glinting from her window at Chemley Court. She had read somewhere that parts of the river had frozen over in a recent blizzard, but she hadn't believed it. As the slender weight of sleep tugged her down, Evelyn imagined herself sprawled across that thin sheet of ice, the soft cries of gulls suspended above the water, waiting to swoop when the surface cracked.

MARCH 1948

NINETEEN

THE KNOCK AT Evelyn's door woke her with a start. She sat up, shivering, her head full of the distorted fragments of a fitful dream—Nina forced into that black car; the shriek of Mrs. Ivanov from the restaurant doorway; the little boy with scabby knees standing across the road, watching it all. She had fallen asleep in the armchair in front of the fireplace and the flat was now cold and very dark. Outside the streets were quiet. When another knock sounded, this time more insistent, she threw back the blanket and went quietly to the door, pressing her ear to the wood.

"Who is it?"

There was no answer. If she screamed her landlord would hear; he lived in the flat beneath her. She could strike the floorboards, or make a terrific racket from the fire escape. That would surely wake the building. Maybe the young couple from next door would make an appearance on the landing, the menacing husband in his drawers, eager for a fight. She opened the door a fraction, peering into the gloom. She stood like that, her breath growing moist against the jamb, until a man's face shifted into focus, the strong odor of whisky blasting through the gap between the chain and the lock.

"*Stephen?*"

He smiled crookedly. "Who did you think it would be—your War Office friend?"

She undid the chain and he pushed his way inside, stomping toward the fireplace, where he stopped, swaying slightly. He was drunk, Evelyn realized. She had never seen Stephen like this before, and for some reason it frightened her more than anything else about the past few days.

"You look like you've seen a ghost," he said with a hiccup.

Evelyn moved behind an armchair, her fingertips kneading the chenille back.

"I fell asleep. You startled me." She squinted at her wristwatch. It was after two. "I didn't think you'd come."

Stephen made a mess of removing his coat and tossed it on the ground. Evelyn stared at it, then looked back to him.

"Did you get your work done?"

"Yes, yes. Went to the club afterward. Had a few drinks with the chaps."

Stephen continued to stare at her, his eyes small. She'd always thought he had lovely eyes, hazel-colored, with neat freckles on his eyelids, but tonight they were blank and spiritless. He was angry, she could see that, but he was also struggling with another emotion. They had never strayed into this territory before, these murky waters of pain and confusion.

"Can I get you anything?" she asked, moving toward the stove. "A cup of tea?"

"Got any whisky?"

"No, just tea, I'm afraid."

She could feel him watching her as she brewed up a pot. She wished he wouldn't—something about his glazed, wounded expression made her want to scream.

"Look here, Stephen," she said, returning to her seat in the armchair once she'd handed him the steaming mug, "I am sorry about the other night, really I am."

He shrugged. Again she thought how odd it was to see him like this; Evelyn had only ever known him to be calm, restrained. Now his fair hair was disheveled, some sweaty strands plastered to his forehead.

"Won't you sit down?" She pointed to the other chair. "Stephen?"

He shook his head, his mouth a hard line. He looked around the flat as if he were searching for something, his eyes finally settling on Evelyn.

"I'm not staying. I'm sorry it's so late and that I gave you a fright, but I came over to tell you something." He laughed raggedly. "Only now I'm here I don't quite know how to say it."

Evelyn leaned back, her eyes throbbing. So it had come to this—this rupture. She had always known the day would arrive when Stephen announced he no longer cared to spend time with her. In many ways, she had been preparing herself for it from the moment they met. She thought about the way he had looked down on her that first afternoon in the gardens. He had sat beside her on that bench, they had got talking, and eventually he had offered Evelyn half of his sandwich. She had already eaten, but she had sensed a difference in this young man that made her accept it anyway; there was something expectant in his eyes, almost hopeful, as he passed over the paper bag. Later she had wondered what he had seen to make him look at her that way.

"It's fish paste," he'd said as Evelyn bit into the bread. "I have it every day. That's rations for you, I suppose. Do you like it?"

"Mm, oh yes." She managed a disgusting mouthful and smiled. "Thank you."

Stephen had watched her for another moment, then turned away with a chuckle, saying, "It's all right. I won't be offended by the truth."

Afterward he had asked for her number, and telephoned the flat the following evening. He wanted to buy her a drink. And though Evelyn had been out with men from time to time, she had felt something unprecedented toward Stephen as she hung up the receiver, something warm and unfurling. She carried this around with her in the days before they met again, unable to pinpoint the exact sensation he had elicited in her. But now she understood, as she stared at Stephen across the room, that it had been a kind of unmasking. That he was the first man since the war who had managed to guide her out, pale and bare, into the light.

Evelyn cleared her throat. "Whatever you have to say, Stephen, just say it." But her voice wasn't steady, her hands trembled in her lap. She didn't want him to say it; she wanted him to sit down and put his arm around her. But he was looking at her like she was wearing that mask again.

He began pacing in front of the fireplace, his left leg dragging behind him. Eventually he folded both arms against the mantelpiece and stood there with his head bowed, still swaying as if he could hear music, until he snapped around to face her.

"You know, Evelyn, for months I've wanted to take you to meet my parents in Bristol. To show you off. My mother is always asking about that clever girl from Lewes and will I ever bring her to visit . . . ? And I want to more than anything, but I've been so anxious about what this introduction would reveal to them—and to me. You see, I've come to realize that after all this time we've spent together I still really don't know you."

Stephen's expression had become entirely sober, his voice clear, as he moved toward the window, gaze fixed on the empty street below.

"I know the small things, of course—where you like to go for dinner, what films you might enjoy—but you shut me out whenever I stray any closer. I'm not sure you know you're doing it. It's second nature, I think. But the hardest part of it all is that the more you pull away, the more I want you. I've never met anyone like you, Evelyn. A woman who gives me room to be myself. Someone I can talk to for hours—for days on end if I could—and still look forward to our next time together, for the possibility of it. Because I think that's what I see in you that you can't see in yourself: I can see the person you could be. You have such warmth just below the surface, yet it's almost as if you're afraid of it, because every time it reveals itself you seem to snatch it from me. And though I've tried to understand why you might do that, and have come up with a dozen reasons, none of them change the fact that it hurts to be treated in this way. To have never had"—here his voice wavered—"your trust."

Finally he turned back to her. His face was drawn, as if some grief had arrived in his life unannounced. He was a good man. Evelyn had always known that, but she had somehow managed to push this understanding to one side, and now her heart was actually aching. A good, kind man—someone she had grown to care for deeply, perhaps even love. They could have a life together. They could be happy. But this goodness was where it had gone wrong for them, she realized. Stephen had no secrets from her; his past held no mystery. He was an open person—no guile, no artifice. How had they come together in the first place? It was nothing short of miraculous!

Stephen was shaking his head, still regarding her with incredulity. "I just wish I could understand what has made you this way."

"What way?" she said tiredly.

"So . . . *cold*."

And then, astonishingly, he began to cry. It was a dreadful sight, his face transforming into a blotchy mess. Evelyn watched for a while and, unable to comfort him, she began to wonder if there was indeed something wrong with her.

"I only want to *know* you," he wept.

"Stephen—"

"You know all about me." His breathing began to slow, his face wan again as he wiped his eyes. "Where I grew up. Where I went to school. My first girlfriend's name . . . And you also know the larger things. The fears, the nightmares." He pointed to his foot. "I watched my friends die in France, I washed their blood from my own skin. I've spoken to you about that terrible time, and it has been a comfort, Evelyn, to share that part of myself."

"But you know things about me too."

"I know the facts. *Some* facts. For goodness' sake, I don't even know what you really did in the war! But most of all I don't know what's going on inside your head." He tapped his chest. "Or what's going on in your heart."

Evelyn looked away. She had never heard him talk like this. Part of her felt light at his words, but she was fighting against her own instincts, even as she sensed herself being towed along by a current toward a monstrous whirlpool.

"No one ever knows what goes on in another person's head, let alone their heart."

It came out more coolly than she intended, and Stephen stared at her with red eyes.

"You don't think that."

"But I do."

"Why?" Stephen stepped closer. "Tell me why. You needn't be afraid of me."

Evelyn looked over her shoulder to the door. The latch was down, the bolt fixed. If I were to disappear, she thought, the world would continue just as it always has. Nothing would change. I would have never made an imprint. I would never be remembered. But she also knew if she kept living like this she would disappear anyway. Dwindle, reduce, evaporate. She could already feel herself diminishing. It had been gradual, wearing her away like the sea against rock. She was exhausted, and it was tempting to simply give in. But give in to what? Didn't she deserve some happiness? Didn't she deserve this man? Stephen was still crying, and Evelyn slumped forward, a low sound escaping from somewhere inside her. She slapped a hand over her mouth, horrified, but she couldn't stop it. Stephen stared, his face shiny and distorted.

"Come to me," she gasped. "Stephen, please."

When he hesitated, Evelyn felt the pressure building inside her. She knew if this burst, something huge and gaping would open up, a wound that might never heal. But when he took a step toward her, now dragging a chair up beside her armchair, she grasped his hands in hers, turned them over, and then raised them to her lips, and for the first time she dared to imagine that she might survive the act of telling the truth.

"You must promise to listen to the whole story." Her voice was raspy. "And when I'm finished, you may want to forget me."

"I could never—"

"You might even hate me."

She sniffed, wiping her nose with her sleeve. She could see confusion in Stephen's eyes, but before he could say anything she spoke again.

"My parents . . ." she said.

"What about them?"

"They're not dead."

"What do you mean?"

Evelyn swallowed. "They're still alive, as far as I know. In Lewes. It was easier to tell you they had died than explain why we're no longer in touch."

"I see." He watched her. "And why is that?"

"Because I'm so ashamed of what happened . . . Of what I did during the war . . . And now that shame has taken over and I don't know how to get rid of it. You see, I've pretended to be something I'm not for so long that I have trouble understanding what is real." She squeezed his hand. "Except for you. I know you're real, Stephen. You have been real to me from the moment we met."

His brow creased, and he looked back across the room. I've pushed him too far and he's going to leave, Evelyn thought, panic and despair building once more. He's going to walk away and never return. But then Stephen turned back to her and crossed his long legs. He hadn't walked out. He was still there, still listening, still waiting. He gave her a small nod, permission to continue.

Vincent had suggested starting at the beginning, but which one? And how could she make Stephen believe she had become a different person? Because she wasn't sure she was—a different person, that was—and she let out a long, shuddering breath.

"Evelyn?"

She had once made the choice to confront the past and that had required a certain kind of bravery. Evelyn looked inside herself now, searching for the resilience she'd summoned all those years ago. Only this time she would be using it for truth and not all the nebulous gray found between the lies. She began to talk, and they sat like that, one chair beside the other, Stephen's soft hands in hers, until the sun rose on the new day, washing the dark sky clean.

MARCH 1940

TWENTY

EVELYN AND VINCENT caught a taxi to the pub opposite the square on Westbridge Road in Battersea. It stank of stale smoke and beer, and above the front door was the eponymous raven, its shiny black eyes trained on Evelyn as she wandered over to a table near the fireplace while Vincent fetched the drinks.

Setting down the satchel containing a small camera, Evelyn scanned the pub's patrons. It was only one o'clock, but already a row of regulars were perched at the front bar, their heads bent to the wireless, the broadcast of the trots ringing through the place. Elsewhere, in the main lounge, a young man sat flicking through a newspaper while another threw darts despondently at a board.

"Right," said Vincent when he returned with two brandies. "The keg room is out the back. I couldn't see anything just now, but I'll have a better peek when I use the gents'. Then we can plan how to take those photographs for White."

"What's the publican like?" Evelyn asked.

"Seems all right. Infiltration is more your sport, remember? I just solve the crosswords."

Evelyn smiled and looked past him to a man who had appeared at the bar. He was older than Evelyn, nudging forty, with thinning hair and chafed crimson lips. He reached across the counter to shake the publican's hand with the obsequiousness of a pastor. His gaze settled for a moment on Evelyn before he took his stout and sat near the billiards table.

"A crumb?" Vincent asked.

"Hard to tell." Evelyn sighed, rubbing at her eyes. "I wanted to work on something new after the Lion Society case, but now I'd prefer to sleep for a hundred years."

Vincent sat back, loosening his tie. "How are you feeling after all that business?"

Evelyn shrugged. "What about you?" she asked. "How were things at Chemley Court while I was in the field?"

"So-so." Vincent smiled grimly. "Bennett has been like a bear with a sore head. I don't know what he wants or what I can do to make him happy."

Evelyn studied the dark stubble on her friend's chin, then his slate-colored eyes. She drank some brandy and wondered what would become of them both when all this was over.

⌒

Evelyn and Vincent went back to the Raven Inn the following week. They chatted with the publican, a jolly fellow from Conwy, and began feeding him pieces of their fabricated backstory. On their third visit, Evelyn managed to distract the Welshman with a query about an old photograph hanging on the wall, giving Vincent the opportunity to sneak into the keg room with the camera. He found the bundle of pro-German leaflets beneath an old metal fan and took several photographs.

Evelyn had begun building profiles of the regulars, but had not found any leads: they were mainly elderly men who could barely stand up straight to toddle off for a piss, let alone distribute propaganda. The man playing darts hadn't appeared again, nor had the chap reading the newspaper, while another fellow in a dark suit with a shifty expression turned out to be only selling bottles of black market French perfume in the lane at the back of the pub.

This left the man with thinning hair and sore lips. He'd been back twice, speaking in the same quiet tone to the publican, but Evelyn had never seen any material pass between them. She had managed to smile at him once when he took a seat close to their table, and there was something boyish about his unblemished face. Colin, his name was. She'd heard the publican say it.

"He's our mark," Evelyn told Vincent on the taxi ride back to Pimlico. "I'll come alone next time and try to strike up a conversation. We'll see if he leads us anywhere."

Vincent made a face. "Better you than me, darling. Colin's not exactly one of life's more glorious specimens."

Evelyn glanced out the window at the blur of the Thames and felt a twinge of humiliation once again. She clutched the suitcase containing the camera tight to her chest.

"Lucky it's for King and country, then," she muttered.

⌁

Evelyn returned to the Raven Inn the next afternoon. She wore her blue tambourine beret and brown felt suit, and made sure she painted her lips, just as White had instructed. She brought along a newspaper and a fresh packet of cigarettes. After a few words with the publican, during which she explained that her brother had found a job moving freight at the docks, she took a seat near the window overlooking the street. At around two o'clock, Colin came in through the front door, this time carrying his own small leather briefcase. He sat at the table next to Evelyn. When the publican brought over her pot of tea, and Colin a fresh pint, she tried to catch his eye.

"Busy day, is it?" She nodded to the briefcase. "You're a businessman?"

Colin shook his head. "Goodness me, no. I'm an engineer. Was, in any case." He sniffed. "I'm doing maintenance work for now while I look for something new."

Evelyn stirred milk into her tea. "My word, an engineer? You must be clever."

"I don't know about that . . ." He spoke in a mumble, grinding grains of salt into the tabletop. His hands were large and callused.

"I'm sure you're too modest." Evelyn smiled at him. "Do you work local, Colin? It is Colin, isn't it? I overheard the man behind the bar . . . I'm Bea Henry."

He nodded, but still he wouldn't look at her. "Yes, just over at the power plant. I've been there a few months. I was in Acton before that."

"What took you there?"

He raised his eyes and Evelyn finally saw they were a startling green color, like forest pools. He stood up and pushed his chair nearer to her table.

"I worked for Siemens-Schuckert. There fifteen years, all told."

Evelyn brought the cup to her lips to blow on the scalding tea. "It's a German firm, isn't it?"

"That's right."

"I heard it closed recently. Some talk of . . . interference, wasn't it?"

"It was a good firm," said Colin, sticking out his chin. "And a very good place to work. I was sorry the day we all received our notice. Management understood the value of hard work—and of a hardworking Englishman."

"Mm," said Evelyn. "Should be more like that, in my view."

"Well, their hands were tied, weren't they? The government set out to destroy them."

Evelyn put down her cup. "They did?"

"Oh yes." Colin leaned forward, his breath oddly sweet-smelling. "Almost from the very beginning. And they destroyed good, honest men who worked for them in the process. So what if some of them agreed with some of the things what—" He paused, blushing, his eyes fixed back on the pint glass. "Forgive me, Bea. You must think it very rude of me to be running on like that."

"Not at all."

But he'd taken fright, and when a shout came from the front bar, followed by the sound of a glass smashing, all his reserve returned, and she knew she'd not get anything else from him that afternoon.

"I should be heading back to work," he muttered. "I've only an hour for lunch." She hadn't even finished her tea and he was already standing up.

"Of course, Colin. Maybe I'll see you here again?"

"Yes, all right. I may drop by again early next week."

Again he blushed, and in another life she might have felt sorry for him. Evelyn studied the lint on his shoulders, the light dusting of dandruff in his wispy hair. There is nothing more dangerous, she thought to herself, than a clever man with an ax to grind.

"Next week it is, then," she said.

⌒

Evelyn found White in his study when she returned from Battersea, Vincent's photographs of the leaflets in the keg room spread across the desk. Rain fell heavily outside, coating the window in a greasy slick, and the room was growing dark. Ted Young sat in the corner at his typewriter, bashing away at another report. White gestured for Evelyn to take a seat.

"So," he said, setting down his cigarette. "Vincent tells me you have a suspect in the crosshairs."

"Could do," said Evelyn. "A fellow by the name of Colin. He's been coming into the Raven regularly, is on good terms with the publican. Otherwise he seems a loner. A bit unsettled in his own skin. He's certainly sympathetic toward Hitler . . ."

White raised his eyebrows. "But you're not sure?"

"I suppose it's a hunch more than anything else." She chewed at her lip. "It was rather odd, actually. This afternoon, when we got talking, Colin told me that he had been an engineer but lost his job some time ago. It's difficult to explain, but there was something about this work, what it had meant to him, that gave me pause." She looked up. "He's angry, very angry."

"Is that so?" White's eyes widened. "Did he tell you who he worked for?"

"The German firm Siemens-Schuckert. They had the plants in Acton and Ealing, didn't they?"

"Yes. We had been watching them, but when war broke out resources were directed elsewhere . . ."

Evelyn frowned as White began scribbling on a piece of paper. She'd never seen him take notes.

"Right," he said, setting down the pen. "Thank you, Evelyn. This is very useful information."

"I thought so too." She sat back, gazing at the ceiling. "I've been turning the thing over and over in my head since I got in the taxi, and I can't help wondering if he's up to something else? Something perhaps bigger than this leaflet operation?"

White watched her levelly before he stood up and wandered over to the window, where he pressed his fingertips against the glass.

"You're due to go away next weekend, aren't you?" he said. "Heading down to Shropshire?"

Evelyn blinked. "Well, yes . . ." She had hardly had time to think about it, but it was finally the weekend of Sally's wedding. "But I wonder whether it might be better to stay on here and follow up this lead?"

Pushing his hands deep into his pockets, White shook his head. "It will do you some good to see your friends. Get out of London for a time. Enjoy the fresh country air. Enjoy a break from all . . . *this*." He gestured around the study.

"But, sir." Evelyn sat forward. "I think there's something to this Colin fellow. I can keep visiting the Raven while at the same time doing more digging on—"

"I don't want you digging," White said. "You were instructed to investigate the leaflets and you've done that. We'll bring in the publican and get him to talk. The rest doesn't matter."

"*Doesn't matter?*" Evelyn was shaking her head. "I can stay on this, sir. I can find out what Colin is part of and—"

"No." Something stealthy had crept into White's voice. "I've given you your orders. Don't go back to the Raven and don't talk to Colin again. I'll pass your intelligence on to Special Branch and ask them to follow up with it themselves." He cleared his throat. "The Lion Society trial is due to start in a couple of weeks. You need to sit tight until then."

"After which I go back to the Scrubs just as you had planned." Evelyn pushed away her chair. "I don't understand this. I'm still useful in the field. You said it yourself: I've done good work. Why do you want me back in John Chadwick's cell answering telephones all day?"

"It's not a question of what I want," White said. "It's what is good for all of us. Please, Evelyn. I have my reasons for telling you to step back from this new investigation. You just have to trust me."

The study dimmed further, and Evelyn heard Ted flick on a lamp and trudge over to the window to close the curtains—in the heat of the exchange, she had forgotten he was in the room with them. When it became clear that White had dismissed her, she went to the door, but paused. Standing there, Evelyn saw White as a stranger might: as nothing more than an eccentric older gentleman. They might imagine him to be a professor, or a doctor—someone distinguished, with integrity and importance. Someone to be counted on. But the truth was that the moment Bennett White stepped outside the flat he disappeared. He left no mark, no shadow, not even a memory. It would be dangerous to defy him—because she had come to realize this was her only choice now if she were to avoid returning to her old life—but perhaps it wouldn't matter. It hadn't occurred to her until that moment that she had placed all her trust in the hands of a ghost.

The following week, Evelyn waited for White to leave the flat for daily briefings with the Home Office before ducking downstairs to catch a taxi over to Battersea. Each time she found Colin waiting in the front bar, a nervous rash spreading up his throat when he recognized her in the doorway. They sat together by the billiards table. Evelyn mostly talked about herself, about her work in accounts at the Deptford plant before she lost her job ("because of all them East End Jews come over from Europe") and how it was lucky she had a little money set aside from when her mother died, otherwise she and her brother would be out on the street. And slowly, like the boiler in an engine room, Colin began to warm up. He spoke more about the war, about how his dicky heart had stopped him joining up, and then about Hitler, who at least wanted to make Germany a nation his countrymen could be proud of.

"He puts Germans first, doesn't he?" Evelyn said. "What exactly is the problem with standing up for the English in our own blinking country? Why has that suddenly become a crime?"

"It's a . . . bleeding disgrace," Colin stuttered, then he raised his glass for a mouthful of stout.

Evelyn brought out a cigarette, aware that Colin continued to watch her like he had been slapped across the face, though once he'd finished his pint there was something newly resolute in his posture.

"I can tell you, Evelyn, that there is quite a bit of it going around," he said.

"What's that?"

"Opposition to the Jew war. I don't know a single man or woman happy about fighting the Germans again. And for what?" He looked over his shoulder. "I don't like to brag, but I could give you names right here and now of people—and people high up, I don't mind adding—who wouldn't shed a tear if Hitler were to march into London and set us straight."

"Really?"

Evelyn drank slowly from her cup, taking in the strange man nodding vigorously across the table.

"In fact," Colin went on, "I'm part of a group of like-minded Englishmen and -women. We've been meeting for the past few months."

"Like a club?" Beneath the table, Evelyn squeezed her fists together in triumph.

"Nothing so formal." Again he looked about. "It's a risky business, of course. I could find myself in a lot of trouble . . ."

He glared at his empty glass and once more Evelyn felt him slipping away. She reached out and put her hand over his, and Colin gaped at it, apparently no less surprised than if she'd taken off her dress right there at the table. But she needed him to tell her more if she was to go back to White and convince him to keep her on the investigation.

"But why? You're only talking, aren't you? Or have they banned that now and all?" She edged forward. "And what do you do, Colin, in this group?"

"Mainly we get together and talk about things that have gone wrong for Britain."

"And about ending poverty in our slums?"

He looked at her oddly but wouldn't say, his eyes darting back to the casement window and the movement of people out on the street. He checked his watch, fidgeting.

"I'm sorry, Colin, I don't mean to pry," Evelyn said. "My mother used to say I should have been a spy, I was that curious." She laughed.

He smiled briefly, studying her as she slipped out of the seat. She thought she'd blown it, but he stayed near as he guided her toward the front door. They stood on the pavement outside the pub, the traffic streaming by, until Colin spoke over the noise. "Listen, about this group . . ."

"Yes?"

"Well, it's only six of us, old workers from Siemens-Schuckert mostly, but we're always looking for more to join. I could put in a word?"

"Would you?" Evelyn squeezed his arm. "It sounds like just my sort of thing. Who knows—I might be exactly what you're looking for!"

Colin smiled properly now and dimples appeared in his cheeks. "I'll speak with the chairman. Well, I say chairman, though there's nothing official about it. But he does run the show, so to speak. He's a splendid chap. Very professional."

Evelyn's heart began to thud. If only White had listened to her . . . Colin leaned in, and for a horrible moment she thought he was going to kiss her. But he only wanted to whisper something in her ear, though there was no one around to overhear him.

"He's ex-navy, you know. Hancock, his name is."

His breath was hot against Evelyn's cheek. She tried not to shudder.

"And won't you look at this . . ."

He brought out a handkerchief from his jacket pocket. Folded inside was a badge with a black cross within a silver casing. There was a small swastika in the center.

"Is that an Iron Cross?"

It hardly seemed possible. She'd read about them during her research for the Lion Society investigation. They were military decorations awarded to German soldiers.

"Hancock said I could have a loan of it. He's generous like that. They're very rare, I believe."

"Yes, I'm sure they are," Evelyn said.

Colin folded the badge away. Then, with a nervous smile, he stalked off in the direction of the Battersea power station.

Evelyn watched until he'd disappeared, then she hailed a taxi, unease gnawing at her stomach. How on earth had this Hancock fellow got his hands on an Iron Cross?

TWENTY-ONE

EVELYN LEFT CHEMLEY Court that same afternoon with her suitcase and dress bag and traveled straight to Euston station. Another blizzard had been forecast, and by the time she reached Birmingham the dozen or so other Wesley guests sharing the same service were told that the local train had been canceled, leaving them stranded. They congregated at the stationmaster's booth while he made a telephone call. Connection was patchy across the county, but eventually he got through and an hour later an estate van pulled up out the front and took the disgruntled party directly to the manor.

By now it was well after midnight, and only Parker was awake to escort them to their rooms, his candle throwing wobbly shadows against the great paneled walls. For once Evelyn had been put up in the north wing, where a fire had been lit, and though exhausted after the long journey she slept badly, tossing and turning against the tight-fitting sheets. She was dreading seeing Julia. How on earth was she going to explain herself? After all this time, she still didn't know what she could say that wouldn't give away her work with Bennett White. Maybe Julia had already said something to the Wesleys; that would explain why she had been given a room on the other side of the house, and why it had been weeks since she'd last spoken to Sally . . . Evelyn rolled over, squeezing her eyes shut, desperate for sleep, but a pair of robins had perched on the ledge outside her window, their high-pitched melodies jolting her awake every time she managed to nod off.

By morning the fire had gone out in the hearth and the room was chilly. Evelyn woke to voices in the corridor, and when she drew back the velvet curtains she was almost blinded by the glare. Overnight the wind and sleet had died away and the grounds were now blanketed in fresh snow, so deep in places she could hardly make out the drive or the groundsmen near the walled garden frantically shoveling out a path. She brought out her House of Worth dress from the wardrobe, running her fingertips over the apricot sash, then she drew the voile behind the curtains together and began to get ready.

At two o'clock, the house guests made their way toward the sandstone chapel overlooking the lake. The day had warmed up and the slushy pathway made for a slow procession up the hill. Evelyn sat toward the back of the chapel next to a boy with a downy top lip. She watched Hugh Wesley at the entrance, avuncular as usual, and then Jonty at the altar in his morning coat, looking nervous. Evelyn recognized Julia's father, Lord Jennings, sitting near the front with a young woman she assumed was his wife. She couldn't see Julia anywhere.

Finally, there was some murmuring along the pews and the organist began "Dear Lord and Father of Mankind." Evelyn turned. All this time she hadn't considered what Sally might look like today, and there she was, her dear friend, exquisite in a silk dress and long scalloped veil, Hugh's arm through hers, looking so calm and confident as she drifted down the aisle.

The wedding banquet began at four o'clock in the great hall. Evelyn was seated on a table near the bridal party with Miranda and Katherine McGregor, a pair of bucktoothed twins she'd known at Somerville College, and while they twittered about their villa at Lake Garda, Evelyn drank champagne, half the bottle gone before they had reached the denouement of their tale.

"Evelyn? There you are!" It was Hugh, his big chest puffed out as he made his way toward her. "And don't you look smashing."

"Not half as smashing as the bride. Congratulations, Hugh!"

He gave her a bruising hug. He smelled of wine and, judging from his stained lips, he'd already had quite a lot to drink.

"She scrubs up all right, doesn't she, old Sallywag. My word, Evelyn, this is the best day of my life. But what about you? It's been too long since we last saw you." He waggled a finger in mock admonishment. "Things must be going well at the War Office if you've no time for us anymore. Keeping the Boche at bay?"

Evelyn felt her smile wane as she looked into his benign blue eyes. They were so like Sally's, she'd never noticed it before. She held her breath, waiting for him to say something about Chesterfield and Caxton Hall, but when he didn't she realized that he mustn't know, that Julia must have kept her secret after all, and she almost cried out with relief.

"Elizabeth and I have always been grateful that Sally has you, Evelyn—and now Julia does too," Hugh said. "She told me she's seen a bit of you in London these past months. I'm so pleased. She's needed good, sensible friends."

He placed a hand on her shoulder and Evelyn studied the large, heart-shaped flower in his lapel—the *Brassavola*, Julia's orchid.

"I've enjoyed spending time with her," she said.

"I don't need to tell you that I was quite worried for a while there. That husband . . . She went quite wild with him, quite wild indeed. Mixing with all sorts in Berlin, all a bit rich for me, and I'm a staunch Tory. Still, I'm glad to know how well she's doing with her charity work and making new friends." Hugh gave her shoulder a squeeze in parting. "So, thank you, Evelyn, for everything."

Evelyn watched him dart between the tables, as nimble as a dancer, before she spotted Sally across the hall and gave her a wide, looping wave. Perhaps everything was going to be all right.

"There you are, Evelyn, come to save me!" Sally cried as she made her way through the crowd. "If I have to talk to another ancient relative I think I'll keel over and die."

Evelyn hugged her, Sally's flushed face warm against her cool cheek.

"You look just marvelous, Sal! You both do." She nodded toward Jonty standing a few paces away, but he looked away, pretending not to hear. "Now, remind me—where are you headed on your honeymoon?"

"The van der Hoort estate on Loch Lomond. We'll be there for a few days before Jonty goes back to the base and me to the manor. Then we'll start looking for a place of our own. Daddy has offered us one of the cottages here, but I'd like to have a house in London." Sally paused, fixing her bright gaze on Evelyn. "Perhaps I might stay with you, Ev, in the meantime? It's been so long since we spent any real time together. You could help me search for flats."

"Stay in Soho instead of Mayfair?" Evelyn laughed. "You do remember 'cozy' being the best thing you could say about my place?"

"I don't mind. It might be fun."

But it didn't sound like much fun to Evelyn, the silence between them growing as Jonty shifted his weight from foot to foot.

"Of course you should stay, Sal," she said at last. "Though I'll warn you, we'll have to bunk together. And I work such long hours . . ."

It sounded feeble, but Evelyn could not find a way to talk her out of it. Thankfully, another aged relative interrupted, diverting Sally's attention, and Evelyn drifted away toward a spot by the paneling beneath one of the pastoral oils. For some reason Jonty followed, leaning against the wall beside her, his face broader and flatter than she remembered, that bump on his nose more pronounced than ever.

"Is something the matter?" she asked when he refused a cigarette.

"Why don't you come out and say it?" he muttered as he toyed with the new wedding band on his finger.

"Say what?"

"That you don't want her to stay with you. In London."

Evelyn blew out some smoke. "Why do you think that?"

"She's *needed* you. She's needed a *friend*." Jonty spat out the words. "But you just disappeared into thin air."

Evelyn looked at him steadily. "I'm not a scullery maid, Jonty. I don't appear on command."

"No, you're much shrewder than that."

"I beg your pardon?"

Jonty tucked in his chin. "Where have you been, then? Enlighten me."

Evelyn stared across the great expanse of the hall, all the smiling heads and blur of dancing, and felt for a moment as a bird must, hovering above human life, seeing everything and yet a part of none of it. She glanced back at Jonty, once again tracing the blunt contours of his tanned face.

"I work, Jonty. I know that must be a difficult concept for you to grasp, but I am busy." She crossed her arms, wanting to create space between them, a buffer against his bulk. "Not that I need to explain myself to you. Sally is my dear friend—"

"Only when it suits you."

"What does *that* mean?"

Jonty stepped toward her and Evelyn saw for the first time the fresh lines around his eyes. He had grown older; it had never occurred to her that he might carry any burden of this war.

"You use people, Evelyn," he said quietly. "That's what I mean. I've thought it for a while—there's something too self-assured about you, too cool. Like you've been playing a great joke on the rest of us. Smug, that's what you are." He paused. "It's not an attractive quality."

Evelyn glanced away again, rage and fright swelling inside her. She had always thought Jonty didn't care much for Sally's feelings—once, long ago, she might have been pleased to know that he did.

"You've got it wrong," she said.

"Then why do you never see her in London?"

"I've told you, it's complicated. My work—"

"Oh yes." He scoffed. "At the War Office, isn't it? Tell me, is it so taxing to make tea and type letters for some third-rate bureaucrat that you can't spend an evening with your closest friend?"

Evelyn smiled. It felt ghastly, her skin stretched tight, but she couldn't help it. The ballroom crowd was getting boisterous, and when Evelyn felt herself being thrust forward with the sweaty surge of dancers almost into Jonty's arms disgust welled up inside her. It was inconceivable that she had ignored his humiliating jibes for so long, believing she must to get on, that she must not be a nuisance, that she must keep Sally out of it. But she wouldn't live like that anymore. She refused to be cowed by those who were so undeserving—here at the manor, and back at MI5. She looked across the hall at Sally, who was now captured in some serious exchange with a different old lady. Surely their friendship could survive this tectonic shift?

"You know something, Jonty?" Evelyn said, turning to look him square in the eye. "I've always thought Sally could do far better than you. She's gentle and kind, and you're nothing more than a bully and a thug. And yet for some mad reason she still loves you. But don't think you can speak to me like one of your border collies. Because if you ever do it again, I'll tell your wife and everyone else at this wedding that you tried to kiss me, and then they'll all know you for what you really are."

She thought she would savor the way the color drained from his face, but somehow Jonty standing there, his thick neck straining at his collar as he grasped at words of protest, made Evelyn feel broken. She shoved her glass at him and strode away, threading a path through the dancers, determined to forget him and have this night for herself. But she soon ran into Hugh again, and he insisted on a dance, and before she knew it she was flying around the great hall, Hugh's incoherent chatter at her ear. After a while she began to let herself go, weightless in Hugh's arms. Maybe John Chadwick had been telling the truth. Maybe it was as simple as locking away all the nasty pieces of life in a box and moving on; among this press of damp flesh it did seem possible.

She closed her eyes, Hugh's grip slippery on her wrists as they made their final whirl. The quartet was thunderous, the strings bringing the tune toward a frenzied crescendo, and Evelyn, overwhelmed by vertigo, let out a whoop, her lungs expanding with a rush of hot air. Then, at the exact moment during the long fermata when the crowds lurched to one side of the hall, she recognized Julia through the line of dancers. Evelyn raised a hand to her eyes, rubbing at them, as if she were seeing a mirage. But there she was, smoking at the foot of the stairs. With her head still spinning from the foxtrot, Evelyn tried to pull Hugh away, to hide herself, but he mistook her gesture and relinquished her from their dance. By now Julia had spotted her and was making her way across the dance floor. Evelyn stood trapped in the crowd beneath the chandelier, but when Julia reached her she only took up Evelyn's hands, her smile glittering.

"I've been looking for you all day," she said.

"You have?"

"Come quick." Julia urged her away from the dancers toward the staircase. "Before Hugh ropes you in for the rumba."

They went to Hugh's study on the first floor—"We can talk here," Julia said as she flicked on a lamp, the shade casting a green hue across the room.

Evelyn sat on the windowsill. A blast of cold air rattled the glass.

"Drink?" Julia made her way toward the trolley in the corner. "Port?"

"All right."

Evelyn stared over the west lawn. The moon had drifted out from behind the clouds to throw some light on the garden, and a few dirty patches here and there had sprung up in the snow.

Julia joined Evelyn. Her dark hair was tied up in a blue band. It made her look almost girlish.

"You're a hard woman to catch up with," she remarked, lighting up a cigarette. "Have you been away?"

Evelyn drank some of the sweet, syrupy port. "No, nothing like that," she said. "It's all been rather frantic at Whitehall. I haven't had a spare second."

Julia pressed her fingertip to the window, leaving a smudge on the glass. They perched there for a few moments, gazing out over the white spread of lawn. The music downstairs grew loud again as the quartet began a new cycle.

The hard line of Evelyn's jaw began to ache—she had to say something—and eventually she set down her glass. "I thought after you saw me in the park . . . Well, perhaps you wouldn't want to see me again?"

Julia swiped at some stray smoke. "Why shouldn't I want that?"

Evelyn blinked. "The thing is, I can explain. What I was doing there. Why I said . . . what I said."

"There's no need, really. There's not much I haven't seen or heard, Evelyn. We're still free to think our own thoughts the last time I checked."

Julia smiled, her head angled in reflection, and though she knew she should have felt gratitude and a sense of reprieve, something about the other woman's expression as she gazed back at her set Evelyn's teeth on edge. No matter how much Julia valued free thinking, this was not the response she had expected.

"You know, London can be a lonely city," Julia murmured. "I'd forgotten that. It can be hard to find your own people, to share in a sense of community. Now, my father, he's a feckless sort of man, not much good with responsibility, or anything else for that matter, but he did teach me the value of finding someone to share your life with. To find yourself in that other person. I don't think Hugh has ever quite understood that—how I wanted an equal in Hans, that I *needed* it. Not only in intellect but in values. In beliefs." Julia's eyes were fixed on Evelyn. "You do know what I mean, don't you?"

Evelyn didn't answer. She watched Julia stand and abruptly walk out of the room, leaving her to follow to the wing balcony, where they had a view down to the ballroom. More dancers had crowded the floor, moving in dual lines to another round of foxtrot, as one of the twins— she was too exhausted to tell one from the other—gave Evelyn a wave.

"There he is," Julia whispered. "Can you see him?"

Away from the dancing loitered a few men and women alongside the tapestries. It didn't take long for Evelyn to locate the tall gentleman with dark hair. From the balcony, he looked sharp in his tuxedo, a shoulder pressed against the paneling, keeping a distance, whether by accident or design, from the other wedding guests. After a moment, he raised his eyes and nodded toward Julia.

"That's your man?"

"Yes." Julia's breath was light against Evelyn's cheek. "He's handsome, isn't he?"

"I suppose so. It's serious, then, between you?"

"You could say that."

"You know, I'm not sure I know his name."

Julia was staring down at the man, smiling faintly. "It's Paul," she said. "Paul Hancock."

Evelyn stared back at her, every one of her nerve endings crackling. "And he's in the navy, you said?"

"Not anymore. He's an engineer, actually. He worked for a time at the plant in Acton."

A dark thrill pressed against Evelyn's chest. "Siemens-Schuckert?"

Julia's smile grew wider. "Now, how did you know that?"

But she hadn't known. She hadn't known a thing, and as she watched Julia lean against the banister, one foot tapping in time with the music on the rug, she felt something give inside herself, as if part of her flesh had been torn away. How could she have been so stupid?

"Paul's rented a room at the Crofton Hotel in Kensington," Evelyn heard Julia say from far away; it was as if she had been plunged underwater. "I spend time there whenever I can get away from Curzon Street. In fact we're driving back to London later tonight. Perhaps you'd like to come around on Friday? We're entertaining a few other friends, then we might go out. Not the Four Hundred Club, I promise. Room number four, eight o'clock? I'm eager for you to meet him somewhere more private."

There was movement on the stairs below them, and Evelyn spied Sally's blond hair, her dress trailing at her feet. She had the wedding bouquet in her hands. Evelyn turned to Julia.

"Does Sally know? About Paul?"

Julia shook her head. "And please don't tell her, or Hugh. They'd only try to keep me away from him."

"Why would they do that?"

"He's not like them. He's . . . different."

Sally had reached the top of the stairs, looking about. *"Evelyn?"*

Her voice was light but constrained by some emotion Evelyn didn't recognize. She drew up alongside Julia, grasping the white roses so tightly the stems looked ready to snap. At last Sally stepped forward, her arm outstretched. The willowy silk of her dress was already crumpled, like the old wings of a moth. "Won't you come with me, Evelyn?" she said quietly. "I'm about to throw the bouquet."

They went downstairs. The crowd had stopped their dancing. Sally stood on the third step, her arms raised for quiet, and when her audience had complied she made a pivot and launched the bouquet. Evelyn watched Hugh among the revelers, his delight stretched wide across his glowing red face. While today had marked a turning point in Sally's life, Hugh's happiness appeared just as absolute. She thought of her own father, and their recent trip to the seaside; how contented he had been with Evelyn and her mother together again. What kind of pain would the truth about Julia inflict on Hugh and the family?

Across the hall, Evelyn spotted Julia standing beside Hancock, her head bent toward his as he whispered something, and when she met Evelyn's eye she felt a dreadful thread between them grow taut once more. Then one of the McGregor twins plucked the bouquet from the air and the ballroom broke into maniacal applause.

TWENTY-TWO

WHEN EVELYN ARRIVED back from Shropshire on Sunday afternoon she ran straight up to the flat, had a quick wash at the basin, and changed her dress. Throwing on a teal cardigan and yanking up a fresh pair of woolen tights, it occurred to her that this day, and the decisions she made in it, would probably be the most important of her life. She grabbed her handbag and rushed back downstairs, catching the bus toward Green Park. As she alighted at the Natural History Museum, she realized she had at last moved beyond that place of careful calculation and was now acting purely on instinct.

Part of this was knowing she had to confront Julia as soon as possible to prize her away from Paul Hancock before she brought ruin on herself and the rest of the Wesley family. It was only a matter of time before Special Branch closed in on the Siemens-Schuckert group. And with Nina Ivanov's trial scheduled to start next week, Evelyn would soon be forced from the field back to desk work at the Scrubs—and no longer in a position to help Julia.

There had been no opportunity to speak to Sally or Hugh about what she had learned at the wedding—Sally had left for Loch Lomond immediately after the wedding, and Evelyn had caught the first train back to London before most of the manor had awoken. A bigger problem was White. Failing to report Julia's involvement with Hancock was risky, but Evelyn had come up with a plan by the time the train arrived at Euston. She would tell White that Julia had discovered her work at MI5 and threatened to blow her cover before the Lion Society trial. The lie was flimsy, but she knew he would be tempted by just how far Julia's cooperation could extend once she came in to Chemley Court, especially if it meant they had an operative embedded deep inside a new cell of German sympathizers. If Evelyn walked this tightrope, it was just possible that everyone could come away from this untainted.

The Crofton Hotel was a shabby hostel near Hyde Park. Before going inside, Evelyn stopped on the street to survey the pedestrians and passing cars, but noticed nothing out of the ordinary. Then she went to the corner phone box and had the operator put her through to the hotel's concierge. An elderly man answered the call, and Evelyn asked to speak with a guest named Hancock—she needed to make sure Julia was alone in the room. After a few rings, Julia answered, and in a gruff voice Evelyn asked for "Paul."

"He's just gone out," Julia said. "He'll be back in half an hour, or I can take down a message . . . ?"

Evelyn hung up the phone and ran across the road, nodding a quick hello to the concierge and taking the stairs to the first floor. She strode the maroon-carpeted corridor until she found number four and knocked.

After a moment, Julia opened the door. "Evelyn?" She looked past her, a confused smile on her face. "You know we're not meeting until Friday. Paul's just gone out."

Evelyn pushed her way inside. The room was small, two single beds with floral-printed sheets jammed together against a mildew-stained wall. The curtains were drawn, casting the place in a reddish light, and an ashtray on the side table smoldered with cigarette ends. Men's slippers had been tossed beside the bed, a pair of braces hanging from the hook on the back of the door. Two toothbrushes in a glass by the basin, a bra flung over the chair.

"Evelyn, what's going on?"

The room seemed to be shrinking. Evelyn went to the window, peering between the gap in the curtains. The street was busy for the early evening, the lights from passing cars flaring against the smeared glass.

"We need to talk," she said quietly.

"Yes, we do. I was going to wait until Friday, but since you're here . . ."

Evelyn turned around. Closing the door with a soft click, Julia crossed the floor toward the chest of drawers. She picked up her packet of cigarettes, lit up, and took a seat on the edge of the bed.

"Did I ever tell you I was there in '34 during the Säuberung? Hans took me. I saw Goebbels address the crowds in Bebelplatz. It was terribly thrilling; all the shouting and crying. The students couldn't throw books onto the bonfires fast enough." Julia blew out a steady stream of smoke. "That's what they don't tell you—that it was the students who began the burning. Or that they didn't require much encouragement. They *wanted* to purge the universities of those books." Julia gazed at her, amber eyes wide and clear.

Evelyn swallowed. "Why are you saying this?"

"Because we are alike, that's why. Two halves of the same coin."

"Why do you think that?"

Julia tapped some ash to the carpet. "Because I was in Nina's flat the first night you visited. I know who you really are."

It wasn't possible. Evelyn put a hand out behind her, clutching at the sill. The floor seemed to pitch and tilt, as if it were about to crack open beneath her.

"I'm sure you can imagine my shock when she said you were coming." Julia chuckled. "Here I was thinking you were a proper little patriot, a real girl guide. But you've surprised me, Evelyn. I found something of myself in you. I found a kindred spirit."

"Wait a minute . . ." Evelyn grasped for words. None of it made any sense. "How could you have been at the flat?"

"There's a door in the corner of Nina's workshop that appears to be locked up, but it actually leads to a small dressing room with a desk and a chair. I sit in there and listen during those meetings or whenever Nina brings in a new recruit, and later, when everyone's gone, we talk. Funny, isn't it, how the biggest things can be right under our noses . . ." Julia flashed a wry smile. "The other women, they never see me either—most of them don't even know I exist. Your friend, Mrs. Armstrong, has no idea! I suppose we only see what we want to. Nina had you all thinking she was running that tight little ship with her loyal troops marching to Valhalla, but the truth is she was working for me."

Watching Julia grind out her cigarette in the ashtray beside the bed, Evelyn thought back to a time, playing fullback at Raheen, when she had been hit in the stomach by a hockey ball. It was the most painful thing she'd ever experienced, like the air had been literally knocked out of her, and she'd curled up on the grass, her vision dim, wondering if her lungs would ever begin working again, as her teammates crowded around her. This felt worse, much worse. Wherever she looked now she saw devastation, as though an earthquake had struck.

"So when I saw you in St. James's Park, with the Jewish boy, that was all an act?"

"Of course!" Julia clapped her hands together. "I had to be sure of you, didn't I, before Nina invited you to join? But you really did exceed my expectations."

"So that's why you returned from Germany," Evelyn said, shaking her head. "It wasn't because you wanted to get away from the regime; it was because you believed it needed to be alive in Britain too."

"We're crying out for our own revolution," Julia said. "It's a Darwinian struggle; it always has been. When I knew I was coming back to London, I got in touch with Nina. A mutual friend at the Italian embassy introduced us a few years ago at a party in Berlin, and we began building our network from then. And for a while things looked like they were working for us, didn't they? We were making real progress. But our work can't stop because of the arrests. We're on the cusp of something remarkable here, Evelyn. We can stop Churchill's ascent to power. We can make a targeted strike."

"I don't understand . . ."

But Evelyn did understand, and it started to dawn on her how misguided this intervention had been. She felt sick. She had always thought Julia escaped from Germany untouched by the fever that had gripped the country, but she could see now that she was just as rabid as the rest of the Lion Society. Those conversations about wealth, about poverty, about injustice—Evelyn had read them all wrong. She had believed what she wanted to believe. Julia had condemned the system, but only because she was convinced that she belonged to a superior group of people who would in time crush those with less power and less privilege. How extraordinary to have been betrayed, to *feel* betrayal, and behind all this was a long, sharp pain at Evelyn's breast, as if Julia had reached inside and ripped her heart from its chamber.

"Paul knows the wife of an old colleague from Siemens-Schuckert," Julia said. "A common sort of girl but sharp as a tack. A few weeks ago, she started working as a shorthand typist at the Ministry of Supply, and she was assigned to the Royal Ordnance Factories' files. You know what they keep there, don't you, Evelyn? It's your department, after all. Consignment lists, transport of artillery, shipments lost at sea. But on Monday she came across something really hot. Oh, Evelyn, you wouldn't believe what she brought me . . ."

Evelyn felt her scalp prickle. "What was it?"

"The coordinates of an RAF black spot on the east coast of England. It's been made up to look like a genuine military base from the air, but no personnel or weapons have ever been stationed there. It's the ideal landing point for German parachutists, with a clear run once they're on the ground . . ."

"But what are you going to do with them?"

Julia looked at her, and for the first time since she'd arrived Evelyn saw something like doubt creep into her eyes, but it quickly disappeared.

"Paul will take the maps to Wilhelm Canaris, the head of German military intelligence. He's leaving on Friday night. Don't you see, Evelyn? We can still help the invasion. We can still play our part, because Paul is working for the Germans. He's a spy."

Evelyn looked out the window. Suddenly, she felt calm. There was a way to make sense of it, after all. Julia was enthralled by this Hancock, brainwashed by him, just as she had been by her husband, Hans. It was still possible to make her see reason. But in order to do this, she needed to reveal her own truth. "I have to tell you something, Julia," she said slowly. "The fact is, I haven't been entirely honest. I don't work at the War Office."

The room was quiet. Julia gazed at Evelyn, resting her chin in her hand. "All right," she said. "Who do you work for?"

Evelyn took a deep breath. If she didn't get it out now she never would. "In September I was recruited to Military Intelligence, Section 5. To begin with I was stationed at Wormwood Scrubs, doing mostly paperwork and transcription—nothing much of real consequence. To keep this work secret, however, it was recommended

I tell everyone, even my family and closest friends, that I had been employed by the War Office. A few months ago I was transferred to counterintelligence to undertake an undercover operation where I posed as a Nazi sympathizer to infiltrate the Lion Society."

"I see." Julia smiled. "Very amusing. And the punchline? Your mother is really Wallis Simpson?"

"There is no punchline, Julia. I'm not joking. Christ, I wish I was."

Julia tapped another cigarette from the pack but set it aside instead of lighting it. Something had changed; she was trying not to show it, but Evelyn could see that she was nervous, and when she spoke again her voice sounded faint. "You really never worked at the War Office?"

Evelyn shook her head miserably.

Julia stood up and took a step toward the door, but she continued to stare at Evelyn, her face drained of color. "Are you saying you never *believed*? Everything you said, the typists, that Jew in the park . . ." She slumped on the edge of the bed again. "What about Mrs. Baden-Marr? You *attacked* her!"

"It was part of my cover."

"But you came to us. To Nina. She trusted you, and all this time you've been *spying* on her, on us?"

Julia brought a shaking hand to her mouth. She looked distraught. Despite everything, it was awful to see her like this, and Evelyn found herself walking across the room to place a hand on her back.

"Listen, Julia, I don't know what this Hancock fellow has promised you, or what lies he's spun, but I can help you before it all goes too far. Come with me now. I can protect you."

"Protect me from what?"

"We don't have time . . ."

Letting out a cry, Julia sat up and shook her fists at Evelyn.

"You're not *listening*! I don't care what happens to me. Don't you see? I want something different. I've always wanted something different—something new and great for this country; I want its dignity and power restored. I want to be part of that—I must be, I've lived my whole life for it. That's why I'll never be afraid of you and your spies. I'm not afraid of what you can do to me."

"Don't think that because of who you are, your family's position, you will somehow be spared," said Evelyn carefully, as though she were speaking to a child. "They're interning people with links to the Lion Society. They will charge you with treason. Do you know the penalties for treason? It's a prison sentence—for years, Julia—or worse."

But Julia only laughed, and Evelyn could see there was some new tranquility to her bearing, an exalted sort of acceptance. It made Evelyn's blood run cold.

"I was so wrong about you, Evelyn. I always imagined you were like me, but you're nothing more than a spineless follower, aren't you?"

"This isn't about me."

"No, I suppose it isn't. You've always been afraid of your own reflection. And now look at you. Still hiding behind a facade."

"You do know what the Nazis are doing to civilians in Europe, don't you? They're *killing* them, Julia! Jews, gypsies—even Poles, I've now heard."

Julia stared back at her mildly. "Violence is merely restitutional in our struggle," she said. "It will save our people."

"*Our people?*" Evelyn shook her head in disbelief. "Can you hear what you're saying? Do you really think this is the best way to save Britain? To side with the enemy? To betray the government?"

"*Your* government," Julia returned with contempt. "*Your* enemy. What I want is for every man and woman in this country to have the opportunity to realize their full potential and know real freedom. You—you're just fighting for the status quo. You think because you follow the rules, report to your masters, cross your t's and dot your i's, that you're somehow advancing a better cause?" Her voice had risen in indignation.

Still breathing heavily, she picked up the cigarette and lit it, then sat for a time smoking.

Evelyn stared at her, willing some recognition, some understanding, but the chasm felt so wide now, as endless as the sea. She thought back to that moment they had shared outside the chapel at Raheen, the smooth feel of the acorn in her palm, the salty breeze nudging at her brow. She hadn't imagined it: when Julia had looked at her, Evelyn had sensed a connection, the kind of knowingness between them she had not encountered in many people since. But now Julia might as well have been a stranger.

"Do you see how much I've risked by coming here?" Evelyn muttered. "What this could cost me?"

Julia made no reply. Instead, she stood up and began gathering her handbag, her room key, her coat.

"I'm leaving," she announced.

"What? No, you can't!"

Disgust flashed in Julia's eyes once again and Evelyn shrank back, afraid Julia might actually strike her. It had taken months to build this friendship, for that was what it had been; it had been real to Evelyn. Yet it had been reduced to ashes in minutes. As she watched Julia stride across the hotel room, a line from Corinthians brushed against her memory: *Do not be misled: Bad company corrupts good character.*

"Don't you dare tell me what to do," Julia seethed. "You're nothing, a nobody, just a bloody shadow creeping around the edges of people. You've spent your life clinging to the skirts of those with more power and money and potential than you, hoping some of it will rub off. But it hasn't and it won't. It doesn't work like that. Sally, Elizabeth, even Hugh—they only care about you in relation to themselves. You were only ever a pet project for the Wesleys, an act of altruism like me working at that damn Benevolent Society. They never believed you could rise above your station—and, worst of all, neither did you. You'll never be one of them, Evelyn, and you'll never be anyone of consequence. You'll always be the jumped-up little prig from Lewes. And when people are done thinking that, you'll be forgotten."

"And you think you'll be remembered?" Evelyn retorted. But she could feel tears burning in her eyes as Julia snapped closed her handbag and slung it over her shoulder.

"I'm getting out of this hovel and I'm telephoning Paul."

"You can't. Don't you understand—"

Julia fixed Evelyn with a cold glare. "No, *you* don't understand. I told you: I don't care what happens to me."

Evelyn moved to stand between Julia and the doorway. This was the last chance—Evelyn's only chance—to stop her.

"Move," Julia demanded.

Evelyn shook her head. "I can't let you go. And I can't let you speak to Hancock. I came to warn you about MI5 and ask you to come with me. You have a choice. I can bring you in to my handler; he can help you, keep you safe. Then we can approach Hancock—"

She stopped. There was something incredulous in Julia's eyes as she began to laugh.

"You want to *turn* me? I don't believe this. Oh, Evelyn, what a fool you are! All this time you've been feeding information back to them, to MI5, betraying Nina and everyone else, and now you think I'll *join* you?"

Evelyn could hear noise from the street: some urgent query, followed by the slap of shoes on the stairs.

Julia must have heard it too, because she took another step toward the door. "Get out of my way," she hissed.

"No."

"I said *move!*"

She shoved Evelyn aside, sending her sprawling, and she was already halfway down the corridor before Evelyn managed to climb back to her feet.

TWENTY-THREE

EVELYN FOLLOWED JULIA along the corridor, wincing at the pain in her side where she'd caught the sharp edge of the dresser. She glimpsed movement in the room next door: two men, one bashing away at a typewriter, the other, headphones on, dismantling a hearing piece fixed to the wall, but she had no chance to wonder what they were doing there.

"Where did she go?" she called to the concierge when she reached the lobby. "The woman—just now?"

"Lass turned right, I think. Cromwell Road."

The underground was only half a mile away. If Julia got on a train she would disappear. As Evelyn burst out of the hotel, two men in dark suits appeared on the steps, blocking her way.

"Whoa! Steady on." In a blink, they had her arms pinned behind her back.

"Hey!" Evelyn tried to shake herself loose. "Let go of me!"

"Keep calm, miss. You need to come with us now."

"I don't have time for this. Don't you know I'm one of Bennett White's agents? We need to stop *her*!"

She scanned the street. About fifty yards ahead she spotted Julia striding along the pavement.

"Look! There! Can you see her? She's heading for Cromwell Road. We have to stop her before she makes it to the underground."

The men glanced at one another, and the taller one took off. He was fast, drawing alongside Julia easily.

"*Ouch*," Evelyn cried as the grip on her arms tightened. "What *are* you doing?"

"Miss Varley?"

She still hadn't seen either of the men's faces.

"Yes, I told you, didn't I? I work for Bennett White of counterintelligence. You're not going to . . . Look, will you let go of me, please?"

The agent dragged her a few yards along the street, deeper into the shadows of some ivy creeping across the length of a tall gate. As her eyes adjusted, Evelyn saw the outline of a man standing before her. His brown tweed suit was crumpled, his bow tie askew, a trilby clenched in one hand as he slapped it against his leg.

"Oh, Evelyn." White was shaking his head. "I wish it hadn't come to this . . ."

Evelyn opened her mouth. A pounding began deep inside her skull, as if something in her brain was about to burst.

"You haven't met Jack, have you? Our colleague from Chemley Court?"

For a second she didn't recognize the man who emerged from the darkness. Tall, well-groomed, younger than he had appeared when she saw him at Sally's wedding. She knew him as Hancock, and he was smiling, his lips upturned in a cruel twist.

Evelyn shrank back, terrified. He wasn't handsome, as she had thought, not at all. His eyes were small and almost black.

"Hello, Evelyn," he said. "So sorry for all this subterfuge. But it seems you haven't been entirely forthcoming with us, have you?"

"I don't understand," she cried. "What are you doing here?"

White stepped forward. "For the past year, Jack has been embedded in the Siemens-Schuckert group," he said. "This infiltration began soon after the plants closed and ex-workers sympathetic to Germany coalesced, including your friend Colin. Jack joined the group under the guise of Paul Hancock and established himself as the leader, all with the intention of exposing these traitors when the time was right."

"No," said Evelyn. "*No.* There's been some mistake. Colin had an Iron Cross. I saw it with my own eyes. Only a German could have come by it . . ."

"A fake, of course," said Jack. "I had to prove to the group I was bona fide; Colin in particular was nervy. I must admit I'm surprised it fooled you, Evelyn." There was that cruel smile again. "Especially after Bennett had spoken so highly of your intuition."

"But what about Julia?"

"Jack was introduced to Miss Wharton-Wells a few months ago at a rally," White explained. "But she had been on our radar long before she came back from Germany. We suspected her of being linked to the Lion Society, but she was careful and never left a paper trail. It turned out she had networks of fanatics everywhere, including in this Siemens-Schuckert group, so we caught up with her in the end." White shook his head at Evelyn, his mouth downturned. "I told you to stay out of it, didn't I? I gave you a chance to keep away from Colin and the Raven Inn. But you didn't listen. It was like a sore that you just had to pick."

"You set me up?"

"No, I tried to warn you."

"But Julia . . ." Evelyn turned to Jack Littleproud. "She must have said something about me. You must have known she was my friend."

Jack shrugged. "Would you believe she never mentioned you? Seems like you weren't so important to her after all."

Evelyn struggled against the agent, wanting to scream, as White edged back into the shadows.

"*Bennett*," she implored. How odd it felt to use his first name. "*Please*. I was only doing what you trained me for."

He wouldn't look at her, and a moment later he turned away.

The hold on her arms sent a fresh bolt of pain across her shoulders, and a cool hand covered her mouth. Evelyn managed to glance down the street, where she could see Julia standing on the pavement with the taller agent, some urgent discussion taking place between them. It looked to be calming down when the man patted her shoulder and Julia began to walk with him back toward the Crofton Hotel. Julia was only about twenty yards away, her gait slow and deliberate, when she locked eyes with Evelyn, and though the light was poor Evelyn could have sworn she saw her smile. Then Julia reached down for something by the curb, the agent following her movement, and as she straightened she slammed what looked like a discarded brick into the side of his head. He slumped to the ground, and Julia took off toward the underground once more.

The agent guarding Evelyn dropped the hold on her arms and ran—not after Julia but to his colleague. Evelyn watched Julia's determined stride and was reminded of how she had been in school, her attention never on those around her, eyes always focused instead on the vanishing point of the horizon. They had both been searching for something no one else could see and, ignoring the tight feeling in her chest, Evelyn began another chase. She was faster than Julia, and within ten seconds Evelyn had reached out and taken hold of her wrist, forcing her to an abrupt halt.

"Julia, please!"

"Why won't you just let me go?"

The street was eerily quiet; people had scattered from the scene as if they'd been alerted to some impending catastrophe.

"Come in with me," Evelyn pleaded. "It's not too late."

The whites of Julia's eyes shone bright like an animal cornered in a trap. She was thrashing at her wildly, but Evelyn had her fixed firm in her grip.

"Why does it matter so much to you, Evelyn? What are you so afraid of?"

Evelyn felt Julia jab at her breast, kick her shin, and amid the tussle she saw the agent lying on the pavement stir, a streak of blood through his fair hair. She grabbed Julia by the coat.

"Is it that you found somewhere you truly belonged?" Julia gasped. "Is that what scared you so much—that you found something to actually believe in?"

"Evelyn!"

It was White. He and the other agent were charging down the pavement toward them.

Evelyn turned back to Julia, tightening her grip.

"Let me go," she heard Julia cry. "Just let me go."

And when Julia struck her in the ribs Evelyn did, and for a brief moment experienced a feeling of perfect freedom, until she watched Julia tilt, stumble, and then fall from the pavement onto the road— and right into the path of a southbound bus.

AUGUST 1940

TWENTY-FOUR

IT WAS LATE summer when Evelyn was told she had a visitor. No one had come to see her in months, not since the solicitor with the plea bargain papers. In the early weeks of her imprisonment she told herself it was because the case had caused such a stir—it had been in all the newspapers and across the wireless. Julia's father had resigned his peerage, and then there had been the scandal with Wesley Buttons. The firm lost the army contract and Hugh Wesley went bankrupt soon after, having taken out a large loan against the equity of the business.

In the end, White had decided not to bring any of his own charges against Evelyn. It seemed he couldn't risk the embarrassment of revealing that his agent Jack Littleproud had been posing as a German spy, or that Evelyn had disobeyed him. Jack never managed to expose anyone from the Siemens-Schuckert group with any real connection to the Nazis, but Evelyn supposed that didn't matter. White had already claimed his big scalps in the Lion Society case and everything else had been tied up nice and neat, just as he liked it to be. In the meantime, the intelligence service had turned its gaze away from

London: France had fallen to the Germans, and Britain's spies now needed to find a way into the Occupied Zone.

But her transgression could not go unpunished, and Evelyn was charged with attempted murder. White had given a witness statement at her hearing, testifying that he couldn't say for certain whether Evelyn had meant to push Julia in front of that bus—his revenge, perhaps, for her conflicted loyalty. It was the last time she had seen him. Julia hadn't been called as a witness. She was still recovering in the hospital wing of Holloway with a broken leg after being sentenced to prison for violating the Official Secrets Act and inciting treason. But the Wesley family still had friends in high places: Julia would be incarcerated for just two years.

Meanwhile the judge had sentenced Evelyn to five years. There had been no mention of her work at MI5 in his summary, nor that her testimony in Nina's trial had been given anonymously in closed court, securing a conviction and a jail term of ten years. No one had spoken in Evelyn's defense, testifying to her strong character; even her lawyer had regarded her with contempt during their brief meetings in her cell. She had entertained a hope that John Chadwick would make an appearance, but he didn't. Her good qualities, whatever they may once have been, had been expunged from her record.

Evelyn followed the warden along the metal walkway and down the juddering stairs toward the main block. She had been housed in B Wing with the other political prisoners, though thankfully Nina Ivanov and Julia were kept in a different part of the jail. They were pleasant enough to her, the other women, mostly because they believed she was a fascist like them. Evelyn supposed they could afford to indulge in pleasantries because they knew they wouldn't be kept in there for long—there was already talk of Churchill releasing certain detainees and allowing other privileges. People of influence like Diana Mosley and Norah Elam. But not me, she thought grimly. Julia had been right: I am not a person of influence.

At the entrance to the main block, they didn't turn into the visitors' room, as Evelyn expected. Instead, she was led around the side of the ancient kitchen and through the wooden door near the bins. They came out into the dining room, a large hall at the south end of the prison. In the far corner stood Sally Wesley—Sally van der Hoort now, Evelyn reminded herself—next to a table on which were tea and biscuits.

Evelyn ran a hand over her unkempt hair. She looked around for the warden, but he had disappeared; only the guard stood at the door, his back to them. Evelyn sat down and, after pouring them each a cup of tea, Sally nudged the plate toward her and took a seat.

Evelyn had not seen Sally since the wedding. In June, three months after her arrest, she'd read an obituary for Hugh Wesley in *The Times*. He had died suddenly in Shropshire. Evelyn had written to Sally but received no reply, though she hadn't really expected one, and with no one to talk to about it the news hardly seemed real—Hugh had always been so present in the world, so corporeal. How was it that he was now gone? She had wept over the newspaper until one of the guards came into her cell and took it away.

Sally pulled out a silver case and handed a cigarette to Evelyn. They sat smoking for a few minutes, Sally picking strands of tobacco from her lip.

"You must think it strange," she said. "My being here."

Evelyn shifted her weight against the bench. After her cool cell, the dining room felt oppressively warm. She drank some tea and said, "I was sorry to hear about Hugh. I wrote, but . . ." She trailed off, staring at the table. "How is your mother?"

Sally shrugged. "She's at the manor. She's not very well. It hit her hard. She found him, you see . . ."

"Oh, Sal." Evelyn swallowed. "How awful."

"Yes, it was rather. Dr. Kitchen thinks it was a heart attack. He'd been warning of it for some time. Daddy's diet was never good, and he always drank too much—more so after the scandal with Julia and the factory . . ." She took a quick breath. "Anyway, one day he went out for his early walk with Tortoise, like he did every morning, but when he wasn't back for breakfast Mummy went looking for him. He was at the bottom of the lawn . . ."

Evelyn pictured Hugh keeled over, hand gripping his chest, those dark woods looming behind him.

Sally gave a brisk shake of her head. "I can't stand the manor right now. Everything in boxes, paintings removed from the walls to be sold." She raised her eyes, squinted. "Still, at least we can keep the Mayfair house. Daddy put that in my name, thank goodness."

"And Jonty?"

"He's flying his planes." Sally's smile was hard. "I hear you won't be going to trial after all. That your lawyer made an early plea."

There was no malice in her voice. She tapped ash into the saucer, her expression inquisitive but unguarded. They could have been back by the stream in the manor grounds.

"He says with good behavior I might be out by Christmas after next." Evelyn didn't say how unlikely that would be, or that since she'd been in prison time had become elastic. Two years, ten years. She was still trapped inside her own head. These past months had felt like a nightmare, but none she had ever experienced before. Buried alive was the feeling that most often came to mind, for its slow suffocation and the endless nights alone in her cell.

Sally nodded. Her hands weren't quite steady as she lifted a cup to her lips.

Dust motes drifted through the air, caught in a shaft of light from the high windows. Evelyn's eyes felt raw in the brightness—she had cried so much since arriving at Holloway, she often wondered if she'd ever be able to produce tears again.

"Why are you here, Sally?"

Sally's gaze skimmed the outline of Evelyn's face, trailing down to her prison-issue long-sleeved woolen blouse and white smock, which Evelyn thought made her look like she worked for the Red Cross.

"Daddy was so fond of you," she said quietly. "He once said that he saw something of himself in you. At the time, this made me love you even more, but now I must confess I'm not sure why he said it. Perhaps it was how you could shape yourself as you needed to. He always thought you were clever, we all did, and he admired your aloofness. Not something he ever really mastered. Always said it was the Irish in him; that we talk too much at the dinner table. That was his weapon, of course—other people's assumptions. I know how many people thought my father was a buffoon, and perhaps even more so now. Lovable, like a teddy bear, but not too bright. Rather like me, *non*? Still, he always believed that we could rely on you. That if we ever needed it, you would help us."

Sally looked past Evelyn, toward the windows, to the glimpse of green at the edge of the courtyard.

"We're all bound by our secrets," she continued. "Even me. And perhaps I should have done more for Julia. If I'm honest, I think I always knew that darkness was still in her. That she hadn't come home reformed like we all said she had. It's the mistake we make, isn't it? To believe that goodness will prevail."

She brushed the crumbs to one side of the table, then back again.

"But I came here because I needed to ask you, Evelyn: why didn't you tell me about Julia? Why didn't you come to me when you knew what she was up to, rather than heading straight to her? If you had, none of this would have happened. My father would still be alive, my family name would be intact, and you . . ." She paused, sucking in a breath. "You wouldn't be in this terrible place."

Evelyn closed her eyes, but when she did she saw Julia, her slow tumble before the bus. The smear of blood across the road like an oil slick.

"I couldn't. The Official Secrets Act forbade me from telling anyone."

"But you told Julia." Sally folded her arms, her look almost triumphant. "You risked it for her."

"I risked it for all of you. Yes, I was trying to help Julia, but I was trying to help your family too."

"But it didn't help. If you'd told me first, I could have spoken to Daddy, and Julia could have been stopped. He would have made her see reason. She would have listened to him. Instead, you had to play the hero."

"I'm sorry," Evelyn mumbled. "I never meant to hurt you."

"But you did." Sally's eyes blazed. "And I warned you, didn't I, that Julia wasn't the answer? I told you that she would only cause trouble. I'd known her my whole life and it was a mistake to put any trust in her. I told you how she used to steal things that belonged to me and that everyone else thought it was a great joke, remember? Do you know what she did with those books and toys when she was sick of them? She tossed them aside like garbage."

The guard had turned in the doorway and was watching them with interest.

"Listen, I don't have much longer . . ." Sally glanced toward the door, her voice strained. "It was hard enough arranging this meeting; I had to pull a lot of strings."

She sat like that, staring at Evelyn for several seconds, then she reached across the table, as if she wanted to touch her. But Evelyn jerked her hand away.

Sally's face went dangerously still, and she seemed to Evelyn a stranger for the first time, full of so much anger but also steely dignity. "I'm not to blame for this, Evelyn. You're in here because you couldn't decide what kind of person you wanted to be, or whose side you really wanted to be on." She shook her head again as if she were now trying to be rid of something trapped inside it. "I thought I'd feel some relief at seeing you, some relief from this relentless grief, but I can see now that I was wrong. There's nothing for me here. It's all gone."

Sally withdrew her hand and began twisting her wedding ring, a frown creasing her forehead. "I'm sorry it's all ended up this way, Ev, I really am . . ."

The guard was approaching the table now, tapping the shiny face of his wristwatch.

Sally got to her feet, her cigarette burned all the way to the stub. For a moment, her face disappeared in the last plume of smoke and Evelyn stared, mesmerized, at that empty space. So *Sally* had been the magician, she thought miserably. The conjurer. Not White or Chadwick or anyone else at MI5. Not even Julia. Evelyn had always believed their friendship could withstand the strongest winds, the bleakest winters; that it could survive a meteor. But she had been wrong. It had been no more real than anything else. Sally had created this make-believe, and for the first time in a long time Evelyn could hear her mother's voice in her head. *It's just how the world works, dear.*

⁓

Later that evening, she lay on her bed facing the chipped brick wall. The cell stank of her own stale body odor and unwashed sheets, as it always did, but Evelyn was more aware of it after Sally's visit, as though she had been shocked back to life. That wasn't the only thing she was thinking about. A letter had come in the afternoon mail with the postmark BN8. While she recognized the handwriting, she could hardly bring herself to open it. She waited until the light grew dim at the window before tearing back the flap.

Evelyn,

I have been told this letter will reach you but that it will be read by half a dozen others before it does. I have always thought there is something shameful about baring one's greatest pain to the eyes of strangers, but I realize I may have to change my mind if I'm to make this correspondence worth more than the paper it is written on . . .

You may write to us, dear, if that brings you comfort. I will keep writing to you. You needn't feel afraid. It would be untrue if I said that our days are not difficult thinking of you in that place, but we know you couldn't have done what the papers are saying you did. Some things in this world aren't fair or even just, but we are proud of you. We want you to know that.

With love,
Dad

Evelyn read the letter twice before she folded it back inside the envelope and pushed it beneath her pillow. Then she settled back down on her bed. In the dark she could make out the desk beside the bed, and the pencil and single sheet of paper she was permitted each day. What a poor correspondent she had been to her parents all these months. Perhaps tomorrow would be the day she squashed down her shame, picked up the pencil, and began composing a reply.

Evelyn put a hand behind her head. The room felt still tonight, quiet: for once she didn't hear the dull thud of Julia's body being dragged under the bus. They had waited days before telling her that Julia had lived; all that time Evelyn had been haunted by the belief that she had killed her.

She glanced at the small grate near the ceiling. She still longed to be outside in the warm air, moving through the city, but simply imagining a journey out of prison would be enough for now. Besides, she had other things to think about. Most evenings before sleep she tried to picture herself sinking deeper and deeper beneath the coarse woolen blanket until she was no bigger than a speck of dirt. Somehow that made the night bearable; she would need to disappear, she had convinced herself, if she was ever going to start her life again. She had made something of herself from nothing before, though she knew now that it had been built on lies. She wasn't going to make that mistake again. When she left prison, she would build herself up, brick by brick, into the sturdiest fortress, the most impenetrable wall. She would be the person she wanted to be. She wasn't afraid, not anymore. No matter what others might think, there was goodness in her, even if she had to dig deep to find it.

Evelyn rolled onto her side. Shadows danced across the wall, but soon her eyes grew heavy, and for the first time in months it didn't hurt to feel the dewy summer grass beneath her fingertips or hear the swirl of air between the reeds by Magdalen Bridge as she surrendered to sleep.

MARCH 1948

TWENTY-FIVE

EVELYN DIDN'T REMEMBER falling asleep, but when she woke she found herself in bed, the curtains drawn. She sat up. The flat was silent, only the groan of pipes from the downstairs bathroom shuddering through the walls, and she sank back into the pillows with a moan, rubbing the heels of her palms into her eyes. Last night she had told Stephen everything and now he was gone. She had felt so close to him, but that had been just another illusion. She rolled onto her side, wretched. How easy it was to prize one person from another, that small space between them having now grown so vast she could have been orbiting a different sun. She pulled the pillow tight around her ears. How was she ever going to navigate a way back without him?

Then Evelyn heard a sound, a distinct rattle, and Stephen appeared, his hair matted, bearing a tray with a pot of tea. He was dressed in his shirtsleeves and a pair of drawers, his pale legs much hairier than she had expected. She glimpsed his foot, the one that had been so badly damaged in the war, bent at an ungainly angle and rippled with scar tissue.

He set the tray down on the edge of the bed and drew back the curtains. The blue light of approaching dawn flushed through the flat.

"You're awake," he said.

Evelyn watched him sit beside the tray and pour the tea. After handing her a mug, he leaned back on an elbow, picking at sleep in his eye.

"Don't worry," he said, smiling. "I spent the night in the armchair."

Evelyn drank some tea. It was milky and sweet. Stephen watched her, an apprehensive look on his face.

"Evelyn, last night you spoke about your parents," he began.

"Yes?"

"Do you . . . Well, have you seen them? Since you got out?"

Evelyn glanced toward the window. The morning was brightening. Noise had begun filtering in from Euston Road. Soon the rest of the city would be awake too. She shook her head.

"Right." Stephen stared at the floor, his brow creased. "But they know you're here, in London?"

"We haven't been in touch since I was sent to Holloway," she said. "My father wrote to me while I was in jail, but I never replied. I felt too . . . ashamed. Everyone in Lewes would have read about what I did—news spreads fast in a place like that. My parents are modest people who valued their good name. I ruined that for them. People in the town would always know what their daughter had done. That's why I didn't write. I wanted to spare them the reminder that I had brought this shame on them."

"Right," Stephen said again, his frown deepening. "And what about me?"

"You?"

"Yes." He cleared his throat. "Is that why you never told me about Holloway and your work with Bennett White? Did you expect me to be ashamed of you too?"

"Worse than shame. Anger, repulsion, even hatred. You fought in the war. You were prepared to give your life . . ." Evelyn let out a bitter laugh. "I've led such a dishonest life. I hardly know who I am."

Stephen shifted on the edge of the bed, a knee bent close to Evelyn's hip. Feeling his warmth, she placed her hand on his thigh. They sat like that for a few minutes, neither of them speaking.

"I can't begin to understand what the past years have been like for you," he said quietly. "And I can't begin to understand what it must take to start one's life over as you have. But I do wonder—what if you were to visit them? Your parents? If only so they know you're all right, I mean. It may begin to heal something in you." His eyes shone. "They must miss you."

"Miss me?" Evelyn laughed again—she couldn't help it.

"Why, yes." Stephen stared back at her. "If they didn't want to keep in touch, I'm not sure they would have written to you so assiduously. Every week, wasn't it? That is dedication. That is devotion. But when you left prison they wouldn't have known where to find you, and that must have taken a terrible toll. I imagine every knock on their front door carries the hope that you are standing on the other side of it."

Evelyn drew back her hand and placed it against her chest. Beneath her breastbone she felt the flicker of her heartbeat. It had never occurred to her that they might be waiting. That they would welcome her return to their home when everyone else had turned their backs. That they would accept her like this—so depleted. She looked past Stephen to her cluttered dressing table and the thick wad of envelopes, and her throat grew tight. Her father's letters. He had written to her each week for four and a half years, and she had kept every one of those letters in her Holloway cell—first under her pillow, and then between the mattress and the wire springs—even though she couldn't bring herself to write back.

"I never really thought . . ."

But she could see it now. They *had* been waiting. The letters said as much; they had shown their constancy. Her parents had never sought her remorse, as others had, or contrition. And she supposed they had never loved the woman she had tried to become, either, preferring the girl she had been, full of imperfections though she was. Perhaps that was why they had kept that awful photograph of her as a child on their mantelpiece; they could see behind the cold, sneering expression. They could see *her*.

Evelyn pushed back the blanket and padded toward the basin in the corner, where she splashed icy water on her face. Then she returned to the bed and, kneeling before it, dragged out her old suitcase.

"What are you doing?" Stephen asked.

She opened her wardrobe and hunted for a sweater and fresh blouse to throw into the case.

"I need to go to Euston," she said. "Right now. I need to catch a train."

"All right." A look of panic flashed across his face. "Can I come with you?"

"No. I'm sorry. I have to do this alone."

Stephen watched her move about the flat, bending down to pick up a sock, tossing aside an unwanted brooch, searching for her purse on the dressing table. She was trying not to look at him sitting there on the bed, his shoulders hunched against the cold.

"I love you, Evelyn," she heard him say quietly. "Whatever happened in your past, I think you are a good, decent person. Someone I am proud to know."

There was such resignation in his voice that immediately she turned around to face him. He thought she was leaving him. He was staring into his lap, the freckles on his nose darkened by the gloom, and for the first time she could picture what he had been like as a boy. Sensitive, curious, vulnerable. Perhaps *that* is the measure of truly knowing another person, she thought. Having the imagination to comprehend the expanse of their life and how it has come to shape them. She walked over to the bed and ran a hand over his fair hair. Tears welled in her eyes.

"I love you too, my darling," she said.

Stephen gazed at her, astounded, until he smiled. Evelyn leaned down and kissed him, his mouth soft and sweet-smelling from the tea, his cheeks scratchy with stubble.

"I'll be back with you in a couple of days," she said. "I promise."

Stephen held her for a moment, his face pressed into her neck, then let go.

The sun had broken through the clouds as she slipped out of the flat and hurried toward the station. The streets were still mostly empty, with only the milk truck trundling by on the main road. She waited outside Euston until the first attendant raised the grate on his ticket booth.

"This is an early start, miss," he called. "Where to?"

"Lewes, please."

He nodded to her suitcase. "Heading home?"

Evelyn had never wanted to go back, afraid that she would never find home elsewhere, afraid that she would never discover the kind of person she wanted to be. But against the odds she had managed to make London her home, and this was the first time in all the years she'd lived there that she felt like she belonged. She pictured the stroll from the Lewes station through the town, across the cobbled bridge over the river, the steep incline of the hill, her father's face when he recognized her in the sitting room doorway. And her mother. What would her mother say? Evelyn bit her lip.

"I'm visiting my family," she said.

"Well, there ain't a train till nine," the attendant said, handing her ticket through the window. "So you've a bit of a wait."

The station was coming to life. The other booths had opened and people were arriving for the early trains. Evelyn bought cigarettes from the tobacconist as commuters began to emerge from the underground and spill onto the street. A warm gust of wind tunneled through the arcade and slapped hard against her cheeks, the force of it shaking the morning newspapers in their stands. She watched a dark-haired woman in a fox fur stride past, her high heels striking bluntly on the stairs as she made her way to a platform. A day ago Evelyn had been terrified of encountering Julia again, but she had finally pushed that fear behind her. She had managed to rebuild herself into something strong after all. She sucked on a cigarette as hunger scrabbled at her stomach; she hadn't had a bite to eat since yesterday's breakfast and now she wanted another cup of tea.

Evelyn came out of the station and crossed the street. There was a cafe near the corner with a light shining behind the counter. It would open shortly, and she would sit inside while she waited for her train. She might use the telephone and call Mrs. Foy to ask for a few days off from the shop, and when she came home she and Stephen could go away somewhere—to the country, or to the seaside—before they talked about the Rome trip again. In the meantime, Evelyn was content to stand beneath the awning and finish her cigarette, watching the sun rise across the vast gray city.

AUTHOR'S NOTE

AN UNLIKELY SPY is a work of fiction, but several of the main characters are loosely based upon real people and the plot is shaped by real events.

I've always been interested in the Second World War—and in particular how London weathered these years. While the stories of the Blitz, the Battle of Dunkirk, and the Normandy landings were familiar to me, I was curious about the quieter, lesser-known period before everything kicked into gear—before the invasion of France in May 1940 in particular, when the United Kingdom was still trying to work out which way the wind would blow. During the so-called Phoney War, the intelligence agencies were at loggerheads with the government and the fear of German invasion was MI5's most urgent spur. This fear drove their campaign to expose influential British men and women ready to support Hitler in the event of the Nazis arriving on English soil.

But, most of all, I wanted to know how an ordinary young woman could become a spy.

Before I began writing the novel, I traveled to London and began my research, spending many afternoons at the National Archives, which had recently declassified MI5 transcripts of interrogations and other procedures from the period. This gave me essential insights into their methods as well as the Service's mindset about the enemy. During my time in the UK, I came across the story of a young woman named Joan Miller, who was, like Evelyn in *An Unlikely Spy*, recruited into MI5 in her early twenties, taken under the wing of spymaster Maxwell Knight (later the inspiration for "M" in Ian Fleming's James Bond novels), and tasked with infiltrating groups sympathetic to the Nazis at the beginning of the war.

This first group she infiltrated was called the Right Club, and their leader was a Scottish MP, Captain Archibald Ramsay. The leader of the women's faction of the club was a White Russian émigré, Anna Wolkoff. Along with Ramsay and an American cipher clerk, Wolkoff was responsible for the theft of classified cables between the Admiralty and high-ranking Americans, and their dissemination. Miller's investigation led to arrests and secret trials, but a few years later she was dismissed from the Service. She died in a mysterious car crash in the 1980s not long after she had published a memoir about her time in MI5.

This woman was fascinating. At an age when I was mooching around university, she was embroiled in suspenseful and dangerous investigations that had real consequences for the Allies and the war effort. What kind of person did you need to be to excel in this role, which required so much deception, ingratiation, and acting? In *An Unlikely Spy*, Evelyn must adopt the persona of someone with unforgivably abhorrent views, while at the same time cultivating intimate friendships with the enemy. What toll does this take on a person and their sense of self? These questions propelled my writing.

I have tried to remain as faithful as possible to the history of these events, but as all novelists must I have made some adjustments to the real timeline to best build the story. For instance, Anna Wolkoff was arrested in April 1940 (Nina Ivanov is arrested in early February) and the Siemens-Schuckert case that Evelyn subsequently investigates took place between late 1940 and early 1941, not in late February and early March, as depicted in the novel. Max Catto's *They Walk Alone* was performed at the Comedy Theatre on Panton Street from May to June 1939, several months before Julia and Evelyn attend a performance. Evelyn's interrogation of Jacob Vermeer, who is a fictional character, takes place in early December 1939. In fact, six agents were picked up from Ireland, though not until May 1940, and according to MI5 files, between September and October 1940 a further twenty-five Dutch agents were parachuted in, expecting to play a role in the imminent German invasion. And while Evelyn's role in the MI5 counterintelligence team has been partly based on that of Joan Miller, her personality, background, relationships, strengths, and foibles are all a work of fiction.

ACKNOWLEDGMENTS

AN UNLIKELY SPY was largely produced on unceded sovereign Wurundjeri country and unceded sovereign Jagera country. I acknowledge the traditional custodians of these lands, and pay my respects to their Elders, past, present, and future.

My dear friend Tess Ley passed away before this novel was published. I was always grateful for Tess's support of my writing, and as a detective with experience in counterintelligence, she provided me with a great deal of insight into this work that I later used to develop Evelyn's character. I miss Tess very much. She has an enduring place in my life, and this book is dedicated to her.

Thank you to Pippa Masson for being my wonderful agent and seeing this project through from beginning to end, as well as to Caitlan Cooper-Trent and the rest of the team at Curtis Brown Australia. Thank you to Dan Lazar at Writers House in the US for believing in the potential of Evelyn's story and helping me to shape the manuscript in its later stages.

Thank you to Jane Palfreyman, Angela Handley, and everyone at Allen & Unwin for supporting my writing and having patience as I developed the novel. Particular thanks to my editors, Kate

Goldsworthy and Ali Lavau, and to Clara Finlay for such an eagle-eyed proof.

Thank you to Helen Atsma, Sara Birmingham, and the whole team at Ecco in New York for taking a punt on a debut novelist. I have been so grateful for all your enthusiasm and hard work.

I would like to thank early readers of *An Unlikely Spy*, in particular Hannah Kent. Thank you to my supervisors Veny Armanno and Natalie Collie at the University of Queensland for their encouragement in my creative life. And thank you to Creative Victoria, who awarded me a grant to work on an early draft of the novel. Arts funding in Australia is a lifeline for writers—we must preserve it.

There were many books that assisted in my research of the period, but I would like to make particular mention of Christopher Andrew's *The Defence of the Realm: The Authorized History of MI5*, which was my entry point into better understanding Britain's intelligence services, along with Mike Hutton's *Life in 1940s London* and Bryan Clough's *State Secrets: The Kent-Wolkoff Affair*. Thank you to the good folks at the National Archives in London for helping me navigate the system, as well as the staff at the Imperial War Museum.

I would like to thank my brother, Ashley, and Bethany Rote, for their love and friendship. Thank you to Roger Griffith and Philippa Milward for all their support over the years. Thank you to Tori Batters for being my one and only Spin, and to Janine "N-P" Rainbow. And thank you to my parents, Peter and Fiona Starford, especially for all their trips up to Queensland; it's been fun.

And to my son, Theo Griffith, who arrived in the middle of all this. You fill each day with indescribable happiness. And last but not least, to Elinor Griffith. You are everything to me.

AN
UNLIKELY
SPY

REBECCA STARFORD

A READING GROUP GUIDE

REBECCA STARFORD ON WRITING
AN UNLIKELY SPY

A few years ago, I came across an article about the late Peggy Harmer, a British octogenarian whose secret life as an agent during the Second World War had only been revealed in detail after her death. She had been just nineteen when she was recruited to the War Office in the 1940s, and soon found herself working in the counterespionage unit code-named "Double Cross," which made a vital contribution to the Allied war effort.

The article was a quiet, unceremonious eulogy; it seemed few people knew about Peggy's wartime exploits at all. But this woman, who had been so modest in her achievements, got me wondering about the role other young women may have played in the intelligence service during the war. The article made claim that Peggy's preternatural beauty assisted in her espionage (and perhaps it did), but I was eager to look beyond that archetype. I wanted to know what kind of young woman was attracted to a life of disguise.

I began my research, thinking to write about a spy who perhaps betrayed her country in some way, even by secretly working for the Germans. I read as many novels as I could depicting that period (William Boyd's excellent *Restless*, Sebastian Faulks's *Charlotte Gray*, and John Banville's *The Untouchable*, to name a few) and extensively researched MI5 and its history (Christopher Andrew's comprehensive authorized history on MI5 was invaluable). I traveled to London for on-the-ground research, too. I spent a lot of time at the

National Archives, which had recently declassified MI5 transcripts of interrogations and other procedures, giving me essential insights into their methods and their mindset about the perceived enemy. I visited parks, pubs, hotels, houses, streets, suburbs, underground stations around London that feature in the novel—all to build a sense of that authenticity. I went to Oxford and visited many of the colleges on the campus. I recorded my thoughts into a Dictaphone and kept a scrapbook of other notes and ideas.

And while I did not find my treacherous double agent, my research did uncover a young woman who would come to inspire Evelyn Varley. Her name was Joan Miller, and like Evelyn she was recruited into MI5 in her early twenties, was taken under the wing of spymaster Maxwell Knight (the inspiration for M in Ian Fleming's James Bond), and was tasked with infiltrating groups sympathetic to the Nazis at the beginning of the war. Her investigations led to many arrests and secret trials, but then she was promptly dismissed from the Service and died in a mysterious car crash years later, not long after she had published a memoir about her time in MI5.

These events were already so novelistic—it seemed like ideal material to adapt into fiction. And I found the psychology of this woman so intriguing. While I was attending university at the same age, she was embroiled in suspenseful and dangerous investigations that had real consequences in the early years of the war. But what most interested me was the substance of this young woman, her inner life, which required so much deception, ingratiation, and performance. In *An Unlikely Spy*, Evelyn must adopt the persona of someone with unforgivably abhorrent views, while at the same time negotiating intimate friendships with the enemy. What toll does this take on a person? In her memoir, Joan Miller spoke about the pain she felt giving evidence against these traitors. What kind of emotions would Evelyn grapple with? Who else would she betray along the way? And, more fundamentally as a writer and reader, who are you if you lie to everyone about your real self?

To create Evelyn, I knew I had to build her up from the beginning of her life. I decided to shape her as someone who, while possessing intelligence, confidence, and ambition (and a dash of Peggy Harmer's beauty), remained nonetheless uncertain of her true self. From her modest childhood in southern England, she molds herself into someone she believes will fit in and succeed in the upper-class milieu she will come to inhabit. Evelyn's school experiences were, in fact, similar to my own: I was a scholarship student who attended a prestigious and exclusive boarding school, and like Evelyn I felt compelled to seek belonging with the wrong sorts of people during my time at school. So although set in both another time and another country, this world Evelyn finds herself in was not totally unfamiliar to me.

But what drives *An Unlikely Spy* is how Evelyn, complex and fraught as she is, responds when placed under extraordinary pressure—the kind of pressure experienced on a grand scale by the United Kingdom at the beginning of the war, when the fear of German invasion was MI5's most urgent crisis. It was this fear that drove their campaign to expose influential British men and women ready to support Hitler in the event of invasion, and it is this fear and frantic activity in which Evelyn finds herself embroiled.

By the end of the novel, Evelyn is faced with terrible choices. It was curious to be working on *An Unlikely Spy* with Brexit, the rise of far-right populism in Australia and abroad, and the ascent of Trump as a backdrop; I couldn't help feeling that this fear and anxiety was making its way into my writing and my characters, too. Ultimately the novel is about self-realization, which I believe is a universal and timeless pursuit. What I tried to create in Evelyn was a young woman who recognizes her own mistakes and weaknesses, and in time finds redemption in building herself into someone who no longer needs a disguise.

QUESTIONS FOR DISCUSSION

1. The idea of who or what makes a traitor is a large theme throughout *An Unlikely Spy*—from Evelyn pretending to fit in with her upper-class boarding-school classmates to the things she keeps from her parents to the exact nature of her role in the war. How do you think the concept of traitorhood changes from the beginning to the end of the novel? Is Evelyn a traitor? Why or why not?

2. The friendship between Sally and Evelyn explores how vast class differences can be. Despite being in separate social classes, what qualities do you think Evelyn and Sally share that made this unlikely friendship a success? Do you think Sally and Evelyn would still be friends if not for the war?

3. *An Unlikely Spy* traces Evelyn's story using a close third-person point of view—the reader never strays from her side. How do you think this shapes our understanding of her as a spy, a witness, and, possibly, a traitor? Did you ever wish to see parts of this story through the perspectives of other characters? If so, who?

4. In chapter eight, Vincent and Evelyn are at dinner and he says, "She [Vincent's mother] understood me. How many

people can you say that about?" Do you think anyone can understand Evelyn and why she has made the choices she has in her life? Can Stephen, by the novel's end?

5. In chapter ten, Bennett White tells Evelyn, "I think that's why I've always found the love of one's country has its limits; we need to see our love reflected in something, or someone." Who or what do you think has Evelyn's love? Do you agree with Bennett's sentiments? Why or why not?

6. In chapter ten, Evelyn recalls the moment when she was exposed to her mother's anti-Semitic beliefs: She told Evelyn that her former classmate Harriet was engaged to a Jewish man and expressed pity for her, saying she would have a hard life as a result. After returning to her room, Evelyn felt confused by the exchange and still is now, thinking, "Behind this feeling was the concern that her father hadn't said anything. Did his silence mean that he agreed? And what of her own complicity?" Did Evelyn and her father's complacency surprise you? Why or why not?

7. Imagine that Evelyn writes her father while she is in prison—what do you think she reveals to him?

8. *An Unlikely Spy* grapples with the obligations of loyalty versus the desire for free will. Throughout the novel, we witness Evelyn often weighing her allegiance to her family against the urge to make her own choices, ultimately creating a tension between the two. Do you think we always have a choice when it comes to our actions? What do you think is more important: Staying true to the people and ideas we have

always known, or taking a chance on ourselves and engaging in new ways of thinking?

9. In the closing lines of the novel, Evelyn is pictured looking at the sunrise in solitude. What do you think she could be doing a year from the novel's end?

10. Evelyn's story is inspired by the life of Joan Miller, a young girl recruited into M15 and tasked with infiltrating groups sympathetic to Nazis at the beginning of the war. What insights and discoveries do you think the genre of historical fiction can give us that biography cannot? Does knowing that Evelyn and her life were inspired by real events change your reading of the novel?